FRAYING AT THE EDGE

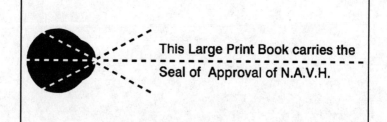

This Large Print Book carries the
Seal of Approval of N.A.V.H.

THE AMISH OF SUMMER GROVE, BOOK 2

FRAYING AT THE EDGE

CINDY WOODSMALL

THORNDIKE PRESS
A part of Gale, Cengage Learning

GALE
CENGAGE Learning·

Farmington Hills, Mich • San Francisco • New York • Waterville, Maine
Meriden, Conn • Mason, Ohio • Chicago

GALE
CENGAGE Learning®

LIBRARY OF CONGRESS CATALOGING-IN-PUBLICATION DATA

Names: Woodsmall, Cindy, author.
Title: Fraying at the edge / Cindy Woodsmall.
Description: Large print edition. | Waterville, Maine : Thorndike Press Large Print, 2016. | Series: The Amish of summer grove ; 2 | Series: Thorndike Press large print Christian fiction
Identifiers: LCCN 2016027739 | ISBN 9781410490926 (hardback) | ISBN 1410490920 (hardcover)
Subjects: LCSH: Large type books. | GSAFD: Christian fiction.
Classification: LCC PS3623.O678 F73 2016b | DDC 813/.6—dc23
LC record available at https://lccn.loc.gov/2016027739

Published in 2016 by arrangement with Waterbrook, an imprint of the Crown Publishing Group, a division of Penguin Random House LLC

Printed in the United States of America
1 2 3 4 5 6 7 20 19 18 17 16

In memory of Iris Summer Woodsmall,
January 15, 2016,
and to all loved and wanted babies
who never drew an earthly breath.
And to the parents who suffer,
searching for ways to survive a lifetime
of missed hugs, laughter, achievements,
hopes, and dreams.

THE AMISH OF SUMMER GROVE SERIES

The story so far . . .

Ties That Bind begins twenty years earlier. At an Amish birthing center, a single Englisch college student, Brandi Nash, gives birth to a daughter as a fire engulfs the building. A few minutes later in a nearby room, an Amish woman, Lovina Brenneman, gives birth to twins, a girl and a boy. The midwife and Lovina's husband, Isaac, struggle to get the women and three babies to safety.

Chapter 2 of *Ties That Bind* moves forward twenty years, and Ariana Brenneman is trying to buy an abandoned café so she can help support her large family. She and her twin brother, Abram, have been working and saving for years to purchase it. As time is running out, Ariana's one-time friend Quill Schlabach offers to help her conduct a benefit to raise money, but Ariana wants nothing to do with him. Five years ago he broke her heart when he left Summer Grove in the middle of the night, taking with him Frieda, Ariana's closest friend. Although Ariana has moved on and is seeing Rudy, a young man she cares for deeply, she resents how Quill and Frieda deceived and betrayed her.

Quill tries to win Ariana's trust, knowing that if she will act on his ideas, she will raise the money she needs. Although Quill continues to conceal why he left with Frieda, he longs for healing between Ariana and himself. But his main purpose for being in Summer Grove is to help an unhappy, disillusioned family leave the Amish — Ariana's eldest sister, Salome, and her family.

Ariana lets down her guard and trusts Quill's guidance. Although Rudy has reservations, he backs her as she, Quill, and Abram hold a benefit, which raises the needed money.

While Ariana and Abram are focused on the café, their brother Mark sees a college performance in a nearby city and is struck by how much one actor looks like Salome. When Mark tells their Mamm, she seems concerned.

Lovina and Isaac ask Quill to investigate the background of this young woman. Quill obtains information that indicates the woman, Skylar Nash, is probably Isaac and Lovina's biological daughter. He contacts Skylar's parents, Brandi Nash and Nicholas Jenkins, and a DNA test confirms that she's not related to Brandi or Nicholas. The test also reveals that Skylar has drugs in her system.

Lovina struggles with the knowledge that her biological daughter seems so lost, and Nicholas, an atheist, is appalled that his daughter has been raised in an insulated, religious society. When he discovers that the midwife knew the two girls might have been accidentally switched at birth and did nothing about it, he threatens to sue her unless Ariana spends a year with him and Brandi, cut off from the Amish community. And Nicholas gives Skylar a choice — time in rehab or time with her biological family. Otherwise he will cut off all financial support.

When Ariana learns that she's not a Brenneman and that Quill helped uncover the truth, she once again feels betrayed by him and asks him never to contact her again.

Ties That Bind ends with Ariana leaving Summer Grove with Brandi and Nicholas to spend a year with them. And Quill picks up Skylar, confiscates the drugs she tries to hide, and drives her toward the Brennemans' home.

For a list of main characters in the Amish of Summer Grove series, see the Main Characters list at the end of the book.

ONE

Summer Grove, Pennsylvania

The dark shadows lying across the living room floor were eerie, seemingly coming out of hiding as Lovina remained kneeling in front of the couch, her Bible open. The pale moonlight only intensified the darkness that surrounded her, as if the blackness were a picture of what was happening to her family. To her daughters.

She tightened her interlaced fingers. Her knees ached from the hours she had quietly sought God for the kind of help only He could give.

The daughter she'd thought she had given birth to two decades ago was gone, spending her first night with strangers in an *Englisch* home that by all accounts was worldly and in disarray. From what little she knew, that home was dysfunctional at best. She was terrified for the daughter she'd raised, the one who had none of her DNA.

Until recently Lovina hadn't realized that even God's faithful ones endured the kind of terror that had now entrenched itself in her heart. But maybe the truth was Lovina hadn't been faithful, not truly.

"God, please don't let Ariana or Skylar pay the price for my sin."

How would Ariana — Lovina's sweet, wide-eyed girl — survive for a year outside the Amish community she loved with her whole heart?

The daughter Lovina had actually given birth to was upstairs, sharing a bedroom with her sisters for the first time in her twenty-year life. The image of meeting Skylar yesterday for the first time made Lovina break into fresh sobs. Her daughter had black nails that matched the dyed-black streak in her blond hair. And she wore jewelry, makeup, and revealing clothes. But none of that had twisted Lovina's heart in a knot like the hardness she saw in Skylar, as if bitterness had already destroyed her belief in life and humanity. The young woman wasn't hopeless. She had dreams but no apparent understanding that life and people were valuable. Even with all that, the most painful part of yesterday was when Skylar's driver, Quill Schlabach, handed Lovina the luggage and suggested she thoroughly inspect it to verify Skylar hadn't brought any drugs with her.

Lovina had set the luggage aside for a while and tried to connect with Skylar about little things — her hobbies, schooling, and such. Later, when the two of them were alone, Lovina went through the suitcase as Skylar sat on the bed, calmly and apathetically assuring her that she'd only popped a few pills on occasion and that a random drug test happened to catch her right after one such rare event. Lovina found no drugs, but Skylar's calm, detached behavior toward meeting her family, having a twin, and the drug search was disconcerting.

"Father in heaven, please strengthen Skylar to overcome all desire for pills — occasional or otherwise."

It was her fault Skylar was in this predicament. Just as it was her fault Ariana had been forced to leave here and go to a dysfunctional home. Would Lovina spend the rest of her life carrying this unbearable sense of blame?

When the floor creaked, Lovina lifted her forehead from her folded hands. Her husband stood in the doorway between the kitchen and the living room, bathed in shadows and dressed in yesterday's pants with suspenders pulled over a white T-shirt.

He eased toward her, knelt, and put an arm around her shoulders. "God, help my Lovina," he whispered, and then he kissed her temple. "It'll be okay. It will."

Lovina didn't need or want false words of hope, but maybe God had spoken to Isaac. Maybe He hadn't. She wouldn't ask.

Skylar had spent a lifetime being indoctrinated in ways Lovina had little knowledge of. In fact, she would be in rehab right now were it not for these crazy circumstances.

Lovina's need to confess her sin to her husband weighed heavily. "The unbearable part is I did this."

"Shh." He held her tight, probably trying to ease her trembling. "No, my love. This isn't —"

"But it is. Please, I have to say it aloud to someone . . . at least once."

He nodded. "Then say it a thousand times if it will help."

Lovina wiped her tears. "When I doubted that we had the right newborn, I didn't push hard enough to get answers."

"But Rachel dismissed your fears."

"Rachel meant well, but as a midwife she didn't have a mother's heart. I should've pushed harder for answers then." She sobbed. "And twenty years later when I discovered the truth about the girls being

14

swapped, I pushed too hard, too fast. Quill tried to warn me, telling me I needed to slow down. But I forged ahead, thinking Skylar needed the faith we could offer her. But we're in over our heads with that one. I see that now. I've upended both girls' lives. Ariana is there, and . . ." She broke into fresh tears. "I'm a horrible person, Isaac."

He wrapped her in his arms and held her tight. "God will forgive us."

Even he couldn't muster another denial of their guilt. This nightmare was Lovina's fault, and no matter how it played out, her daughters — yes, she considered both of them her daughters — would pay the price. Who knew how high a price? All the regret of her past failures and all the fear of her daughters' futures weighed on her mother's heart, squeezing and pressing until she didn't think she could take any more.

As much as she believed in forgiveness and redemption, she wasn't sure any existed for her. God could forgive her, and He could redeem her from eternal damnation. But that wouldn't undo or erase two decades of planting and harvesting in Skylar's life.

Clarity came to her like dawn dispelling night, and she knew why the burden of her sin was so very heavy tonight. Darkness was stretching toward Ariana, and Lovina needed to pray fervently, because her sweet girl would soon be in a fight for her sanity.

Two

Bellflower Creek, Pennsylvania

Ariana stood in her biological father's kitchen, listening as he and her birth mother screamed at each other. Her heart raced in a way it never had before, and she felt she needed to make a conscious effort to remain connected to her body, but that didn't even make sense. Was it her lack of sleep for weeks? her inability to eat? stress?

Whatever was happening and why, she seemed to leave her body and hover above the room, looking down. She appeared as out of place as she felt — an Amish girl fresh off the farm and in full Plain attire while in the home of strangers who, as God would have it, were her parents. Despite being twenty, she felt like a five- or six-year-old child as her parents kept screaming at each other.

Emotions suffocated her, just as they had when she'd arrived thirty-six hours ago, and

17

there was no one to talk to about any of it. The only tie to her past that she was permitted to contact was Quill — former Amish man, current con man. Was he skilled at deceiving everyone or just her? She didn't care, not anymore. Truth be told, she'd rather keel over dead than call him.

What she desperately needed was to talk to *Mamm* and *Daed.* She missed them so badly it hurt, but they weren't her parents. The DNA testing had revealed she belonged to these people.

She wasn't angry with Quill because he'd investigated her birth and had uncovered the truth that landed her in this nightmare. She was angry because he did it behind her back, along with a thousand other sneaky things, after once again having won her trust. She was the poster child for the saying "Fool me once, shame on you; fool me twice, shame on me." And she felt ashamed. But she would not give him a third chance to deceive her.

"Do the words *culture shock* mean anything to you?" Brandi hissed at the man Ariana would never call Dad, but apparently he was her father.

The tension rose as her parents shouted at each other even louder. Surely there had been a mistake. How could she go from being a beloved third daughter in a caring and gentle Amish family to . . . this? But missing home was easier than missing herself, and she did miss who she'd once been or at least who she'd thought she was. Would she ever again be that innocent young woman full of hope and love? Or would confusion become her shadow, tracking her every move?

"I will not agree to this, Nicholas!" Brandi shook her finger at him.

He laughed, but his face was scarlet. "You think I expected you to? Here's the deal. You don't have to. She's as much my daughter as yours, and I have just as many rights as you do."

Brandi's arm bangles clinked and jingled as she stabbed a finger toward him. "You were never like this about Skylar."

Skylar. The poor girl who should have been raised Amish. How was she faring in an Amish home?

"And just whose fault was that?" Nicholas asked. "You need me to admit that twenty years ago I wasn't invested in having a child with you and that not living in the same house made things tough to navigate? Okay, I'll admit both. But you pushed me away at every turn. You know you did, and I let you. Not this time, Brandi. Not this time."

Her biological parents hadn't wanted her, and they weren't living in the same home when she was born?

Floating to the ceiling wasn't far enough away. She wanted to go home. The air continued to crackle with unfamiliar tension, and the angry voices bounced off the four walls. The room seemed to shift, changing shape and color as it tilted on its side.

Both parents stood mere steps from their current spouses. They had been introduced to Ariana as stepparents, which wasn't a completely new concept. Sometimes one Amish parent died and the other remarried, but she'd never thought about the possibility of one child having two parents and two stepparents simultaneously.

Just one of the million things she'd never considered before being removed from her home.

"I want to be fair," Nicholas said. "But you have to be reasonable, Brandi. I won't give in. You know I can outlast you."

"Give me a break. Who doesn't know what a loudmouth you are?"

"I'll split the time with you equally." Nicholas held out one palm and then the other, as if each represented a home. "But for the first time I've taken some family leave. I have two weeks off and then some extra time here and there over the next six months. Let me use next week to get her feet under her and get her started on some goals. A bucket list of sorts."

"Good name. One of your bucket lists might just kill her."

"That's absurd. Stop fighting me, and give her and me some space. She'll have fun. I promise."

Maybe Brandi was right about the culture shock. Ariana simultaneously felt like a loose helium balloon and feed corn being run through a grinder. Clear thought seemed impossible, but she knew Nicholas was wrong to use the word *fun*. Fun was being home and spending time with Rudy. Fun would be running the café she'd finally purchased a few weeks ago. *This* was miserable. But she would learn to cope, because if she didn't, Nicholas would take legal action against Rachel, the Amish midwife and family friend who'd known for twenty years that she and Skylar might have been swapped when she delivered them back to back before a fire engulfed the birthing clinic. Ariana hadn't known a person could be sued for negligence. If she left here, would Nicholas stop at suing the midwife, or would he also sue Mamm and Daed? Within a few days of her birth and Skylar's, her Mamm and Daed had a hint that something might be amiss. The blanket Ariana went home in differed slightly from the one Rachel swaddled her in following delivery.

"You listen up, Nicholas. She's not ready for all that." She pointed at the stack of books on the kitchen table. "Good grief. On Saturday she stepped out of her world, a world that more closely resembles the eighteenth century than the twenty-first."

Gabe, Brandi's husband, nudged her and opened his eyes wide, as if asking, "Seriously?" Brandi glanced at Ariana and gasped. Apparently in the heated exchange Brandi had forgotten for the moment that Ariana was standing there.

Brandi smiled, her eyes holding an apology as tears filled them. Ariana supposed Brandi missed Skylar as much as Ariana missed her Mamm. This whole mess was so new to all of them. Brandi and Nicholas had no idea Skylar wasn't their biological daughter until four weeks ago.

"Look." Nicholas took a deep breath. "I don't want to fight with you like this, but I'm not backing down. I have one year to . . ."

Their voices faded as Ariana slipped into memories of last Saturday when Rudy kissed her and held her tight, promising to wait for her return. Neither of them had ever desired life outside the Amish. Then she learned she wasn't at all who she'd thought herself to be. When she first heard the news, she feared telling Rudy. He had felt sympathy for her heartache and hated being separated from her for a year, but he hadn't minded that her DNA was Englisch.

All she had to do was live here for a year, and then she could return to Rudy and her café and her family that wasn't actually related to her. Would they love her just as much after they'd had a year to ponder that the ties of blood had been broken?

"Ariana?" Gabe spoke softly.

Ariana seemed to float down from the ceiling and return to herself. The stack of books in the center of the table still looked overwhelming, but the fury radiating from Brandi and Nicholas was the most disconcerting. She tightened her grip on the edge of the kitchen table, hoping to remain on her feet.

Gabe held his hand toward his wife and snapped his fingers. Within seconds the room fell silent. He angled his head. "Can you tell me how you're feeling?" His calm voice brought a bit of peace.

She should be fine — a little rattled maybe, but nothing more. What difference did this short time of upheaval make? Her life was back home, and this mess was just a slight detour. So why did her skin feel as if it were on fire? She wanted to ask if divorced people always argued like this. They didn't understand. Not one of them. She'd spent a lifetime having ingrained into her every thought that all these things — from divorce to higher education, from nail polish to television — were wrong, and now she was living in the middle of them. If she could get her mind to slow, to absorb what was happening. "A . . . a little confused."

"Yeah. I imagine so." His eyes radiated gentleness.

"Could . . . I mean . . . Would it be okay if I went for a walk?"

Nicholas moved forward. His face was so unfamiliar, and yet she recognized the parental concern. "We shouldn't have . . . I'm sorry, Ariana."

She managed a nod.

He drew a deep breath. "You're right. Some fresh air would probably be good for you. What if one of us goes with you?"

"Nee." The word came out fast and sharp. "I mean, no thank you."

"Okay, but it's a confusing subdivision, laid out strangely. So don't leave this block, and you'll be fine. If you go around two or three times, we'll have a plan when you get back."

Did that mean they would know where she would sleep tonight — here or at Brandi's? That's what began the argument. She'd slept at Brandi's Saturday night and here last night. Brandi had come to pick her up, and Nicholas said no. Then the argument shifted to everything concerning Ariana, including her clothes and hair. The threat of Nicholas suing her loved ones is what kept her here. Otherwise, she would walk out and never return.

Ariana pointed at the stack of books. "I can do this."

"Yeah?" Nicholas sounded hopeful. He'd been disappointed to discover he had a daughter with an eighth-grade education, but surely he knew she could read. He picked up the thinnest book. "Do you think you could learn to drive?"

If that's what it took to cause peace, she could. *"Ya."* That wasn't the right word. She was used to floating between Pennsylvania Dutch and English at home, but here the wrong language kept slipping out. "Yeah."

He motioned from Ariana's head to her feet. "Look at you. I told your mom you're a smart, capable girl."

Then why do I feel like a prized horse? she

25

wanted to ask. If her sister Susie were here, Susie *would* ask.

Awash in embarrassment, she walked past them and out the front door.

She looked to where the horizon had been her whole life, but it wasn't there. A multitude of huge houses covered every inch of the horizon, and there was barely the width of a lawnmower between them.

So many homes. Yet the emptiness Ariana felt was overwhelming, and the thought of calling Quill came to mind again. Nicholas had said she could reach out to Quill because he had left the Amish to live as the Englisch did. That's what Nicholas hoped she would choose to do by the end of her time here — leave the Amish and live Englisch. She would return home, but a year without anyone to talk to who knew or understood her was a very long time. Still, she wouldn't call Quill, no matter how bad things got.

The cool fall air felt good. Autumn meant a lot to the Amish — a time of refreshment, a season when life without electricity was easy. Spring also had gentle weather, but it was filled with planting and tending crops. In contrast, fall was a season of relative ease and weddings.

I want to be there, God. Or at least be al-

lowed to reach out to my family, friends, and, maybe most of all, Rudy. You have a reason for all this, right, God?

She felt no stirring of God in her spirit, only loneliness. Before learning she wasn't really a Brenneman, she'd never understood the pain of being alone. How had Quill's mother withstood her older boys leaving one by one? Then, a couple of years after her husband died, Quill, her youngest son, left the Amish, taking Ariana's good friend Frieda with him.

What kind of person did that?

A car stopped abruptly, and she realized she was crossing a street. It was dark? She supposed she'd known that, but it hadn't actually registered. It was also rather cold. How lost had she been in her thoughts? How long had she been gone?

"Sorry." She hurried back toward the sidewalk, tripping over the curb in her haste. It was time to get back to Nicholas's house. But nothing looked familiar, and now that she thought about it, she realized she'd stepped off the curb several times, crossed roads, and then gotten back on other sidewalks.

So where was she? And why was a man getting out of his car and coming toward her?

27

THREE

Mingo, Pennsylvania

Quill poured batter onto the hot skillet. The last time he'd made pancakes he was with Ariana while they worked to fix up the abandoned restaurant. That was a really good day.

"Yeah, sure." His oldest brother walked into the kitchen, talking on his cell. "This Saturday at four. Can you hold, please?" Dan removed the phone from his ear and pressed the Mute button. "Smells good."

Quill and his four brothers took turns cooking or bringing in takeout food during the week, and tonight was his turn. "It'll be ready in five."

"Listen, McLaren is flying in on Saturday. He says he wants you to be at the meeting too. Any chance you'd stay in Mingo this weekend rather than go home?"

McLaren was a wealthy developer, maybe even a billionaire. When he made a request of Schlabach Home Builders, they took it as a demand. But Dan's question was phrased as if Quill had a social life. He didn't. And that needed to change. Soon. "Sure. No problem. Any idea what he wants?"

"To discuss 'issues.' That's all he's willing to divulge."

Schlabach Home Builders had taken on a lot of responsibilities to win the bid for this job, and they were often close to being in over their heads with the workload and legalities. Had they messed up? They'd learned the hard way there was no end to Englisch laws and regulations regarding construction.

"I'll be there. No problem." Quill turned over the sizzling bacon.

Dan disappeared down the hall. "Thanks for waiting. I can confirm . . ."

Quill shoved a spatula under the pancake, opened the warm oven, and stacked the pancake on top of the others. The tiny trailer wasn't much, but it provided sufficient living space when they were working this far from their homes in Kentucky. Staying here was difficult. It was hard on his brothers because they had wives and children in Ashton and hard on Quill because he liked solitude — lots of it. In Ashton he lived alone in a tiny home he'd bought. It wasn't much, but he loved the old place.

His golden retriever stood near him, staring as pets do, unwavering and unabashed. Why weren't people, the creatures with the ability to speak, as direct with their thoughts and hopes? Lexi whined, a barely audible noise, hoping she'd get some of the bacon. Quill broke off a small piece and tossed it to her. "That's enough for now. Go lie down." After circling her bed several times, she plopped in the perfect spot to watch his every move — just in case he dropped a morsel.

Elam walked to the sink, his cell propped between his ear and shoulder while he washed his hands. "Sure, we'd love to see you and the kids, honey. When do you think you girls could head this way?" Elam grabbed a stack of plates from the cabinet and a handful of forks from the drawer while listening to his wife. The "girls" were Quill's four sisters-in-law, and when their husbands worked out of town too many weeks in a row, they would visit. The trailer was supertight during their visits, but Quill understood the girls' reasoning. "In two weeks?" Elam's words faded as he moved to the kitchen table.

Quill's thoughts drifted back to Ariana.

He'd helped her buy the café, but she didn't know most of what he'd done. Despite his efforts to support her, he — and his vast array of secrets — had alienated her again. He called them confidentiality issues; she called them secrets. Either way, the last one had broken their relationship.

His cell phone buzzed, and he pulled it from his pocket. Speaking of people who mattered . . . Frieda had sent a text, asking how he was. He pressed the microphone to dictate a response: "I'm good. Fixing dinner. Call after. Okay?" He hit Send and quickly received a smiley face in response. He tucked the phone back into his pocket.

He removed the last of the bacon, added the sizzling strips to the rest, and turned off the eyes and the oven. With a potholder in hand, he reached into the stove and took out the plate of hot pancakes. "Food's ready," he yelled.

Within a few minutes he and his brothers fixed their pancakes to their liking, loaded bacon onto their plates, and were ready to give thanks. Each of them had left the Amish at a different time, and none of them had kept many of the traditions they'd grown up with, but they did say a silent prayer before every meal.

Unlike his brothers, Quill hadn't felt a

need to pursue life outside of the Amish culture, and he hadn't been filled with a desire to explore the world beyond the Amish. For a while he'd hoped to stay and build a life with Ariana — not that she'd ever been aware of his feelings.

There was five years' difference in their ages, and before she was old enough to ask out, he had to make a decision concerning Frieda. Ariana had never professed her love, but he knew how she felt. He left anyway, keenly aware that he was destroying the love she had for him. He had no choice. With the deeply ingrained principles his Daed had taught him and his Mamm's hushed but steady nudges, Quill took Frieda and left, burning all his bridges behind him. After a five-year absence, he had the opportunity to rebuild the bridge to Ariana's life. It took both of them to build it, and it was really important to him. Then he watched it burn. It wasn't anyone's fault, not really.

He and Ariana were different people now. And despite wanting to be her friend, he knew that getting along with her was nearly impossible. Temporary truces ended with deeper and wider fissures between them.

Dan said, "Amen," and his brothers dived into eating.

If given the chance, Quill would rekindle the friendship. Still, Ariana was Rudy's girl now, and Quill was grateful. He wouldn't change that if he had God's powers to do so. She and Rudy were a good match; she and Quill were not. They didn't view anything similarly — not faith, not politics, not the meaning of life. She was honest and open; he was indirect and locked away.

Leaving the Amish life had brought more heartaches than just his brokenness with Ariana. The complications of his mother not having any children who'd remained Amish was one. But the hardest part was Ariana. Always Ariana. He prayed for her, but she'd been clear — he was to leave her alone. He had lied to her for years. About seven years, actually. It had been easy to justify his lies when she was a teen and he was trying to protect her from knowing the ugly side of life. And he still wanted to protect her from that knowledge.

Erastus gestured toward Quill's plate. "Is there something we need to know about the food?"

Quill's stack of pancakes had one bite out of it, and his brothers were halfway done. He'd been lost in thought again. "Very funny." He dug his fork in and took a bite.

"I disagree." Elam gave a lopsided, sad

smile. "You find nothing funny these days."

Leon removed the glass of apple juice from his lips. "And you do, Elam?"

"All right." Dan leveled a look at the two. "No one here finds anything funny, not right now. Drop it and eat." He poured himself some more juice. "We'll get through this most recent upheaval with the Amish just like we have all the other times."

"But it's not like the other times, is it?" Elam shoved away his almost-empty plate. "Seems like we ought to admit that and let Quill admit it."

Just what Quill wanted, to air his feelings to a room full of brothers. "I'm fine. Change the subject."

"Who's going to look after Mamm now that Ariana's gone?" Erastus took a swig of juice.

Quill couldn't think of any Pennsylvania Dutch words they still used other than *Mamm* and *Daed.* But from the time he and his brothers had learned to speak, they had called their parents by those names and probably always would.

"Maybe some of the other Amish will step up," Erastus suggested.

But Quill knew better. The Amish usually looked after their own, but none in the community were quite sure about Mamm. When

Quill's parents first married, they left Indiana and moved to Summer Grove, Pennsylvania, where they had no relatives. Then they had five sons. Once grown, four of them left, one by one, over a twelve-year period. Not out of rebellion against their parents or God but because of an unwillingness to conform to the *Ordnung*. Their Daed was faithful to the Amish beliefs, but he was also an analytical, independent thinker who taught them well. He believed that staying was the right thing for Mamm and him, and his goal was to bring some reform to the Old Ways, where shunning scarred a person's reputation for life and yet did nothing to stop an abusive alcoholic or a mentally unstable head of a household.

When Quill was eighteen, his Daed died of a heart attack while trying to get justice for Frieda. Quill hadn't understood all the circumstances that led to Frieda's leaving Ohio and moving in with them two years prior, but he learned about them soon after his Daed passed. When there was no justice or protection for her, Quill knew he had to finish what his Daed had begun. So at twenty years old, he disappeared with Frieda, making everyone in the community, including Ariana, believe he'd run off with her to get married. The community would let her go if she was married, but if she wasn't, they would hunt for her and try to force her to return.

Poor Mamm was caught in the middle. Her husband and sons were gone, and the community treated her as if she were contagious, as if she could infect them with her tragedies. When several offspring leave over time, the church leaders become stricter with the ones who remain. The greater supervision isn't to punish them but to make sure the children of other family members understand the hardships facing both sides — those who stay and those who leave.

Some thought his Mamm had committed a secret sin that caused her to be alone. But Quill knew the truth. Mamm was innocent. However, she had given birth to four mavericks. Then her fifth son had left for different reasons, and now he was a maverick too. Maybe he had been all along, but the desire to be present and to provide for his Mamm and his desire to build a life with Ariana had kept him from considering leaving.

"I've been thinking," Elam said. "We sank all that time and money into preparations for Salome and her family to leave the Amish. Since Salome has now promised Ariana to stay, at least until Ariana returns, maybe we could ask Salome to help Mamm the way Ariana used to."

After years of prayer Ariana's oldest sister and her husband had decided to leave the Amish, taking their children with them, of course. But like others who wanted to leave, they needed help to do that, including places to live until they could support themselves. That's where Quill and his brothers came in. They provided funds and temporary homes. Even if Ariana spent a decade among the Englisch, he doubted she would ever agree with him about helping Amish people to leave.

"No." Quill glanced at each brother. "Ariana's family is off-limits."

"Salome and her husband owe us. We've invested time and money . . ." Elam hushed when Dan gave him a stern look.

"Quill's right," Dan said. "Besides, no one asked Ariana to help Mamm. It was voluntary. Since having contact with us is not allowed, if we ask someone directly, we're asking them to disobey the bishop. So the whole community is off-limits."

Ariana had gone by their Mamm's place at least once a day for five years, often staying for hours. Neither Ariana nor anyone else in the Amish community had any idea that the brothers took turns secretly visiting their Mamm. If Ariana came during one of their visits, the son would slip out and hide in the barn or the shed until she left.

"We have to do something," Leon said. "If Ariana hadn't been looking after Mamm two months back, she would've died from simple dehydration because of that virus."

"But that was a fluke. Mamm gets lonely, and everyone could use a little help with daily chores, but she's generally healthy, right?" Elam asked.

"Sure, but another fluke could happen at any time, and she could be dead before anyone checks on her," Leon said.

Their Mamm's health wasn't bad, but her being a widow without family in the area raised issues that were difficult enough when Ariana was in Summer Grove. They seemed insurmountable with her gone now.

"Josiah Gingerich." Leon dropped the name and fell silent.

Josiah was from an Old Order Amish family in far northern Pennsylvania. He had left home as a teen and lived Englisch for a decade. Now he lived with his Old Order Amish folks. He had electricity, television, and other modern conveniences on his side of the house. He didn't attend the Amish church or wear their clothing. Yet on the other side of a simple door that separated the two sides of the home, his parents lived according to the Old Ways.

"Who?" Elam asked.

"Josiah Gingerich," Dan said. "You probably know him as Joe."

"Oh yeah," Elam said. "He was injured on a loading dock, right?"

"Yeah, that's him."

"That's all it took — becoming wheelchair bound — for his church ministers to decide that allowing him to live with his parents so they could help him was the Christian thing to do."

"Then that's all we need to do — take turns getting sick or injured." Erastus's chuckle sounded more like a groan.

"As brilliant as that plan sounds, we have wives who could care for us."

"Quill doesn't. I volunteer him. That would solve all the issues of Ariana not being there."

"I know you're teasing, trying to lighten things up, but I hate this conversation." Quill dropped his fork on the plate and pushed back from the table. It wasn't just about Mamm being lonely, or worse, but they talked about Ariana's departure from Summer Grove as if the only hardship was how it inconvenienced them and their Mamm.

Dan drew a deep breath. "Sorry, Quill."

Quill nodded.

"For what?" Erastus asked.

Dan sighed, shaking his head. "Ariana wasn't just a companion and helper for Mamm."

"Oh . . . ," Erastus said. "Yeah, I didn't . . . Sorry about that. It's easy to forget she's more than someone who watched after Mamm. I haven't seen Ariana since she was four or five, so I doubt I'd even recognize her." He gestured at Elam. "Would you?"

"I don't think so. Like you, I only saw her from a distance, mostly as she was walking away or hidden by the laundry she was hanging out."

Leon shrugged. "Doubt I would either."

Apparently Quill's brothers weren't as good as he was at finding a spot where they could see her without her seeing them. Catching glimpses of her as he sat in the loft of his Daed's cooperage shop had helped Quill cope during those first few years after he left. She was light and air in a heavy and dark world.

A memory hit, and Quill chuckled. "Dan would recognize her." His eldest brother had left the Amish when Quill was seven and Ariana was two, so it was ironic that he was the only other brother who could identify her.

Dan laughed. "Yes, I could . . . I think. Although I have to admit she startled me, and she was toting a hunting gun." He pointed his index finger at Elam's chest, as if his finger were the barrel of the gun and Ariana had him in her sights.

The table broke into laughter.

"Do I know this story?" Leon asked.

Dan leaned back in his chair. "I went to visit Mamm late at night about two years ago, and I fell asleep. I woke to the sound of Ariana calling out to Mamm."

"The voice I know," Elam said. "I can hear Ariana calling to Mamm now. 'Berta?' She says it like honey rolled in powdered sugar, as Mamm would say."

They laughed, but Quill wondered how badly Ariana was missing her loved ones right now.

"Anyway, I rushed to the closet to wait until Mamm could distract her and I could sneak out. I thought I was being quiet when I finally left the closet and tiptoed toward the back door, but I came face to face with her, and she was carrying Daed's Remington Mag." He laughed. "I promise that huge rifle looked twice its size at that moment."

"What was she doing brandishing a gun?"

"Good question. I had that same thought

after the incident." Dan pointed at Quill. "The reason is his fault."

"True." Quill couldn't help but smile, and it felt odd.

"He'd told her that if she ever heard an intruder, get the gun, and if the person didn't run off, put a bullet in the chamber and fire it at the floor near them. I was afraid to move."

Leon roared with laughter. "You were afraid she'd miss that huge floor and hit your tiny heart."

The room vibrated with laughter.

"Hey," Dan said, "I need this Grinch-sized heart."

"So what happened?"

"I glanced at Mamm, and I knew coming clean with Ariana wasn't the answer." Dan paused. "Am I right?"

Quill nodded. If Dan had revealed who he was or why he was there, Ariana would've had to carry the secret or to expose Mamm for seeing her sons behind the bishop's back.

Dan lifted a glass and waved it about as he swayed in his chair. "So I acted like I was drunk and had accidentally entered the wrong home, and I begged her not to shoot me."

His brothers broke into laughter, but Quill didn't join them.

"Okay, guys. Enough." Dan put the glass down. The merriment quickly faded. Dan laced his fingers, sighing. "It was an act of trickery, and in one way or another, we've all lied to Ariana over the years. She deserved better."

His brothers nodded and mumbled apologies.

"So," Elam said, "circling back to the topic, maybe we should talk to Mamm again about returning to her family in Indiana."

Dan stood and gathered plates from those who had finished. "She's made it clear that she's not leaving."

"Why is she so stubborn about this?" Elam lowered his head, looking weary.

"Apparently only she and God know why," Dan said. "But we can't stand for freedom, helping the Amish leave if they believe that's right for them, and then pressure Mamm to move because it's what *we* think is best."

"So what do we do?" Elam asked.

Three of his four older brothers looked at Quill.

It dawned on Quill that their looking to him said something about his nature. He was a planner. A schemer. He hadn't started out that way, and when he stepped into that life, it was because he saw no other way to finish what his Daed had begun. But in every decision, he'd put his personal beliefs and mission above Ariana.

Sounded ethical.

Felt very different.

FOUR

Ariana couldn't figure out what was going on. Once the man was at the front of his car, he returned to the driver's side and reached in for something. Blue flashing lights came on, disturbing the serenity of the night. A cold wind sliced through her thin sweater. How had she not noticed before now the sharp drop in temperature?

"Ma'am." Despite the numerous lampposts along the sidewalk, he shined a flashlight in her eyes, and she couldn't make out his face. He then lowered it a little. Evidently she'd stepped in front of a police car. Was it a coincidence, or had Nicholas sent for the police? Did police routinely ride through neighborhoods looking for signs of trouble?

For a brief moment he swept the light from her head to her feet. "Is everything okay?"

"I'm turned around." Her heart palpitated, and a surge of confusion seemed to numb her mind. Looking at the maze of sidewalks, she couldn't recall how she'd gotten here.

"Have you been drinking?"

"What?"

"You walked in front of a car and stumbled when retreating, ma'am. You're clearly confused. And you look underage. Have you been drinking?"

"No."

"It's the time of year for parties. Maybe some friends had a costume party nearby, and you —"

"Costume? These are my clothes."

"Do you know where you are?"

She shook her head. "I'm from Summer Grove, three or so hours from here, and I . . . I only arrived here on Saturday." Did she sound as terrified as she felt? "And I wasn't in this subdivision until last night." She studied the street. "They were arguing. So unkind and . . ." Tears threatened, and she dropped the rest of her sentence. It would be best to focus on concrete issues. She cleared her throat. "I hardly know them, and I went for a walk, lost track of time, and now I don't know how to get back." Her voice trembled.

He studied her for a moment before nodding. "Okay, I can help you with that. I assume you don't have a cell phone."

She took a deep breath, trying to settle her nerves, but it seemed as fruitless as trying to stop the wind. "I don't own one."

"Not a problem. Do you know the address of where you were?"

"No." A gust of wind made the pleats in her dress billow, and she shivered.

A robotic voice mixed with static came through some device attached to his shoulder, but she didn't catch what it said. He grasped the thing and responded, "Lost pup at Richland. Should be walkin' the dog in twenty." He released the device. "I wasn't calling you a dog. 'Walking the dog' means going on break. But you were the pup, so . . . I guess . . ." He cleared his throat and went to the passenger's side door and opened it. "Let's get out of the wind."

Her whole body shook, and she needed to sit. Maybe it would help her to regroup her thoughts. She got in, and he went around and sat in the driver's seat.

"How about the homeowner's name?" He pointed at a computer. "I can look it up and drive you there."

She should know this, and her heart moved to her throat. "Quill told me Nicholas's last name, and it should've stuck."

47

But when Quill told her, she'd just learned she wasn't really a Brenneman — a truth she had not wanted to accept, still didn't want to accept. She covered her face and broke into sobs. "I was so sure it was all a mistake." As best she could, she had put on a front with her family and community, pretending to be fine. Today she was falling apart.

"It's okay. Here."

She lowered her hands, and he passed her several tissues. "I've heard so many names over the last few days." That alone had her head spinning. Why wasn't Brandi's last name the same as Nicholas's or Gabe's? But knowing Brandi's last name wouldn't help. She lived several miles from here, and she wasn't at her house.

"Ma'am?"

"I can't recall it. I'm sorry. It's all so confusing." Tears welled again. Maybe because of embarrassment or maybe because it was fully dawning on her that neither God nor life was anything like she had believed them to be.

"The database won't be any help without an address or name." He pulled a cell phone from his pocket. "Do you know someone you could call? Your parents?"

"They only have a community phone."

When they did get the message, which could be late tomorrow, this incident would terrify and grieve her whole family.

He looked from the phone to her. "A friend? Someone who might know your host's name, address, or phone number?"

Only one person knew the information she needed.

Quill Schlabach.

"I'm not calling *him.*" She shook her head. "I'm not."

The officer held out his cell. "You could text him."

"I . . . don't know how."

The man seemed speechless, but then he held the phone with both hands. "What's his number?"

Ariana told him, and his fingers flew over the screen.

"Your name?"

"Ariana."

"I'll use voice texting." He pressed an icon. "This is Police Officer Barnes." His words appeared on the screen. "I'm with Ariana. What is Nicholas's street address or phone number?"

"You can't send that. He'll flip out and be on Nicholas's doorstep in no time flat. I don't want to see him."

The man pressed a circle that was off

screen and then pressed some more icons. "Look, I'm supposed to go on break soon, and I'd really like to get you somewhere safe and warm first." He held out the phone. Quill's number was on the screen, ready for her to push the green icon. "So I can call or text him, or you can."

It would do no good for either of them to text Quill. His knee-jerk protective mode would override all else, and he wouldn't respond to a text. He'd immediately call her on this number, and he'd refuse to tell Officer Barnes anything unless he talked to her first. She would have to talk to him to get the information. She pressed the Call button and waited.

Would he answer? He had two phones, one for everyone and one for just a handful of people. She was calling the number he'd given her, the one only a few had. Less than six weeks ago he'd bought her a phone, and she'd called him regularly as he helped her plan a benefit to raise money to buy the café. When she discovered that he was meeting with Skylar, the real Brenneman daughter, at the same time, she returned the phone and told him to leave her alone.

Her heart pounded harder by the second as the phone rang.

"Hello?" Behind Quill's greeting she

heard other voices and dishes rattling.

Why couldn't she speak?

"Hello?" Quill repeated.

Drawing a shaky breath, Ariana hoped the tears didn't return. "It's me." She breathed.

Something made a snapping noise three times in a row, and the background noise vanished. "Ari?" He waited. *"Iss sell du?"*

Hearing her language, one of the many things she missed desperately, caused tears to brim. Her lungs were begging for air as she tried to remain in control. "Ya, it's me."

Beside her, the robotic voice returned, static mixing with odd words.

"A police dispatch? Where are you?" Quill's voice remained calm as if none of the uproar in her life worked its way past his tranquil emotions.

"I didn't want to call, but I . . . went for a walk, and I can't find my way back. I need Nicholas's address, please." The words were the right ones, but did they come across to him as frantic as she felt? She hoped not.

"Sure. That's easy. I'll text it so you'll have it without having to write it down. Listen, I'm only an hour from Bellflower Creek. I could be there —"

"No."

"You're still angry with me. I get that. But I've been where you are — fresh from the

51

Amish community and feeling displaced. You don't have to go through this transition alone."

She wanted to say, "Of the two — alone or with you — I choose alone," but that would be excessively unkind, especially since she was asking for his help.

The dispatcher spoke again.

"You sound as if you're at a police station. I could pick you up, and —"

"It's a car. An officer is helping me." She couldn't have imagined what this new world would do to her, but she would manage without him. "I'll find others to help as I go along. Not you, please. Just text the address. That's all I need from you. Okay?"

"If you change your —"

"I won't. But thanks." She disconnected the call.

The phone pinged seconds later. Officer Barnes swiped his finger across the screen. "Here's the address, and he said to call him anytime, night or day, and that you can trust him."

Ariana swallowed the lump in her throat. "Could you take me back to Nicholas's house now?"

FIVE

A clanging noise startled Skylar awake. It had to be the crack of dawn. She looked to her left where a digital clock usually rested on the nightstand, but it wasn't there. During her few hours of sleep, she'd almost forgotten where she was, but the mooing of cows and the clanking of dishes downstairs were quick reminders. The past three nights had been spent on scratchy sheets, listening to the sound of restless farm animals.

The sharp pain behind her eyes signaled her desperate need for nicotine. She glanced at the other two beds, where Susie and Martha were when Skylar finally fell asleep. The beds were empty. Good. At least one thing was going her way. She got up, went over to her suitcase, and pulled out a pack of cigarettes.

Someone tapped on the door. "Skylar, honey?"

She recognized the voice of a nearly

unknown person, the woman who'd given birth to her. "Uh, just a sec." Skylar shoved the cigarettes into a compartment of her suitcase and zipped it shut. Thankfully, when the woman had gone through her suitcase, feeling for pill bottles, she hadn't noticed the squishy pack of cigarettes. "Come in."

She didn't even know what to call her birth parents. They said to use their first names — Lovina and Isaac — but she'd yet to do it, not because using a first name was disrespectful, but because it was too intimate. She felt nothing for these people. Unless they counted disdain.

The door eased open, and her birth mom smiled. "You're already up."

Did she have a choice? Maybe if the Brennemans didn't start banging around in the kitchen so ridiculously early. "Yeah. What did you need?"

The smell of coffee floated into the room. Amish coffee was perked, made by boiling water bubbling up and spilling over the grounds. The process made for a nice aroma, but apparently they used hardly any coffee grounds in the brew. It'd been distastefully weak her first two mornings here.

Lovina's eyes moved to the zippered section inside the suitcase, and Skylar realized one corner of the cigarette pack was peeping through. Could the woman tell what it was?

Sunday evening a bunch of teenagers had come to the barn and sung. Supposedly it was a fun tradition for single people, but Skylar had stayed in her room — a room she regretfully had to share with two younger sisters. At least they'd been out of her hair that evening. After the singing was over, she'd watched the young people through the window, and a few of them stood in the driveway smoking cigarettes. Still, she was unsure whether the Brennemans would approve of her doing so. Not that she cared what they thought or felt. It was just in her own best interest to keep her smokes a secret for now.

"I need for us to talk. Remember, I mentioned needing that on Sunday and again yesterday?"

She remembered. "Can it wait? My head is pounding again." Besides that, whatever Lovina needed, Skylar didn't have it to give.

Lovina studied her, looking a little anxious. "Ya, okay. We're making pancakes for breakfast." She gestured toward the stairs, looking every bit as uncomfortable as Skylar felt. "But then . . . do you even like them?"

Probably not. Skylar liked the way her mom fixed them — with a specific mix, hot cakes slathered in store-bought butter, fresh fruit, and whipped cream. But this home probably didn't have any of those things. She'd been here for days and hadn't yet seen a stick of store-bought butter or a carton of milk. Forget something like pancake mix. They produced their own food or did without. Every towel was threadbare, and the sheets had been patched. If her dad, the one she'd grown up knowing, wanted to teach her a lesson about using drugs, this was the way to do it. Amish living at its best was absolutely miserable.

"Pancakes will be fine. Thanks. Is there water this morning?"

Skylar had a lot to adjust to — new family, Amish rules by the silo-full, no modern conveniences, and the frustration of living in a poor home. Every time she turned around, another water pipe had broken, which meant someone had to haul water into the house so she could brush her teeth. And if she wanted to bathe, the water had to be heated on the stove. Forget having a shower. Who lived like this — no electric lights, washing clothes by hand even when the water worked, and having a rule for every little thing? But they hadn't put any of the gazillion Amish rules on her, not yet anyway.

Lovina looked sympathetic. "Your Daed . . ."

"*Dat?* What's a dat?"

"It's Amish for *dad.*"

"Oh." She'd heard the term numerous times, mostly from her stranger siblings.

"Anyway," — Lovina closed her eyes and swallowed hard — "Isaac is milking right now, but he will fix the issue after breakfast. I was hoping you would get dressed and join us at the table this morning."

Skylar wasn't a morning person, especially not crack-of-dawn morning, but today was her third morning here, and apparently her family thought it was time she joined them. "I'll be down shortly."

"*Denki.*" Lovina smiled and closed the door.

Skylar didn't understand much Pennsylvania Dutch, but she knew the word for "thank you." And *Bobbeli,* because there was no shortage of babies around here. In her other life Skylar was an only child. Now she had nine siblings and fourteen nieces and nephews — too many of whom shared this home. Mind boggling, really.

She put on a pair of jeans and a short-sleeved shirt. Thankfully no one had asked her to dress the way they did. What would she do if her birth parents wanted that? She removed the cigarettes and her lighter from the suitcase, slid them into her jeans pocket, and pulled the hem of her shirt over the bulge.

The hardest part of this ordeal thus far was the lack of drugs. The first two nights were the worst. Her feet started burning, and her legs wouldn't stop moving, and all she could think about was a couple of tablets of Xanax, Ativan, or Valium. Anything to stop the incessant restless legs.

She had to get something somehow. But sneaking out of a shared room was problematic. There was never any white noise to cover the sounds of her movements — no music, no iPhone app of ocean waves, no television left on by accident. Nothing.

Everyone — all umpteen hundred of them — watched her as if trying to wrap their heads around the fact that someone so different was related to them, or they watched her as if they feared she'd run off. And she would if she had any money, any prospects of getting money, or anywhere to go.

She was stuck. Maybe people who were smarter and braver would just leave and figure it out as they went along, but being homeless and penniless sounded to her like an easy way to wind up dead.

She *had* to get to a phone today. She left her room and walked down a large wooden staircase that groaned with every ounce of weight she put on the steps. It would be impossible to move around in this old house without the floors creaking. When she had a set plan with Cody, how was she supposed to sneak out?

Anxious tones between some of the women caused Skylar to pause on the stairway.

"Then I guess we need to make a trip to the bank." Martha sounded very upbeat and singsongy. Martha was the youngest daughter and the same age as Skylar's stepsister, Cameron, but the two were nothing alike. Cameron was tough, like sandpaper glued to old leather, and Martha was springy sweet, like wedding cake.

"Banks aren't open this early, Martha." Lovina got a pancake off the griddle, opened the oven door, and set it on top of a stack of pancakes.

"Then customers won't get any change back. They'll love that, right?" Susie had a whisk in hand, beating some white fluffy stuff in a bowl.

Salome poured coffee from the percolator into a thermal carafe. "The days of living as if Ariana can step in and rescue you are gone. Grow up and think for yourself. Getting change and other errands have to be done in the afternoon as soon as the café closes."

"Now those are helpful tips," Susie quipped. "Not."

"Things like correct change and opening on time aren't going to matter at all if —" Salome saw Skylar and motioned. "*Kumm.* Breakfast will be ready shortly."

"No rush. I'm not hungry." She wasn't lying. She'd felt ill ever since her arrival in Amish country on Saturday. "Coffee would be nice though." Maybe it would be better this morning.

Salome got out a mug and poured her a cup. Skylar walked to a chair at the kitchen island. Looking at Salome was like looking into a mirror, except Salome's eyes drooped, probably from years of weariness or unrest. And despite the pleated dress she always wore, Skylar could see that her belly sagged, probably from bearing five children. Why did she, her husband, and their children have to live here? Wasn't this house already brimming?

"Here you go." Salome set the cup in front of her.

Skylar could easily see through the light

brown liquid to the bottom of her mug. "Great," Skylar mumbled. "Canoe coffee."

Salome's eyes narrowed. "What's canoe coffee?"

"Like floating in a canoe, this coffee is as close as one can possibly get to water."

Martha angled her head, looking from Skylar to the mug. "That's how we make it at the café."

"Any return customers?" Skylar asked, sarcasm oozing.

Susie tapped Martha on the shoulder and whispered to her before Martha turned to do something.

"Sleep well?" Salome asked.

"Sure." That wasn't true, but what difference did it make? Salome returned to helping the others get breakfast on the table. Skylar added cream to her coffee, hoping to give it some flavor.

Lovina passed her a bottle of Advil, and Skylar got out two gelcaps. Watching the others move about, she tried to recall their names. She had most of the siblings straight now — at least those who lived under this roof: Abram, who was her twin, Salome, Mark, Susie, Martha, and John. It didn't feel as if they were related to her, and they seemed as frustrated by the situation as she was. They obviously missed Ariana.

Skylar took several deep sips of her coffee, hoping the caffeine would provide some respite.

Isaac walked in, immediately spotting her. His eyes probed hers, as if seeking confirmation that she hadn't yet lost her mind. In his own quiet way, he looked far sadder than Skylar.

What could she say? *Sorry, bio dad, my dad's gain is your loss?* She knew that Nicholas had been more than happy to learn that Skylar wasn't his, and he hadn't wasted any time threatening this Amish community in order to convince Ariana to leave with him and Mom. What were the odds that Skylar was switched at birth and that she had three sets of parents — Mom and Stepdad Gabe, Dad and Stepmom Lynn, and now her very Amish birth mom and dad — and none of them liked her? Her mom loved her, and no mom had worked harder to support her child's dreams, but Skylar wasn't at all sure her mom liked her, not really.

Mark and John, two of her brothers, came into the room chuckling about something. She couldn't imagine anything being amusing when they got up around four to start the milking. Besides that, the milking barn stank, and from her few days here, it seemed that cows were particularly stupid animals.

Abram eased into the room behind the other men, but unlike their birth dad, he seemed determined not to look her way. Some twin he was. He wanted less to do with her than anyone else in this home.

The next few minutes were chaotic as the men washed up and the women set plates of steaming food on the table. After everyone was seated, they bowed their heads, and there was a long pause as they prayed silently. Just as she'd done during every mealtime prayer, she watched each face. Did they really believe that God existed and, if so, that He actually heard their prayers? That was just crazy.

When her birth dad shifted, making some of the flatware jingle even before he removed his napkin, everyone opened their eyes and lifted their heads. Synchronized swimmers had nothing on these people. Isaac glanced at her birth mom. "So, Skylar, have you made your decision yet?"

"Decision?" Skylar asked.

Lovina pursed her lips, looking uncomfortable. "I haven't had a chance to talk to her yet, Isaac."

"Why?" Isaac took three pancakes off the stack and flopped them onto his plate.

"There hasn't been a good time." Lovina flicked a thumbnail against her index finger, looking a bit nervous.

"Did you sleep in again, Skylar?" Isaac reached for the wooden bowl that had a weird, whitish butter in it.

"A little." Skylar hated mealtime conversations. The siblings were usually noisy and boisterous, except when their parents pinpointed one of them for interrogation. Where was the privacy for adults?

Disbelief showed in Isaac's eyes before he nodded. "How many hours of sleep are typical for you?"

"Seven or eight, but I'm not sleeping well at night yet." And by *yet* she meant she wouldn't sleep well until she was no longer living like a pioneer.

"Sure, I get it. Sometimes our bodies need us to take it easy. You've had a lot to adjust to, and that's fine for another day, but it's also important to work. Staying busy is good for the mind and body. It's also good for us when we pull our weight."

"Pull my weight?"

"Every single thing you eat, wear, or need, someone had to work to pay for it. In this home we work together to make ends meet."

"I'm supposed to work for food and the roof over my head?"

"Honey." Lovina put her hand over Isaac's and patted it. "Are we supposed to get rain today or tomorrow?"

Skylar knew a distraction move when she saw it. Her birth mom didn't like the path of this conversation.

Isaac paused and smiled at his wife. "I don't think so. It'll be cloudy, and some wind may kick up." He returned his focus to Skylar. "Doing your fair share may sound unusual to you. Maybe your Englisch parents assumed all responsibility for paying for your needs. I think that's a mistake."

"Wow." Skylar rubbed her aching forehead. "So you believe the saying that idle hands are the devil's workshop?"

"What I believe is you should be bored by now, and I can't fix most of what goes wrong in life, but *that* I can fix."

"I'm mostly exhausted from not sleeping."

"Sometimes that sort of thing is circular. We can't sleep at night, so we sleep late and rest a lot the next day, and then we can't sleep the following night because we rested too much. That's not always the case, but we won't know until we break the routine, right?"

Did this man think he was a doctor? The desire to get up and walk out was so strong, but Skylar wrapped her fingers around the edge of the table and held on. They'd been kind to her up to this point — Saturday evening, Sunday, and Monday — but starting this morning she was expected to pitch in like a hired hand on a farm? She had to get away from here.

"Is there a problem?" Isaac asked.

"No. Maybe. I mean, I don't mind work, but it should be toward a worthy goal — like getting a break in the entertainment industry or finishing a semester of college."

"That's on hold for a while. And would have been whether you came here or not, right?"

He knew the answer to that. She'd been found with a concoction of illegal substances in her system, and her parents were going to pull her out of school and send her to rehab . . . or she could come here.

She nodded.

"So" — Isaac dipped his head to look her in the eyes and smiled — "let's focus on what can be done. Like pitching in with the work. Okay?"

He ended his sentence as if he'd made a request. He hadn't. It was an absolute. Man, she didn't want to be here for one more day. She had no money, and for the first time in her life, neither Brandi nor Nicholas would bail her out. Stupid drug testing. If her blood work hadn't revealed her secrets, she wouldn't be stuck here.

But Cody said he'd help her escape after he got a few things squared away. She just had to wait until he could get to her.

Salome put a serving bowl in front of her. Was that whipped cream? "We were wondering if you would like to help Susie and Martha at the café today."

Oh yeah. That's exactly what Skylar wanted to do — have her stage dreams taken from her and miss the rest of this semester while she helped keep Ariana's dream alive. "I wouldn't be much help."

"It probably sounds scary, but what's needed isn't hard." Abram lifted a coffee carafe from the table and refilled her mug. "See, that's pretty much all the girls need from you. Well, that and a few other simple tasks that would be a lifesaver for us right now."

She stared at the ripples he'd caused in her mug. Did he think she was so stupid that he had to show her how to pour coffee? Even if she was, she didn't need the lesson in front of the whole family. "Sorry, I'm just not feeling too well today."

Lovina passed one of the platters of pancakes to Martha. "Anything wrong besides not sleeping?"

"Headache." Skylar pushed the coffee mug toward Abram, giving him a silent *thanks but no thanks.* "I think resting will help." If she was going to cope with life until Cody could get her out of here, he had to bring her something stronger than Advil.

"Sure, you rest." Isaac smiled, nodding. "You can use today to decide whether you're going to help in the café or on the farm."

"That's the choice — help fulfill Ariana's dream or stay here and muck out the stalls? No. But thanks."

Everyone stopped eating, and the room fell silent, all eyes on her. What? Had no one ever told this man no?

Isaac pushed his plate away. "You don't have to help with either."

"Thank you."

"There's plenty of other work — laundry, housecleaning, meals, gardening."

"There's gardening in October?" Skylar's surprise made her sound interested. She wasn't. But the garden produced stuff in mid-to-late October?

"It's been a good year," Isaac said. "Much to be grateful for. The kale is still standing. There's more red cabbage to make into coleslaw. Some beets and Brussels sprouts are continuing to produce. Some years we're still gardening during the first snow flurries."

"No way." Why did she continue to sound like someone who cared? She glanced at Martha, imagining the sweet wedding-cake girl in a tattered winter coat and no gloves while gathering food for supper. Why did that image bother Skylar?

"Maybe you should choose gardening," Isaac said. "It's coupled with the chores of canning and meal preparation, but a lot of people find working with the dirt to be healing. I do. No matter what difficult thing is going on, when I'm planting or harvesting crops, I feel better and think and sleep better."

"I don't need any healing." Did these people just say anything that was on their minds while everyone was in the room?

And to think she'd almost felt bad for planning to go behind their backs in order to reach Cody. Not anymore. They didn't want to connect with their new daughter. They wanted slave labor. That's all.

When she left here, she didn't intend to be a part of either family — Brenneman or Nash. And certainly not a Jenkins, because Nicholas was a pain. She would head to New York or L.A., and she would never look back.

SIX

Abram slung a bundle of shingles onto his shoulder and toted the sixty-plus pounds up the ladder. This part of the neighborhood had no residents, only homes in various stages of completion.

"Abram." Jackson's tattoo flattened and inflated as he slid a shingle into place and shot several nails into it. "You okay?"

"Ya." Abram tossed the bundle onto the roof and dug in his pocket for his lock-blade knife. He pulled out the blade, ready to rip the paper off the shingles.

"Hold up. Don't open those."

Abram closed his knife. "Why not?"

Jackson rocked back to sit on his haunches while looking at Abram. "Because we don't need any more bundles of black shingles, especially since that color doesn't go on this house."

Abram looked to the ground below at the two stacks of roofing materials, one on this side of the driveway and one on the other. He'd spent the last thirty minutes getting bundles from the far side of the driveway. How had that not dawned on him?

"I just realized the mistake as you were climbing up." Jackson shifted until he was sitting on the roof. "You've been distracted lately. No biggie. Just take a breather for now."

Abram's knees were a bit weak, and he sat. He knew exactly where his mind was — Ariana. She had been the confident one, his safety net when he needed to talk, someone who could help him get through everyday encounters. Now that she was gone, he wasn't quite sure how to function. He was sick with worry about her, and he didn't know what to do about that either.

Sitting on this roof, looking at dozens of unfinished homes, watching other workers on the ground moving about, he had one clear thought: he couldn't let the café go under while Ariana was gone.

"I don't think I can keep this job."

"Why? We've been a team for three months. And you're good at roofing when your mind is where your body is. I gotta say it's bothered me to watch you go from extremely focused to superscattered over the last month. I'm not the boss, so there's no need to explain anything to me. I just wanted to get that off my chest."

Abram should string together a few more words. Ariana would want that of him. "I'm not dying. No one I know is dying. So you know . . . I'm fine."

"Ah, so that's how it is. If you're not gut shot and none of your buddies are gut shot, everything is just fine." Jackson propped his forearms on his knees and interlaced his fingers. "The Amish guys you arrive with each day seem to have had your back since your focus disappeared. I'm guessing they know what's going on, right?"

"Ya. They know."

The local Amish community knew the story, and maybe the Amish communities around the country knew. But since Abram's family didn't want the story picked up by the news, the Amish were keeping it to themselves.

"That's good," Jackson said. "Everybody needs at least one person who knows."

"But they don't get it, not really." Why had Abram said that?

"Yeah, what people know and what they get are very different, but take it from a former marine, it's still important to talk to someone."

Abram's sounding board was gone, and it

was hard to sleep and eat. Every time he looked at Skylar, it made things even harder. He had to remind himself that she was as innocent in this as Ariana.

Jackson pulled a stick of gum from its package and offered it to him.

Abram took it. "Thanks." Would the walking boss see them sitting around and yell? "I better take the wrong shingles back and get the right ones."

"You can do that tomorrow." Jackson held up his wrist and looked at his watch. "It's almost quitting time." He gestured toward the driver, Mr. Carver. The older man was half a block down the street, but he'd removed his tool belt and was slowly walking toward the work van.

"My sister bought a café, and I'm needed there. My two younger sisters are struggling to run it."

His whole family was struggling under the weight of the new café and Ariana's absence. If Jackson thought Abram was making a mess on the construction site, he should see what was happening at the café. Susie and Martha could barely cook anything on the menu, run a register, or keep enough dishes washed. If Ariana were here, she'd have that café running like water in a crystal-clear creek in summer — inviting and rippling with energy.

"I didn't know you had sisters or a café. Amazing what a person can learn when the quiet man actually speaks." Jackson chuckled as he unwrapped a piece of gum and shoved the trash in his pocket. "Is the food any good?"

"I doubt it."

"That's a great recommendation. I'll be sure to spread the word." Jackson's laugh echoed off the half-built homes around them. "But you'll forgive me if I don't eat there."

"Can't say I blame you. Hopefully, Susie and Martha are getting the hang of cooking what's on the menu."

"Your sisters bought a café, but you don't know if either can cook? I thought the Amish were practical."

"We are. I think. It's just . . . well, things didn't go as planned." Abram had said plenty, at least to an outsider.

"Where is this topnotch café?" Jackson got up.

"Old town Summer Grove." Abram stood. Nausea and lightheadedness made him feel a bit wobbly. A man who couldn't eat or sleep shouldn't be on a roof. "My sister Ariana can bake, and she bought it the first of the month."

He took baby steps down the slanted roof and to the ladder, thinking about all he and Ariana had been through to buy the café. They'd worked and saved for years. When time began to run out on the option to buy it and they were still short on funds, Quill walked her through the steps for having a successful benefit. She went to closing less than a week after the benefit. Abram started down the ladder.

Jackson waited nearby. "So why isn't Ariana running it?"

"She had to leave unexpectedly. In the two weeks between buying it and leaving, she tried to teach us how to prepare everything on the limited menu, but apparently that hasn't worked so well." Abram hushed and stepped off the last rung.

He couldn't stop thinking about the café. No matter what he did, the café forced its way to the forefront of his mind like a punch to the head. Something had to be done. They couldn't afford to hire anybody yet, and Susie and Martha couldn't keep up with the baking, serving, cleaning, ordering, and picking up supplies.

Ariana could, but Skylar couldn't even manage to pour refills for the customers.

Without having Ariana to talk to, he actually had a hankering to talk, but he had already said too much to Jackson. The man was just being polite.

The other men who rode with Mr. Carver were loading the van with their tool belts and lunchboxes. Abram told Jackson bye and climbed in the van, tuning out everything as the others got in. Mr. Carver started the van, and once the tires hit the main road, the vehicle seemed to fly.

Abram had decisions to make, and there was only one girl to talk to about it — Cilla Yoder.

An hour after leaving the job site, Mr. Carver dropped off Abram at his house. He needed to eat something so he would feel better, but instead he went into the barn and hitched a horse and buggy. He hoped none of his family had seen him get out of the van, because he wasn't in the mood to tell them where he was going. Or how work had been.

With the buggy set, he headed out of the barn and soon was going down a gravel road. Seeing the small pond to his left made him feel nostalgic. He and Ariana used to go to the pond, lie on their bellies, and lean into the water with buckets in hand to scoop up minnows. But once they had the minnows, they would let them go. Since Ariana left, everything reminded him of her.

Pulling onto Cilla's driveway, he realized he'd been hoping she would be outside. But she wasn't. He parked his buggy and walked to the house. After hesitating a few seconds, he knocked on the door, rapping three times. They probably had their door open earlier, letting in the fall air, but with the sun setting it was getting nippy.

He heard footsteps, and when the door opened, Barbie stood on the other side — the girl he'd finally gained the courage to ask out, who had said yes, and who had then jilted him before their first date. Abram nodded at her, frustrated at feeling nervous in her presence.

"You here for Cilla?" Barbie acted friendly.

"Ya."

"I'll tell her. Want to come in?"

That was the last thing he wanted to do. "No, just let her know I'm here."

Barbie gently shut the door. He moved to a rocking chair and stared out at a wide field, bare except for large, round bales of hay.

Cilla came out of the house, looking chipper and healthy, as if she didn't deal with cystic fibrosis. "This is a pleasant surprise." Her smile made his heart warm. She sat in the rocker next to him. "You know you could come inside."

"This is good."

They sat in silence for some time, gazing at the field and the pale orange sky. His head felt a little clearer already. "Do you think she'll like it there?"

"Ariana?" Cilla turned, studying him. "I don't know. I hope not."

"Ya, me too." He wanted assurance, but Cilla was too honest to tell him only what he wanted to hear. A silence stretched out for a few moments as he thought of all the Amish who had turned Englisch. Was the Englisch way of life as appealing as it looked from the Amish side? Appealing enough for people to leave their families forever? "I think I might need to quit roofing."

"Why? You're not thinking of searching for Ariana, are you?"

"No. She has to do what Nicholas wants, or it could cause trouble for the midwife." Abram watched the sky as the clouds moved across it. "It's so hard to believe Ariana has different parents than me. It always felt as if we were twins. We were so close."

"You and she *are* close, Abram, not *were.*"

The clouds changed shape, looking so different from a few minutes ago. How much would circumstances change Ariana between now and when she returned? "*Are* close," he mumbled.

"How's your Mamm doing?"

"Not great, but she tries to hide it. I overheard her talking to Daed, and she's carrying unbearable guilt. And now that Skylar is living with us, she seems to blame Mamm too. It's as if neither of them remembers that Rachel, the midwife and Mamm's friend, spent twenty years hiding her suspicions from Mamm."

"I heard at the Sunday meeting that a blanket brought everything to light."

"Sort of, I guess, in a roundabout way." He imagined that a lot of what was being said wasn't accurate. Other people could think what they wanted, but he wanted Cilla to know the truth . . . as much as he knew it. "What happened is while Mamm was in labor, she had time on her hands, and she embroidered a small set of baby's feet in the corner of two blankets, one blue and one pink. Since she didn't know she was having twins, she thought she would need just one of those blankets. Hours later as Mamm was delivering us, the birthing center caught fire. Rachel and Daed got everyone out safe — Mamm, Ariana, Brandi, Skylar, and me."

"Ya, I know about the fire. Everyone had to be really shaken and not thinking clearly for a while after something like that."

"I'm sure that was part of it. Brandi and Skylar were taken to a hospital. Mamm and Daed came home with Ariana and me. A few days or weeks later Mamm realized Ariana's blanket didn't have the embroidery on it like mine did, so she talked to Rachel about it. And Rachel wasn't just the midwife; she and Mamm were good friends. When Mamm questioned her about whether there was any chance the girls had been switched at birth, Rachel assured her the answer was no."

"Your poor Mamm must feel betrayed."

"Probably. Rachel told her the blankets fell off the infants and were mixed up but not the girls. That's the story Rachel stuck to until my brother Mark saw Skylar performing on stage, and he couldn't get over how much she looked like Salome. He came home and told us about it. Not long afterward Mamm and Daed approached Rachel, and whatever she said caused them to ask Quill to investigate the issue secretly."

The knot in Abram's stomach began to ease. Talking changed nothing, so why did it help him feel so much better?

"It seemed to happen so quickly."

"Some of that was Mamm's mistake, and she admits it. Once she suspected the truth and saw Skylar on stage, she felt God was directing her to connect with Skylar, and she let Brandi know that the girls were likely swapped at birth. But when the father, Nicholas, caught wind of what was going on, he rushed in, got blood work done on Skylar, and then started threatening lawsuits if Ariana didn't leave this life and spend time with them in the Englisch world." He intertwined his fingers. "So Ariana is doing that to keep Rachel out of jail. Part of me wishes they'd let Rachel pay the price instead of Mamm and Ariana."

"But how could Ariana stay here and let her biological father send a sixty-year-old Amish woman to jail?"

"She couldn't, which brings me back to why I'm thinking about quitting my construction job. I can't let the café go under while she's gone." Abram wasn't used to being so sure of something . . . of anything. He wasn't a leader, but he had to take matters into his hands this time. "The benefit left the café in pretty good shape to pay its bills for the next few months, but if it is run so poorly that there aren't any customers after that money runs out, we'll lose the café before Ariana returns. I can't allow that."

"Do you know anything about cooking or running a café?"

Abram shook his head. "Nothing."

81

"By all means you should quit your paying job." Cilla smiled.

Abram laughed. "I know. It's crazy talk, isn't it?"

"Not completely." Cilla's brows furrowed. "You're pale. Are you feeling poorly?"

"A little, but only because I haven't eaten right. That can wait. I need answers."

"Are you hungry?"

"Ya, but I'm fine. I wanted to talk for a few minutes, just us."

"Sure, but let me fix you a plate. Stay here, and I'll be back in two shakes of a lamb's tail."

He started to protest, but his stomach overruled him. "Denki."

"Glad to do it." Cilla went inside, and it seemed he'd barely gotten comfortable when she returned with a plate of food. "It's just leftovers from supper, but they're still warm."

"Denki." Homemade mac and cheese had never looked so good, and she'd given him an extra-generous portion of beef tips. He forked the beef and noodles together. "*Ach,* that's good." He felt better and more like himself with each bite.

Cilla set a glass of water on the table beside him. She waited quietly while he ate, and they watched as the late afternoon turned into the dark autumn night. "What about Skylar? Couldn't she be enough help that you could keep your job?"

"I don't know that she'll warm up to the idea of helping out at the café, but even if she does, I doubt she'll be much help. She never offers to do anything, including putting her own dishes in the sink. Daed won't put up with much more of that, but I doubt she's ever held a job or had a chore list."

Cilla blinked, her eyes wide. "Oh." She leaned back in her rocking chair, staring forward. "I can see why you're thinking about quitting."

"Ya, but jobs for poor Amish folk don't come easy. Not unless your grandfather or Daed or an uncle owns a business."

"It seems to me that you have your answer, don't you?" Cilla buttoned her sweater. "I could help at the café a couple of days a week. With both of our efforts, we might equal one slightly skilled person."

"That's very generous." Especially considering her health. "But I'm not in favor of that idea."

"Why?"

"Most important, your health. And we don't have money to pay employees yet."

"I'm fine now, could be for months. That's how CF works for me. And I don't want to be paid. Being a volunteer is perfect, no?"

"I . . . I don't know, Cilla."

"Would it help if I begged?" She clasped her hands together.

"No."

"Gut." She stuck out her hand. "We have a deal."

Abram hesitated. She was definitely pushing for her way and for all the right reasons. "Deal."

He shook her hand, noticing how very soft it felt in his.

What would it be like if he never let go?

SEVEN

"Sweetheart," Isaac said, "if you keep that up, you're going to wear off the enamel."

Lovina glanced in his direction. Her husband peered at her over the top of his newspaper. His gentle smile said he understood, but it did little to settle her emotions.

"At least then I would get past one hard coating around here." Lovina turned away from the stovetop she had been attacking with a rag. She would be encouraged if she could see one tiny victory in penetrating Skylar's armor. Despite helping with some chores yesterday, the girl skillfully avoided contact as much as possible through sleep, sarcasm, and indifference. Maybe those were defense mechanisms, but she seemed to detest everything about the situation — their faith, their large family, and their lack of electricity, cars, phones, entertainment, and education. They had to talk to her.

Isaac folded the newspaper and laid it on

the table beside him. "Skylar's only been here five days."

"Ya, five days without her letting down her guard once. Five days without her setting aside her disdain for us long enough to have one truly good moment, a moment where she connects. All she sees are poor people who aren't worth her time."

"Do you think Ariana is embracing Brandi and Nicholas any better?"

Lovina eased into a chair. "May God forgive me, but I hope not. They're . . . worldly, probably dangling every shiny bauble known to man in front of her." Did feeling that way make Lovina a hypocrite? She wanted Ariana to return unscathed by her new world, but she wanted Skylar changed by the power of God.

Isaac glanced at the clock, but he said nothing. Usually at this time of the morning they would be busy with their workday, but they remained in the kitchen, hoping Skylar would wake and the three of them could talk.

"I don't know if I should tell you . . ."

Isaac frowned. "If we're going to make any difference, we can't hide anything from each other concerning Skylar."

"Okay." Lovina glanced at the stairway and lowered her voice. "The whole time she and I were together yesterday — working some in the garden and then making lunch — she gave me nothing, Isaac. Not one kind word, not a smile, not really even lifting a hand to do any real work. She dragged herself through every hour and disappeared if I so much as blinked."

But Skylar had logged time on her feet and not in her bedroom. That had to count for something. Today she'd slept in, waking only long enough to say her head hurt again.

Since everyone else was gone in a dozen directions now, Lovina thought it might be a good time to try to find something in common, something fun or interesting they might begin to bond over.

Her guilt about the girls hadn't eased, nor had her grief. The situations Ariana and Skylar had been forced into were unfair, and Lovina carried the most responsibility. But she couldn't let that drown her. There was work to be done in both their lives — prayers to be prayed and battles to be fought. Lovina had to keep moving forward. This was no time for immobilizing regret.

But one of the undeniable realities was that the hole Ariana had left — her tender heart toward everyone and her love of hard work — felt as deep as the well in the side yard.

Lovina picked up Isaac's mug and took a sip of lukewarm coffee. "I hope Ariana is putting forth good effort for Brandi and Nicholas."

"She is."

"I'd sort of hoped that Skylar was one of those Englisch people who was enamored with Plain life."

"That would have made the transition easier, but she would realize we're not on that pedestal, because no one is. At least this way we get to work our way up, and it'll be based on who we are, not who she thinks we are."

Lovina slid her hands over Isaac's. "That's a good way to look at it, I suppose."

He glanced at the clock. "It's almost ten. Perhaps you should wake her."

"What if she didn't fall asleep until nearly morning?"

"Then she'd fit in with the rest of us, I think." He shrugged. "No one is sleeping well right now." He opened his paper and began reading again.

Lovina put a fresh pot of coffee on to percolate. She had a bacon biscuit sitting in a warm, covered frying pan. Surely Skylar would be up soon. In the meanwhile Lovina started scrubbing the inside of the oven. Twenty minutes later she heard the floor overhead creak and light footsteps on the stairs.

Still in her red silky pajamas, Skylar walked into the kitchen. Her blond hair with its black streak was tousled, and her gait resembled that of a wobbly-kneed senior citizen. She spotted them and froze, as if surprised to see them. Usually by this time Lovina was up to her elbows in outdoor chores — mostly laundry, some gardening, and helping with the never-ending farm work.

Lovina smiled. "Kumm. Sit." She took a mug from the cabinet and poured hot coffee. She put the bacon biscuit on a plate and placed both in front of her.

"Thanks," Skylar mumbled and leaned her temple against her palm.

Lovina passed her cream and sugar.

Skylar gave Lovina a sleepy halfhearted smile before returning her focus to the coffee.

Lovina sat across from her, and Skylar shifted. Were they making her uncomfortable? Lovina waited for the words to come to her, but her brain was just dead weight, and she looked to Isaac for help.

He fiddled with the edges of his newspaper. "We are wondering how you're doing. You know, how are you feeling about the transition?"

His words were as stiff as the oak table between them. How were they going to reach into Skylar's heart to make a difference when they couldn't get past their own awkwardness?

Skylar took a sip of coffee. "Not much to compare this to, is there?"

"True." Lovina stopped her fingers from fidgeting. "Still, you should know how you feel, right?"

"Considering how surreal this tabloid 'switched at birth' thing is, I'm fine. It feels as if I'm being punked."

"Punked?"

"It's a television show, and I can hear the hook — 'Aspiring actress college student has been sent back in time, a time before electricity and cars, where people live off the land. Will she adapt or go insane?' " Skylar set the mug on the table. "I'm leaning toward insane. You?"

She sounded every bit as apathetic as she was sarcastic, and once again Lovina looked to Isaac. His eyes were glued to the table, probably trying to keep from lecturing Skylar. Lovina couldn't let the awkward silence settle into nothingness. "There's no chance of going insane. People are built to adjust to their surroundings. But I also don't think you are, as you said, *fine.*"

Skylar set down her coffee. "How would you know how I feel?"

Her tone bothered Lovina. It wasn't accusatory. Her question was more like an observation.

Lovina put her hands in her lap and clutched them, holding tight. "This is a tough situation, and no one expects you to be happy, but you seem particularly unhappy, and we thought you might have a couple of suggestions for ways we could help."

"Maybe seeming unhappy is my personality. You don't really know me well enough to have a clue, do you?"

What could be done to break through her defenses, her apathy? "So what would you like to see happen between us — parents and daughter — while you're here?" Would reminding her they were her parents help her *want* to try?

" 'See happen'? You mean other than being allowed to return to the twenty-first century and attend college?" Skylar took a bite of her biscuit.

"I meant relationshipwise." Lovina couldn't keep her hands still. "This is our chance to get to know one another. We don't want it to feel like a punishment."

Skylar took another bite of biscuit. "I don't know what else to call it. I was given the choice of rehab or living here. Quill talked me into coming here, and I thought it would be better than rehab. For the record, it's not."

If this young woman weren't their daughter, Lovina would be tempted to show her the door.

Isaac shot his wife a look. "You see being here and doing chores as a punishment, but our only wish is to get to know you."

"That is just so shady."

Lovina wondered if Skylar thought they didn't know she was calling them liars.

Isaac sat up straighter, his face taut. "Why?"

"You're not trying to get to know me. Nobody here cares who I am, which is fine. But be honest about it. You want to use me as another worker. When I arrived, I wondered why anyone would have this many children. Now I know."

Isaac closed his eyes and rubbed his forehead. "That's not true, but, more important, what's your point for saying those things? Do you need to vent, or do you hope to keep pushing us away?"

Skylar blinked, and her guard seemed to drop momentarily, as if she was shocked that Isaac had pinpointed her desire to keep them at bay.

What would this relationship be like if they hadn't missed out on her childhood: seeing her blow out candles on her birthday cake, watching her clap and beam with excitement over dozens of things each month, kissing a scraped knee to make it better, walking with her to her first day of school, greeting her with homemade snacks when she came home, helping with homework, having daily devotions. But Lovina was never given that opportunity, and she feared Skylar would never want to have anything to do with her.

Skylar raised an eyebrow. "Don't you already have a daughter my exact age?"

Was Skylar being aloof and difficult because she thought they had no room in their hearts for her? Lovina had so many unanswered questions. If they didn't understand Skylar, they wouldn't be able to find a way into her heart.

"We have other daughters. That's true," Lovina said. "But each one is equally valuable and means the world to us. We would do anything to help them, and that focus is especially directed at our third daughter right now."

Skylar flinched at the words "third daughter." An awkward silence filled the room. "Don't you think referring to me as your third daughter might strain your relationship with Ariana?"

Lovina had practically thrown out Ariana for the chance to make sure Skylar knew God. Clearly she couldn't undo how swiftly she'd pursued connecting with Skylar. And Ariana would always be her daughter, but would she see it that way? "Love is weird. Its boundaries are able to expand, and each time that happens, it brings unexpected joys. Gifts from God."

Skylar's light brown eyes held suspicion. "All the joy of having a bouncing baby girl was centered on Ariana . . . for twenty years. I arrived too late to that party, and it's over. If you think otherwise —"

"Skylar." Isaac leaned in. "You're right that opportunities have been missed, and we're strangers for now. There will be a learning curve for us to connect this many years later, but we'd like for you to give us a chance."

Lovina shifted uncomfortably in her seat. "Ariana will always be our daughter, just as you will always be your parents' daughter."

"Yeah, *that's* the sentiment."

"What do you mean?" Isaac asked.

It was becoming clear that Skylar didn't

show much emotion. She just nonchalantly spoke in a sarcastic tone. "My mom was weary of trying to make me better, and my dad was all too grateful to have a new daughter."

Lovina ached to touch her daughter — to hold her hand or place a hand on her shoulder — but she didn't reach out. "I'm sure —"

"It's okay. I'm not complaining. Or looking for sympathy."

Was that true? Were Brandi and Nicholas worn out from trying to raise Skylar? "Look, we know this isn't an ideal situation, but —"

"That's a bit of an understatement."

"Regardless of how awkward and unpleasant this situation is, God can cause it to benefit all of us." Would Lovina regret talking about God to someone who didn't wish to hear about Him? "You can talk to us about any struggles." Was that true? What did they know of the kind of issues Skylar was dealing with?

"Struggles?" Skylar lifted a brow. "If you want to talk about drugs, say so directly . . . as if I could get my hands on any around here."

Looking at her in this moment, Lovina was convinced her daughter intended to make connecting with her impossible, and Lovina had no idea what to say to her.

"We weren't talking about drugs," Isaac said, "but since you brought it up —"

"I really don't want to hear about my sins."

"Then we won't touch on that topic." Isaac went to the stove and got the percolator. "But a laws-of-nature chat might be in order." He refilled her cup. "Not only am I a farmer, but I'm from a long line of farmers. Whether growing crops or tending cattle, we know the yield is a gift, but that gift is affected by whatever it comes in contact with. If crops grow in tainted soil, they can make a person sick rather than give nourishment. It's the same basic principle for livestock. If livestock eats something as harmless as onion grass, their milk or beef will taste strange, ruining the gift. Laws of nature are true whether we like them, agree with them, or are ignorant of them. Your life is a gift, and it's meant to yield good things to you and others. Drugs, whether a sin or not, will negatively affect your gift."

"Laws of nature." Skylar pinned Isaac with her stare as he sat back down. "Like the one that says if you don't care enough to look for or reach out to your child until she's twenty, she's not going to care by that point."

Isaac abruptly stood up, and Lovina knew he was fighting with himself, trying to weigh his words rather than unleashing them to straighten out this girl's thinking. He went to the cabinet, got a glass, and filled it.

"Is that what you think?" Lovina's insides shook.

She'd asked herself time and again why she hadn't pushed to learn the truth sooner, why she hadn't acted on her mother's intuition. She hadn't dreamed Skylar would piece together enough to blame them so fully.

"What should I think?" Skylar asked.

Isaac downed the glass of water and refilled it. "You should think that mistakes have been made on all sides. But we're your parents, not the enemy."

Skylar slunk back against her chair, looking disinterested in the whole conversation.

Lovina's heart ached for her child. Skylar was more than walled off and defiant. She was skilled at debating, and she wasn't interested in accepting where they were and moving forward but in assigning blame and pushing people away. Lovina was beginning to see why Susie bristled whenever Skylar entered the room. But whatever irked Susie about her new sister, she was keeping it to herself.

Isaac set a fresh glass of water in front of Lovina.

"Skylar . . ." Lovina took a swallow, trying to gain control as she prayed for the right words. She set the glass on the table. "You seem to understand the laws of nature well, and our hope is that you will apply that knowledge toward all sorts of things in your life, including the use of illegal drugs." Lovina drew a breath. "We don't want to impose our Amish beliefs on you or use you as free labor. That was never our hope."

"Then, do tell, what is it you want?"

The question stung. Was her only desire to figure them out and be on her way? "To get to know you," Lovina said. "To assure you that wherever you go in life or whatever you do, we're here for you. To give you a chance to get to know us and your nine siblings."

Skylar still had the same melancholy, apathetic look on her face. But she wasn't firing back a witticism or an insulting observation, which Lovina took as a small triumph. "How do you feel about our wishes?"

"I feel that if I refuse, I won't have a roof over my head by this time next week."

Lovina opened her mouth to refute that, but Isaac shook his head. Skylar's eyes bore into Lovina, making her shudder. They had no idea who this young woman was.

EIGHT

The aroma of steamy hot water, perfumed soap, and expensive body lotion filled the bathroom as Ariana finished pinning her prayer *Kapp* in place. She felt as if bees had taken up residence in her chest. Nerves, she imagined. She eased open the door and tiptoed past Cameron's closed bedroom door, hoping not to disturb the snooty, difficult teen. The whole house had been completely quiet since Ariana awoke an hour ago. What time did the Englisch wake on a Saturday?

She glanced into the room where she was staying — Skylar's bedroom at Brandi's house — making sure it was in good order. Ariana had made the bed and straightened everything, but nothing looked as it should.

A driver's license manual with her name scrawled on it sat on a French provincial vanity with three huge mirrors and a marble top covered with silvery containers of makeup, creams, and colognes, along with a jewelry box. A canopy of red lace was attached to four bedposts, a thick satiny bedspread of golds and reds covered the mattress, and a mirror ball hung from the ceiling. Ariana hadn't even known what a mirror ball was until she arrived. So who decorated a young girl's room like this?

Feelings she detested settled over her. When had she become a judgmental biddy? Had it always been there? She grabbed the manual, closed the door, and went downstairs to the kitchen. Her stomach growled, and she looked in the pantry. It had lots of stuff — cold cereal, macaroni and cheese, Hamburger Helper, raw sugar, breakfast bars, protein drinks. She spotted an uncut loaf of french bread and grabbed it. The one thing she knew how to do was to turn limited ingredients into something wholesome and delicious. She pulled eggs, cheese, and bacon out of the fridge before moving to the spice rack.

She had everything she needed to make cinnamon french toast. Her family loved it. If Cameron had friends over again, maybe they'd enjoy a nice breakfast when they woke. So far things between Cameron and her were uncomfortable. How could they not be? Cameron whispered and snickered with her friends, and she constantly referred to Ariana as different movie characters.

Ariana walked to the stove. It was time to win over Cameron, and a good meal would help. But the stove had no dials to turn and no burners. She studied it. There was writing inside various painted squares on a flat panel. Clock. Clean. Start. Off. It had other things too, including a number grid like a touchscreen phone.

She pushed various spots on the panel, and blue digital symbols and numbers showed up where it had been blank moments earlier, but nothing else happened. She pushed more painted squares, hoping to find the right combination that would make this cold block of silver and black come to life. It was pretty, and it was the cleanest stove Ariana had ever seen. Unlike the lace canopy on her bed, surely the oven served a purpose. Fine. Forget the oven.

She would simply make french toast on the stovetop. But . . . how did she turn it on? She pressed different squares of words this time. The stove beeped. Actually more like howled, making long shrieks that she didn't know how to stop. More shrill beeps started coming from somewhere in the house. What had she done? She followed the beeps and discovered a book-sized electronic plastic thing on the wall that was screeching and blinking. How had pushing buttons on the oven made this thing go off? Heat burned her skin, a sure sign of once again feeling completely stupid. She pressed the red button with the outline of a home on it, and it beeped louder and faster. Perhaps she should run upstairs and get Brandi. No one could be sleeping through this anyway. As she started up the stairs, a phone rang, the noise echoing off the walls.

The back door swung open, and Brandi and Gabe hurried inside, followed by Cameron and her friend. Brandi had on shiny, skintight pants that came just below her knees, Gabe's sleeveless shirt was as tight as his wife's clothing, and Cameron had on something that hardly covered her underwear. What was wrong with these people?

Such thoughts made Ariana uncomfortable, but they came nonstop from morning to night. Would she get used to the sentiments or figure out how to stop them? A reprieve of thirty minutes would be greatly appreciated.

Gabe grabbed the phone. "Hello?"

Cameron stood in the doorway and studied Ariana. Now a week after they first met, she apparently still hadn't decided whether Ariana was friend or foe, animal or human, slow witted or intelligent.

"We went for a run." Brandi's eyes were wide. "Are you all right, honey?"

Ariana nodded. "I'm fine. I . . . think I may have set off a couple of alarms."

"Ya think?" Cameron glanced at her friend, looking smug, before she moved to the stove. After confidently pressing a couple of buttons, Cameron silenced the useless thing. But another alarm, a much louder one, was still shrieking throughout the house.

"You're sure you're okay?" Brandi again looked Ariana up and down.

She wasn't okay. She never would be again, but she nodded.

Gabe said a few words, answering questions for whoever was on the line. His eyes centered on Ariana. "Hold on, please." He lowered the phone to his chest. "It's the security system people. They said the emergency button inside the house was pushed. Is everything okay?"

"I . . . I guess." Ariana shrugged. "As far as I know. I was trying to turn on the stove, and . . ."

"The stove?" Gabe repeated.

"Dad," — Cameron rolled her eyes — "tell the guy all our secret code stuff, convince him the house hasn't been invaded by body snatchers, and let him get back to the people who aren't trying to figure out how to use electricity."

While Gabe wrapped up the call, Cameron went to the plastic box Ariana had been at a few minutes earlier and pressed some buttons, and silence reigned. Cameron pointed at it. "This is a control panel for the security system. Because Dad and Brandi feared the apocalypse would take place while you were here alone, they set it."

Ariana looked Brandi in the eyes, and the realization of just how much they favored each other made the walls around Ariana's heart quake. Brandi's blond hair and green-blue eyes were a darker shade than Ariana's but very similar. Brandi had a willowy, hourglass figure, almost identical to Ariana's. She didn't want to be like this woman, to embrace her in any way, and yet the reality was staring back at her. "Until just now I didn't realize you weren't home."

"Oh, honey, I'm sorry. You've hardly slept all week, so I thought —"

"I was in my room awake, studying the driver's manual while trying to stay quiet so I didn't wake you."

Cameron went to the back door and closed it. "My guess is that while Dad was disarming the alarm so we could come in, it caused loud beeps inside, and you pressed some buttons trying to make it shut up. And, voilà, just like that we had a perfect storm of chaos." Cameron motioned from her friend to Ariana, shaking her head. "Disney's Giselle lives, and I'm sharing a house with her."

The girl laughed, opening her eyes wide and blinking, probably mimicking the character.

"Cameron!" Brandi pointed at her. "You be nice."

"I'm only teasing." Cameron shrugged and pulled a wide red band of some type off her wrist. "It's a whole new world for you, isn't it, Princess Jasmine?"

"That's enough, Cameron." Gabe spoke softly as he put the phone back in its cradle.

"What?" Cameron's eyes were wide. "You don't think I'm being nice either? She and Toto aren't in Kansas anymore. Is anyone in this house surprised by that?"

"I am." Ariana's words were more of a growl than anything else, and she grabbed the eggs and cheese and all but threw them back into the refrigerator. She wasn't cooking anything for anyone. "I'm totally surprised by it. Shocked. Miserable. But it's just funny to you, isn't it?"

"I didn't mean —"

"Ya, you did, Cameron. You like poking fun and comparing me to movie characters because I can't call you on exactly what your rudeness implies. I had siblings, good ones, even a twin. But like that" — she snapped her fingers — "no more. Now I have *you.*" She fluttered one hand toward a window. "And Nicholas's two stepsons. And none of you are actually related!" Ariana opened the pantry and tossed the french bread onto a shelf. "Tell you what. You learn Gabe isn't your dad at all, and trade him for someone as difficult as Nicholas. You give up your comfortable life and put yourself, by yourself, in, I don't know, maybe the Middle East, where the culture is totally disrespectful of you and all you've been taught to believe. Then we'll talk about how nice you've been, okay?"

Cameron stood there, eyes narrowed and locked on Ariana as if she was about to unload on her.

What is wrong with me? How could she stand in her birth mother's kitchen and yell at Cameron, or anyone, really? Nevertheless, Ariana snatched the driver's manual off the countertop and shook it in Cameron's face, daring her to speak up. "Today I have to give up my Amish clothes. Is that funny too? I'm being forced to wear Englisch ones because the irony of Nicholas being disgusted by Amish rules while he burdens me with his decrees somehow goes over his head. And I have to change my hairstyle. And when that's done, I get the fun of trying to pass some Englisch test to get a driver's license. None of which I ever planned or wanted to do, but, you know, that's okay as long as my life is fodder for you and your friends. Do you know why I'm agreeing to those things, Cameron? Has it dawned on you that this isn't just about the joy of learning I'm not Amish?"

Cameron looked at Gabe and then Brandi. "I . . . I never thought about it."

"Because if I fail to please Nicholas, an Amish midwife who is probably the age of your grandmother will go to jail. So, ya, I'm here, and everything about me is hilariously out of sync with this world, only nothing about it is funny." Ariana turned and hurried up the stairs, no longer hungry or caring if she and Cameron ever got along.

She closed the door behind her, leaned against it, and fought for air. *God, what are You doing to me?* Life seemed so unfair. Skylar had magically inherited wonderful parents and nine siblings. *She* was Abram's twin, not Ariana.

Ariana had lost everything and gained nothing.

Nothing.

The only thing that had been hers that still remained hers was Rudy, and she missed him so much. He wouldn't have a lot of advice for how to cope with going from the Amish world to the Englisch one as Quill might, but Rudy was the one she longed to talk to. Thankfully her new status as the only daughter of Brandi and Nicholas hadn't changed Rudy's love for her. He was spending this time with his parents in Indiana to save money so they could start a life together after she returned to Summer Grove. All she had to do was survive, be obedient to her biological parents, and return home.

Well, she also needed to avoid Cameron as much as possible.

"God," she whispered as tears fell, "when I do finally return home, will Mamm, Daed, my sisters, and my brothers still consider me family?" Or would everything change after a year of pondering her non-Brenneman status and the natural shrinking of the hole her absence had made?

Ariana shuddered.

She needed to talk to someone about all this craziness that weighted down her shoulders like the yoke of a workhorse. Who could she talk to? Brandi? Nicholas?

Quill.

The idea of calling Quill annoyed her. Angered her actually.

"Ariana." Brandi tapped on the door.

Ariana wiped the tears off her face. "Just a minute, please." She stood upright, willing the tears to stop as she drew a deep breath and moved away from the door. "Come in." Ariana went to the window seat and sat looking out at the neighborhood.

The door eased open, and Brandi stood in the threshold. "Hi." She stepped inside and closed the door. "You okay?"

Ariana opened the learner's manual, giving herself something to look at other than Brandi. "I'm sorry for losing my temper. I don't know what came over me."

"I know. Your world's been stripped away, and Cameron isn't a parent you feel you have to be respectful to, and then she trounced on your last nerve. A perfect storm, as she would say."

"I guess." Ariana flipped some pages, catching glimpses of road signs.

Life had a new and unfamiliar weight to it. She'd thought she was reasonably tough after being raised poor, and in some instances that was probably true. But she was no match for the weight of worldliness. And loneliness.

"You want to talk?" Brandi sat down a foot away from her.

Ariana's throat started to close again, and she knew tears were close to the surface. "Thanks, but no."

"Nicholas and I have really botched this. I was hoping by some miracle we'd do things right, but I guess that's beyond our parenting skill set."

"It's fine." Ariana dog-eared a page, opening and closing the tiny triangle. "We're all three trying to cope and adjust."

It'd been a long, tough week, one in which Nicholas had spent a lot of time teaching her about things she'd never heard of as well as teaching her how to drive. When Officer Barnes had brought her home, Nicholas and Brandi were visibly less hostile to each other. They apologized for their argumentative behavior and said they had worked out a lot of their plans and they wanted to compromise with her on things she strongly opposed — like wearing pants and sleeveless tops. She'd won that battle.

"Do you feel ready for the driver's test?"

She'd spent a lot of time behind the wheel, either with Nicholas or an instructor. A lot of time. "Probably." Her Daed had started teaching her the rules of the road at fourteen. He had her driving everything from rigs on the road to a team of horses in the fields. A vehicle with power steering and brakes seemed pretty easy after that.

"I know you're not happy, but it'll get better, and I'm determined to do better."

"Ya, me too."

She'd thought God let her be raised in an Amish home and then brought her here to lead Nicholas and Brandi to faith, but now that seemed naive of her. She'd spent a week splitting time between Nicholas and Brandi. He wasn't absent of faith. He had plenty of it, but none of that faith was in God. He was well schooled in why her faith was misleading and was based in fear. How did one explain faith to a man who was an atheist because of his vast knowledge of things she'd never heard of? What was the Higgs boson? She wasn't even sure what physics was.

"If it helps any, Skylar didn't get along with Cameron either."

That didn't help at all. Ariana was supposed to be skilled at bridling her tongue and turning the other cheek.

"I need to jump in the shower," Brandi said. "As soon as I'm dressed, we'll go to the mall. We won't have time to shop until we drop, but we'll do some good damage before it's time for you to meet Nicholas at the Apple Store."

The mall. Nicholas demanded that Ariana couldn't leave it until she had four dresses, a new hairstyle, and an iPhone. Once those things were accomplished, he would take her to the DMV so she could get her license.

"Any chance Nicholas changed his mind about letting me wear my prayer Kapp?"

Brandi looked sympathetic. "No. But I've been thinking about that. You know, a lot of Bible scholars feel the passages about a head covering are meant to be taken as symbolic, not literal."

Nicholas had already explained that line of thinking to her. "Okay." She forced the obedient word to leave her mouth and held up the manual. "I'll be ready when you are." That wasn't completely true. She would never be ready for the changes being forced on her.

Halfway to the door, Brandi turned. "I wanted to show you some of my favorite cafés. Going to different ones is sort of a hobby of mine, and we'd have time to go by the closest one before going to the mall. They have pumpkin spice coffee and donuts this time of year."

"That sounds nice. Thanks." She wasn't sure she could see someone else's café without tearing up, but she would try.

NINE

Quill's feet hit the ground with precise pacing as he ran, and his breath was as frosty as the ferns along the wooded path. He focused on the rhythmic beat of his steps, the swaying trees overhead — red maple, box elder, and white ash — and the brown leaves falling like snow.

Why can't Ariana just call?

He tensed at the thought and refused to dwell on it. He put his eyes on the path in front of him and took note of the late October air. It smelled of hydrangeas and forest dirt.

But five minutes of decent conversation would help both of us . . . Okay, maybe only me.

Quill picked up his pace. If running ten miles on a Saturday morning wasn't enough to shut out thoughts of her, he'd do fifteen — and push even harder.

His phone rang, and he almost tripped

over his own feet. He dug the cell out of his fleece pants and glanced at the screen. *His brother.* He slid his finger across the phone. "Hey."

"Something came Priority Mail Express, and it's addressed to Mr. Quill."

Whoever sent it obviously didn't know him well. So how did the sender get the address for the temp house in Mingo? "Dan, the whole idea of my going for a run is to put life on hold for a while."

"Then don't take your phone."

Quill kept the phone with him 24/7 in case Ariana called, which meant that he stayed keenly aware she wasn't calling. His brother was right. "I'm at the Y in the road. I'll be there in a minute." He ended the call and turned left at the fork in the path, heading out of the woods and toward the trailer rather than taking the three-mile loop again.

Dan was at the mailbox, shoving the phone into his pocket and holding a Priority Mail Express envelope.

Quill slowed, breathing hard.

"Sorry." Dan walked toward him, closing the gap. "I saw 'Mr. Quill' on the envelope, and I forgot about your preference for solitude when running." He passed him the envelope.

"Not a problem." He'd just leave the

phone in his bedroom next time. As Dan and he walked toward the trailer, Quill peeled back the perforated strip on the thin cardboard envelope. A quick glance at the contents revealed a newspaper clipping of maybe two hundred words, three invoices of some sort, a photo, and a note. He opened the folded note.

Dear Mr. Quill,
He needs your help before it's too late.
Sincerely,
Jake

The note appeared to be written by someone young, maybe under twelve. So who was the "he" and who was Jake? As he skimmed the short newspaper article, Quill followed Dan up the small steps and into the trailer. The key person in the article was Nate Lapp, who'd been found unconscious after falling from a hayloft.

Lexi lifted her head and wagged her tail, but she didn't budge from her spot on the couch. She'd run with him the first three miles, but then she started lagging behind, and he brought her home before hitting the trail again.

The kitchen table had an array of business papers spread out, ones that hadn't been there when Quill left for his run. "Been busy?" Quill looked at the many items on the table as he unfolded the invoices from the envelope. Love might make a person's world go round, but paperwork made the business world go round.

"Yeah." Dan tapped a yellow legal pad that had a long list of items, most with a red check beside them. "Trying to get all the work orders, plans, bills of sale, and memos in order for today's meeting with McLaren. Speaking of which, I can't find the electrical plans you used for the new phase of the development. I searched the storage bin in your room, and they aren't there. Could they be in your car?"

Quill looked at the three invoices. "Maybe. I don't think so." He passed the newspaper clipping to Dan. "Read that."

"Quill." Dan snapped his fingers. "I need you to look in your glove compartment and trunk and under the seats before the meeting. Okay?"

Quill glanced up. "Yeah, sure."

Dan didn't look convinced and for good reason. Quill would dump paperwork and receipts in his car for a year or more before sorting through everything, which often meant getting a garbage bag and throwing it all out. He hated paperwork.

Dan dropped the topic and read the article while Quill studied the invoices again. They were bills from trips to an emergency room for Nate Lapp.

"Nate Lapp." Quill mulled over the name while looking at the postmark on the envelope. It had come from Glen Rock, a town about forty miles west of Summer Grove. From where he was in Mingo, Quill could drive there in less than two hours. "Why do the names Nate Lapp and Glen Rock sound so familiar?"

"Because Glen Rock has a lot of Amish, and you must know a dozen Nate Lapps."

"True." Quill studied the info, trying to draw a memory to the front of his mind.

Dan turned the short article around to face Quill. "This is completely outside our abilities."

"Maybe." Quill took it back and looked at the picture. A scrawny kid, maybe sixteen or seventeen, was asleep in a hospital bed when someone took this picture, and he was as thin and frail as an old man. Something about the kid looked familiar.

"There's no *maybe* here, Quill. We don't offer to help anyone this young, and for good reasons."

"Frieda was this young."

"Totally different. Daed brought her to

live with you and Mamm. You were able to see all the puzzle pieces and know what was really going on. We can't know those things about this person's life."

"So whatever we do, we'll walk slower and lighter than usual." Quill returned the newspaper clipping to Dan. "Did you catch where the article says he's accident prone, and yet an unnamed family member used the word *suicide*?"

"I saw it. Followed by 'said Nate's twelve-year-old cousin.' We can't stick our foot in the door based on something a kid said — not to mention the severity of the word *suicide*." Dan clicked his tongue. "And you know if Ariana got wind that you're even thinking of dabbling in —"

"Dan. Good grief. Breathe, man." He picked up the envelope and dropped it on the table in front of Dan. "First, you're jumping way ahead. All we'll do is get some idea whether Nate is accident-prone or trying to take his life. If he has tried to end his life, it doesn't mean we'll get involved. He could have the best of homes and be mentally ill. We won't touch this request if that's the case. Second, I would do anything to help Ariana, but I can't and won't stop being who I am."

"That gotta-be-me comment may be

directly linked to your don't-ever-date singleness."

"Good." Quill went to the refrigerator and grabbed a bottle of water. Despite his quip to his brother, maybe Dan was right. Maybe the two things were connected, but he didn't think so. His inability to put effort into building a relationship with someone seemed directly connected to the baggage and emotional ties between him and Ariana.

After he opened the bottled water, Quill returned to the kitchen table and again looked at the newspaper clipping. "I know this kid. He used to come to Summer Grove with his family every other year. He's a second cousin to the Brenneman family."

"Great. Your looking into this ought to help you and Ariana make peace."

"Can't be helped, can it?" Quill knew he sounded flippant. That's not where his heart was, but his calling, if one could describe it that way, was to help any Amish person who needed him. Most Amish were good, loving, faithful souls, but when one wasn't or a family wasn't, there simply were no safety nets to help the victims, no safe harbor to run to, because the closed system allowed limited knowledge of who to reach out to and how to get help.

Even his love for Ariana couldn't make

him turn a deaf ear to those who needed help. He pulled out his cell and, using the information on the bill, called the hospital. After a couple of transfers, a nice woman confirmed that Nate was still there, and she gave Quill his room number. He thanked her and disconnected the call. "Let's make an upbeat visit, walking lighter than helium." He peeled out of his T-shirt. "I can be ready in fifteen. You?"

"How? We're going to sneak into a hospital room, unseen and unnoticed in broad daylight? And then we're going to ask this kid questions without him realizing what we're asking?"

"That's about the size of it. Where's your sense of adventure?"

"I don't have one. Never have." Dan gestured toward the stacks of paperwork he needed to organize. "The meeting with McLaren is at four."

"It's barely nine, and we'll be back in five hours with, at the least, a gut feeling about Nate and, at the most, some solid answers. That puts us back before three, plenty of time to make the meeting." Quill went down the hallway to the bathroom. This kind of visit was much better if two people went. It was usually strained if two strangers tried to talk, but throw a third person into the mix and have the two who know each other talk about their Amish childhoods. Then the third would chime in, and the ice was broken.

"What if he has relatives there?" Dan asked.

"Don't know. We'll figure it out as we go."

TEN

Ariana stared in the mirror, examining the scoop-neck, gray knit dress that molded to her body. Was this as good as it would get when it came to modesty?

Probably.

Dressing rooms were strange. The man-made illumination reminded her of something she'd never actually seen — an indoor, gloomy maze with electric lights that played tricks on the mind. How could electricity shine superwhite light that looked grimy and murky? It seemed to be another contradiction of the Englisch world.

She turned, looking at herself from one side and then the other. She would be self-conscious in this, but at least it had sleeves of some sort and came below her knees, barely. This room revealed flaws in her skin and body that Ariana had never noticed before. She looked pale and pudgy. Was she?

She stepped out of the dressing room, and

the jingling sound of arm bangles let her know which direction to head to find Brandi. She spotted her browsing a rack of jeans. Brandi's blond hair was shiny and flouncy, and her nails were manicured with a fresh coat of burgundy. Was it her birth mom's outward appearance that nagged at Ariana so much? She pondered that for a bit and decided it wasn't, not really. The issue seemed to be that Brandi's life was molded to the world's ways and she was comfortable with it — in fact, pleased and happy with it.

There was suddenly a bitter taste in Ariana's mouth, as if her judgment against her mom was making her sick. She wanted to accept her parents, but it was so much harder than she'd expected. She'd become harsh and unkind on every topic, but she didn't know how to free herself. Were those things a part of her heart, or was she simply overwhelmed and irritable? A better question was how could she esteem God's Word as literal for herself and not judge others who viewed it differently . . . or in Nicholas's case didn't view God as God at all? God was clear about what was right and wrong, but how could she hold on to that while not judging others who didn't hold to it?

Brandi looked up, immediately smiling. "That looks very nice. Does it pass muster?"

Ariana didn't really understand the phrase *pass muster,* but she knew what Brandi meant. The answer was *not really.* But if she didn't find something acceptable today, she was afraid Nicholas would pick her clothes for her.

Ariana tugged at the waist. "Perhaps one size larger would fix it."

"Oh, honey," — Brandi moved closer and pulled in the sides — "I could easily take four inches out from under the arms to the hem. It just feels snug because it follows the curves of your body, but there's plenty of room."

Ariana tugged at it. What would Rudy think of her dressing like this? "It's kind of you to take the time and to spend good money on me. Thank you."

Brandi's brows furrowed. "Let's buy this and keep moving. Time is flying."

Whatever thoughts had run through Brandi's mind a moment ago when her eyebrows knit, she wasn't voicing them. They found four dresses, and they hurried to their next destination. Their long strides took them by a blur of scantily dressed mannequins, more styles and colors of women's clothing than Ariana had imagined existed, and rows of bright counters with beautiful women selling makeup, perfume, and jewelry. Soon enough Ariana was in a hairdresser's chair and facing a mirror while a girl not much older than she fussed over her, asking a gazillion questions about what she would like. She wanted to wear her prayer Kapp and keep her hair in a bun. It had taken all of Ariana's willpower to remove her prayer Kapp in public without bursting into tears.

"We have to cut some of this." The girl stared into the mirror, looking at Ariana.

Ariana's pulse raced. She glanced at Brandi and shook her head. "We're not supposed to cut our hair."

"We?" The hairdresser's eyes reflected confusion, and she glanced at Brandi. "Well, whoever *we* is, it's your hair, and it's great. But it's so long, the last five inches are really thin."

"No, I . . . can't."

Brandi stepped forward. "Could you give us a minute?"

The hairdresser nodded and left.

Brandi stood behind Ariana's chair as if she were the hairdresser. She stroked Ariana's head. "Honey, I don't know if my opinion counts, but I'm going to share it. There is a lot happening every second on this planet: life and death, joyous events and horrendous suffering. I don't know which outweighs the other, but humanitarians — Christian and otherwise — log a lot of money, energy, and hours trying to ease the affliction of millions on a daily basis. It's been a lot of years since I've opened the Bible, but I remember it says that all good things come from God, so He's bound to be on the side of fighting for good. Right?"

"Yes."

"Can you see Him looking down on Earth and being so narrow as to say, 'Ariana, you cut your hair . . .' or 'You wore a dress that didn't have pleats . . .' or 'You removed the fabric covering from your head . . . so to hell with you'?"

Was that what kept Ariana so uptight about following the Ordnung — the thought of going to hell? That wasn't it. Couldn't be. She had moral objections and felt strongly about following her conscience.

Brandi cupped a bundle of Ariana's hair and showed her the ends. "You need a few inches off to shape it up since you won't be wearing a bun all the time. But more than that, you need to look yourself in the eye and say, 'I'm not afraid to live, not afraid to step outside of what anyone thinks, including Amish people.' Okay?"

Brandi's words tilled fresh ground in Ariana's heart, and a tiny piece of the hardened earth gave way. But one question niggled at her: In obeying the Ordnung in every way, was integrity or fear directing her?

She stared at herself in the mirror as if maybe the anxious young woman looking back at her had an answer.

Brandi put her hands on Ariana's shoulders. "Refuse the fear."

Was that what kept tripping her up — fear? She managed a nod. "Okay."

Brandi smiled, kissed her head, and motioned to the hairdresser.

The girl returned and picked up a spray bottle of water. "Since it's long enough to sit on, I doubt you'll miss five inches."

It's only hair. Be cooperative. Ariana nodded. Despite Brandi's convincing talk, Ariana's heart raced, and she wished she could flee back to her home.

Instead, she remained in place, drained and emotional, while the girl cut off a few inches, blew her hair dry, and styled it in what she called a really long, messy bun. Ariana turned her head, and the stylist held up a mirror so she could see the back. Actually . . . it was sort of cute. The clothes weren't so bad either. But it felt wrong.

Everything felt wrong, and she was growing weary of it.

Once done at the salon, Brandi walked with her to the Apple Store. Ariana's clothing and prayer Kapp were in a bag, and it seemed like an abomination to walk through the glitzy mall while all signs of the real Ariana were hidden in a bag. Did God mind?

Nicholas was waiting outside. "You're late." He checked his watch as if verifying his words.

Brandi nodded. "Yeah, I know. It took longer at the salon than I'd planned."

"I got the phone already." He held it up, pressing various icons.

Ariana noted the bright pink covering. At least he hadn't bought one adorned with fake jewels, like Brandi's phone. "Thank you."

"Sure. My pleasure." He didn't glance up from its screen. "I've set it up, entered Brandi's and my information so you can easily reach us. You're sure to need help learning to use some of its features, but that will have to wait. We have to leave if we're going to make it to our appointment at the DMV." When he held out the phone to her, he seemed to notice her for the first time. "You look nice." He glanced at Brandi.

She nodded, giving a slight shrug. "I think so too, but she's not feeling good about any of it."

Nicholas shifted. "Then it's probably something we need to talk about, but right now we have to go."

The man liked to talk about things, and sometimes it was helpful, but usually he explained how she needed to feel rather than listened to how she felt. Sometimes it seemed her Englisch parents only wanted to mold her into someone they could learn to like. Thus far, neither one was willing to consider going to church. Nicholas said he would listen about her faith after she read a book called *Religious Poison.* She read a bit a few nights ago, but its opening was horrible, saying that man made up God's existence and that the author would explain, through research and reason, why that was a fact. She had closed it and hid it in the closet before reading her Bible. But the words still haunted her.

Brandi waved at her and remained in place as Ariana hurried to keep up with Nicholas. He walked into the parking lot and pulled out his keys. "You excited about the next step?"

Excited was the totally wrong word, but she had to keep moving toward Nicholas's goals, and she had one more hurdle to get over today — taking her driver's test. "You're sure they'll let me take the test?"

He opened his car door. "You worry a lot. You know that?"

She shrugged and got in on the passenger's side.

"You have an appointment, and it's as I said earlier this week." He pressed the brake and pushed a button to start the car. "The laws for getting a license are different because you're not a teen."

He backed out with ease. Despite the hours he'd spent teaching her to drive this past week, she always felt she was on the verge of having a wreck when she was behind the wheel.

He turned on his left blinker. "If you can pass the written and driving tests, and if you have car insurance, which you do, you can get a license." He pulled onto the main road. "Oh, and you have to have ID to prove who you are, which I have right here." He patted a leather portfolio.

It was ironic. A man she barely knew had all her true identification information, and yet with each passing day she was less sure who she really was.

"Will the driving test include toll booths?" She hated those. They were confusing, and the cost seemed extreme.

"No toll booths. You did great learning how to drive." He merged into the far left lane. "I still can't believe it."

"Learning to steer something that doesn't have a mind of its own and doesn't have wheels that only go straight was incredibly easy."

"Interesting. I never thought about that."

"The worst is when it's raining or snowing or the winds are howling, and the horse refuses to come to you."

Nicholas laughed. "Gives new meaning to 'catching a ride,' doesn't it?"

"Not to mention the idea of 'can't catch a ride.'"

They chuckled, and she pointed at the driver's manual.

"Oh yeah." He nodded. "Study."

She focused on the rules of the road while he drove. The number of laws seemed to be increasing by the minute, and when they arrived, she was shaking.

He turned off the car. "I'll go in with you to make sure you get in the right lines and fill out all the paperwork correctly. Then I'll wait for you out here."

"Sure." She took a deep breath. Her will was set. She would keep putting one foot in front of the other, and maybe at some point she would stop feeling as if she were about to shatter. He held the door for her, and she went inside.

The busyness of the DMV looked like organized confusion.

"Just relax. You simply go through the steps until it's done."

Would it be that easy?

Two hours later Ariana walked out of the DMV with her driver's license. Part of her felt like a traitor. What was she doing with a license? On the other hand, she had something that was frowned on but allowed during one's *rumschpringe.* Very few Amish girls got one, but a lot of the guys did.

As polluted as she felt, she also had a few niggling moments of something she couldn't define. She felt . . . good about herself. Even so, the new things she'd gotten today weren't worth chasing after. But was there any harm in letting herself enjoy the victory?

Nicholas was leaning against his car, talking on the phone. When he spotted her, he ended his call and stood up straight, grinning. "Let's see it."

She held it out, unsure if she felt like a dying cow caught in the mire or a new calf in springtime.

"I'm proud of you, Ariana."

Remorse crept up her spine. If he was proud of her, then she'd crossed a line to feel good about getting her license.

He dangled the keys in front of her. "Care to drive?"

She shook her head. "Not if I'm given a choice."

Disappointment showed in his green eyes. "Why?"

"I'd just rather not, okay?"

"Yeah, it's fine. It's just not the typical response when people get their license. That's all." He withdrew the keys and got behind the wheel.

She went to the passenger's side and got in. Was Skylar struggling to adjust to her surroundings as much as Ariana was? No one seemed willing to talk about Skylar, not even Brandi. "Can I ask you something?"

"Sure."

"How's Skylar?"

His face became taut. "I don't know."

"Why?"

"We're trying to abide by the same guidelines we've given Isaac and Lovina — no contact."

"If I were Skylar, I would feel abandoned."

"Abandoned?" He glanced at her. "Why?"

"If my parents had the power to reach out

135

to me and didn't, my feelings would be hurt."

"Yeah, well, it's different with Skylar. She's not emotional like that, and I think she needs this time away from us. If Brandi or I reached out, she would use every trick in the book to get us to rescue her. If her friends knew where she was, we'd probably be looking at the same scenario."

Ariana couldn't imagine wanting to be rescued from her home. They rode in silence until they were almost back to his house. "Am I staying here tonight?"

"You're welcome to, but I brought you here because I wanted to give you a few things, and we need to talk." He pulled into the driveway and shut off the car.

"Give me a few things? All you've done today is buy me stuff."

"Indulge me. I've missed twenty years of your life. Besides, my dad's dad invested two grand in The Gap for me in 1980, and that gives me a little more spending money. All of that aside, I have a used car that's yours for as long as you want it." He gestured toward a white car parked by the curb.

"A car?" She sounded offended. She hadn't meant to. But a car? Why would he do that?

"I guess hoping for you to feel any excitement about it is asking a bit much." He pursed his lips, a faint smile shining through. "The plan was that you'd be so thrilled about having a car you wouldn't mind the next part." He shrugged. "We have a ways to go before we understand each other." He pulled out the large, thick manila envelope that held all the papers he'd needed to prove her identity. "Still, I have some goals for you, a sort of bucket list." He handed her a small stack of papers that were stapled together.

"Bucket list?"

"Yeah, it's usually a list of things people want to do before they die. In this case it's a list of items you need to accomplish before you return to Summer Grove."

She skimmed it. He wanted her to get ten manicures and pedicures and five massages. She thumped the paper. "Manicures? Pedicures? Massages?"

"They're an indulgence that most women I know enjoy, and I want you to see that there isn't anything evil about them."

"Ten?"

"I thought it might take you a while to chill about it and see that it's fun."

Why did he put such a premium on buying and enjoying things? She continued reading. "Attend an outdoor fund-raising concert?"

"I'm helping with a charity event next Saturday for a student of mine who's battling cancer. I saw that you held an Amish benefit, and I thought it'd be good for you to see how we hold an English fund-raiser. It'll have a concert, a talent show, food, games, and whatever else the committee comes up with to earn some money for the family."

That was certainly something she could agree to. "Okay."

"Really?"

"Yeah, sure. Something like that didn't need to be on this list."

"Good."

She returned to the list. He also wanted her to find a friend, go shopping with an Englisch friend four times, stay in a hotel, watch twenty-five movies, pick one religion and learn enough about it to pass a college-freshman-level test, and pick a destination at least seven hundred miles away and drive there by herself. "This is a lot of stuff."

"You have a year to chip away at those items. Twenty-five movies over the course of a year is only one movie every other week."

She read more. "Go to a bar?" What kind of dad *wanted* his child to go to a bar? Especially an underage child!

138

"Yeah, a bar. Just to see that neither the bar nor the people who go there are something to fear. If you learn anything this year, I'd like it to be that life should be lived with bold, brassy courage."

"I'm not even of legal drinking age."

"Then don't drink while you're there. But if you ever do drink, it's okay as long as you never, ever get behind the wheel of a car afterward. Just call me, and I'll pick you up."

"It's against the law, hence me telling you I'm underage."

"You don't have to color inside the lines all the time. Even the law allows for a little underage drinking in the privacy of your home for religious reasons."

"You don't even believe in God."

"That's not the point, Ariana. I'm just saying there's some leeway." He gestured toward the list. "But if you don't want to do that one, choose something else. I've listed ten categories, things like education, travel, relationships, electronic entertainment, novels, and the like. Under each heading there are fifteen to twenty-something suggestions. Each one is worth at least one point, and you only need to earn a hundred points."

"And then what? Do I get to go home?"

"Not home, no. Then you don't have to do anything else on the list. Look, if you spend the next year doing the things on the list, I'll be able to deal with whatever decision you make at the end of the year."

Did he think she would change her mind about returning home and joining the faith if she completed his bucket list? She lowered the papers and looked at him. "I've already made my decision."

The lines in his face mirrored his frustration and his effort to be patient. "Okay." He stretched out the word. "Until then, we do things my way."

"Yeah, that much I'm clear about." She went through the pages again, and this time her eyes caught the words "four dates." "You've listed dating, but I'm seeing someone back home. We're not officially engaged, but we are talking of marriage."

"So find a male friend, go on a few dates, and don't even hold his hand. But go out and get involved in life differently than you ever have. That's what I want. If a specific suggestion crosses your sense of moral rightness, don't do it."

"Why does *dating* have an asterisk?" She flipped through the pages again. "Several on the list have two or three of them."

"Those have more value. As I said, you

have to reach a total of a hundred points. Each suggestion is worth one point, and each asterisk is worth five points."

Could she figure out a way to earn a hundred points quickly so she would be done with this? "If I finish this list early, will you add more to it?"

"No, I promise." He motioned at the used car he'd bought for her. "It's apparent you're not thrilled about your car over there, but can we at least look at it?" He got out and went to it and opened the driver's-side door for her. "I got a great deal. It's an automatic 2006 Acura RSX. Since it's a two-door, it has a bit of a sporty look." His eyes met hers, and his shoulders drooped a bit. "You don't care, do you?"

She didn't mean to be rude or hurt his feelings. It was obvious that today meant a lot to him. "It's pretty."

"Skylar was over the moon when I got her a car."

"I'm not Skylar."

He flinched. "No. Of course not. I didn't mean . . ." He sighed. "Could you just sit in it?"

She got behind the wheel and laid the bucket list in her lap.

He passed her the key. "Leather seats and steering wheel."

She looked for the ignition and found it on the steering column, but she didn't put the key in. "It's nice. Really. Thank you."

"Look," he sighed. "I know all this is hard. I do. And I'm trying to walk lightly, hoping to find a balance between what you want and what I think is best for you."

"How is asking a minor to go to a bar and drink good for her?"

"That was wrong of me. I see that now. I should've seen it earlier. I guess I assumed all young people either drank or wanted to."

Ariana didn't know what else to say, but she wondered how messed up Skylar's thinking was.

Nicholas propped his arm on the open car door. "Imagine if you discovered you had a child who couldn't read and had never experienced the beauty of the outdoors or seen a sunset. You would want to change that, right?"

"This" — she picked up the list — "isn't about learning to read so someone can know God's Word, nor is it about seeing God's sunset." She shuddered to think of fulfilling his list. "The list is . . . unfair."

"It's not. I promise. I don't want you to do anything you'll regret. I've done more than enough of that for both of us. I was careful in deciding what to put on the list and what not to, although I should've left off the bar and drinking. I've admitted that. But somewhere between where you are as a person and where I've been as a person, there's a good balance, and I want us to find that for you."

"So your plan is for me to sin."

"Based on your definition of sin, yes, I absolutely want you to sin. You're afraid to wear your hair wrong. Even if I believed God existed, I would never accept Him as one who stood in judgment over half the things you consider wicked. If anyone understands the power of doing wrong, it's me. I've caused more people more pain than I'm worth, and that's the truth of it. I would never want to lead you into anything that's truly against good, strong morals."

Ariana looked from the bucket list to him. "You mean that?"

"I do. I needed a better moral compass long before I got one. God or no God, it was immoral for me to be married to someone else when you were conceived, but even so" — he gestured from her head to her feet — "that time clearly brought a lot of good. You were born because of it. So even when wrongdoing is at its worst, it's not as bad as you seem to feel about how you wear your hair."

Her heart turned a flip. What did he say? "You were married when I was conceived but not to Brandi?"

All the vigor drained from his face. "Wait." He looked desperately remorseful. "You didn't know?" He clutched his head with both hands and moaned. "Not again." He drew a deep breath, gaining control. "I . . . thought . . . I assumed you knew."

Her chest felt as if it were on fire. She was a bastard? That wasn't possible. God wouldn't . . . Her insides quaked, and her faith of knowing what God did and didn't allow — everything that had been a sure foundation of solid rock under her feet — seemed to crumble as if it were bone-dry, unbaked pottery.

Her head spun. She was illegitimate?

That meant her mom and dad were adulterers, and she had been conceived in sin. She'd been a mistake of the worst kind.

God, I can't do this. I can't be this person.

But she was, and the pain in her chest was so bad she could only take shallow breaths.

"Ariana?" Nicholas said. "I'm sorry."

She needed to get away. "I . . . I think I'll take the car for a drive."

"I'd rather you come inside and talk."

"Later. Okay?" She grasped the handle of the door.

He hesitated but let it go.

Her hands shook as she shoved the key into the ignition and turned it. Illegitimate and unwanted. Unlike her Amish parents, who were excited and proud to welcome her, Brandi's and Nicholas's lives had been torn apart because of her. And it seemed pretty clear to her that neither had fully recovered from her ill-timed, unwanted appearance. A bastard? Tears fell from her eyes. The Amish community would never look at her the same. She'd heard of illegitimate Amish babies, not that she knew of any personally. The gossip arrived on the winds of a tornado, filled with debris and destruction of the character of the mother and child.

Ariana drove for miles, barely able to see. Not only was she not who she thought she was, but neither was God.

Then who was He?

Her lifetime had been spent in a small community that spoke its own language and listened to preachers who spoke in the believers' homes or barns. Her education came from teachers no older than herself who taught in a one-room schoolhouse. Every one of them — believers, church leaders, schoolteachers — believed and taught the same thing. How much of what she'd been taught was true? And how much was based on the bishops' and preachers' interpretations of what was true?

She pulled into a parking lot and shut off the car. Her hands trembled, and the tremors intensified until her whole body shook. *God, I can't do this.*

All dignity and honor were gone now. If she hoped to survive this test of endurance intact, with enough of her left that she could return home and begin to heal, she had to talk to someone.

ELEVEN

The wind whipped brown leaves across the Brennemans' yard as Lovina checked the hanging laundry and found it was dry. She unpinned several dresses and laid them across her arm as she moved down the line. Her grandchildren's voices echoed as they played in the sandbox and play area on the far side of the house.

A gate clanged and rattled, and Lovina looked in that direction. Skylar held open the gate to the pasture as Salome pushed a wheelbarrow of compost out of the field and toward the garden area behind the house. Neither looked happy, and neither was talking. Isaac had paired them as chore partners today, and they were doing some gardening — harvesting and prewinter prep — while keeping an eye on Salome's children.

Her daughters couldn't be more of a mismatch. Skylar wore jeans and a sweatshirt with the name of her college stamped in bold letters across it, and Salome looked to be an exemplary Amish woman. But how Salome looked or acted didn't reflect how she felt. Otherwise, she wouldn't have planned for Quill to help her abscond during the night with her husband and children.

Dogs barked in the distance, and cows mooed as if they were uneasy. The men and her eldest grandson were gleaning feed corn from Englisch fields that machines had already harvested. Usually they picked up enough leftover cobs to feed the horses through the winter.

Lovina tried to reel in her meandering thoughts. She returned to getting clothes off the line even though her heart was as heavy as the laundry. Mondays were laundry days in these parts. All Amish knew that. But here she was on a Saturday afternoon standing at the clothesline for any passerby to see. Then the Amish community would have more gossip to add to the rumor mill.

She wasn't sure she cared anymore what people outside her immediate family thought. What anyone believed wasn't the problem. Truth was the problem, and the truth was that Lovina had failed her family.

What Mamm doubted that a newborn was hers and yet didn't fight to uncover the truth? What Amish woman couldn't keep her home in order, couldn't do laundry on the right day, because worry and grief had come her way? And what good Christian failed to seek wisdom and to use patience before searching for the truth?

Lift up your eyes unto the hills.

Lovina immediately looked to the hills at the horizon, longing for insight and a whisper of God's wisdom to her heart. She neither saw nor felt anything helpful — just the eerie beauty of half-barren tree limbs swaying in the wind as they were entering a deep winter sleep.

Suddenly loud barks pierced Lovina's thoughts.

"Esther!" Salome screamed. "Run! *Dabber schpring!*" Salome thundered toward her children. "James! Henry! Get behind a tree!"

One glance informed Lovina of everything — the gate to the pasture was open, and the dogs were chasing the Holsteins. As the cows rushed through the gate, they gained momentum. Lovina threw the clean clothes at the basket and took off running. The herd was headed straight for the children's play area.

Lovina urged her aging body to go faster. Why was she going in this direction? *Stop! Go the other way!* But her body didn't listen, and she kept running toward the front of the house.

Skylar seemed frozen, and Lovina cupped her hands around her mouth. "Skylar!" She pointed behind her daughter at several cows that were heading straight for her. "Get behind a tree!"

Skylar flailed her hands heavenward as if she had no idea what Lovina had said. Had Lovina spoken in Pennsylvania Dutch? Lovina pointed. "The tree. Get behind it or climb it!"

Skylar sprinted, but she seemed to be heading away from the closest tree. Should Lovina go after her? Maybe. But her legs kept going toward the front of the house. Soon four-year-old Esther was in sight, running as fast as her little legs could go. She was ten feet ahead of the first cows, red faced and losing ground. Although exhausted, Lovina somehow ran faster, grabbed the girl's hand, and dragged her around the corner to the front of the house. Gasping for air, she lifted her granddaughter and held tight, flattening her back against the house. The cows thundered past them, dogs still barking and chasing.

Where was six-year-old James? And eight-year-old Henry?

"James!" Salome screeched.

Time seemed to move in slow motion as terrifying thoughts whirled in Lovina's head. Where was Katie Ann, Salome's two-month-old? Surely she was safe in her bed, sound asleep, and not on a blanket in the yard. Lovina's heart thudded, and her wobbly legs threatened to melt to the ground, but she stayed upright. *"Bischt allrecht, Liewer?"*

Esther nodded. *"Ich bin gut,"* the girl whispered, panting hard. The burn scar on Esther's face was extra bright red, but she'd assured Lovina she was good.

The cows continued onward, gradually scattering and slowing down. Lovina peered around the side of the house and saw two straggling Holsteins. Cows didn't usually need to be feared — as long as they weren't stampeding across the ground where children were. Lovina ignored the stragglers and held Esther's head against her chest as she wobbled along, praying neither her grandsons nor Skylar had been trampled.

Salome jumped up from behind the woodpile, her son Henry beside her. Salome spotted Esther and broke into tears. "Denki, *Gott.* Where's James?" She spun. "James!" The panic on her face made chills run up and down Lovina's body.

"Here." Skylar came out from behind a

151

tree, pointing up. "James is here."

Henry ran to Lovina and wrapped his arms around her waist. "You saved Esther!" He hugged his *Grossmammi* tight.

"Denki." Lovina rubbed his back. "But Gott saved her."

"I'll go close the gate." Henry ran off, but Lovina thought the whole herd may have gotten out. They needed to round up the cows as quickly as possible, but right now Lovina didn't care if it was midnight before they were all corralled. The women and children needed a few minutes to restore calm.

James was still standing on the lowest branch and holding tight to the tree.

"It's okay." Salome sounded calmer now. "Kumm." She reached for him, but he was too high. How had he gotten up there?

Salome directed him gently in Pennsylvania Dutch, and James slowly released the tree, lowered his belly onto the limb, and then hung from the limb by his hands. Salome wrapped her hands around his belly and steadied him as he let go and dropped to the ground.

Lovina moved in closer toward Skylar. "Are you okay?"

Skylar took several steps back. "I'm fine."

The girl seemed just short of hating

Lovina. Was Lovina expecting too much progress in a week? *We will move past this, right, God?*

Lift up your eyes unto the hills.

Lovina again looked to the closest hill. The wind played with the trees, leaves fell like spring rain, and gusts of wind pushed the limbs to and fro.

The two boys grabbed their Mamm and Grossmammi by their black aprons and pulled them into a group hug. After a long squeeze all of them laughed with relief. Skylar stood ten feet away, arms folded and as aloof as the day she'd arrived. The group finally released one another.

"For such stupid creatures they sure can cause trouble." Henry looked a bit bewildered. He'd been helping with the milking for a while now, but nothing like this had ever happened. "Those were cattle dogs herding the cows, but I've not seen them before."

"Me either." Lovina held Esther tight, so grateful she was safe. "We'll tell your *Grossdaadi,* and he'll set the matter straight."

Salome held out her hands for Esther, and the little girl scrunched into her Mamm's arms. For the first time in weeks, Salome looked into Lovina's eyes. "Denki."

Lovina cupped Salome's cheek with her

hand. *"Mei Lieb."* *My love.* Lovina had called her that since the day Salome was born. Even after Salome's plans to leave the Amish in the dark of night, Lovina loved her. Did Salome know that? Lovina was angry with her. And hurt. But her love for Salome hadn't wavered.

Salome gazed into Lovina's eyes, and tears ran down her face. She took a step back. "James, go inside and check on Katie Ann. Henry, get a bridle on the two horses so we can begin rounding up the cows."

Was Lovina's eldest daughter trying to get a moment alone with her? If so, it would be the first in a long time.

James went to Skylar and put his arms around her waist. Skylar pursed her lips and rolled her eyes — neither of which he could see — but she put her hand on top of the boy's head.

He beamed up at her. "Denki."

Skylar nodded.

Salome closed the gap between her and Skylar. "You put him in the tree." The awe in her voice was undeniable.

Skylar shrugged. "He was trying to climb it. I just gave him a boost."

Salome glanced from the tree to Skylar. "That was quite a boost."

"And it wasn't the closest tree to her,"

Lovina added. Now it made sense why Skylar hadn't ducked behind the nearest tree. She'd put herself in danger to help her nephew.

Salome grabbed Skylar by the shoulders and pulled her into a hug. "Thank you."

Lovina half expected Skylar's face to soften, but the lines across her brow grew harder. "Geez, people, all I did was give a kid a boost into a tree. And I'm the one who didn't shut the gate properly."

Salome released her. "But that was an accident. Helping my son to safety was on purpose."

James took Skylar by the hand. "Kumm. I'll get you some water."

Skylar wriggled her hand free. "I'm fine, kid."

"Kumm." James motioned for her.

Skylar sighed, but she followed him. A moment later James dropped back, walking beside her. She looked disgusted and weary when she glanced at Lovina.

As Henry strode toward the barn to harness the horses, Salome turned to Lovina. "You saved my precious girl, and the words I've held back for so long won't stay penned up." Salome's eyes again filled with tears.

Lovina looked to the hills, hoping for wisdom as she nodded. "Go on."

"I know I hurt you and Daed deeply when I went behind your back and made plans to leave the Amish," Salome whispered. "I can see that now. Missing Ariana the way I do, even after a good farewell and her promises to return, makes me realize what I would have done to you and Daed if I'd left without warning. But, Mamm, look." Salome gently ran her finger down the side of her daughter's scarred face.

Esther had closed her eyes, ready to take a nap after the exhausting incident, clueless as to what her Mamm was saying. But Lovina knew.

The memories of that day nearly three years ago played in her mind like a bad dream. The family had gathered in the yard, and Isaac had built a fire. Esther fell near the firepit. Like most nightmares, parts of what followed were a blur. They rushed to an Englisch neighbor, who drove Esther and her parents to the hospital. The doctors recommended skin grafts, and Salome wanted to follow their advice, but the Amish community pressured her to bring Esther home and follow the Old Ways, using herbal poultices instead. Salome's husband, Emanuel, sided with the elders and the community, as did Lovina. Salome caved to the pressure, feeling shamed into trusting

God over educated doctors. So she relied on the Old Ways.

Salome was faithful night and day to make the best poultices and apply them numerous times a day. But what the church leaders had promised would happen ultimately didn't. Esther suffered severe pain. Salome's agony turned to depression. What Lovina hadn't known until recently is that at some point during that arduous time, Salome and her husband contacted Quill, asking him to help them leave the Amish. Apparently the process with Quill went slowly, probably to give Salome and her husband time to pray and reconsider. They sold their home, moved in with Lovina and Isaac, and waited until Salome gave birth to Katie Ann, who was ten weeks old now. If the situation with Ariana hadn't come up, Salome and her family would've been long gone by now.

"Mamm?"

Lovina drew a deep breath, coming back to today. "Salome, I have no stones to throw. Of course I forgive you."

"You mean it? Because I don't get any sense that you really do."

"Ya, I mean it."

But she understood Salome's reluctance to believe her. Lovina sounded hurt and weary rather than loving and forgiving.

She'd spent more than three decades raising children, trying to give her all. How had she gone from a whole family to this broken disaster? It seemed to have happened overnight, but apparently the only thing that had happened overnight was her eyes were opened.

Salome inched forward. "I love you, Mamm. My need to leave was never about how I feel toward you."

"Denki." Lovina took Salome's hand into hers and squeezed it. "Can I ask you something?"

"Ya." Salome shifted Esther onto her other shoulder.

Lovina patted the little girl's back. "You promised Ariana you would be here when she returns, but for how long, Daughter? Is your decision to remain Amish permanently, or is this merely something you feel obligated to do for a season?"

Salome's eyes moved to the ground, and the shards of Lovina's broken heart were ground into powder. Salome lifted her head, looking her Mamm in the eyes. "I don't know. I . . . I'm sorry. But I give you my word that if we decide to leave, I'll come to you first."

Lovina looked at the tree that had protected James only minutes earlier. God had provided protection in a variety of ways as the cows had stampeded across the yard — a woodpile, a tree, the corner of the house, and three adults — one for each child. Where was His protection for her and her daughters' hearts in all of this?

Something at the base of the tree caught her eye. Peeping above the grass was a brown bottle with a white cap. She went to the tree and picked up the bottle. It was filled with round white pills, and the label had the name Charles Cook. Lovina's heart sank. She didn't need anyone to tell her they'd fallen out of Skylar's pocket, probably as she helped James onto the tree branch.

When did Skylar get these and from where . . . and from who? Had she managed to conceal them despite Lovina patting her down and going through her luggage? Or had she sneaked out at night and bought them from someone?

Lovina closed her hand around the bottle, suddenly feeling like a woman who'd feared her husband was cheating and had just discovered the proof.

"Mamm?" Salome walked to her. "Are you okay?"

Lovina opened her hand, revealing the bottle. "Why do I brush aside reality until it

159

sinks its teeth into my jugular?"

Esther's eyes were heavy as she snuggled against Salome's shoulder. Lovina would give almost anything to return to that simpler time of being a young Mamm. Before decades of mistakes pressed the life out of her. Before her weaknesses tainted the harvest in her children's lives, crops from seeds she'd never meant to plant.

TWELVE

Quill put his palms on the hood of Dan's truck, studying the electrical plans that were spread over it. He hadn't found his copy, in part because the trip to see Nate Lapp had taken longer than he'd planned. Still, the three of them — Nate, Dan, and Quill — had managed to have a good conversation, one worthy of their time. Quill wasn't completely sure what was going on with Nate, so he would visit again and investigate a little more. But Nate seemed in good spirits, and Quill was leaning toward believing the young man was simply accident-prone.

"So what happened?" Liam McLaren, a gray-haired, broad-shouldered man with a thick Irish accent, gestured at the plans.

"I'm not sure." Quill studied the plans in front of him, and they didn't look accurate. If he'd messed up as badly as it appeared, it would take a lot of time and money to fix them. Still, this wasn't the kind of thing a developer cared anything about. The general contractor usually addressed these types of issues, and McLaren himself doing it stuck out as very strange.

"It's obvious" — McLaren thumped the plans — "that you didn't order or install the right-sized electrical panels."

"I agree that's how it looks."

The new phase of building had begun about the same time as the upheaval in Ariana's life. His time and attention had been spread very thin at that point as he'd tried to do right by her and help her get the café — for all the good it'd done either of them. Had he missed seeing the changes in the plans for the new phase?

"That's all you have to say?" McLaren asked.

Quill looked up, studying McLaren, and the hairs on the back of Quill's neck stood up. This man had more on his mind than Quill's mistake. "Maybe I overlooked the info in the new plans. I would need time to locate my plans and go over my notes." He wasn't sure how much experience this man had with the construction process. "The project manager updates the plans as needed, and he's responsible for adding a new date, sealing it, and writing *superseded* on all the old plans." Quill pointed to each part of the plan as he talked about it.

"So it's Sanders's fault?"

"I'm not saying that. It may be completely my fault." All the information on this set of plans was right. But what did the information say on the plans he couldn't find? And where was the set of plans he'd used to order and install the panels and wiring for all those homes?

While trying to sort through possible solutions, the private cell phone in his jeans pocket buzzed. McLaren would be furious if he took a call now, but Quill wouldn't take the chance of missing a call from Ariana. What if she needed his help? He pulled it from his pocket and saw a number he didn't recognize. "Excuse me. I'll be brief, but I have to take this call."

McLaren slammed his hand on the hood of the truck. "I'm talking to you, Schlabach!"

Quill held up his index finger. "Hello?" He heard nothing. Was anyone there? "Hello?"

"I . . . I can't do *this.*" The husky whisper sounded nothing like Ariana at first, and she was sobbing.

"Whatever it is, I'll help you. And not just me. You have my brothers and sisters-in-law who would do anything. You're not alone, Ari." When he'd left the Amish, the one overwhelming feeling was loneliness. He'd been confused, angry, sad, and a lot more, but loneliness was what dragged him under time and again.

Her breathing was labored. "No. No one can fix *this*."

Chills ran up his spine. Whatever was happening, she was overwhelmed, and the way she'd twice said *this* stuck out like a warning flag. "What can't you do, Ari?"

She cried harder, and Quill ached for her. She'd had the same desire her whole life — to have the Amish dream: the simple life of faith, family, and hard work.

"Ari, it'll be okay. We'll find solutions. Just talk to me." He could only imagine the demands being put on her. He waited, and even though she said nothing, he heard her brokenness. "Ari, what can't you do?"

She said nothing, but the short, ragged breaths continued.

"Ariana, what's happened?"

She hesitated and stammered. "I can't say it. I can't tell anyone," she finally whispered.

Panic unleashed within him, and he fought to temper it. What new thing had happened to put her in this state?

He needed to look her in the eyes and will

her to get control and find the strength to work through this transition no matter what it dished out.

He dug in his pocket for his keys before remembering he'd come with Dan. He walked back to where Dan was. "Tell me what you need, Ari, and we'll work on it together, just like we did when we were kids."

"I have to get home, Quill. I have to."

"Okay, then we'll make that happen . . . somehow."

Could they find a way to convince Nicholas to release her without suing Rachel?

"I had to remove my prayer Kapp, wear Englisch clothes, read and study Englisch things, but I kept holding on, thinking that I'm still me. Thinking that somewhere beyond all these changes, I'm still the same girl who grew up in Summer Grove . . . but I'm not her at all."

"Ari, where are you?" As soon as he asked, he pushed Mute on his phone. All he heard was her crying. "Dan, give me your keys." He held out his hand. "I have to go."

Dan reached into his pocket.

McLaren pointed. "You're kidding me!" He slammed his hand on the hood of the truck again.

Dan passed him the keys and grabbed the

plans off the truck.

"Look." Quill fumbled with the keys until he had the right one. "If the mistake is my fault or if there is no evidence saying otherwise, I'll make it right, working however many hours are necessary to get the homes rewired in time for their closings. And the cost and time will be covered by Schlabach Home Builders. Okay?"

McLaren's bushy eyebrows knit, and he glared at Dan.

"He's right. He has the full backing of Schlabach."

Quill hopped into the truck, leaving the door open as he started the engine. "Dan, call the family. Get everyone praying." He closed the door and pressed the Mute icon again so Ariana could hear him. "Ari, please, tell me where you are."

Neither her sobs nor her breathing had calmed. "Did you know?"

Before she learned she'd been swapped at birth, he was familiar with every tone in Ariana's range of emotions. Whatever this was, he didn't recognize it. What had she found out?

"Focus on your future, Ari." The truck wheels screeched as he pulled out of the job site. "You'll return home to Rudy, join the church, marry, and have lots of babies.

That's your dream, and it will happen. Today will be a distant memory."

"Rudy . . ." She sobbed even harder.

Why? His name usually brought her immediate hope and peace.

She finally took a deep, jerky breath. "He's as good as gone already. He just doesn't know it."

Quill prayed not. If Ariana could come away from this mess with Rudy waiting for her, she would weather everything else. "He loves you."

"He loves a woman who doesn't exist."

"That's not true. You are you no matter what — the kindest, gentlest, strongest, and most honest and loyal woman I've ever known. Nothing that's happened can take that away."

"Did you know?" she asked again.

He hoped he wasn't about to get caught in something else he hadn't revealed to her. It had destroyed their friendship when she discovered that he'd known she wasn't a Brenneman and that he'd kept it from her while getting to know Skylar. He'd seen it as a necessity. She'd seen it as a betrayal of her trust. "What I know is that Rudy's love is deeper than you're giving him credit for."

"Quill." Her firm whisper hinted at her exasperation with him, but at least the weeping had slowed. "Did . . . you . . . know?"

"I'm not sure what you're talking about."

"That . . . that . . . I'm a bastard."

His heart plummeted, but that explained why she was in such a state. All she'd been taught for twenty years gave this news the power to push her to the edge. "I didn't know. I . . . I had some suspicions. That's all. But how you were conceived doesn't mat—"

"Ya, it does! My father was married, and I'm the result of adultery. I'm just an inconvenience. Even the term *love child* doesn't fit because my parents hate each other. I have no siblings, no Amish heritage, and adulterous parents!"

"*You* are a gift, a miracle. You were the godsend that held me together when my Daed died and my life shattered. You are the cement that has held the bricks of the Brenneman family together time and time again. You are half of my mother's heart, and you watched over her as if she were your own. You are among the best that this earth holds for a little while, and Rudy knows it."

"That's how you want me to see myself. But who I am is a —"

"Ariana Grace," he spoke softly, "stop. Do

not use that *b* word again."

"Why, because hearing it offends you? It's who I am!"

Despite her anger she was calmer than at first. Talking would help, especially with someone who could absorb her deepest hurt and angriest blows.

"The word is derogatory and belittling. There isn't a person alive who couldn't be described with some ugly narrative. And you're saying it as if it's the most significant thing about you."

"The Amish ways are built on the life and times of Jesus. In His day when a woman was discovered as an adulterer, she was stoned to death, and I would've died with her, never seeing a day of life. If I'd been born before her sin was discovered, we both would've been stoned."

Ariana's Achilles heel was her legalistic, unrealistic view. It was her nature to be obedient, to figure out what God and her parents expected of her, and to give a hundred percent effort. "Jesus changed that, remember? He said, 'Let he who is without sin throw the first stone.' And he wanted children — all children — honored and protected."

"I don't recognize myself, Quill. I thought I knew who I was, but I have no love or compassion. I can't stop judging people for even a minute. Cameron was out of line, and I told her off, screaming like an outraged teen. In all my years of living with my Daed, I've never talked to him with hints of sarcasm and anger the way I do Nicholas. It's been a tough week, and now there's illegitimacy to contend with."

Finally she was letting him in, allowing him to know what was going on inside her. He'd traveled some of this same path, the one that went from Amish dreams to Englisch brokenness. "It gets easier, and you'll get stronger."

"My hair, my clothes, my way of life can be just right — and none of that matters. I'm an illegitimate, judgmental mess."

Quill merged onto the highway, pushing the speed limit a bit. "We can't get life right enough. You've known that, and you've lived by His grace, Ari. The only thing that's changed is now you feel a deeper sense of unworthiness."

"I can't imagine having to tell Rudy I exist because of an affair."

In a few minutes Quill would ask again where she was, but he was headed toward Bellflower Creek. She couldn't be far from there. And right now she was calm and talking. He needed another thirty minutes to get there. "Rudy will not care. He sees you — the one and only woman who will make his life a thousand percent better just by being in it."

She sniffled, and he knew she'd started crying again. "I miss him so much, and I can't even talk to him."

"There are acceptable ways around every demand Nicholas has made."

"Scriptural ways?" She sounded doubtful. " 'Cause I don't need you tempting me to disobey my parents. Rudy wouldn't want that either."

"We can talk about this later." It made no sense to tax her right now by introducing a different way to look at the scripture on obedience to parents. An exit sign with the words "Bellflower Creek" directed him to merge right. "So where are you?"

"In a car in the parking lot of a brown clapboard building called Long Shots. Why?"

"You're outside a bar."

"Am I?"

"With that name I'd give it a ninety percent chance of being a bar. Ten percent chance it's a gun range. You're in a car by yourself?"

"Ya." She sounded disgusted. "I got my license today."

He knew she wouldn't want him to congratulate her. "After driving a horse and carriage, it feels weird, doesn't it?"

"It feels as if Nicholas has managed to strip away another layer of my Amish life." She seemed to be fighting tears again. "I doubt getting your license distressed you."

He passed a slower car. "True, although I wasn't planning on leaving the Amish at the time. Still, I didn't mind going outside the Ordnung."

"I do. Nicholas says I'm afraid to live."

Quill had no decent response for that.

"You agree with him?" Her voice quivered as if tears were too close to the surface. "He is determined that I face my fears, and he's given me a list of challenges. He called it a bucket list."

The term *bucket list* sounded about right. Her biological dad would consider her life over when she returned to the Amish.

"So what's on it, Ariana?"

"Hundreds of things I don't want to do." She listed some of the options Nicholas had provided.

"He's given you choices. That's good. A little adventure might —"

"You're going to take his side?" Was she crying again?

"No. I didn't mean —"

"You do agree with him, don't you?"

"He seems to be going about this wrong, but his desire for you isn't all bad. He's giving you room to make decisions. Dan and Regina do that with their children all the time. It's a good method. Rather than telling their children no or insisting they do as they're told, they give their kids two options each time. So if my brother needs to walk across a parking lot, he gives his children a choice — hold his hand or be carried."

"So in this scenario I'm the child."

"What? No. I wasn't saying that."

"I called you crying, so I guess I deserve to be called a kid."

"Ari, come on. My point is he may be trying to be a good parent. He wants to draw you out of your Amish shell, and afterward you can return to it."

"My Amish shell?"

The phone beeped three times, as if the call had dropped. But it could also mean she'd hung up on him. That was more likely.

"Great, just great, Schlabach." He sighed and pressed the button to dial the number she'd called from. "Go right ahead and share your opinion no matter what the cost. It's a brilliant plan, really."

The phone rang, but she didn't answer. When it went to voice mail, a computerized message gave the phone number and said to leave a message. "Ari, we were disconnected, or maybe you hung up. Either way, would you call me back?"

THIRTEEN

Ariana stared at the phone. She'd needed him. She'd called him. She'd hung up on him. What was wrong with her?

But he thought like Nicholas? Disappointment rolled over her. Apparently there was no one she could talk to. No one who understood.

A neon sign in the window of the brown building flashed the word *Open.* When she'd pulled into the parking lot, it had been practically empty, but now, as twilight eased into darkness, the place was coming to life. She glanced at the clock: 6:54. Maybe she should go home or at least call Nicholas or Brandi. But she was tired of trying to do the right thing and too embarrassed about their affair to look them in the eyes or speak to them on the phone.

So now what, genius?

Music vibrated the air, and she realized that while talking to Quill she had seen several young men carrying instruments into the place. A familiar song caught her attention, one she and her sisters had heard while cleaning Englisch homes. She turned the key in the ignition just enough so she could lower the window. Nicholas had taught her that trick earlier in the week.

The song "We Are the Champions" filled the air. Susie used to love that song, and Ariana smiled, thinking about her younger sister dancing through the Englisch house and singing loudly while cleaning. Even though they had been alone in the house, Ariana thought it was inappropriate to turn on secular music and dance around, but Susie never saw the harm. Was Ariana right or simply a dinosaur?

Feeling a bit defiant, she grabbed her purse, put her keys and cell phone in it, and got out of her car. She took a few steps and then stopped. Going to a bar was on the list and had two asterisks beside it, but could she even get in? Her feet did not want to move. Had she lived a restrained life because she was godly or because she was afraid of everything?

The music stopped, people clapped, and she remained in place. A young man with brown shoulder-length hair and a beard was smiling as he walked out the front door, talking to someone inside the bar. The door slammed behind him, and he chuckled. He glanced her way. "The good times are inside."

"Are they?"

"I think so." He went to a car and pulled out a folder of papers before heading back to the bar. He paused near her. "It's like a person — okay looking on the outside, but the interesting stuff happens on the inside."

Oddly enough, the man reminded her of Jesus. He had dark brown hair and eyes and a warm, welcoming smile.

"I'm not sure I would be allowed inside."

"No money for the cover charge?"

"What's a cover charge?"

His eyebrows rose. "You have a bit of an accent." He waved his hands, fingers splayed, as if about to do a magic trick. "Your aura is a little different from what I'm used to. I have no doubts you're sober, and yet you seem a bit . . . unglued. Any chance you recently stepped off a boat and onto US soil?" He grinned.

Ariana was weary of feeling serious about everything, so she aimed for some humor. "Yeah. The *Mayflower,* I think."

He laughed. "That would explain it." He tapped the folder against his leg. "Brice."

Nicholas had shoved a lot of vocabulary

at her this week, hundreds of words. Words like *dolman, acerbic,* and *trenchant,* but *brice* wasn't one of them.

"Brice?" As soon as she asked, it dawned on her that it was his name. She felt her face flush. Where was her head? "It's your name. Sorry. It took me a minute. See, I was happily on the *Mayflower* for twenty years and was forced to leave a week ago. It's been a tough week."

He nodded as if he'd been in a similar predicament. "Let's try this again." He held out his hand. "I'm Brice."

She shook it. "I'm confused."

He chuckled. "I can help with that." He pointed at the building. "See, that's what we call a watering hole, only no one drinks water."

"I would. I'm not twenty-one."

"Don't worry, Prudence Bradford, no one is going to put you in the stocks." He motioned toward the bar, welcoming her. "We serve water and soft drinks, and I can get you in despite the age thing. It'll be fine. You'll enjoy the music."

She couldn't keep standing in the parking lot, wavering between wanting to run and doing something new. "Okay." While walking toward the door, she dug into her new purse and came up with a ten-dollar bill

Brandi had given her. "It's all I have. Is it enough for the cover charge and a drink?"

"It'll be plenty." He took the cash and held open the door.

When they stepped inside, she was hit with a stale smell she couldn't define. Glasses clinked, and the room had a dingy amber glow. Unlike the dressing room at the mall with its bright-white gloominess, this was a dull radiance with more shadow than light. Did the Englisch have different color light bulbs?

Brice gave her money to someone at the door, and several people spoke to him at once, some sounding jovial and some frustrated, but he smiled and answered accordingly, never missing a beat. He recommended the annoyed ones get another drink, and he responded to the friendly calls with the same energy. The person who took the ten gave Brice a five back, and he handed it to her.

"This way." He walked ahead of her.

She scanned the strangers in the room. A man in his midtwenties wearing a black T-shirt with the name of the bar on it stood behind a long counter, and behind him was a wall of variously shaped bottles and glasses. It clicked — the counter *was* the bar.

Two men at the end of the counter glanced at her with disinterest, as if she weren't really even there. One wore a camouflage shirt and pants, and everything about him was neat and orderly — from his haircut to his pants tucked into his boots. The man next to him looked totally different. He had on a tattered, sleeveless shirt, and tattoos ran down his neck and arms. Only one woman was on the row of stools. She had long, straight black hair and was in jeans and a sweater. Ariana could only see her profile as she turned up a bottle and drank, looking at ease inside this strange room filled with people who, with their distinct clothes and various hairstyles, looked nothing alike.

Were they pagans?

"Here." Brice pulled out a chair for her.

Ariana appreciated that he'd picked a spot at the back where she could see everyone but wouldn't be seen by many, and it occurred to her that in this moment she was glad not to be dressed in her Amish clothes.

"I'll have a drink sent over, something more enjoyable than a soft drink. You can get that anywhere at any time. Okay with you?"

"Yeah."

"Good. I have to get back onstage. I get a

break in about forty. Can you hang around until then?"

"You're part of the music?"

"The band, yeah. Lead singer, guaranteed to make a couple hundred bucks a week if I can find enough confused people in the parking lot and convince them to come inside."

She held out the remaining five-dollar bill.

He laughed. "I'd much rather have your name."

"Oh, Ariana."

"Nice name, Ariana. Better than Prudence. Just try to relax. It'll be fun."

"Do I not look relaxed?"

"You don't, no."

"Makes sense. I only agreed to come in because you remind me of Jesus."

He lowered his head, chuckling. "No one has ever said that before. Is that a good thing?"

"Yeah. Why wouldn't it be?"

He nodded. "It's a *Mayflower* thing, right?"

"Amish, actually. Old Order."

"Really? Meeting someone Amish in the parking lot isn't an everyday event. And you seem like a good girl to me. But they shoved you out?"

"No." What an awful question, and yet on

second thought . . . "Maybe." She shrugged. Leaving had been her decision, hadn't it? Right now she wasn't certain of one thing about herself or her life.

"I have to hear the rest of *this* story. Any chance you have a phone?"

"Yeah." She pulled it out of her purse.

"In case the Puritans come for you while I'm onstage, I'll text myself from your phone so I have your number, and I'll put my number in your contacts." He typed in letters and numbers twenty times faster than she could. "Any song requests from the Pilgrim section?"

"I . . . I wouldn't really know any names to tell you, but maybe something about home."

He gave her a warm, sweet smile that said he knew exactly what he was going to sing. "You got it. And just so you know, I think there's a first-bar-visit rule — drinks on the house." On his way to the stage, he stopped by the bar and said something to the man behind the counter.

Once on the small stage, he took some papers out of the file he had gotten from the car and put them on a music stand. He turned to the band members and said something. The next thing Ariana knew, she was listening to beautiful lyrics about country roads taking her home, to the place where she belonged. And suddenly this place didn't seem ungodly or sinful. It just seemed like a place to be less lonely.

While Ariana was enjoying the song, a woman set an interestingly shaped glass in front of her filled with a slushy, orange-colored drink. "It's on the house."

"The house?"

"Free."

"Oh, thank you." She took a sip. Brice was right. This was a lot tastier than a soft drink. She sipped on it and got lost in the beauty of the song. The lyrics tugged at her heart — about gathering memories and feeling that he should have been home yesterday. But tears welled in her eyes as Brice sang, "Country roads, take me home to the place I belong . . ."

The words reached deep, and the cold drink seemed to relax her. She realized she could breathe easy for the first time in way too many weeks. Within seconds of the song ending, Brice started another one, something about sweet Caroline, and the crowd joined him. He continued to sing one song after another, and on the fifth song the woman brought her another drink. The people no longer looked like pagans. They were just people loosening up after the workweek. What was so wrong about that? The muscles in her shoulders relaxed a bit more with each new song.

"Ariana." Quill pulled a chair from across the table and set it next to her. "What are you doing?"

Her heart should have picked up its pace or jolted at the sight of him, but it didn't. Should she be embarrassed to be here? "I'm not totally sure, but I'm enjoying myself." She had to speak over the music and the singing of the people around her.

"I didn't think you'd be *inside* the bar."

Based on his body language, he was talking loudly, but it didn't sound that way.

"I've been searching up and down the street for thirty minutes." His eyes held anger, a very different kind than when they'd argued before. "Why didn't you return my call?"

"I didn't hear my phone ring. But why would I want to talk to someone who agrees with Nicholas? Go home, Quill. I'm sorry I bothered you."

The music stopped.

"Are we really going to do this again?"

"Do what?"

The man at the piano made more beautiful music, and no other instruments joined the soft melody. Brice moved to a stool and adjusted the microphone stand, apparently waiting for his cue to sing again.

Quill glanced at the band. "You let me into your life, and then a few minutes, days, or weeks later you kick me out again."

Brice sang the opening of an unfamiliar song.

"We have a pattern, Quill. It goes something like this: I think you hung the moon, and it feels as if you did it just for me. Then you do me wrong. Or I simply discover that you've been quietly dismantling my life behind my back. Either way, at that point you're very sorry. Rinse, repeat."

Brice sang, "Speaking words of wisdom, let it be. Let it be, let it be."

She was glad the song was soft enough that Quill could hear her speak her mind.

He studied her, his piercing blue eyes taking her in. "We're struggling right now." He picked up her drink, took a sip, and set it in front of him.

"Right now?" She scooped up her glass. "For me it's been five years of struggling, Quill."

"You're right. I get it. Can we go somewhere quiet and talk?"

"Nope." She looked past him, watching the stage.

"Ari, you called because some part of you

trusts me, because some part of you knows I would do *anything* to help you through this time."

"Maybe." The song ended, and she lowered her voice. "Or maybe I called because I'm not allowed to call anyone else."

The musicians set aside their instruments, and Brice put his microphone in its stand.

"That was nice." Quill sighed. "Really."

"No one deserves it more than you." She sat back, an eyebrow raised as she held his stare. A few moments later she saw Brice heading her way.

"Hey." Brice stopped at the table. "You have company."

"No one important." She gestured toward the remaining chair.

He turned it around and straddled it. "Brice." He held out his hand to Quill.

Quill drummed his fingers on the table. "Let me guess. You ordered that drink for her."

"You can't shake the man's hand?" Ariana played with the condensation on the glass. "I wanted something tasty to drink."

Quill shifted. "That's not the problem. It's a sweet beverage laced with schnapps."

Schnapps? That was German for a strong drink. She hadn't detected any alcohol, not that she'd had any before. But she'd always

186

thought liquor tasted bitter, and this was the best slushy ever. Embarrassment worked its way through her. Why did Quill *always* have to know things she didn't? It was so humiliating. And infuriating.

Brice shrugged. "She was a bit uptight, and I asked if she'd like something more enjoyable than a soft drink, and she said yes. I thought a frozen fuzzy navel might help take the edge off. Problem?"

"Several. For starters, it wasn't your decision to make. It was hers."

Brice turned to her. "Do you have a problem with the drink?"

"No. I would've ordered it myself had I known to." That wasn't true, but she refused to admit Quill was right.

"Then no harm, no foul." Brice turned toward the bar and raised two fingers. The man behind the counter nodded. "Would you care for something, on the house?"

"No, thanks." Quill intertwined his fingers. "Look, Brice, I need you to back off. No harm, no foul. Okay?"

"Ariana and I made plans to talk. If anything, you're the one who's interrupting."

Ariana finished her drink and nodded. "Definitely."

187

"See." Brice motioned toward her. "Ariana agrees."

"She is currently under the influence. So for the moment her opinion has no value."

Ariana wanted to slap him. "Why don't you tell him the truth, Quill? In your eyes my opinion never matters."

"That's not true, Ari."

The server set a beer and another fuzzy navel in front of Brice. "Thanks, Nancy." Brice slid the drink toward Ariana before he took a sip of his beer. "Who is this guy?"

Ariana rolled her eyes. "I've been asking myself that question for years. I guess the easy explanation is we used to be neighbors, and he and my brother were friends."

"Ah, so you were the kid sister he got used to bossing around."

Quill took her purse off the chair, took out her keys, handed the purse to her, and stood. "It's time to go, Ari."

She leaned back, folding her arms.

Brice took another sip of his drink. "Looks to me like she doesn't want to go anywhere with you."

"Sounds true enough to me," Ariana said.

Quill put her keys in his pocket and sat. "Fine. But I'm not leaving you until you are inside your home."

"That could be a while, because I don't

actually have one. But you knew that long before I did, right?" Brandi and Nicholas just provided a roof over her head and four walls shared with people she didn't understand or particularly like.

Quill said nothing.

"What? No great words of wisdom?" Ariana asked. "No pep talks to help me survive? You're so good at those." She grasped the glass and brought it toward her.

Quill put his hand over her drink. "Before you take another swallow, I need to say one word."

"What?"

"Rudy."

Her face flushed, and she set the glass down. Again she wanted to know what was wrong with her. "Brice, I . . . I can't be here." Ariana stood, and suddenly the floor felt like a trampoline.

Quill wrapped his hand around her arm, steadying her. "You got your footing?"

She nodded. He let go and got out his wallet.

"Who's Rudy?" Brice asked.

Quill tossed a twenty onto the table. "Pretty much her fiancé."

They wound their way around the various tables and to the front door.

"Well, that was fun." Quill pulled a set of

keys from his pocket. "This way."

She longed to get into her car and drive away from Quill, but he had her keys, and even if he didn't, she felt disoriented.

Quill opened the passenger door of the truck for her. "You want to ride for a bit and talk?"

She got in. "No."

"Fine." He started to close the door, but her purse fell out, spilling its few contents onto the pavement. He shoved them back into it, except the folded papers. He opened them, glanced through the pages, and shoved them into his pocket. He closed the door, went around to the driver's side, and started the truck. "Which house? Nicholas's or Brandi's?"

She was supposed to stay with Nicholas tonight and Brandi tomorrow night, but how was she going to look either of them in the eye again? "Nicholas's."

"Do Brandi and Nicholas know that you know?"

Leaning her head against the car window, she closed her eyes and shrugged.

"So you're not talking to me?"

"Apparently not." She longed to ask him the questions that were churning inside her. What did she need to do to survive a year of this? What was happening to her? Why didn't she feel anything like herself? Did God care how confused she was? But she was too embarrassed and too . . .

The next word — the one that welled up and she knew was true — shook her. *Bitter.* She was too bitter. When had that happened? She'd thought it took people years to go from angry to bitter.

She opened her eyes. Power lines crisscrossed the land, and she saw businesses and houses with pretty yellow lights, and she caught glimpses of flat-screen televisions. If all the miles of power lines were gathered into a single mound of twisted cables, they would match her jumbled thoughts.

They rode in silence until he pulled into Nicholas's driveway. "Ari, how clearly are you thinking?" He no longer sounded angry.

"Decently." Her head felt as though it were full of butterflies. "Why?" She stared out the front window, unwilling to look at him.

He put the truck in Park and turned it off. "I need you to hear me. I want to help you. Nothing means more to me. Do you understand?"

She nodded, waiting for him to finish.

He removed the keys from the ignition. "No matter how much I want to help or how guilty I feel for past wrongs, I can't keep doing this — jumping every time the phone rings, turning my life upside down for you. If you're going to survive this and get back home, you have to forgive all of us — me, Brandi, Nicholas, your Mamm and Daed. In our own ways each of us has seriously let you down." He turned on the dome light and waited for her to look at him. "Don't call me again unless you're ready to stop beating me up for things I can't change."

His words burned away the chaff, and she saw the truth. Her heart pounded, and every erratic beat held rage. An unfamiliar, uncontrollable fury. But why was she angrier with him than the others? Was it because his betrayals had been the most purposefully deceitful and they'd hurt the worst?

She wasn't sure, but he was right. She was angry with Brandi, Nicholas, Mamm, and Daed too. But as she began to recognize her anger, she knew they weren't the only ones. She was also furious with God. She lifted the door handle. "None of us has the power to change anything, do we?"

"Of course we —"

She opened the door. "It was a rhetorical question."

"Fine."

They got out, and he walked with her to the front door. She opened it and went inside, knowing Nicholas would reprimand her if she knocked.

Nicholas bolted out of his office. "I've been trying to reach you. What's going on?"

She headed for the stairway without answering.

"Ariana?" Nicholas called to her.

"I'm going to bed. Quill knows far more about me than I do anyway. Ask him."

Quill watched her stagger up the stairs. Once on the landing, she stopped and stared down at him, their eyes locking. No matter where life had taken him, he'd always been able to gauge to some degree what her reaction and response would be. Was he seeing her at her worst, or was she beginning to spiral out of control?

She lowered her eyes and walked away.

After they heard the door close, Nicholas turned to him. "Is she okay?"

Quill's pulse quickened. He needed to say as little as possible and get out before his angst and anger spilled onto Nicholas and made the situation even worse. "She's pretty beaten up."

"I guess she told you about the affair and . . ."

"Yeah."

"I didn't mean to blurt it out. I thought she knew."

"She knows now, but it'll be a while before she's okay with it."

"I don't really understand why the news hit her so hard. It happened twenty years ago."

"It happened in your life twenty years ago. It happened in her life today." He handed Nicholas her keys. "The car is at a bar called Long Shots." He pulled the bucket list out of his pocket. "You can put a check mark beside 'go to a bar' and 'have a drink.' She accomplished both. I guess this means you should be proud."

Quill tucked his resentment down deep and went to the door to leave. Then he stopped and turned to face Nicholas.

"Your method of welcoming Ariana into the Englisch world will, without a doubt, ensure she returns to Summer Grove. I think that's where she belongs, so I should be fine with what you're doing, but you're ripping her apart." He shook his head. "And that, Mr. Jenkins, is probably the worst thing you've ever done in your life." He walked out.

Nicholas followed him outside. "I don't want to hurt her. I'm just trying to keep my daughter from returning to the eighteenth century."

"Why?"

"What do you mean *why*? Those people are . . . weird and closed minded, and they believe in myths."

"For the sake of argument, let's assume you're right. That bothers you because . . ."

"Because it's wrong to live that way."

"Wrong?" Quill's temples throbbed. "You think it's wrong? Why? Because people like you and me have it right? Because we're so happy with our lives?"

"She doesn't know enough yet to have a clue about what could make her happy. She's tied in knots about pleasing a God that doesn't exist."

"If, as you say, He doesn't exist, then all we have is this brief life. What's so wrong with letting her do what she wants with it? Let her go home, marry Rudy, raise the babies she's always wanted, and die having lived a simple life."

"I . . . I want her to grow as a person. There's nothing wrong about that."

"Grow?" Quill couldn't stop himself. "Ever known a gardener to rip a plant out of the ground and stomp on the roots until they're crushed *and then* expect the plant to grow?"

"It's been clear from the day she arrived that I need to be more tender. I actually thought I was being very gentle this past week."

"Just because she's not fighting you, that doesn't mean you're being gentle. You insisted she remove her prayer Kapp. That's no big deal to you, but to her, God told women to wear a head covering. That makes it a big deal. Removing it feels like a violation. Would you condone violating a non-Amish woman over her choices, Nicholas?"

"Okay." Nicholas rubbed the back of his neck. "Apparently I've missed being gentle by a lot. But there's so much she needs to know before the year is up."

"Your goal should be to get to know her, to embrace who she is — not to mold her into who you think she needs to be."

"You think I'm being intolerant? Religion is intolerant —"

"We aren't talking about religion. We're talking about your daughter. It's obvious you think religion is evil. But you can't set anything right by force-feeding Ariana books written by atheists or threatening to sue the faithful people she loves unless she goes against her conscience and accomplishes certain goals. She's not a cause or an issue you can do battle with to win a

Supreme Court decision. She's your daughter, and you get one year to be with her . . . maybe."

Nicholas's brows furrowed, and Quill knew he'd made some headway.

He drew a deep breath. "Good night." Quill exited and got into Dan's truck, hoping Nicholas would start cutting Ariana some slack.

If something between Nicholas and Ariana didn't give soon, Quill feared what would happen to her.

FOURTEEN

Skylar looked back over her shoulder as she hurried along the road toward the community phone. She hoped no one heard her slip out of the house right before midnight. When she'd done the same thing four nights ago, no one was the wiser. But she hadn't expected to need a repeat performance this soon.

Cody had met her near the Brenneman house at two a.m. on Tuesday and had given her a good stash. But now it was missing. If she called him, surely he'd find a way to get more to her. She opened the weather-beaten door to the phone shanty and stumbled inside. While searching for a light switch, she cursed. When would she stop trying to turn on the lights?

She ran her fingers across the makeshift desk until she felt the now-familiar shape of a box of kitchen matches. She struck one and searched for a candle or kerosene lamp.

There was a lantern near the old push-button phone. She lit it and pressed the buttons, calling Cody.

"What." He sounded as if he'd been asleep.

"Hey, it's me."

She heard shifting.

"What's up, Skylar?" He seemed both annoyed and glad to hear from her.

"The pills are missing."

He cursed. "Missing?" He still sounded groggy. "All those uppers and downers are missing? Do you know what it took to get those? Were they stolen?"

"No, I had them in my jeans pocket, and the bottle must've fallen out."

"Bad move, Skylar, and I feel for you, babe. But I'm fresh out and can't get any more for a day or so, and if I had them, I couldn't make another late-night run out there on short notice. You're in the boondocks, and I work for a living. Are you sure you can't find what I brought you last Tuesday?"

"I've looked. The cows got out, and after the stampede was over, we were on foot for hours, covering miles while corralling them back into the pasture."

"You, on foot, herding cattle? I'd have paid good money to see that." Cody laughed.

"I'd pay good money not to be here . . . if I had any money. Look, I'm really sorry. I know you're covering all the costs right now, but you can't possibly hate more than I do how inconvenient the missing bottle is."

"It's okay. Chill already. I can handle the money part."

"When can you get me out of here?"

"In a few weeks, I think. I'm working on a deal, a big one. When that happens, I'll have some cash. And the first thing on my list is getting you, okay?"

His words brought hope, and she was grateful. "Okay, thanks, Cody."

"I can't leave my best girl stuck in Amish country, can I?"

She cursed. "I hope not. I'd die. When can you bring me more pills and cigarettes?"

"Any way you can meet me during the day? I'm wiped at night, babe — working on the deal and holding down a job."

"We'd be seen during the day."

"What can they do to you — take away your social life, your cell, your allowance? They've already done all that."

"If they call my dad, he'll follow through on his threat to come after you for distribution and put your butt in jail for as long as possible."

"Oh yeah." From the slurred speech and breathing pattern, she assumed Cody had started to smoke a cigarette. "I didn't think of that. I guess he has the means to target me and keep you out of it. So let's play it safe. Maybe there is a place we could meet during the day. What if you worked at that café you told me about?"

"I'm not helping keep someone else's dream alive."

"Then sabotage their efforts. Have it in ruins by the time you two switch places. Since no one there has a clue what I look like, if you're at the café on Tuesday, I'll bring you another stash."

"Tuesday? It just turned Sunday like fifteen minutes ago. How am I supposed to wait until Tuesday?"

"Raid the medicine cabinets, Skylar. You said there are family members with homes of their own. Visit them. See what you can find. Someone has to have something. What about the midwife? Would she have something at the clinic? Is there an Amish doctor who might have some goods at his office and not have them locked up like they are in other places?"

"Yeah, I hadn't thought about any of that."

"That's because you don't think like a junkie, and you should."

The word *junkie* sounded so wrong. She wasn't one. Not even close. "Everything in my life is upside down, and I need some uppers and downers to get by."

"If you say so, babe. Funny how those drugs were in your system before any of this started."

If she weren't desperate for drugs, she'd tell him off and hang up.

Why did guys always ruin everything for her? She wouldn't even be in this mess if it weren't for that other guy. Quill Schlabach. Oh, how she wished she'd never spoken to him, never told him her birth date, never learned she'd been switched at birth. Her old life wasn't the best, but it was better than this. "I'll be at the café on Tuesday. It's open from seven to two. Please don't get there after hours."

"Yeah, okay, Skylar."

"Bring Xanax and Ritalin this time, not Valium and Bontril." Valium and Bontril just didn't do the trick. They were older drugs, and her reaction to them wasn't the same from day to day. What might knock her out one day barely calmed her the next.

Xanax helped her chill, just the right amount of chill. And since she wasn't hyperactive, Ritalin gave her mounds of energy, and in the right dose it made for some really interesting hallucinations. Nothing too bizarre. If the television was on, it was as if the characters left the box and became holograms in the room with her — stretching oddly like Picasso paintings. She liked the feeling, and despite what the law said, what she took was nobody's business but hers.

Abram sat on the steps of the back porch, waiting. Tonight was the second time Skylar had sneaked out. He had some concerns she might not return, but if she did, he didn't know what to say to her. Accusations wouldn't help.

He wished he were capable of talking to people like Ariana was. She could quickly get to the heart of complicated matters. He needed to form some sort of bond with Skylar, but it'd been hard even to look at her, let alone talk to her. She was a constant reminder that Ariana wasn't his biological sister.

Across the backyard near the fence line to the pasture, he saw a shadow moving briskly. Despite the stiff movements that made Skylar look angrier than usual, he remained on the steps, trying to be calm. She stopped in front of him and lifted her eyebrows. "What?"

"Nothing." He had to come up with something better than that if he expected a conversation.

"Good." She climbed a couple of steps and tried to go around him.

He didn't budge. "Wait."

She stepped back down. "Can I help you?"

A rush of embarrassment spread over Abram's face as he tried to gather his thoughts. "This is the second night you've left the house."

She put a hand on her hip, staring at him. "Are you spying on me?"

"What? No. I just noticed, that's all."

"You noticed, but you aren't spying." She sounded condescending, and it made him miss Ariana even more. Of all his sisters she was the nicest.

Abram steadied his nerves. "I just wanted to make sure everything was all right."

"So that's why you're waiting here?"

"Could you stop answering everything with a question? You aren't defending yourself to Mamm and Daed, and I'm not accusing you of anything." Abram was surprised at his tone. He sounded assertive, but Skylar seemed to relax.

She propped a foot on a stair. "Maybe not tonight, but you'll tell them."

"I know you aren't accustomed to this

204

whole brother-sister thing. Trust me, I won't tell anyone."

She laughed as if Abram had said something funny. "You think we're brother and sister?"

It felt weird, but he said, "Yes."

"I'm not interested in being anyone's sister."

He did his best not to flinch, but it hurt. He wasn't all that interested in being her brother, but they were twins nonetheless. "That's fine. I just don't want you to walk out one evening and never come back."

"I'm not a child. I'm twenty, and I can do what I want."

Abram nodded. "I know your age. We were born minutes apart, remember? And, ya, you can do what you want. But if you do, then Ariana's leaving will be meaningless."

"Everyone around here seems keen on making Ariana happy."

Was she envious? Maybe her behavior had more to do with feeling insecure than just being irritable. "Leaving was really hard on her, just like being here has been hard on you. We care about her and you both."

"You care about her and just threw me into the mix to be nice."

"Being nice because someone is related is

part of what it means to be family. Another part is trying to be supportive and honest." He scooted over in case Skylar wanted to sit. "I start full time at the café on Monday." Why had he told her that? She didn't care. But he'd turned in his notice Thursday morning and told them he'd finish out the week. Susie and Martha couldn't keep things going at the café while he worked out a two-week notice. Every customer who left dissatisfied was one more person who wouldn't return and one more person to spread the word that the café wasn't worth going to. Besides, there were plenty of skilled Amish men waiting to take Abram's place.

Skylar pulled her cigarettes from a pocket. She paused, looking at Abram. "You sure about confidentiality between siblings?"

He smiled. "Between us, I'm sure. You smoke in front of Martha or John, and they'll tattle before you get it to your lips."

"Good to know." She lit a cigarette and breathed in heavily. "You showed me how to pour coffee."

"What?"

She shifted, leaning against a post and looking up at the stars. "A few days ago when we were at the kitchen table, you showed me how to pour coffee as if I was too stupid to know how to do it."

Was that how he'd come across? "I didn't mean it that way." He needed to tell her the truth. "In case you haven't noticed, I'm not too good at communicating."

"Anyone over the age of seven doesn't need to be shown how to pour coffee."

"I know. I'm just trying."

"Trying what? To be annoying?"

Abram watched Skylar's smoke disappear into the black night. "Trying to have a conversation with you. Could be about pouring coffee or about the weather. Anything to stop the silence between us."

She held out her cigarette to Abram.

He shook his head. "I don't smoke. I've never tried it."

She gestured again for him to take the cigarette. He took it, put it to his lips, and sucked in. It felt as if something had caught in his throat, and he coughed as he handed the cigarette back to her. He gagged and spit on the ground. "That's disgusting."

She laughed, looking at the cigarette as if she were seeing it for the first time. "You're probably right." She put the cigarette to her lips and inhaled. "But I'm hooked."

He didn't know what to say, so they sat in silence until she finished her cigarette.

"Do you still need help with the café?"

FIFTEEN

Ariana pulled the pillow and covers off her head, stretched from the fetal position, and put her feet on the floor. Spending most of Sunday morning wallowing in remorse and regret wasn't helping. She had to pull herself together.

She reached toward the nightstand and ran her hand across her tattered Bible. Some witness for God she'd turned out to be. She pulled the Bible into her lap and opened it, feeling the thin, delicate pages before skimming a few passages. It was no coincidence that the Word fell open to Luke, and her eyes immediately connected with the passage "Judge not, and ye shall not be judged: condemn not, and ye shall not be condemned: forgive, and ye shall be forgiven."

"Sounds great, God," she muttered. "And I mean no disrespect, but how? I have no idea how to stop judging. Apparently I would fare just as well if You told me to stop longing for home. How?"

A clinking sound pulled her from her reading. Was a bird pecking on the glass? She set the Bible back in place, put on her housecoat, and walked to the french doors that opened onto a balcony. She peered out. There weren't any birds tapping.

She turned and went to her closet and heard the noise again. Something was definitely hitting the glass on the doors. She unlocked the balcony doors and stepped outside.

Something tiny and sharp struck her forehead. "Ouch," she yelped.

"Sorry." Cameron's eyes were large with an oh-no look, but she laughed and held up a straw-type thing. A horn tooted, and she looked at the car waiting by the curb and held up one finger before turning back to the balcony. "I guess slinging rocks at you when you're at Brandi's isn't sufficient. I felt it necessary to travel across town to bring my game to Nicholas's."

A hint of mirth stirred deep inside Ariana, as if it were waking from a long winter of sleep. "Thanks."

"Anytime." Cameron grinned, looking free of embarrassment or resentment over their argument yesterday. It was pretty cool outside, but the girl just had on shorts and a thin, baggy jacket over a T-shirt.

Ariana wasn't sure how to feel about Cameron, but she liked the girl's fearlessness in being herself and not taking life too seriously. Ariana could use a dip in that pool.

Cameron held up the peashooter. "I really am sorry for hitting you just now. I found it funny because if I spent all day trying to smack you with a pebble, I couldn't do it again." She shoved the peashooter into her pocket. "I only have a minute, so let me say what I need to say."

"You're going to throw pebbles at me just to talk to me from there?"

"Yes, it's all very Romeo and Juliet of me."

"And look how well that story ended."

"True." Cameron laughed. "I don't need to say much, and I'm not knocking on Nicholas's door for anybody."

In this moment Cameron reminded Ariana of her younger sisters. She had Susie's pluck and wit, and although Cameron looked and sounded older, she was the same age as Martha. Because of those things, Ariana wasn't letting Cameron go as easily as she'd hoped. "Yes, we need to talk."

"Not really." Cameron glanced back at the car. "I was wrong to make fun of you and think it would go over your head. You were right to call me on it. The end."

That was it? Ariana heard no remorse whatsoever. "Why, Cameron?"

"Why what? Why am I standing here and apologizing for something I did wrong?" She held both hands out, palms up. "Because Dad said it had to be face to face before I could meet my friends at the park for a game of extreme Frisbee. I've done it now, so —"

"Why would you make fun of me in front of your friends? I can tell you exactly why I screamed at you and why I shouldn't have."

"I don't know." Cameron scoffed. "Because you were an easy target?"

"So that's what you do to everyone who's an easy target?"

"What? No." Cameron's carefree and dismissive attitude disappeared. "Okay, okay. If we're going to do this, could you come down from your ivory tower?"

"Give me two minutes, and I'll let you in."

"Are you hard of hearing as well as technologically impaired? I'm not coming into Nicholas's house."

It sounded as if a door below Ariana had swooshed open. "Cameron?" Nicholas's voice was matter-of-fact, and the humor of it skittered through Ariana.

Cameron backed up as Nicholas stepped onto the front lawn.

He looked up at Ariana and then at Cameron. "Ladies, is there no cell phone service? Did an apocalypse take place and you're unable to text each other?"

Cameron dug her hands into her shorts pocket. "I needed to talk to her."

Nicholas gestured toward the front door. "I'm sure the neighbors would like a quieter approach on their Sunday morning."

"Really?" Cameron asked Ariana. "You can't just accept an apology and let me go?"

It wasn't what Ariana wanted, but she would free her. "Go." Ariana gestured toward the car.

"Wait." Cameron studied her for a moment. "I know how this works. You say *go,* but then you'll tell Brandi I did a drive-by smoothing, and Dad will ground me."

Before Ariana could respond, Cameron pursed her lips and walked to the car waiting at the curb. While she talked to someone in the vehicle, Nicholas studied Ariana, and his face held parental concern. He had dark circles under his eyes, and she wished she could redo yesterday and respond with grace. He turned his focus to the cell in his hand and began tapping on the screen.

Ariana remained in place, watching her dad. She no longer needed to ask herself what was wrong with her. After a fitful night of drunken sleep, it was very clear — she was like those she judged. Regardless of her knowing right from wrong, shortcomings of many kinds easily entangled her. They might not be the shortcomings others had, but, nonetheless, they were a part of her, and they were strong. Her disappointment in others caused her to hurt them, and that wasn't at all Christlike. The perfect One didn't throw stones at sinners or those who'd hurt Him — although she'd like to know how He'd managed that.

Still, no matter what she saw or understood, it wouldn't stop her personal struggles with this mess. It wouldn't end the grief of losing a family that wasn't hers or help her love the family that was hers. But for now she saw her dim reflection in a mirror instead of the sins of others. She understood more today, her grief and offense were milder, and she was more ready to repent than accuse.

The cell phone in her housecoat pocket pinged, and Nicholas looked up again. She knew the message would be from him, and she pulled out her phone and read it.

Your life is just as precious and important regardless of the situation you were conceived in.

Tears welled. The words reminded her of what Quill had said about her value to him and his family, and Ariana closed her eyes and took a deep breath. Would God want them to undo the affair? She wouldn't be here without it. Did *she* want them to undo the affair? Seems as if she should because of the sin, but the whole situation left her miserably confused. What had happened to her black-and-white world?

She needed to talk to Quill. If anyone could make sense of her thoughts, he could. Even if he viewed her similar to how Nicholas did, Quill had gone out of his way last night to get to her and to protect her from herself. She needed to apologize *and* thank him.

She wiped her eyes, looked up from the text, and smiled at Nicholas. "Thank you."

His taut body seemed to relax.

Then she texted:

I'm sorry for yesterday.

Nicholas read it and nodded, a faltering smile slowly forming on his lips. "Me too,

Ari," he said.

Cameron walked toward the house, waving at the vehicle as it drove off. Nicholas gestured from her to the front door, and while they ambled in that direction, Ariana hurried inside to brush her teeth and hair and change. But she stopped cold when she saw an envelope under the door. She picked it up and opened it. Inside was the bucket list with a note on top.

Let's rethink this bucket list. If you don't want to do anything on it, I accept that. If you're willing to do the ones I've highlighted, I'll be very grateful, so much so I'm willing to reward you with various types of contact with family and friends.

Her heart jolted, and she pulled the papers to her chest. *Denki.* She breathed the prayer and glanced at the highlighted sections. Relief surged. Mostly he was asking her for reasonable things — to make an Englisch friend, to work in a typically male job for at least a day, to travel some with him, and a few other things.

No more reading books by atheists? Gratefulness hit so hard her knees were shaking. She could do this . . . at least enough to

215

earn a visit with Rudy. She shoved the papers into the pocket of her housecoat as she hurried into the bathroom. By the time she brushed her teeth, there was a knock on her door.

When she opened it, Cameron wasted no time sliding into the room and closing the door. "That's the most time I've ever spent with Nicholas in my whole life." She opened her eyes wide and clutched her chest.

"Seems as if Nicholas rattles you."

"Ya think? For years I've watched Skylar come here for a weekend and return home an emotional wreck."

Skylar . . . Rather than Ariana being angry with God or doubting Him or feeling sorry for herself because she was pulled from a life she loved, maybe she should be on her knees thanking Him that she had twenty years with the Brennemans. Otherwise, she wouldn't even know them. Or Rudy.

"Hello?" Cameron waved a hand in front of Ariana. "You there, Giselle?"

"Oh, sorry. So tell me, all your jabs and poking fun — have I done something to offend you?"

Cameron sat on the bed and stared at her tennis shoes, tapping her feet against the thick carpet. "No. I was just teasing and having some fun. And I'm really sorry for it."

Ariana had no choice but to accept her apology, but she felt sure there was more to it than Cameron was admitting.

Cameron leaned back on her elbows. "Your turn."

"Okay." Ariana pulled one of the new dresses out of a shopping bag to remove the tags. She was weary of being down and serious. "I'm sorry you did things that made me yell at you." She kept a straight face while going to the dresser and getting a pair of scissors.

"See that right there." Cameron pointed at her, chuckling. "That sounded just like Brandi. You barely know her, but even some of your gestures look like hers."

"Do they?" That was a little alarming, but she had to identify with more than just the Brennemans as family now. "I'm not doing much better with Brandi than I am with Nicholas."

"Blended families take time to bond. You've been here a week. I have plates of food under my bed that are older than that."

Ariana reached into her pocket, feeling the bucket list. "I could use a friend."

Cameron opened a drawer in the nightstand and searched it. "Should we get a piece of paper and a crayon and write 'Will you be my friend?' and put a box above *yes* and one above *no*? You could slip it to me during recess."

"If it makes you feel better. But to be really honest, I mean I could really *use* a friend."

"You want to use me? Are you sure you're not related to me?"

Ariana plunked beside her. "I'm not even sure *I'm* related to me."

Cameron laughed. "You're not nearly as dull as I thought."

"Thanks."

How did one cope with the depth of pain of knowing her life had been a mistake of catastrophic proportions? Her Amish parents had considered her a gift from God, and yet the reality was her existence had wrecked lives. What would Rudy think of her newly discovered status — illegitimate?

"Hey, Giselle?"

"Hmm?" Ariana came back to the present. "Who is this Giselle? Is she a friend of yours?"

Cameron buried her face in her hands and laughed. "Okay, you win. You have to have someone who knows the ropes to help you. Stick with me, kiddo. I'll have you speaking the English lingo in no time flat." Cameron used one thumbnail to click the other one over and over again. "Giselle is a clueless, innocent klutz in the children's movie *Enchanted.*"

"For children? That doesn't sound so bad. I'm supposed to watch a few movies." She didn't have to, and that posed a new issue. Was she selling out her faith in order to see Rudy? "Could that be one?"

"Sure. I have a boatload of movies we can watch."

"I appreciate that, and I'll make some desserts and snacks."

"I heard you bought a café and can really bake. Can I watch you do some of your cooking magic? I don't want to miss an opportunity to see you set off the smoke alarm while trying to flip on a light switch."

Ariana giggled. "I'd watch my step if I were you."

"Yeah, why? Do you plan to litter the floor with the appliances you can't operate?"

Ariana pushed her shoulder into Cameron's. "You're not the only smart-mouthed little sister I've had to deal with, so I have the upper hand."

"Sister?" Cameron scowled, but her eyes held a hint of pleasure.

"Ya, forever and ever, so let's make the

relationship work for us and not against us, okay?"

"Sisters," Cameron mumbled again, narrowing her eyes as if trying to decide if Ariana was setting her up for something.

"I'm a useful sister to have — not perfect but not a pain on a regular basis. What more could you want?"

"To be an only child?"

"But you didn't ever have that, did you?"

"I'm my dad's only child." Cameron shrugged. "Truth?"

Ariana had no idea what truth Cameron was talking about, but she nodded. "Please."

"I've only seen my mom ten times in the last ten years, once a year, and none of those visits lasted more than a few hours. It's not supposed to be that way with moms." She shrugged. "I was four when I met Brandi, five when my dad married her. I was so excited to have a mom. Skylar was ten, and within a few years she started causing trouble, and I've been the good daughter ever since. I needed that, but I never realized how much until you came along. Then I heard that your Amish mom didn't want to let go of you, not even for a month, and you're grown. And Brandi was willing to sell her soul for time with you, and I . . ."

"Wanted to make me feel unwelcome and

unwanted."

"I guess. I don't think I actually knew that was my intention until now."

Ariana wouldn't comment on Cameron saying "Brandi was willing to sell her soul," not right now. But it bothered her. "Friends?"

"Friends." Cameron scoffed and flopped back on the bed, staring at the ceiling. "What are we, four?" She propped up on her elbows. "What you don't know about how normal people talk and act is a lot."

"By normal, you mean fifteen-year-old schoolgirls?"

"That's right, until I turn sixteen. Then that will be the new fifteen."

"What?"

Cameron swung her feet back and forth. "You've got a lot to learn so that later we can say 'you've come a long way, babe.' "

"Right now I'd settle for going a short way — fifty miles, from here to Quill's place in Mingo."

"You're gonna go in your housecoat? I vote for that over the Amish clothes."

Ariana tossed the now-tagless dress in her lap.

Cameron held it up. "A little school-marmish, but better."

"A little revealing is what it is."

"This? No way. You know what your problem is?"

"My newest friend?"

"Hey, mess with me, and I'll turn off the lights, and you'll be lost in the dark."

"Uh, it's daylight."

"Minor detail." Cameron stood and held up the cream-colored knit dress that was the same basic style as the one Ariana had worn yesterday. "Okay, back to what your problem is. You have absolutely no sense of style. Wear a belt with it and some boots."

"No. Why would I do that?"

"It would be cute. Really cute."

"Clothing isn't meant to be cute. It's meant to cover."

"Says who?"

"The Bible . . . I think."

"I don't think it does." Cameron shrugged. "I go to church with my friends sometimes, and I haven't heard anything about that."

"You go?"

"Some."

"Could we go together next Sunday?"

"Sure, why not? Let's go to the Methodist church on Spring Street. I've been there before, and it has a youth group that meets during preaching. And there is this one guy who is the cutest —"

"Cameron." Ariana snatched the dress. "It's God's day and His house."

"So in Summer Grove there aren't any cute guys who catch your eye during church?"

"Well . . ." Ariana had liked Sunday church more since Rudy moved to Summer Grove.

"There must be, because you're blushing." Cameron pointed her finger at Ariana's cheek. "We have to get you to be real, which means dumping the hypocrisy."

"Hypocrisy?"

"You know there are cute guys at church. You even like it. But when I said it out loud, you corrected me. Come on, Ari. Get real." She held the shoulders of the dress up to Ariana's shoulders. "Definitely needs a belt and boots. I have both back at the house."

"I'm fine without that."

Cameron tapped the toes of her shoes together. "My feet are bigger than yours, so my boots may not fit you, but I bet Brandi's will."

"I'm curious. You wanted a mom, were grateful to get one, but you don't call Brandi *Mom*. Why is that?"

"I called her *Brandi* for a year before she married Dad, and it felt right. The name *Mom* came with lots of hurt feelings for me,

so I stuck with calling her *Brandi* or sometimes *Brands.*" Cameron pointed at the
dress. "More important, you can't let your
culture dictate your wardrobe. We studied
about this in school. Some cultures fear
women showing any skin, and they strap
this heightened sense of overly sexualized
thinking onto women so that anything less
than a burka is wrong. Chill. Get a new
perspective. I'll help you."

What had Ariana gotten herself into?
"Maybe another time. I need to get ready
to go to Mingo, but my car isn't here."

"You know the obvious answer, right?"

"Plug the name of the place where my car
is into the GPS app and walk there?"

"N-o-o-o. That won't get me to the park
either. Call Brandi. She can chauffeur both
of us, and it would make her day. Trust me."

"Yeah, you're right. Call her."

"Not me. She needs *you* to call her."

Cameron seemed to understand Brandi
and have a connection with her that went
beyond that of a typical fifteen-year-old. If
Brandi hurt, Cameron wanted to fix it, and
in that revelation, for a moment Ariana saw
Brandi with a tiny bit of the respect Cameron had for her. Did Cameron know her
superhero stepmom was an adulterer?
Maybe she did but didn't care.

Was Brandi aware that Ariana knew about the affair? She eased the phone out and stared at the screen. Was she ready to look Brandi in the eyes and ignore the awkwardness between them? Or would she disappoint herself once again by being an overwrought stone thrower?

Ariana swallowed hard, praying she could see Brandi through Cameron's eyes of love.

Sixteen

Abram stared at the low-burning fire in the hearth of the living room as he listened to Skylar explain her ideas of what they needed to change about the café.

For the second week in a row, their home didn't have the usual Sunday feel. Last Sunday had been a church meeting day, but since Skylar had arrived the night before, none of the Brennemans had gone. Today was a between Sunday, and they — the café team — were talking business while the rest of the family had dispersed around the farm. Everything about life felt so different these days.

Susie doodled on a legal pad, and Abram knew her mind was spinning. She'd already skimmed the catalog, checking the prices of the items Skylar suggested they purchase. Now Susie looked like he felt: concerned. But he also knew that Susie was praying for her new sister.

"Does anyone even show up at seven?" Skylar flipped through the catalog Ariana had used to order supplies.

"Not many people at this point," Martha said. "But we're trying to stick to what Ariana said would build a customer base."

"What if she's wrong? She's not here to see how it's going or how exhausted everyone is." Skylar tapped a specific page in the catalog. "You need an espresso machine, an espresso grinder, a gourmet brewer, and a commercial blender for making frozen espresso drinks."

"You do know the café doesn't have electricity, right?" Susie asked.

Skylar blinked. "Is that even legal in this country — serving food in a place without electricity?"

"It's unusual, not illegal," Susie said. "Quill rewired the old building, bringing the electrical wiring up to code, and it passed inspection. So the setup is legal, at least in this state. But everything in the café uses gas, including the refrigerator. If Ariana, as the actual owner, had an Englisch business partner, the church would allow the Englisch co-owner to bring in electricity."

"That's weird."

"It's a way to hold on to our culture and

yet allow Amish-owned small businesses some flexibility. But that would also give the Englisch co-owner a good share of the profits, so it's not a solution for us."

Skylar thumped the catalog. "Is that why the barn has that huge generator?"

"Ya, it powers the milkers and runs the refrigeration for the milk tank," Martha said.

"Would the café be allowed to use a generator?"

"Ya. But everything you're talking about doing would cost a lot of money." Abram moved to the fireplace, grabbed the poker, and crouched down. "Odd, really. You've yet to set foot in the café, but you have strong and really expensive ideas of what would work better for it."

"And very Englisch ideas," Martha added softly.

"Fine." Skylar held up both hands. "Forget I mentioned anything. But I'm right."

Susie tapped the pen against the legal pad. "You seem so sure about what needs to be done. Why?"

"My mom loves coffee shops. As far back as I can remember, finding new coffee shops and going to them every Saturday morning was our thing. Apparently I learned a few things without realizing it."

The room was silent as Abram poked the

logs, causing sparks to fly and flames to leap. Was Skylar asking to change the opening time of the café because she wanted to sleep later?

Skylar closed the catalog and tossed it onto the coffee table, looking disinterested. "Do it your way. Exhaust your creative energy getting up superearly six days a week. Serve weak coffee and only the regular kind. Have no breakfast breads. Doesn't matter to me."

"The strength of the coffee is my fault," Martha said. "Ariana wrote down on an index card how to fix it, and I lost it. Her coffee was good, but I've been making it like Mamm and Daed do."

Abram hadn't realized that they had been using different instructions for the coffee than what Ariana had given.

"It's not as if your ideas are bad." He put the poker back in its stand and added a log to the fire. "Some — maybe all — have merit. But we would have to take on debt to purchase the things you're talking about."

"It's an investment," Skylar said.

"It's a gamble." Abram stood.

"You know" — Skylar picked up the catalog again — "one would think the Amish were used to taking gambles. You take your life into your hands to ride in a carriage on the road — no seat belts, no reinforced steel anything, and moving at the pace of a turtle. But apparently buying a commercial blender and coffee machines is over the top." She held out the book to him. "It's no skin off my nose whether this café makes it or not."

Martha flinched. "Are we struggling that much?" Her eyes were large as she looked from Abram to Susie.

"Nee." Susie shook her head. "I mean, it's been a rough start. And you know we've yet to have our croissants or scones turn out well enough that customers would buy them a second time."

Skylar held her two fingers as if she had a cigarette between them and tapped them against her thumb. "So let me get this straight. You and Martha are in over your heads, and Abram has quit his day job to help with the café, but all my suggestions are useless?"

Susie rubbed her forehead. "It's just your ideas are . . ."

"Different from what Ariana wanted, right?" Skylar asked.

"I was going to say *expensive.*" Susie looked at her notes. "Everything you've mentioned will take several thousand dollars, and that's if we go with the less expensive versions."

"Never buy cheap or used equipment for coffee. Your customers will know it first thing."

Susie looked to Abram. "I guess we could tap into the reserve cash from the benefit."

"That's for making sure the bills can be paid in the coming months," Martha said.

"Ya, I know. But it's not enough to keep the bills paid until Ariana gets back," Susie said. "We have to get more people coming in. Right now we have no repeat customers other than Amish friends who would support us if we were serving mud."

Martha pulled her knees to her chest and wrapped her arms around them. "Do you even know anything about making these different sorts of coffee?"

"Apparently more than you know about baking croissants and scones, which actually brings me to another topic. If you can't do a good job of making what's on the menu, change the stupid menu."

Susie's lips puckered to one side as she looked to Abram. "I think she's right," she said, appearing terrified by the idea. "We don't have to purchase everything at once, but we need to change how we're doing things, starting with a commercial generator, coffee grinder, and a change of menu."

Skylar grinned, not really looking happy but more like the cat who'd swallowed the canary.

Abram caught her eye, and she held his gaze. About twelve hours ago she'd asked if they could still use some help in the café, and now she was brimming with ideas about making the café better. Strange, very strange. But Skylar wasn't holed up in her bedroom, and she was engaged in a positive conversation. That had to count for something.

"Okay." Abram motioned from Susie to the catalog. "You take a few days to figure out exactly what you need and fill out the form. When that's done, I'll get a cashier's check from the bank and put the order in the mail."

"Is there an Amish reason you don't own a debit card? Because if you had one, you could place the order by phone."

"No Amish reason. We're just new to having a little money and running a business."

"Get a debit card, Abram," Skylar said. "It'll make life easier. Trust me."

But that was the question, wasn't it? Whether or not Skylar could be trusted.

SEVENTEEN

Ariana's stomach was queasy as the GPS said, "You've reached your destination." A trailer sat fifty feet off the road, but the entire side yard seemed to be a parking lot, and it was filled with vehicles. Was she really going to do this? Thoughts of how well things had gone with Cameron came to mind. If she and Cameron could clear the air and choose to be friends, surely she and Quill could.

She pulled in and turned off her car.

A woman emerged from one of the vehicles. Was Ariana at the right place? The trailer wasn't very big. How could five brothers live here?

Ariana stepped out of her car. "Excuse me?"

The woman had opened the trunk and one of the car's back doors and was doing something, but she didn't seem surprised by Ariana's presence. "Yeah?" She lifted a child out of the car and put the adorable blond-haired, blue-eyed boy on her hip. The little one caused Ariana to miss her nieces and nephews, that is, Skylar's nieces and nephews. Pushing that heartache aside, she tried to stay in the moment.

"Hi. I'm not sure I'm at the right place. Does Quill live here?" Ariana asked.

"He does, but I don't think he's here right —"

Ariana thought she heard a door opening, but she couldn't see around the open trunk of the car.

"Honey," a man said, "you need a hand?"

"Please. Is Quill here?"

"He's on a run," the man said.

Quill was a runner? Did Ariana actually know anything about him?

"Ah." The woman shrugged. "One never knows how many miles he'll log." She appeared disinterested in who Ariana was and why she'd come. Was it an everyday thing for a young woman to come looking for him? Seemed like it.

Quill's golden retriever came toward Ariana from the direction of the trailer, wriggling with excitement.

"Hey, Lexi." Ariana rubbed her ears, and Lexi licked the sleeves of her coat.

"Ah, she knows you." The woman sounded

curious now, and she gestured toward the trailer. "He's stopped carrying his phone with him on his runs, so I can't reach him. But you're welcome to wait."

A man came around the side of the car, strolling into view. He wasn't just any man. He was the drunk who'd stumbled into Berta's home maybe two years ago, thinking it was his own. His eyes met Ariana's, and he froze.

The pieces fit now. He hadn't been a confused drunk. He was one of the Schlabach brothers.

The woman studied them, looking from Ariana to the man and back to Ariana. "So you two know each other?"

"Ariana," the man said as if announcing it to a crowd.

The woman's eyes widened, and her curiosity seemed to turn into surprise. "Oh." She motioned. "I'm making lasagna. Please join us for dinner."

Respond to her. But Ariana couldn't. All her energy was focused on the man in front of her. If he was a Schlabach, he and Berta had worked together that day to trick her. Ariana had watched out for Berta for five years after Quill disappeared, and she'd learned only two months ago that Berta's sons had occasionally visited her during those years.

The Schlabach brothers needed to choose a side and be bold about it. Either live Amish or leave the Amish alone.

Ariana's mouth was dry. "You are . . ."

"Dan."

"Berta's oldest."

He nodded. "I can explain about the day I was in Mamm's house."

Movement near the trailer caught her attention. At the foot of the steps to the trailer were three men, three women, and several children. Quill's brothers, no doubt. Until this moment they'd felt more like a myth than real people, but there they stood with the women who loved them and the children who relied on them.

How many other deceitful, somewhat embarrassing stories about her did they know that she didn't? Her ears pulsated to the beat of her heart, and if she was going to control her response, she had to say something. "I . . . I just . . . need a minute. Okay?"

"Sure." His eyes showed respect and understanding.

She hated to turn her back to them, but she had to, taking in deep breaths while looking skyward. Had she played the fool for Berta? After Dan had startled her that day, she'd spent months worrying that the drunk might return when Berta was alone. Ariana had asked her brother-in-law to install better locks, which he did, and she started going by Berta's more often.

Berta . . . If Quill and his brothers were cloaked in secrets, their mother was too. Ariana had sort of realized that after learning about the sons' visits, but the weight of how deep that secret life went hadn't unloaded on her until now. Berta had known how worried Ariana was about her after the incident with the supposed drunk. But Berta continually discounted the event, talking as if it'd been nothing and telling Ariana she had nothing to worry about. Why hadn't Berta broken her silence and spared Ariana the concern?

Breathe, Ariana. Cold air rushed into her lungs time and again as she tried to put the event into perspective. She had come to apologize to Quill, and she would *not* stir discord with his siblings. "Okay." She turned back around and realized the brothers and their families had moved closer. They were still hanging back a little, as if unwilling to remain where they couldn't hear what was going on but not wishing to crowd her.

She held out her hand to Dan. "Ariana."

What was she doing? He knew who she was.

He shook her hand. "This is my wife, Regina."

Ariana shook her hand.

"Listen, Ariana," — Dan rubbed his clean-shaven jaw, and the gold band on his finger gleamed — "I feel the need to clarify that Mamm had little choice. She longed to see her children on occasion. You can understand that, right?"

Dan was the eldest, and it had seemed he had drawn each brother away from the Amish. But maybe not Quill. Last month he'd told her he hadn't connected with his brothers until two years after he'd left the Amish. She didn't know why he'd waited that long any more than she knew why he'd left in the first place.

"Yeah, but —"

"There are really no *buts.* The bishop decreed there was to be no contact between her and us. I'm sorry we had to deceive you, especially my pretending to be a drunk. Mamm had to choose either not to see any of us or to see us without making you a party to disobeying the bishop."

If Ariana had learned anything since leaving Summer Grove, it was the heartache of longing to see loved ones. How could a mother not want to see her children? Maybe

Ariana's viewpoint of either live Amish or leave the Amish alone wasn't as easily done or as right as she'd thought.

"Mamm misses you." Dan lifted the little boy from Regina's arms. "She's counting the days until you get back. You won't hold the incident against her, will you?"

How many people were lied to and tricked the way Ariana had been and still kept the relationship intact? "It's a lot to ask."

"It is. But in our own way, we — you and us — try to help the world go round for people we care about. Mamm is one of those people. You can disagree with how we keep her world moving, but don't hold Mamm responsible."

Ariana wasn't sure that people like Dan helped the world go round as much as they helped pull it apart. "I'll need more than a moment on that one."

"Sure. I get that, but —"

"Guys?" Quill came to a halt on the far side of a red car. He put his hands on his knees, staring at the ground and breathing heavily. "What's everyone doing out here?"

"You have company," one of his brothers answered.

Quill took a few more breaths before he stood upright. "Yeah?" His dark blond hair was disheveled, and he looked very different in shorts and a T-shirt. A few moments later his eyes landed on Ariana, and he said nothing as he walked toward her.

"Okay, guys," — Dan looped his finger through the air as if it were a lasso — "everyone inside."

Regina grabbed some grocery bags out of the car and hooked some on Dan's hands as he held the little boy in the crook of his arm.

Dan turned back to Ariana. "You're more than welcome anytime, either here or at our homes in Kentucky. If you arrive here and nobody's home, we keep a key in a toy under those rickety steps."

She looked at Quill, who'd moved in closer, easily able to hear what Dan had said.

Clearing her throat, she hoped to speak without her voice wavering. "That's a kind invitation, Dan." But she wouldn't return. Quill's family lived between two worlds, and she found it dishonest.

Quill studied her, but neither spoke until everyone else was inside. "I wasn't expecting you."

She took in the man in front of her, the stranger she knew all too well. "I had things I needed to say — an apology — but now my emotions are all over the place, like that crazy roller coaster we used to tease about . . . the Thunderhawk. And I'm on it once again, and I . . . I can't think straight."

"It's fine, Ari. You're here, which is nice. Let's talk."

His calmness settled her jittery nerves, and she took a cleansing breath, trying to slow the roller coaster. "Nothing about us is ever normal or easy, is it?"

He leaned against the car parked next to hers, looking tranquil. "Our relationship is unique, but then again, for better and worse, we're unique. So it fits."

"Are the lies and trickery befitting of us too?"

"Every deception had a purpose, and none of it was done for selfish reasons. Some were poor decisions, but not selfish. What's this about apologizing?"

Was he serious?

But he was right. That is what she came for. "Ya, about that."

Some birds dipped low and rose again with such uniformity they reminded her of a huge flag waving in the wind. She closed her eyes, listening as the wind rustled through the trees, birds cawed, and thunder rumbled in the distance. Her thoughts began to gather again.

"Sometime during last night's fitful sleep,

I realized I've been angry with you since you left five years ago. Then when I learned that I wasn't a Brenneman and that you were involved in uncovering the truth, being angry with you was the only familiar thing left in my life, and I've been clinging to it with all I had."

"That's a tough thing to have to use as your anchor. I'm sorry for my part in —"

"Shh." She leaned forward and touched his arm, shaking her head. "I know. We've been there before — you apologizing, me forgiving. Let's not rehash it. I'm here to say I'm sorry. I'm sorry for how I behaved last night, and I'm sorry for waffling in my forgiveness, allowing old hurts to rise up and control me, making me feel justified to invite you in or kick you out of my life at will."

His eyes never moved from hers. "Apology accepted." His voice was hoarse. "Thank you."

The air between them seemed to vibrate with awkwardness . . . and some indefinable emotion. Maybe he felt it too, because he looked away. And then Lexi dropped a tennis ball at his feet. He picked it up and threw it a long way.

"You're welcome. Also I really appreciate your help last night. You came when I called, and you protected me from myself."

"Ari, we're friends, and that's what friends do."

"Are we friends? Because if I'm really honest, this relationship" — she pointed at him and then herself and then back and forth — "is a one-way street. It's pastoral care by you, and I'm the flock."

When Lexi dropped the ball at his feet again, Quill picked it up and threw it even farther.

"What you do for Mamm makes you the best friend I have."

"That's just so not how relationships work."

"I'd say it works pretty well. We are two very different people, working through frustrations. Maybe your idea of friendship is people who hold the same views about right and wrong."

"Maybe." She was a long way from knowing how to accept her parents, herself, her new role as their daughter, and the Englisch ways without criticism and discontent. She longed to at least close the distance between Quill and her, but there was so much debris to deal with. "It's just hard to think in friendly terms when I hate what you do, sneaking in to help Amish people leave. My sister? Really?"

He threw the ball for Lexi again. "Friends also argue, as we've proved all too well already. What if we talk about something else?"

Salome had used Esther's scars on her face and neck as a reason to leave the Amish. That didn't make sense to Ariana. "No one forbade Salome to use Englisch medicine to treat Esther. Despite some pressure from the community, the choice was hers and Emanuel's. So I see no reason for you to offer to help them leave during the night."

"You're just determined to have this conversation."

"I am."

"Okay." He picked up the ball and threw it. "Let's have it. Only a very few Amish feel they need a way out, and of those, even fewer choose to leave after we've worked and prayed with them for at least a year. But in the end the decision is theirs. I don't have to agree with someone's conclusions or decisions to support their right to choose. I feel that freedom dictates I take a stand for the Amish who feel chained to a way of life they no longer believe in."

"But it's wrong. They've taken a vow. And for those who haven't, they have a family, a whole village that loves them and has helped raise them."

"Ari . . ." Quill threw the ball again. "There seems to be a number inside your head, and every person's life — including Salome's, Brandi's, Nicholas's, mine, and yours — is supposed to add up to that number. It never does, not for anyone."

"It could, couldn't it — if people tried hard enough?"

"It can't. Even if everyone wanted to do the *right* thing, the possibilities of what's right for individuals are endless. God beats out a different rhythm for different people, and despite all you've been taught, people shouldn't wall out each other because of it."

Was that right? Did God have different beats for people to march to? Longing for answers, she looked skyward.

"Hey." A little girl about six years old, wearing jeans and pink boots, hurried outside. Ariana's prayer scattered with the wind.

"Hi, Kylie." Quill sounded upbeat, as if it wasn't an interruption at all. "What's up?" He grabbed the tennis ball and threw it much farther than before.

The girl's arms were full, and she stopped several feet away. "Mom said you'll be cold staying out here after your run. She's not trying to interrupt, and I can't stay."

"Ah. Tell your mom I appreciate it." Quill removed everything from her arms. He set a bottle of water, a thermos, and a container of hand sanitizer on the hood of the car. Then he slid the gray hoodie over his head and stretched his arms into the sleeves. "I'm much warmer now. Thanks." He rubbed the top of the little girl's head.

Kylie stared up at Ariana as if she was in awe of her. "I heard that you know our *Mammi* Bertie."

Ariana smiled at the nickname. "I do."

"What's she like?"

The question knocked the wind out of Ariana. This sweet child didn't know her wonderful grandmother? Clearly Berta was a bit secretive, but, still, she was an amazing woman. "Well . . ." Years of good, fun memories of Berta flooded Ariana, and her heart ached for the position Berta had been put in. "She's really smart, very energetic, and a bit prickly if you fuss over her when she's sick."

"My dad's like that." Kylie grinned. "Would you give her a hug for me?"

Ariana knelt. "If you give me a hug, I'll see that she gets it."

Kylie threw her arms around Ariana's neck and squeezed hard. Ariana returned the hug. "Mm-mm," Ariana groaned lovingly. "That's from Mammi Bertie."

Kylie backed away, pointing a finger at Ariana. "When I'm big like you and I have a car, I'm going to go see her."

If only it were that simple. "I'll be sure to tell her that."

The door to the trailer opened. "Kylie Peyton," Regina called.

"I gotta go." Kylie took off running, but before she disappeared inside, she blew kisses and waved at Ariana and Quill.

Ariana waved. "She has no memories of Berta?"

Quill blew Kylie a kiss as if he'd done it hundreds of times. "Visiting Mamm is complicated. We've never tried to sneak in any of the kids." He held up the water bottle and the thermos, offering her a choice. "Water or coffee?"

She pointed at the thermos. "Berta's never held any of her grandbabes?"

"Not yet." He poured hand sanitizer into his palms and rubbed them together before he removed the cup and lid to the thermos. Steam rose as he poured the hot liquid into the small mug.

"Couldn't she come to them?"

He passed her the mug. "That would mean directly disobeying the bishop. She wouldn't do that. The most she can handle is not telling the bishop that we drop by unannounced from time to time."

She studied him, seeing a tower of restraint. They were nothing alike, didn't seem to view life from the same planet, yet they seemed to need each other. But she could see this conversation was just another painful reminder for Quill that his Mamm was in Summer Grove without any family. "Do you ever get relief . . . you know, concerning your Mamm being without all of you?"

He opened the water bottle and leaned against the car. "Some, mostly because I know she has you, a girl she loves like a daughter. So when you return, please don't be angry with her for keeping our necessary secrets."

Hard lines were drawn between the church and those who left, but usually if someone hadn't joined the faith, like Quill and his brothers, the boundaries weren't strict — not like this. But for reasons Ariana knew nothing about, the bishop had made inflexible rules where the Schlabachs were concerned. Maybe it was a message to other Mamms to do a better job of ensuring their children stayed. Or maybe the church leaders suspected one of the Schlabach brothers was the Nightcrawler, as the Amish referred to him, the one who occasionally sneaked in at night and helped an entire Amish family leave.

Ariana could still feel the warmth of the hug from Kylie, a beautiful connection to life that Berta had yet to experience. And she might not experience that until Kylie was old enough to hide quietly in a barn or shed for hours. The whole thing grieved Ariana. "It's all so confusing. Not long ago I was completely confident and peaceful in my faith, and now I have no idea how to meld my beliefs with what's taking place in my life — not just with your family, but with the people who apparently are *my* family."

"I wish I could tell you it'll get easier." He threw the ball for Lexi again.

"Yeah, I wish you could tell me that too." Ariana sighed.

She was beginning to think Quill was right about that number in her head. That explanation didn't clear up everything, but if she could refuse to judge people based on that imaginary *right number,* it would help her a lot — and everyone who came in contact with her. "I won't hold anything against your Mamm. She's been my second Mamm since I was your shadow."

"My shadow." Quill smiled before he guzzled half of the bottle of water. "See, we are friends."

She took a sip of coffee, realizing it had the perfect amount of sugar. "Yeah, I guess we are. And it's a good thing because" — she pulled the bucket list out of her pocket — "I need your help."

He took the papers from her, barely glancing at them before again tossing the ball for Lexi. "Absolutely. There are a few things I could use from you too."

"Like?"

Night continued to close in, and a misty rain began to fall, but there was nowhere for them to go. The trailer or a restaurant lacked privacy, and sitting in a car to talk seemed awkward, maybe inappropriate. This is who they'd become — people who stayed put and dealt with the storm between them, whether in his mother's dark home on a rainy night, or working on a rundown café, or here in Mingo.

Quill opened the thermos and refilled her mug. "One, don't meet any more single guys at bars. You're going to get me beat up."

She peered at him over the mug. "You could've taken him."

He set the thermos on the hood of her car. "Maybe, but not all his friends, which seemed to be everyone in the bar."

"So friends don't help friends get beat up. Got it."

"Exactly." He studied her through the misty darkness. "Have you heard from him?"

"No. Do you think I will?"

"Yeah, absolutely. You should block his number."

"Seems excessive and rude. Shouldn't I take his call and tell him the truth? I probably owe him an apology. I was the one who forgot about Rudy and —"

"Ariana, for Pete's sake." Quill's eyes bore into hers, his brows knit, and his voice was filled with concern. "Better yet, for *your* sake, don't be the kind of woman who is too nice, giving users the benefit of the doubt. I call that giving the benefit of the doubt to the death — often the death of someone's good sense and the death of wise decisions and anything else men like that will tromp all over. And apologize? To him? Come on, he was aiming to lower your defenses and see just how far he could get."

So Quill felt a lot he rarely showed. "He really got under your skin."

Quill's brows barely lifted, and a stony coldness etched his face. "He's a creep who tried to use his nice looks and gentle manner to disarm you."

"I believe you." Ariana pulled her phone out of her pocket. "Block his number." She held on to the phone until Quill looked at her. "Thank you, not only for last night, but also for helping me understand creeps and how I should think about them. So what else can I do for you?"

Quill pressed numerous items on her touch-screen phone before handing it back to her. "Write a short, friendly text to Frieda. I can't give you her number, but if you send it to me, I can forward it along with your number . . . if you're willing."

"I can do that."

"About a month ago she offered to tell you her story. Maybe she would have followed through, maybe not. It's hard to tell. But I didn't think the timing was good, so I declined her offer."

"You're unsure whether she'll respond."

"A little. She seems to be doing really well right now. But when Mamm was sick, Frieda hired a driver and traveled seven hours to visit her. Then she couldn't make herself go into the hospital. Still, whether she responds or not, it would be good for her to hear from you."

Ariana couldn't imagine what had happened to Frieda . . . or that she and Frieda had been friends without Ariana knowing what was happening to her friend. She knew Frieda was sick, knew she dealt with depression and anxiety. Ariana never tried to understand why or if their roots were in specific events rather than generalized anxiety.

Should she ask him any questions? Would he answer this time? "Why did you disappear with her?" Ariana had thought he was in love with Frieda, but clearly that had been a smoke screen. "I know you can't say much, but what was happening in Frieda's life that I didn't know?"

He threw the ball for Lexi again. "Something a little similar but totally different from what caused Salome to want to leave."

A little similar but totally different. "She needed something that the bishop frowned on?"

"Basically, sort of. Okay?"

"Yeah, that's enough." Anything else would need to come from Frieda. "Thanks."

"While we're on the subject" — he picked up the ball again and threw it — "I feel I should tell you that I'm looking into a situation with a cousin of yours."

She hated this part of who he was. "Which cousin?"

"A single guy who doesn't live in Summer Grove."

"And you're going in as the Nightcrawler to help him leave?"

"It's way too early to know what the situation will call for. But, yeah, it's possible."

"Quill." The edge in her tone didn't compare to the frustration running through her.

"Look." Quill's slow splaying of his fingers with his palms up seemed indicative of how gently he tried to respond to her. "I know how you feel, and I get it. I don't in any way discount your feelings, but I can't ignore a possible cry for help."

"Possible cry? Sounds more like you need to let my cousin work this out with his family."

"It's not open for debate, Ari. I just want to be honest with you."

"Okay." What else could she say? She would stand a better chance of winning an argument with Nicholas than with Quill, but she was no match for either. Nicholas's beliefs were based on books he'd read and lectures he'd attended. To her, Quill's foundation was much more solid. He based his actions on years of experience inside and outside of the Amish community.

Life was so complicated. No wonder the Amish strove to hold on to the Old Ways, clinging to a time when life was simple. And no wonder the Englisch strove for modernization in everything, looking for new and better ways to navigate the turbulence of everyday life.

"*Okay* as in you accept that, or *okay* as in you're outta here?"

"I accept it. I don't like it, and I never will, but I guess I'm beginning to get the whole need-to-follow-after-freedom thing. If I had freedom, I'd escape back *into* my Amish life."

He picked up the ball and threw it again. "And I'd help you do it."

She knew that was true, and somehow it helped. Lexi's sides heaved as she chased after the ball time and again, and her fur glistened with droplets from the mist.

A shiver ran through Ariana, and she buttoned her coat. "Uh, Quill?"

"Yeah?"

"Your dog is going to run herself to death if you don't stop throwing that ball."

Quill's eyes opened wide. "Lexi, stop!"

The dog came to an abrupt halt.

He whistled. "Here, girl."

Lexi looked from him to the ball.

"Here." He snapped his fingers. "Now."

Lexi tucked her tail, but she hurried to him.

"That is one incredibly obedient dog."

Ariana sipped on her coffee.

"She's a good one." Quill crouched, patting her. "Sorry, girl. I wasn't thinking. You okay?" He looked up at Ariana. "Her heart is pounding like crazy."

Ariana dumped out her coffee and poured water into the cup. "She looks like I've felt almost constantly since last month." She passed the plastic lid to Quill.

"Like *we've* felt, Ari." He gave Lexi the water and stroked her. "We've been hung on the Thunderhawk for a while now."

Was that true? He always looked and sounded so calm, but after a moment of reflection, knowing all she did now, she realized it was true. *They'd* been on a roller coaster for a long time.

Quill stood. He stepped closer, leaned in, and pulled the hood to her coat over her hair. "This, here tonight, means the world to me."

This moment felt like one from their past, before secrets and disappearing acts ripped them apart. But she didn't live in the past. Neither of them did. And it was time to focus on the future.

"I'm desperate to see Rudy."

Quill opened the bucket list. "Then let's see what we can do about that."

Eighteen

Skylar was behind the counter, near the cash register, wiping off endless crumbs from muffins and biscuits. Apparently there were breakfast breads that Susie and Martha knew how to bake. Skylar had made the coffee the last two days, and she wasn't the only one who'd enjoyed refills.

"Hey," Martha whispered while peering out of the pass-through that separated the kitchen from the dining area. She gave a thumbs-up while mouthing the words *you're doing a great job.*

No she wasn't, but Skylar nodded. Customers' food had found its way under her nails. She had spent most of her time hurrying back and forth as she took orders at the counter, handled the cash register, picked up plates of food at the pass-through, and delivered them to the diners. In between those things, she cleared tables and took the dirty dishes to Martha, who thanked her each time and washed every item, including whatever Susie used while cooking.

So much for Skylar just pouring coffee.

Early Sunday morning, while everyone was distracted with life, Skylar took Cody's advice and went through the Brennemans' medicine cabinets. In Salome's side of the house, Skylar found some pain pills that had been prescribed around the time Salome's last baby was born. The prescription was for just ten pills, but there were still six in the bottle. Skylar had stolen three of them, confident no one would be the wiser.

She used the last one yesterday before her first day of work. So last night she sneaked back into Salome's bathroom to get the rest of the pills, but the bottle was missing. Why? Had Salome realized what Skylar had done? Or maybe Salome had needed the medication. Whatever happened to the last three pills, it wasn't as if Skylar could ask anyone about them.

Susie came out of the kitchen, pulling something out of the hidden pocket of her black apron. "Hey, Sky, would you look at this?" Susie unfolded a page from the catalog. "Do you mind if I call you Sky?"

Actually Skylar minded everything. Absolutely everything. But even in her state of forced detox, she could see the sincerity in

Susie's eyes and hear it in her voice. "Sky is fine." She took the slick page and noted the circled espresso machine. Skylar had the jitters from the lack of drugs, so the paper trembled, and on a scale of one to ten, she was an eight when it came to irritability. Cody's words about sabotaging the place tempted her.

When talking to Abram, Susie, and Martha about making changes to the café, she wasn't certain of her motivation for making various and expensive suggestions. But after brainstorming solutions, she got a weird sensation that she knew what this place needed . . . and she actually wanted to lend a hand. Now she knew that her desire to help had come from the drug high.

Skylar laid the paper on the counter. "Whatever. It doesn't matter which one you choose."

Susie blinked. "But I thought —"

"Look, any machine that works would be better than no machine." Skylar took her damp rag and a dish bin to a messy table.

"Okay, thanks." Susie sounded baffled, but she folded the paper and returned to the kitchen. She'd been cooking nonstop since before dawn. Abram moved from one jam to the next, helping whoever needed it the most — Susie, Martha, Cilla, or her. Skylar had been surprised at the amount of work required for just a few customers at a time.

Of course half of the reason every job was so labor intensive was that the Amish were skilled at doing everything in the most time-consuming, difficult manner possible. Like making toast. Rather than buy bread from a bakery or grocery store, Susie and Martha made loaves of bread from scratch, sliced it, and used a camp-stove toaster, which toasted only one side of the bread at a time.

Making toast and squeezing fresh orange juice was Cilla's job. At least for the fresh juice they had a hand press for Cilla to use.

"Excuse me?" An old man held up his empty glass. "Refill of water."

Skylar nodded. If she didn't get out of here soon, she'd start screaming at the customers or, worse, at the stranger sisters, who were definitely making an effort to welcome and be kind to her.

What would it be like if the café was ever packed?

She got the pitcher of water and returned to fill the man's glass. Abram glanced from behind the pass-through, clearly checking on her. Could they stop that? Especially him. He had barely spoken to her today. But like Martha, Susie, and Cilla, he was a worker. He seamlessly moved from serving customers to cooking for them. When he had a minute, he cleaned tables and floors. She'd yet to see him take a break. Was this what she would have been like if she'd been raised as his twin — an unfriendly, stoic pack mule?

She glanced at the clock. Only an hour before closing. On the one hand, the end of the day couldn't come soon enough. She had tip money, which meant she could buy cigarettes from the gas station up the road. Maybe she'd ask to walk to the Brennemans. That would allow her the time and privacy to make her purchase.

But why hadn't she seen Cody yet? He'd promised to come today. Maybe he was lost. That thought brought some comfort, except he'd found a lone tree near the Brenneman home in the middle of the night last week. Maybe he was waiting until they were about to close, thinking the café wouldn't be as busy then and she'd be freer to talk. That made sense, and she took a deep breath.

Only a few people remained, scattered throughout the small café.

The door opened, and a man walked in. He was muscular with a beard and black tattoos on his arms and what appeared to be a genuine grin. Other than his size and tattoos, he didn't look the least bit intimi-

261

dating. She returned to the cash register and set the pitcher on the counter.

He looked around while walking to the counter. "What kind of Amish are you?"

She stifled a sigh. "I'm not." Surely he was joking. What Amish girl wore tattered jeans and a red cashmere tennis sweater? If he was serious, today could be her final day, and it was only her second day.

His grin grew a little. "You don't look thrilled at my joke. Truth is, you don't pass for Amish any more than I do . . . Though I do think I would look good in one of those straw hats."

Glancing out the front window, she searched for signs of Cody. She grabbed the pen from behind her ear, ready to take his order. "You don't have to be Amish to wear a straw hat."

"No, but you do have to be Amish to make a straw hat look manly."

"Yeah, sure." Could he just place his order and take a seat already? "So what can I get for you today?" She looked out of the window again. Where was Cody?

The man leaned against the counter, examining the café. "I've never been to an Amish café before. I was halfway expecting a horse-and-buggy drive-through."

She couldn't tell if he was flirting or just

being friendly. "That's actually clever, but if you suggest it to the owners, I'll have to poison your coffee."

His smile disappeared, but his light brown eyes held amusement. "Suggest what?" He tapped the counter. "Is Abram here?"

He wanted to speak to Abram? She looked at the pass-through and saw him vigorously cleaning the stove.

"You seem confused." He grinned. "He's an owner, I think. Your age, thin, wears straw hats. Doesn't say too much."

"I know who he is, and, yes, he's here."

"Can I speak with him?"

What did a man like this — a worldly looking, tattooed man — want with Abram? Rather than raise her voice, she walked to the pass-through. "Abram, you have a visitor."

He looked up from the grill and stared at Skylar as if she were speaking an alien language.

She rolled her eyes and went back to the counter. "He'll be right out . . . I guess."

"He's sort of hard to read, isn't he?"

Seemed to her he was sort of difficult, but whatever.

Abram came out of the kitchen and walked directly to the tattooed man. Abram smiled, the first genuine smile she'd seen from him all day, maybe since she'd arrived.

"Jackson." Abram stuck out his hand. The two shared a firm handshake without breaking eye contact. She hadn't expected that. Abram normally seemed so . . . immature.

"It's a good-looking place, whether the food is any good or not."

Abram laughed. "Thanks, but I had little to do with how the place looks. How's work?"

"It's only been a couple of days, but it's moving a good bit slower without you there." Jackson shifted his weight. "What do you recommend on the menu?"

Abram moved behind the counter. "The special, Amish shepherd's pie, is good. For dessert, whoopie pie."

Jackson lifted his brows. "What's a whoopie pie?"

"Two cookie-sized cakes with filling between them." Abram gestured with his hands. "Sort of like a MoonPie but much better. Fresh ones are best, and Martha is making a batch right now. They'll be ready by the time you're finished with the shepherd's pie."

Jackson looked at Skylar. "I'll have what he said." He turned back to Abram. "What do you recommend to drink?"

Abram grabbed a mug off the counter.

"Coffee?"

Jackson nodded, and Abram filled the mug with hot coffee.

Skylar rang up the order. "Nine seventy-five."

Abram moved to the register, clearing the amount from the machine. "No, he's a friend."

Jackson reached into his wallet. "A friend who pays for his food." He pulled out fifteen dollars and handed it to Skylar. "Keep it."

That was generous. Would she be allowed to keep the tip? She couldn't believe she was wondering about that. Money had been free and easy when she belonged to Brandi and Nicholas.

Abram waved at Jackson while walking toward the kitchen. "Enjoy your meal."

"Sure thing."

Skylar put the money in the register. "Thank you."

Jackson stayed at the counter for a moment. "What makes a shepherd's pie Amish?"

She shrugged. "It comes with a prayer cap thingy?"

Jackson laughed. "Think I'd look as good wearing that as a straw hat?"

"Definitely." She motioned toward the tables. "Take a seat wherever you want, and

I'll bring it out to you as soon as Abram has it ready."

"Sure, but remember, I didn't share my suggestion with him about the horse-and-buggy drive-through, so don't poison my food." He held up his mug to her as if to say *cheers.*

When Abram set Jackson's plate on the pass-through, she picked it up and the pot of coffee. She set the plate in front of Jackson.

"Thanks. Looks good."

"It's not bad." She glanced out the window.

He turned, looking in the same direction. It took him one second to lose interest, and she envied that.

"Coffee?" He nudged his empty cup toward her.

"Oh." She refilled his cup, examining the tattoos on his arms.

He took a bite of food. "Wow, that's really good."

Some of the ink on his arms had symbols and markings she didn't recognize. One tattoo was mostly hidden under his right sleeve.

He set down his fork and pulled back his sleeve. The tattoo was of an American eagle on top of a globe, with an anchor resting in the background. Below it were large letters: USMC. He ran his palm across it. "Marine Corps."

"Sorry. Didn't mean to be nosy."

"Don't apologize. If I didn't want people to see it, I wouldn't have put it on my arm." He lowered his sleeve. "I'm proud of my service, but it was a long time ago."

"Couldn't have been that long ago. You're too young. Midtwenties? Maybe thirty."

"Feels more like fifty. Seen too much to feel my age."

The way he said it, the haunted look in his eyes, made her want to know more.

Suddenly the door swung open, and a greasy-haired young man with a stubbled face walked in. His eyes were sunk into his skull, and his skin was so white it was almost translucent.

Cody.

The last time she saw him he looked rough, but it'd been dark, and she couldn't tell how rough until now. It was as if Cody was going through some sort of reverse metamorphosis, like a butterfly changing into a slug. He passed her without a word and stepped up to the counter. She lingered.

"You have a customer," Jackson said.

"Yeah." She was supposed to know this customer, but she wasn't sure she did. She went around the counter to her place behind the register. "What can I get for you?"

He stared as if looking through her. "A coffee would be fine."

"Anything else? Today's special is shepherd's pie."

"No." He looked around the place before taking a few dollars from his pocket. He held them out, and when Skylar took the bills, she felt a little baggie stuck in with the cash. A quick glance said there were more than a dozen pills. She quickly stuffed the pills into her jeans pocket and put the money in the register.

"Are you okay?" She grabbed a mug and poured coffee, hoping they didn't look suspicious.

"Sure. Everything is rosy." Cody pulled his cell from his pocket. He picked up the mug and walked off, looking at his phone while going toward one of the empty tables on the far side of the room.

She waited a few minutes before she took the pot of coffee to his table and refilled his mug. "You don't seem like yourself."

Cody looked up from the screen and finally focused on her. "I am myself. This just isn't the ideal situation."

"Us?"

He hesitated and drew a deep breath.

"We're good, Sky. We'll figure out the rest. I need to go, but I'll see you in a few days. Okay?"

Her heart pounded. Was he losing interest in her already? She hadn't been here two weeks yet. Did he already have someone else? It wasn't as if their relationship was built for long distance, but all her hopes were pinned on him getting her out of here and keeping her supplied with drugs. She picked up the container of sugar packets and set them closer to him, brushing his fingers with hers. "I'll be waiting. Okay?"

His lips formed into a lopsided smile. "Yeah."

"You'll come back to the café in a few days, right? And regularly after that?"

"Yeah, of course." He read a text on his phone.

"Cody?" she whispered.

He looked up.

"I need you."

"I know. I won't let you down." He got up and walked out, leaving his coffee on the table.

She took the mug with her and returned to the register. She pulled the baggie out of her pocket and saw more than two dozen pills, maybe ten of which were unfamiliar. Pain pills, she imagined. Whatever they were, he'd added them for extra relief, which was nice, but if she stuck to two pills a day, she had at least two weeks' worth. Maybe he was giving her a few extra in case she needed them or lost some. But if he was returning in a few days, why would he give her this many?

"So . . ." Jackson startled her.

She closed her fist and jammed the baggie into her pocket.

"Is that whoopie pie ready by any chance?"

Had he seen what was in her hand? "Let me check."

NINETEEN

Music vibrated the crisp fall air as Ariana sat on the grassy seats of the amphitheater and watched the stage. Nicholas's hands moved effortlessly across the piano keys as he accompanied a singer. The beautiful sound of his playing seemed almost miraculous, and it filled her with emotion. How could such a challenging man stir her soul with music?

And why were all instruments forbidden among the Amish?

The midafternoon sun warmed her back through her winter coat. She missed home and all who were there, but she had moments, like now, when she felt as if she would survive this time intact. Well, relatively unbroken. Whatever damage occurred between now and when she was allowed to return to Summer Grove, she would gather up the pieces and take them home, where she could mend. Had Frieda survived emotionally and spiritually when she left the community? After talking with Quill on Sunday evening, Ariana had sent him a text the next morning to forward to Frieda. Ariana had said that she'd like to communicate with her via texts or calls or a visit, but Frieda had yet to respond. Should she send another text through Quill?

Cameron walked across the wide grassy area toward her, carrying hot dogs in a paper tray and a napkin in each hand. The park and its wide sidewalks were covered with people, and the acres of green spaces had booths galore with games and food. But the gorgeous amphitheater had only a smattering of people, maybe fifty, spread across ten long, semicircular rows.

Cameron held out a hot dog. "A late lunch or an early dinner. Call it what you will, but it's better than nothing." She eyed the food. "Hopefully."

"Thank you."

"Yeah, well, if Muhammad won't go to the food, the food must come to Muhammad." Biting into her hot dog, Cameron sat.

Ariana hadn't left this spot since arriving at the fund-raiser almost four hours ago, and it would continue five more hours before moving indoors. She'd come here with Nicholas yesterday afternoon as the performers did a quick run-through for today. The music in all forms — cantatas, symphony orchestras, jazz and marching bands, and duets to quartets — was mesmerizing. Maybe it wouldn't be so magnetic if Ariana's father, the person God had put over her as an authority, wasn't fine with it, but he was, and he'd convinced her to relax and enjoy it. If it was wrong to listen and enjoy it, God would have to take it up with Nicholas.

According to the handout the stage events would shift gears throughout the day. At the opening Nicholas's college students had sung a cantata as he conducted. As one of many teachers and musicians helping out today, he was now accompanying individual singers, using an electric keyboard that looked like an upright piano. In a few minutes a talent show would begin, followed by various high school orchestras and at least one college orchestra, and at the inside venue a professional band would perform last as the grand finale.

Ariana wiped her mouth on a napkin. "So where did you ditch Brandi and Gabe?"

Cameron swallowed hard before speaking. "They were playing games like a couple of kids. They had sticks with magnets and were fishing for something. If you hear embarrassingly loud laughter, that'll be our mom."

Any reference to Brandi being Ariana's mom still felt odd, as if it were a mistake, but the truth of it no longer shredded her. Cameron saying "our mom" also brought a new sensation with it. As an only child, Ariana not only felt less isolated, but it also helped her see Brandi through Cameron's eyes as a savior mom rather than an adulterer mom. Ariana wished she could erase all knowledge of the affair from her mind, but she was at least determined to stop viewing Brandi through tainted glass. It would just take time. And maybe Cameron's use of "our mom" helped, because Ariana had thought all Englisch teens were rude to their parents. Cameron freely gave them her opinion, often wrapped in over-the-line humor, but she wasn't bugged by her parents' existence or disrespectful to them. That was refreshing too. Ironically, Ariana seemed to be the child with the attitude problem as she struggled to accept who her parents were and who they'd once been.

When the song ended, everyone clapped. Nicholas grinned, motioning to the singer. A woman moved to the piano, and a new singer came onstage. Nicholas walked down the steps, looked for Ariana, and strode toward her.

"Hey." He smiled and sat beside her. "Enjoying your time?"

"Yeah." It was strange how different she felt this Saturday from last Saturday. As much as she had hated changing out of her Amish clothing and setting aside her prayer Kapp — and those things still bothered her — today she had enjoyed blending in with the people around her. No one was glancing at her and whispering, as if impressed by or questioning her faith. The feeling of invisibility she had in her Englisch clothes was very different from the feeling she had in her Amish clothing. Maybe Nicholas wasn't as wrong as she'd thought in some things he pushed her to do.

A smiling Brandi and Gabe walked up on the other side, Brandi carrying a drink in each hand and Gabe carrying bags of cotton candy. Clearly Ariana wasn't the only one doing better this Saturday than the previous two. It wasn't as if everything was rosy for her or for them. The difficulty of the situation and the grief came in waves, and sometimes it pulled all of them under, threatening to drown them. But then low tide came, and they gulped in air and rested.

Her parents spoke to each other and gave an awkward nod. But like her, they were trying.

Nicholas peered around Ariana to look at Brandi, as if wanting to make sure she would hear him. "There will be an impromptu, anyone-can-participate talent show in a few minutes."

"That should be interesting, and that's all."

It wasn't what Brandi had said as much as the way she'd said it that made Ariana realize Nicholas was doing more than informing them of what would come next.

The bucket list.

"Five minutes onstage and a few hours helping Quill wire a home tomorrow, and you're free to spend a day with Rudy as soon as it can be arranged with him."

"Like next Saturday?" Ariana couldn't believe she was asking him. Wiring a home with Quill was lined up, and on a Sunday no less, but that's when she could be at the job site without being too disruptive. By doing what was typically a man's job, she would earn points. But what was she thinking? She couldn't get on that stage.

"Yes, next Saturday. The whole day."

Ariana turned, looking at Brandi, Cameron, and Gabe.

"Go for it," Cameron whispered.

Brandi looked less sure. "Don't let anyone move you around like a chess piece. If you want to see Rudy that badly, I'll take you myself *for the whole day.*" Her eyes flashed angrily at Nicholas.

But Ariana couldn't allow that, because Brandi didn't have God's authority to dismiss Nicholas's will.

"And now," a woman onstage said, "we will begin the impromptu-talent-show portion of the day. If you're a singer or dancer and have music or musicians, let us know. If you need a pianist, Professor Jenkins will do his best to accompany you."

"I have to go." Nicholas stood. "If you decide to do it, just tell me the song. If I don't know it by heart, I can download the sheet music to my iPad." He put his hand on her shoulder. "This isn't about proving anything to anyone but yourself. No one here knows you, and you don't have to give your name. Who you are is no one's business . . . except yours." He walked off.

Cameron leaned against Ariana's shoulder. "All these years I thought he was just a hothead, and I was scared of him. I stand corrected. He's a weird hothead. Definitely more weird than hot."

"Thanks." Had she nailed the right sarcastic tone while aiming to tease?

"You're welcome." Cameron elbowed her. "You gonna do it? Huh? Huh? Huh?"

A young girl, maybe ten, went to the stage and picked up the microphone. If a little girl could do it . . .

"Cameron," — Brandi put her hand firmly on Cameron's knee, giving her the mom squeeze — "leave her alone."

"Hey, I'm just curious," Cameron said. "You and Dad have always encouraged me to ask any and all questions that come to mind." Cameron's playful energy bowled right over Brandi's correction.

Gabe looked around his wife and daughter to make eye contact with Ariana, silently asking if she needed him to wrestle with his high-energy, says-too-much daughter.

"She's fine," Ariana assured him. "Annoying, but fine."

Gabe and Brandi laughed. Gabe tossed a bag of cotton candy onto Cameron's lap. "Eat and be quiet."

"Oh, the good stuff." She ripped open the bag, plucked out a wad, and held out the bag to Ariana.

The girl onstage was really good, but she sounded nervous. Still, she was up there. Couldn't Ariana do that so she and Rudy could see each other?

Ariana took a big pinch. "You called him a hothead, and I know he's an opinionated stickler, but I thought musicians were supposed to be mellow."

Brandi was leaning in, listening to Ariana and Cameron.

"Yeah, that's the stereotype," Cameron said. "But your dad breaks the mold. Still, he seems different with you." Cameron looked at Brandi. "Doesn't he?"

"Yeah. He's different with her." Brandi smiled, but there was hurt in her eyes. Even though Brandi appeared to be glad that Nicholas felt strongly about her, she was probably hurt for Skylar's sake.

Cameron put another wad of cotton candy in her mouth. "He's, like, human and being only half-throttle difficult rather than full throttle."

"He's right that I don't know anyone here except you four." Ariana finally put the sticky stuff in her mouth. "Wow," she mumbled, licking her fingers, "that's even better than it smells."

"Told you. Stick with me, kid. I know everything."

"Cameron," Brandi said, "that is just so not true."

"I don't know *everything*?" Cameron mocked being offended. "But you could fill a thimble with all I know, right?"

Brandi laughed. "Definitely. Maybe even two."

"There you have it. I know more than enough, a whole thimbleful, maybe two."

Ariana looked at the sparse audience. Most people were milling about in the rest of the park, playing games and eating. "I could have Nicholas's blessing to see Rudy by this time next week, and almost no one is here to see it."

Cameron pulled her cell phone from her jeans, cotton candy sticking to her fingers, and directed it at the stage. "No one, except however many thousands of people watch this on YouTube."

Ariana looked at Brandi. "If I go onstage, confiscate her phone."

"Done." Brandi snatched it from Cameron, smiling as she tucked it away in her purse. "I had to get it while the getting was good. Just in case." Brandi patted her purse. "So, Ariana, if you went up there, what would you perform?"

"I'd sing, I guess." It was nuts even to consider doing that and crazier that it was Skylar's singing onstage that had brought to light the bizarre truth about their being swapped at birth. But it felt right to defy fear and Amish tradition and sing onstage. Who cared whether she could sing or not? She and Susie used to sing Englisch songs while cleaning other people's homes, so she

280

knew she could carry a tune.

While she wrestled with herself, different performers went onstage, did their thing, and received applause as they returned to their seats. It wasn't a spotlight event. It was a community enjoying themselves. Not really much different from playing volleyball while onlookers cheered for them, was it?

The emcee was onstage again. "Anyone else?" She looked around, waiting. "Last call. Anyone?"

Ariana couldn't believe she was on her feet with her hand up. Fear clutched her, and she turned to Brandi.

Brandi grinned with an I'm-in-your-corner motherly look. "You want me to go with you?"

Relief skittered through Ariana. "Would you?"

Brandi glanced toward the stage, probably seeing Nicholas, and she looked a bit unsure, but she handed her cup to Cameron. "Let's do this."

The beautiful fall day seemed to tilt, and as Ariana approached the stage, she feared she'd trip over her own feet. She stopped at the bottom of the steps. What was she doing?

Brandi came up beside her and placed her hand on Ariana's back. "You need a nudge or a place to run?"

Ariana wanted to run. What was she doing? "A nudge."

Brandi took her by the hand and moved ahead of her, leading her up the steps and toward the piano.

Nicholas smiled broadly. "What are you two singing?"

" 'Bridge over Troubled Water' by Simon and Garfunkel?" Ariana asked Brandi.

"Fine by me. Nicholas?"

"Good choice. Go." He nodded toward center stage.

Looking at the stage from this spot, Ariana couldn't budge. Her eyes filled with tears, and she could hardly breathe. Why was she volunteering to disobey the Old Ways? Rather than protecting simplicity and humility, she was offering to get on stage and showcase herself. This wasn't something Nicholas had mandated.

Brandi's hand was warm against her back. "We can still bow out. Ask yourself, do I want the reward bad enough?"

Ariana had no doubts about that part. "Ya."

"Then let's do it." Brandi nodded at Nicholas, and he began playing. "Energy and smiles," Brandi whispered. "If we can't get it right, we'll make it entertaining." She swaggered onto the stage.

Ariana followed, looking back at Nicholas as if he might change his mind about the reward and come rescue her. The lead-in music seemed to last longer than usual. Brandi moved to the microphone. When Ariana missed her cue to begin for the second time, Nicholas said, "Her first time onstage, folks."

The people clapped, and Nicholas played the lead-in again. Ariana missed her cue, and Brandi started singing. Ariana could see Brandi's lips moving, but she couldn't make out the lyrics or the tune. Tears spilled from Brandi's eyes, and when her voice wavered, Nicholas joined in with his beautiful tenor voice: "Like a bridge over troubled waters, I will lay me down."

Chills ran over Ariana's body as she saw the earnestness on his face. Was he having a change-of-heart moment as he sang? It seemed so.

He continued singing, and when his eyes met Brandi's, he smiled. She gained her composure and joined him. It soon became clear to Ariana that they were singing to her — promising to be a bridge for her over troubled waters.

Maybe they hadn't tried to be a bridge for her before now, but in this moment, as truth seemed to float on the notes, the words seemed to pierce their hearts, and she was certain they meant them.

When the song ended, he began another tune, one that he'd learned last week was a favorite of Ariana's: "Hello" by Adele.

She took a deep breath, and when he played the cue, she didn't miss it this time. "Hello, it's me. I was wondering if after all these years you'd like to meet . . ."

The words had never meant more, and she sang loud and clear, grateful she had four parents who loved her. Each set was as different as she was from Quill, but determined love was the unifying factor, not the stress and anger brought on by their differences.

In her mind's eye she sang to her Amish parents — singing her hellos from the other side — and her Englisch parents sang with her.

TWENTY

Abram's face tingled from the cool air. The sun was hiding behind clouds, and he should've worn a coat, but he'd forgotten to grab it before leaving the café. The place was now closed for the day, but his sisters were still there, cleaning and reorganizing the work stations. He'd hurried out the door to go to Cilla's without thinking about how cool it was outside.

The usually fleeting buggy ride to Cilla's house felt more like a pilgrimage this time. Was it because he was eager to see her? He'd insisted she take off today except for going with him to the store to pick up supplies. The café needed staples, lots of them. But the need for supplies wasn't why he'd asked Cilla to go with him. The more time he spent with her, the more he wanted to see her. He was almost glad Barbie had stood him up a few months back. Almost.

The scents of fall filled the air. The leaves

had changed from green to reds and yellows, but now, on the last day of October, most of their beauty was muted by brown. Abram pulled his buggy onto Cilla's driveway, parked by the shed, and walked to the front porch. Before he knocked on the door, she came out of the house.

Her smile was weaker than usual, and she moved slowly toward a rocker. "Good afternoon."

"Hi." Abram took her hand and helped her to the chair. "You all right?"

Her gentle smile didn't falter. "Oh, definitely fine."

"You don't look it."

She chuckled, and he heard a rasping noise. "I'll give you a break, Abram, and pretend you didn't say that."

He grabbed a nearby rocker and turned it to face her before he sat. "You're working at the café too much, aren't you? And now you've agreed to go shopping with me."

"Work has nothing to do with it. I arrive hours after you do and leave hours before. My lungs are giving me a bit of trouble today. That happens regardless of what I do."

"Ya, maybe so, but you're there from the time we open until we close, and work is tiring for those without breathing issues.

286

You don't have to do so much at the café."

"Are you already getting tired of me?"

He smiled. "Not hardly. I just don't want you doing too much."

"I think overdoing it is going from having a full-time roofing job to working at a café and not having a social life."

Abram gestured toward her. "*This* isn't a social life?"

A hint of shyness briefly crossed her face. "Only a person who has never had a social life would have to ask."

Abram laughed. "What about you? I don't see you running around much."

"My sister Barbie has enough of a social life for both of us."

He'd rather avoid that topic. He studied Cilla. "Are you up to grocery shopping?"

She put her hands on the armrests and pushed, shakily getting to her feet. "Yep."

Abram didn't know whether to try to help her or not. Sometimes pulling on a person hurt more than helped. "Are you sure?"

"Ya, I fear what Susie and Martha will have to bake with next week if you shop alone."

"Really?" Abram sighed. "I'm concerned about you, and you're cracking jokes."

She held out her forearm. "Not just any jokes. Potshots at you specifically."

He took her arm and was surprised by how much support she needed to get down the steps. "Susie gave me a list: bread flour, sugar, salt, coffee . . . Besides, what's so bad about my shopping?"

"You ever shopped before?"

"Well, no, but —"

"The list says coffee. What kind do we serve?"

"Uh." Was this a trick question? "Regular."

Cilla laughed. "No, the correct answer is local dark roast, and Skylar requested a light gourmet."

He opened the door for her and helped her get in. "Well, luckily, you will be able to keep me straight."

Cilla lifted one brow. "Good grief, Abram, no woman has that much energy."

He laughed and was still chuckling as he got into the rig on the other side.

Cilla sat up straight as if trying to expand her lungs. "I've been watching Skylar this week, and I think you need to find a way to be her friend."

"A friend? She's not interested in being anyone's friend. I get the feeling she's using great restraint to avoid acting like we're the enemy."

"That's probably a fair assessment. Seems as if she thinks she wants to be left alone to do her own thing, but she's wrong."

Abram thought for a moment. "Wrong in thinking that's what she wants or wrong to want it?"

"Yes."

No one made him smile as easily as Cilla did. He leaned over and nudged her with his elbow. "You're a little free with the advice, aren't you?"

She teasingly slapped at his arm. "Remember, this relationship started by your coming to me to ask my opinion."

"True."

"I'm just helping by noticing ahead of time where advice is needed."

"Like knowing I'd need you on this shopping trip."

"Exactly. My body may be frail, but I can still outshop any man."

"Good to know." He tugged on the reins, slowing as they came to a stop sign. "I'll make new efforts with Skylar."

A beautiful grin stretched across Cilla's face. "Good."

They rode in silence until they pulled onto the gravel lot of a small grocery store. Abram set the brake on the buggy and went over to Cilla's side and helped her down. She wobbled as she walked, and he left his hand on her arm. She smiled and gently pushed it away. "I'm fine." He nodded, but he didn't release her until they had a grocery cart for her to lean on.

The store had hardwood floors and rows of staples. A young Amish woman stood behind the counter. Abram nodded at her, and she returned his gesture with a smile.

"*This* is the wholesale store?" Cilla asked.

"It carries bulk and is within driving distance for a horse and carriage."

"This place is bound to be expensive. We probably need to do some research."

Cilla guided the cart, using it to steady herself. When feeling well, she seemed to move as freely as anyone her age. But bouts of weakness came on so suddenly it bothered him.

They discussed each item on his list and found the right ones, and he put them in the cart.

"Ah, the coffee." Abram loaded ten burlap bags.

Then he saw that Cilla looked paler now.

"We have enough for this trip." He looked toward the front of the store, thinking he shouldn't have let her come. "Let's check out."

She gestured at his list. "Let's finish."

"No, I think —"

"Please don't do this." She paused, taking

shallow breaths. "We came with a list, and when it's filled, we'll head home."

He nodded, but as they continued, her breathing worsened. He could hear her rasping even when she was several feet away. By the last aisle, she was leaning against the cart as if it was the only thing keeping her feet under her.

Abram thought it would be best not to ask again if she was ready to go or if she was okay, because she would give the same answer. How often did her breathing get like this? He didn't dare ask right now.

Instead Abram put his left hand on the cart, and Cilla leaned against him. As they walked slowly down the aisles, Abram examined the prices. "The café could get more items for less if we went to a real wholesale store instead of one that just sells in bulk." He picked up a twenty-pound bag of sugar. "But I'd need an Englisch driver, because there's no way to get there except high-traffic roads, including the highway."

Cilla covered her mouth with a handkerchief as she coughed. "But hiring a driver would cost more than you would save, wouldn't it?"

"I didn't think about that." Abram paused for a moment. "If I asked Jackson, I'm sure he would take me."

"Hm. That sounds an awful lot like friend-ship."

"I'm not following."

She smiled. "Sometimes friendships lead to social lives."

Abram chuckled. "You're worried about that, aren't you?" He checked the basket. "I think we have plenty for the next couple of days."

He would call Jackson and ask him to drive him to the wholesale store.

By the time they paid for the items, Cil-la's coughing spells were growing worse. Did she need to go to the hospital? He put the bagged items in the cart and got Cilla to the curb. "Wait here." He hurried to the rig and pulled in front of the store. After he helped her into the carriage, he threw the bags in the back.

When he got in, she was leaning against the headrest, trying to catch her breath.

"Where to — home or hospital?"

She frowned. "It sounds worse than it is. Just take me home so I can get a breathing treatment."

He hoped that was true, but clearly she downplayed her health issues. Before they were halfway back to her house, night fell, and the air turned much colder. Cilla's breathing was short and raspy, and he urged the horse to hurry.

Something was wrong. Really wrong. In all his years of knowing her, he'd never heard her breathe like this. When they finally arrived at her home, Abram briskly walked over to help Cilla get down. She almost fell out of the buggy, so he scooped her in his arms and carried her up the porch steps.

He jostled her a bit as he grabbed the doorknob and opened the door. *"Hallo?"* He saw no one and heard nothing. Cilla's eyes were closed. Had she passed out? "We need some help," he called out louder and immediately heard footsteps. Barbie entered first, and her mother trailed quickly behind.

Barbie hurried to Cilla and unbuttoned her coat. "How bad?"

Abram didn't know how to respond.

Cilla's mother went to the sink and doused a kitchen towel in water.

Barbie caressed her sister's face, rousing Cilla.

"Seven," Cilla whispered.

Barbie darted away.

Steam rose from the towel in her mother's hand as she laid it over Cilla's chest, soaking her dress. "Can you carry her to her room?"

"Ya. Where?"

Emma led him up the stairs. "She needs

to be fully on the bed but sitting upright."

"Okay." By the time Abram eased Cilla onto the bed, Barbie was already on it, a breathing mask in hand.

"Will she be all right?" he asked.

"She'll be fine." Barbie eased the mask over Cilla's nose and mouth. She then cupped her hand and hit her sister's chest again and again.

Emma moved tubes and cords out of the way, and Abram noted the electric cords went to a small adjoining balcony where there was apparently some sort of generator. "She won't be able to work for a few days."

Guilt almost knocked his feet out from under him. Had working done this? Had going out today made it worse? "I never thought . . ."

Barbie glanced at the machine and then went over to it and turned the knobs, making it beep. A mist entered Cilla's mask.

Cilla sucked in air. "Barbie —"

"Sh." Emma sat on the side of the bed, reaching for her daughter's face. "Save your oxygen." She brushed the back of her fingers across Cilla's cheek.

Abram hadn't realized any of this. He'd known she was sick, but she had a generator to operate medical equipment and set methods for getting relief?

Emma stood. "We need some privacy now, but she'll be herself next time you see her."

Abram clutched Cilla's hand. "I'm sorry." Those were the only words that came to his mind.

Cilla's eyes reflected sadness, but she gave a weak smile and squeezed his hand.

TWENTY-ONE

Once again Ariana stood in front of a full-length mirror, tugging at clothes that didn't feel right. She wasn't sure Brandi and Gabe's bedroom was any more comfortable than the dressing room at the mall. She had on blue jeans because Nicholas said her day wouldn't be a true experience in shadowing Quill on a construction job site if she wore a dress. His logic was sound, but it didn't ease her conscience. Yesterday she'd performed onstage, and today she had on jeans with the intention of working on a Sunday.

Her need to see Rudy was undeniable, but how many boundaries would she cross to win that victory? Singing at the fund-raiser had been intimidating, but once she was halfway finished with the song, it hadn't felt wrong. Daunting, but not wrong. And ultimately the experience had landed her parents and her in a really good place, a healing place. But this? What would Rudy want her to do?

Sitting in a chair beside the bed, Brandi leaned forward, nibbling the inside of her lip. "Those were mine when I was your age. My favorites. But you were three months old before I could fit into them again, and it was a tight squeeze at the time."

What a weird feeling to know that. Brandi had gained the weight while carrying Ariana, and yet Skylar was the baby in her care as Brandi returned to her former figure. It was a bit unsettling to think about, but Ariana couldn't let the emotion derail her goal. She tugged at the seams along her thighs.

Brandi leaned forward. "You have at least two extra inches around the waist and in the thighs. You're smaller than I was back then. I say they're not too tight. But even with the shirt not tucked in, you still don't like them, do you?"

"Women aren't supposed to wear pants. That's men's clothing. And I can't wear this. It's just . . . immodest and unacceptable." Ariana turned one way and then the other, studying the look before she lifted her eyes to Brandi's. The moment their eyes met, she realized what she'd said. "Sorry, these were your favorite jeans, and that was rude of me."

Brandi got up and stepped behind Ariana,

looking at her in the mirror. She stroked Ariana's long ponytail. "Listen, kiddo, if we're going to make this relationship work, you have to let what you're feeling about me form into words." Still behind her and looking into the mirror, Brandi put her hands on Ariana's shoulders and gently squeezed. "You were disappointed to learn about your father and me. But I'm not easily offended, so stop bottling up what you think and feel." She traced her fingers down a curly wisp of hair that dangled along the side of Ariana's face. "I am your mom, and as great as being together onstage was, it would mean even more to me if we could move past where we are right now. I think the only way for that to happen is for you to say what you think. If you need to call me names, do it, and let's get it out in the open."

Call her names? Ariana swallowed hard. What she thought and what she said were rarely the same when it came to Brandi and Nicholas. Did both of them know that about her? "I want to be okay with everything."

"Wanting to be okay with things is a good start. Unlike Nicholas, I grew up in church, and it took me years to learn how to be okay with what I had let happen. I did eventually forgive myself and find peace with my past.

So it's okay for you to take some time to adjust to the truth of that dirty little secret."

Brandi's lack of offense over Ariana's struggle not to judge her helped a lot. "Do you mind telling me some of what happened, like how you and Nicholas knew each other?"

Brandi moved to the bed and sat. "I was his star voice student, and he was my professor. I fell head over heels. It was all very cliché."

"You were in love?"

"I was." She patted the bed and waited until Ariana sat beside her. "I thought he was too, but probably not. I believed his marriage was a mess. Maybe it was. Maybe it wasn't. But later I understood that the state of his marriage didn't matter, and whatever shape it was in was no excuse. But all I knew at the time was what I wanted."

"And after he divorced, he didn't offer to marry you?" That kind of marriage would also be considered adultery for the Amish, but if his being married didn't stop them from being together, what had?

Brandi fidgeted with Ariana's hair. "Whatever love or attraction we had between us just disappeared. By the time his marriage fell apart, Skylar was a toddler, and we resented each other so much that we couldn't be in the same room without a war breaking out. And before you were born, I had determined to prove I didn't need him or my parents or the judgmental church I'd grown up in." Brandi paused, studying her. "I hope you can relate to some of those emotions — the overwhelming desire, resentment, and a need to stand on your own two feet."

"I've had some of those feelings." Ariana hesitated to say what came to mind. The Amish didn't talk about such things. But right then she knew the best way to stop judging Brandi was to bond with her, to be open and honest and real, because that was love, and love would banish judgment. "The strongest of my feelings is an overwhelming desire for Rudy." Heat rose from her core and moved to her face.

"Rudy must be quite the young man."

Ariana nodded. "He's perfect."

"The words of a woman in love." Brandi chuckled while grabbing a brush. She removed the elastic from Ariana's hair and began brushing it. "How did you two meet?"

"It's sort of a long story."

Brandi continued to brush her hair. "I've missed twenty years of your life. I would love to hear the long version."

Ariana explained about not dating until

she was seventeen. "I went to the homes of various cousins outside of Summer Grove. At first I was just looking for a distraction because I was sick and tired of thinking about what Quill and my best friend had done a few years earlier."

Brandi paused. "What had they done?"

"They ran off together." She rolled her eyes. "They did me a favor. I know that now, but they were my friends, and their betrayal was every bit as difficult and instrumental in changing my future as learning I wasn't a Brenneman."

Brandi began brushing her hair again. "That's saying a lot."

"It is. Anyway . . ." Ariana talked on and on about Rudy and her.

"Do you think I could meet him one day?" Brandi looked at her in the mirror again.

In that moment Ariana saw a mom looking at her — her mom. "He's very Amish."

"More than you?" Brandi wound the elastic into her hair again.

"We are equally yoked in that." Or they *were*. According to the mirror, she wasn't sticking to the Old Ways very well.

"I'm not going to hold his extreme Amishness against him, but you're concerned how he'll feel about me."

Ariana found Brandi's honesty very disconcerting. "A lot has gone on that he doesn't know about yet — about me — and I'm unsure how he'll feel when he finds out."

"Ah, I'm not so sure Mr. Perfect is all you're hoping for if he expects everything about you to be perfect."

"What's happened in my life over the last couple of months has nothing close to perfect in it. It's been a mess, and he's not complained once. So if some of the information is too much, it doesn't mean he's a bad person or the wrong guy for me. It just means it's too much for him."

Brandi smiled. "See." She touched her own lips. "You voiced your heart. In your own way you told me to back off, and yet we're both still here, neither one broken or vaporized by God. If you want Nicholas to hear you, you have to speak up for yourself."

But nowhere in the Bible did it say she could do that with her father. She had to honor her mother, but the Bible was much stricter about what could and couldn't be said to her father.

Ariana's head was beginning to ache. "If I can earn the right to see Rudy, will Nicholas let me wear my Amish clothes?"

"We'll talk him into it." Brandi put a finger through a belt loop and tugged. "But for today can you wear a pair of jeans?"

"I'm not sure God or I approve."

"You're a tad uptight, girl." Brandi held her index finger and thumb an inch apart. "I'm beginning to understand why Nicholas put 'have fun' on your to-do list." She rested a hand on her hip and raised an eyebrow. "What did you used to do for fun?"

"You mean besides going to singings?" Ariana stood. "Being poor is pretty cheerless, I guess. Fun to me was working hard enough that no one went hungry or naked or dirty."

"I'm proud that's who you are, and I'm sure your Amish family appreciated it, but could you try to relax and enjoy yourself a little now?"

"It's Sunday. I have on jeans, and I'm going to work."

Part of her reward for doing this today was that Nicholas and Brandi would attend church next Sunday — different churches. But it seemed to Ariana that she had a lot of spiritual lessons and life truths to learn outside of church. She'd judged her parents as sinners while aiming to get them to church. Why? Was it because she cared about them or because she could better tolerate their past and present if they went to church? Or was it because she felt obligated? Where was her love and acceptance? Church existed because of love and forgiveness, not because of man's accusations and disapproval.

"The Amish milk their cows on Sundays, right?" Brandi asked. "I don't see the issue, but the decision is yours."

"Decisions were a lot easier back home."

"I can imagine." Brandi held up one finger. "Hang on. I have an idea."

God, am I selling out?

Brandi returned and held out a black sweater. "Try this cardigan."

Ariana put it on, and the bottom came below her backside. "That helps." But she wasn't sure it was enough.

Gabe came to the bedroom. "How's it going, ladies?"

Brandi turned, a slight smile on her lips. "Good, I think."

Ariana nodded. Gabe and Cameron had gone for a run. Of late it seemed the whole world made time to run.

Cameron glanced in as she passed, and then she stopped and backed up. She stared at Ariana. "*That* I like. Uh . . ." — Cameron rubbed the side of her neck — "could I go with you?"

That was definitely the voice of a little sister wanting to tag along. "Not wearing that, you can't."

Cameron tugged at the hem of her shorts. "Prude." She sighed. "I'll be right back." She pointed at Ariana. "Don't leave without me."

Gabe's eyes met Brandi's, and he raised both brows, as if he couldn't believe what was going on. He looked at Ariana. "Thanks."

"She may regret asking, but I'm glad she's coming with me. Quill is subdued and quiet, very restrained, and she's stuck on wide open. It should be an interesting day."

"That's one word for it." Gabe chuckled. "But I think you have the big-sister bug, and Cameron can feel it." He gestured toward Brandi. "From what she's told me, she had the mom bug from the moment she heard your heartbeat when you were just a ten-week-old fetus."

Ariana studied Brandi. That didn't compute somehow.

Brandi tossed the brush onto the bed. "He's right. It took me a month to adjust to the news that I was expecting you, but once I heard your heartbeat, I fell so in love, and despite the stresses of single parenting, I enjoyed it."

Enjoyed it? Hadn't she wallowed in guilt and shame? Ariana would have. Not only did this new information go against the image Ariana had of how she'd entered this world as an unwanted mistake, but it also made her realize that judging was easy. It came naturally. But not allowing the expectations of society or the church to ruin one's joy had to be far harder. It had to take a strength Ariana was completely unfamiliar with.

A cell phone pinged, and Brandi went to the nightstand and picked up her phone. While she read the text, her phone rang. Barked actually. Her ringtone. "It's Nicholas." She glanced at Gabe. "A text and a call. I need to take this." She swiped her finger across the screen and put it to her ear. "Hey, what's going on?" Brandi listened, nodding. "Okay. Yeah, I'll tell her. If it's a problem, I'll call you." She disconnected the call. "Uh, sweetie." She reached for Ariana's hand. "Our performance yesterday was posted on YouTube. No one has your name attached to it, but it's live and gaining hits."

"What's a hit?"

"Views." Brandi touched the link in the text. "There we are."

Ariana peered at it, and her face flushed hot. What would Mamm, Daed, and her siblings think if they knew about this?

"It's my fault," Brandi said. "I should've warned you that there are cameras everywhere these days. This is from someone's cell phone, but the amphitheater has security cameras that recorded it too. Are you okay with this?"

What could she do about it? She'd been naive to think that, other than Cameron, no one would record it. And security cameras had never dawned on her. Did anyone even look at them?

TWENTY-TWO

The nagging sound of a dog barking caused Quill to open his eyes. The light on his headlamp revealed pink insulation and the bare wood of the framing mere inches from his face. His eyelids were heavy, and his eyes felt as if they were coated with grit. A second night with almost no sleep was taking its toll. While rewiring this home, he had crawled into this black space between the rafters of the roof and a particle-board wall. And apparently he'd dozed off.

He drew a heavy breath, taking in the smells of a newly built home. Had he slept a few seconds or a few minutes? From somewhere more common to humans than this crawlspace, Lexi barked and then whined.

"Yeah, I'm alive, girl." He moaned while trying to work the kinks out of his body. "I'm just fine. How are you?" He imagined her tail was wagging, but he couldn't see her. It wasn't typical for him to get into a tight space and lie still. So if dogs breathed sighs of relief, she was probably sighing now.

Quill still had the thick gray cable in his hand, and he tugged on it as he finished working his way toward the hole in the side of the house.

"Quill?" Regina called.

"In the attic."

Her footsteps on the stairs came quickly.

"You need food. We brought food. Come eat," she hollered down the dark, kite-shaped tunnel.

"Okay." He matched her volume so she could hear him.

His sisters-in-law, nieces, and nephews were returning to Kentucky after a quick picnic in a nearby unfinished home. He'd agreed to this break with the family when he'd thought he would be further along by now. With the exception of a couple of naps, including the one that had been unplanned, he'd worked round the clock since Friday evening. Each of his brothers had taken a six-hour shift to help him.

An electrical inspector would arrive on the job site first thing tomorrow, and Quill's goal was to have every house rewired and ready for inspection. *If* that could happen, McLaren's anger against Schlabach Home

Builders would ease off. Maybe the man would reconsider his plan never to hire Schlabach Home Builders again.

When approximately fifty feet of cable was shoved through the opening to the outside of the home, Quill began to back out of his claustrophobic space. "Are you guys packed and ready to go after lunch?" He angled the beam of the headlamp onto his watch. Eleven thirty. He had about an hour and a half until Ariana was scheduled to arrive . . . if she came.

"Yeah. It was a nice fall break."

He inched his way to the open space of the attic. "Good. I'm glad." He stood upright, dusting off his clothes before patting a wriggling Lexi.

Regina held out a mug of coffee. "We looked for the plans. Your room at the trailer has never been cleaner, but we didn't find any plans, let alone the right set."

"Okay, thanks." He hated that news. He'd gone over everything in his mind again and again, and he finally recalled a conversation he'd had with Sanders, the project manager. Quill had talked to him during that bleak, confusing time when he was trying to help Ariana, and Sanders had said there was a new set of plans but that none of the architects' and engineers' updates would affect the electrical system Quill was putting in. Quill had jotted that on the plans, and he'd had Sanders initial it before he ordered the supplies and installed the systems. But without that set of plans, it was his word against Sanders'.

"I'm worried about you," Regina said. "You're logging too many hours and carrying too much guilt because of the wiring mishap."

"Ah, I'm fine. I haven't set aside my goal to have all the houses rewired by morning."

"You're exhausted, and that huge task would be easier if you hadn't agreed to let a complete novice shadow you today of all days."

"Whether every house is rewired by morning or not, I have done enough to keep the inspectors busy, and the contracted houses will be able to close on time. If that's not good enough to get us out of the doghouse with McLaren, sooner or later Schlabach Home Builders will get another chance to prove ourselves, and he will make the offer again. We may have to work for someone else for a while, but when McLaren once again sees our value, we'll be in a position to negotiate properly, and we'll make up for not getting the promotion this time around."

Until McLaren learned that Quill had

installed the wrong electrical panels in the new phase of homes, he'd been planning to promote Schlabach Home Builders from subcontractors to contractors on the next job. That was huge, and it would have come with a good raise and job stability. It appeared as if Quill's mistake of wiring the houses wrong had caused them to fall from McLaren's good graces, but Quill thought something else was also going on.

She drew a deep breath. "You're good at making things lighter than they are. You need to find a girl who appreciates that about you."

Quill motioned to the stairs and waited for Regina to go first. "Think so?"

"Yep. A girl who would welcome your beautiful idiosyncrasies does exist, you know."

He laughed. " 'Beautiful idiosyncrasies'? Been reading poetry lately?"

"You're a quirky guy. Don't try to say otherwise. And there are girls who'd be thrilled with your unconventional ways."

"Maybe."

Once on the main floor, she turned. "Maybe?"

He went to the side door and opened it, Lexi right behind him. "You do know some people are content being single, right?"

"Yeah, sure." She went down the two steps to the garage. "I just don't think you're one of those people. Do you?"

"I've had one date in twenty-five years, so apparently I am."

Lexi stayed at his side as they went to the sidewalk and turned toward the least-finished home in the subdivision. That's why the family had decided to meet there for a quick lunch. The children could do no harm to new floors and carpets if none had been installed. It was also missing its doors and windows. Quill had given Ariana the address of the house next to it, thinking he'd be ready to rewire it by the time she arrived. Even though he was behind schedule, he needed to take time to see his sisters-in-law, nieces, and nephews before they returned to Kentucky.

Regina pulled her sweater tighter. "Before your life went crazy with Ariana's stuff in August, you'd finally met one girl at church that you liked well enough to ask out. What happened to that budding relationship?"

"It was over before it started."

"So what happened?"

"She was cute. I was lonely. I thought we might be an okay fit. Date one proved I was wrong. End of story."

Regina narrowed her eyes. "What'd she

do or say that was so wrong?"

He shrugged. His reasoning would sound shallow. But even in one date, he'd seen that she didn't have the capacity to understand him or the patience to try. No harm, no foul. While they had talked over dinner, she'd asked about the necklace he wore — the one Ariana made for him right after his dad died — but his date had been condescending, as if he should be embarrassed to wear it. He had tucked it inside his shirt, not because he was embarrassed by it, but because it represented things personal and close to his heart. However, it'd worked its way free. It was made of three leather cords that, according to Ariana, represented God, her, and him. She had forged the medallion by hand, but it showed its age and probably looked like a fourteen-year-old had made it, which she had. Still, if his date was so picky about outward appearances, he was done.

He and Regina went up the sidewalk and into the house. A couple of his nieces and nephews were running and playing. Gavin, the youngest of the group, was awkwardly stomping about, and the others were sitting on the floor with paper plates beside them filled with a simple lunch. He had eight nieces and nephews in all — ages fifteen months to nine years — so gatherings were a chaotic oasis.

Six-year-old Kylie and seven-year-old Jenna ran to him, and he scooped up one in each arm and spun them around while they giggled. Quill set them back down, and as they hurried off, he glanced at his watch. If Ariana was coming, she'd arrive in about an hour. Makeshift tables had been set up using doors and sawhorses, but the food was more lavish than he'd expected. He opened a thermos. "You guys know I only have a few minutes for lunch, right?"

His sister-in-law Piper put two egg-salad sandwiches on a plate, some chips, and a couple of ladles of fresh fruit. "What we know is you need to eat, chill, and breathe." She held it out to him. "And we were hoping to hang around and visit with Ariana."

He didn't like that plan, but he took his plate and coffee and sat on the particle-board floor near the others. He leaned against the unfinished Sheetrock. How could he word this?

"Look, it's fine with me if you're here when Ariana arrives, but you need to know that my relationship with her is on thin ice. She doesn't like or agree with my choices," — he gestured at the group — "our choices. So be very careful with your questions and statements, okay?"

315

The lines around Regina's eyes deepened. "Is your relationship *that* fragile that all of us need to walk lightly?"

"Maybe. I'm not sure, and I'd rather not test it."

Piper gave a plate of food to one of her children. "We just want a chance to get to know the girl you've loved all these years."

Quill's skin flushed hot. "Hey, speaking of thin ice . . ." The topic of how he felt about Ariana was supposed to be off-limits.

Piper turned to face him. "Ariana's on the outside now and has Englisch parents. Don't you want to grab this opportunity and see if the two of you —"

"If we what, Piper?" Quill tried to steady his raw nerves. "Can form a relationship like Mamm and Daed had, where one is fully Amish and one has the heart for rebellion?" He needed to reel himself in, but exhaustion had taken over. "Ariana is no more capable of happily leaving the Amish than Mamm is. And Ariana and I are a universe apart in our views of God, our political beliefs, our hopes for the future. She wouldn't do anything to prevent herself from having all the children God could bless her with, and she seriously hopes to have at least twelve. But you're right. I love her . . . enough to do all I can to get her home again so she can marry the right man for her, a man she's in love with."

"Twelve children." Regina sighed like a schoolgirl in love. "Won't your Mamm enjoy every moment of that?"

"Yeah, she will," Dan agreed. "So, Piper, would you really want Ariana to stay on the outside with us? Because if she did, Mamm would be alone for the rest of her life."

It was almost unbearable for all the adults in this room to be cut off from their families, but they had each other, and that helped. Three of his four sisters-in-law had been raised Amish, and they had grown siblings who remained Amish, so their parents still had a bevy of children and grandchildren near them. It was easier when at least one child stayed, and Quill would've been that child if Frieda's situation had been handled differently by the Amish community.

"Quill, I want you to find someone," Piper said.

"I will, I think." He just needed to find peace with his past, and much of that centered on Ariana. They had achieved forgiveness between them. Now he hoped for healing, and it would do him a world of good if he could help her accomplish the most important thing to her — getting home and marrying Rudy. Then he would take a relaxing breath and begin life fresh. Something he'd been unable to do since leaving the Amish and shattering Ariana's heart in the process.

TWENTY-THREE

Ariana pulled up to the curb, looking at numerous unfinished homes. This section had dirt for yards, and the houses had no windows or doors. But the roofs, sheathing, and subflooring were in place. What little she knew about home construction she'd recently learned from Quill as they prepared for today.

"Are we there yet?" Cameron asked for the umpteenth time, teasing.

This spot fit the directions Quill had texted to her. The GPS got them to the subdivision, but these homes didn't have addresses, so the GPS was no help. She hoped she'd followed the directions correctly.

"Close enough. Come on." She got out of her car and dialed Quill's cell. She immediately heard a phone ring. "This way." She motioned for Cameron, and they headed for a doorless, windowless home.

When they were halfway up the sidewalk, Quill came out the front door. "You're early."

"That's because she has a lead foot, driving like a bat out of —"

"Cameron . . ." Ariana pointed at her.

Cameron waggled her eyebrows, smiling.

"Quill, this is my sister, Cameron."

He reached out his hand. "Nice to meet you."

"Same here, and I was totally kidding about her driving fast."

Ariana heard chatter coming from the house. "Is your family here?"

"Yeah."

Without waiting for an invitation, she headed toward the house, drawn to the little ones inside like a Mamm to her cooing infant. The sight of them reminded her of how much she missed her nieces and nephews back home.

Cameron stayed beside her, and she leaned in toward Ariana. "I never say this about someone as old as he is, but wow," she whispered. "He's like handsome times a hundred. Just wow."

Ariana glanced behind her to see Quill, but she wasn't sure why. Was it to confirm what Cameron had said or to see if he'd overhead her? "What difference does it make how he looks?"

"Oh, it matters. You know it does." Cameron grabbed her arm and whispered, "He's definitely in there with the best-looking *GQ* men, right?"

Ariana stopped just outside the doorway. "Children are, by far, more adorable than any adult." She watched a little boy on the floor as he devoured a plate of fruit. She allowed the boy's preciousness to wash over her. Two girls were holding hands, dancing round and round as they sang. She and Susie used to do that for what seemed like hours.

She turned her head, speaking to Quill, who was right behind them. "I miss the little ones so painfully much. Katie Ann won't even remember me, but time will heal that . . . if Salome doesn't leave."

Quill simply nodded. She'd wanted him to assure her that Salome would stay. But he couldn't. No one could.

She turned back and spotted the toddler again. She looked up and singled out Regina. "Is he yours?" It was a reasonable question since the little boy had been on Regina's hip when Ariana first saw her a week ago.

Regina nodded and came toward her. "Our youngest, Gavin."

Ariana moved into the room and crouched, careful not to get too close and scare him. "He's entirely too cute."

Gavin grabbed a piece of strawberry out of his mouth and offered it to her. Ariana was tempted to laugh, but she kept herself in check so she didn't startle him. "Is that for me?" She held out her hand.

Gavin gave it to her.

"Thank you."

Gavin pushed his hand toward her again, palm up, wanting it back.

Ariana chuckled. She'd figured he would want it back, and she gave it to him. "I'm guessing you're somewhere between fifteen and eighteen months old."

"Fifteen. He and Quill share a birthday."

Ariana's heart felt lighter than it had since leaving Summer Grove. "So you were born on your uncle's twenty-fourth birthday. Fun stuff." She rose. "He is so cute, Regina."

Regina smiled broadly, looking as if she was just shy of grabbing Ariana around the neck and hugging her.

Ariana motioned to Cameron. "This is my sister, Cameron."

The adults spoke and nodded, as did Cameron.

"Come." Regina put her arm around Ariana's shoulders. "Let me introduce you to everyone."

All the children except Gavin circled in closer to Regina, wanting to be introduced. Regina appeared to begin with the youngest and worked her way to the eldest. Ariana thought of something fun to say to each one, and the children responded well. She glanced at Quill, and he seemed to be enjoying this as much as she was.

"This" — Regina put her hands on a boy's shoulders — "is Logan. He's nine and the oldest of Berta's grandchildren."

Logan glanced from Ariana to Quill. "I never knew Uncle Quill could string that many words together until I saw him talking to you."

"Really?" Ariana raised a brow at Quill. "I knew that about him since I was your age. See, the trick is getting him started, which is easy if you make him angry."

Quill rolled his eyes, but he was amused. She could see it in his eyes. It felt good to be doing well enough that she could interact in this way.

"You're an adult, Ari," Quill said, "and there's a roomful of children. Try to be a good influence."

"He's right." She nodded. "It would be completely wrong to try to anger your uncle, mostly because who wants to hear him when he's angry?"

Logan laughed. "You should keep this one, Uncle Quill."

"Life advice from a nine-year-old," Regina said. "Ariana, this is Piper . . ."

Quill's brothers and sisters-in-law began stepping forward, and Ariana met each one. She greeted Dan even warmer than the others, hoping to convey that the baggage between them had been hauled off.

The children started to play games as Ariana continued to meet the adults.

Finally the last brother stepped forward. "Elam."

She shook his hand.

"So how are you adjusting?" Elam asked.

"To the news of being Englisch and my new temporary life?" Ariana asked. "Similar to a toddler during a transition — lots of tantrums and tears." She smiled at Cameron. "But it has some unexpected perks." She turned to watch the children play. Would life ever have that kind of joy again?

Piper poured water from a plastic jug into a cup. "You're in a room of people who, in one way or another, had a high-magnitude earthquake hit their lives, Ariana." Piper gave the cup to her. "Quill had it the worst, but none of us did well at the start. Quill has said precious little about you, but from what I can see, I think you're doing great."

"That's nice of you." Ariana's eyes searched his, wanting to know. *The worst? Why the worst?*

Regina offered Ariana and Cameron a sandwich, and they each took one. The brothers asked general questions about her car and driving and what grade Cameron was in. It seemed they wanted to keep the conversation light.

While Piper asked Cameron about her tennis shoes, Ariana overheard Dan talking to Quill. Dan said that Quill's sisters-in-law had turned his room in the trailer upside down and that Frieda had searched his home. Apparently a set of plans was missing, causing trouble on the job. Dan seemed to be assuring Quill it was okay that he hadn't been able to fix the issue.

Quill nodded and shrugged as if it wasn't important, but Ariana felt sure it was. She was bad at reading herself, so was she reading him right? She doubted it. If she didn't know herself, how could she know him?

When Quill finished talking to Dan, he made his way toward her. "You about ready to start work?"

She could be, but first she wanted to talk more about that night at the bar. If she thought it would do any good, she would ask about the missing plans. But his response would most likely be a polite refusal to answer. Still, it was possible the topic would come up as they worked and he'd open up a bit. That was about the most she could hope for.

She put her unfinished sandwich back on the paper plate and carried it to an opening where a window would be installed. Quill followed her.

Cameron remained near the table, talking with Quill's family. She seemed to be enjoying herself as she animatedly talked while others laughed and injected a few words here and there. Ariana hoped she wasn't regaling them with events of her life from the last two weeks.

Ariana fidgeted with the edge of the plate. "That night at the bar, what made you suspect my drink had alcohol? I was the one consuming it, and I didn't know."

"That's out of the blue."

"Was I slurring my words without realizing it?"

"No." He propped his palm on a stud. "My gut said something was off."

"It bothers me that I don't know myself better. I should've realized what was happening before you did. I want to change that, to know myself better, but I have no idea how."

"When was the first time you thought something was amiss with Frieda and me?"

"I didn't."

"You did. You had to. There had to be a moment, however quick, of thinking something was a little off."

"I trusted you and her. I never —"

"And Brice wanted you to give him the benefit of the doubt, and you gave it to him. Nicholas wanted you to accept that he has full parental rights over you, and you gave that to him. I wanted you to stay oblivious to what I was planning with Frieda, and you gave that to me. If you're going to know and trust yourself, you can't willingly accept what's being fed to you. Don't lose yourself under the mounds of what others want of you."

"So in your eyes I'm wrong all the time."

"Not even close to true. You have the best heart of anyone I know. You're smart and kind and disciplined in your responses to others and in your efforts to obey and honor God. Few come close to those attributes, especially not me. But you're too giving when it comes to what others want of you, and because of that, you give up the ability to truly know yourself because you're so determined to make others happy. How can you do what's best for you when you're running in circles for others?"

"What about submission to authority, obedience to parents, sacrificing for others, and dying to self?"

"All good things in their place, but you need to decide what that place is. What about when Jesus and His disciples didn't submit to authority? What about when Jesus said, 'Let the dead bury their dead,' talking about a man's father? What about living unto God and making sure what you're dying to is what God wants, not man?"

"You know that's not what we've been taught."

"But it's not opposed to it. It's simply a wider, more encompassing view of God and the Word. Now think. When was the first time you knew something was going on with Frieda and me?"

She wrestled with the offense pumping through her. No one prodded her or got under her skin like Quill. Memories of him freeing a caged bobcat that had been illegally captured came to mind. He had been fearless in finding a way to rescue it and return it to the wild. Quill seemed to see her in a similar way, as being held captive in this area of her life, and he couldn't help but say what needed to be said to free her.

She studied the patch of woods outside the window, and after replaying dozens of memories of him and Frieda, one surfaced. "You and she were in the old shed when I came to your home one day and, by accident, realized where you were. I decided to sneak up on you and jump out, but when I did, you both seemed really worried about something."

"Bingo. We tried to act as if our shock and fear were from you startling us, but we were trying to have a private conversation about leaving the Amish without Mamm or you overhearing us."

Other memories started coming to her. "There were a few times that felt weird and off."

"There were."

"I just assumed I was reading things wrong."

"Never discount anything your senses are telling you, not at first. Let the information sink in, and trust your ability to reason out the truth. If you're wrong, that will become evident soon enough. Usually when one part of us is telling another part of us what's going on, it's a gift from God. Use it."

"Brandi said today that if I could find my voice and use it with Nicholas, he'd likely hear me. But my voice is supposed to reflect what God wants, not what I want."

Quill slowly shook his finger at her. "You know what you need?" His eyes reflected hope. "You need a new view of the heavens."

"Of the heavens?"

"Ari, our God is so much bigger than we can grasp. As children we saw Him as if we were inside a snow globe and He was just outside it, on His throne, out of sight, looking down at us. For those of us raised to believe in a jealous, angry God, we see Him with a frown, scowling. And as all Amish know, being frowned on is one tiny step from being shunned."

She imagined God watching her and others with a continual look of displeasure, but perhaps worse than that . . . "It does seem as if He's just outside my snow globe world."

"A great place to start changing your view of God is where you can see the great expanse of who He is through the concrete images of His creations — a planetarium." He glanced at his watch. "I have a favorite one that is open today and giving a program designed for families. It's open until five, and it's less than forty minutes from here. Are you game?"

"You said you had a lot of work to do today."

"I still have a few tricks up my sleeve for finishing the work when we get back. Besides, if going there helps you one tiny fraction as much as it helped me, that's far more important."

He would do that for her? She should give him an award for being the most confusing person in her life. "This much I know about myself: you regularly offend me and honor me within the same few minutes."

"Good thing for me some of your strengths are humility, resilience, and a desire to make peace. Will you go? We can take Cameron too."

"Resilience?" she scoffed, positive that a resilient person wouldn't have been an emotional train wreck the last few weeks.

But he seemed so sure it would help her, and God knew she needed her thinking realigned before she drove herself up the wall and before she was crushed under the weight of feeling isolated and the weight of judging people — both the strangers she needed to reach out to in love and those who cared about her.

"I came here to be on the job site, working in whatever way I can so I could earn a day with Rudy."

"We can still get your time in. You only have to do a few hours, and we set up some lighting days ago, so we can accomplish whatever is needed after it's dark. We can't go to the planetarium after hours."

If she was correctly using the cues Quill had been talking about — trusting her senses, noticing body language and tone — he thought she *needed* to see the planetarium. "Okay, but what got my mind on this whole 'understanding myself and others' topic is that I overheard a little of what Dan said to you, and your reaction to him didn't seem to match how you really felt."

He ran his hand through his dark-blond, Englisch-cut hair. He nodded as if agreeing with himself that he could tell her. "You nailed it."

"Since you know absolutely everything about my life, you could tell me about it."

His expression indicated she had a point. "Okay." He glanced at his watch. "But let's talk in the car."

"In front of Cameron?"

"I'll deal with it. We need to go."

They said quick good-byes, and the three of them got in Quill's car. His was an older, more worn model than hers, and she assumed it had come with a lot of sacrifice and a large payment. She'd paid nothing for hers, and it dawned on her that, despite the emotional toll of the last few weeks, shifting lifestyles from being poor to being upper middle class had been unexpectedly easy.

The three chitchatted about minor things until Ariana asked Quill what he and Dan had been talking about.

Quill turned on his blinker and merged onto a highway. "I installed the wrong electrical panels and wiring in a lot of houses. A lot. And it's costing Schlabach Home Builders money out of pocket, long hours to make things right, and a promotion."

"Whether building barrels in your Daed's cooperage or helping someone leave the Amish, you plan well, triple-check everything, and carry out the goal with caution. *That* much I know about you without any reservation. So what was going on that you weren't being you?"

He shrugged. "Everyone makes mistakes, regardless of their natural tendencies."

"Children laugh. Birds fly. You focus."

He tapped the steering wheel with his thumbs, looking as if he was deciding what to divulge. His hesitancy to speak up and the timing of his rewiring the homes began to add up.

"So while you were in the thick of helping me get the café and discovering the truth about Skylar and me, you made a mistake."

"It's not your fault, if that's what you're driving at." He exited the highway and turned left at the end of the ramp. "Yeah, that's the timing, but the situation is more complicated than just a mistake. Updated plans are always put in flat files and permit boxes, and I think the project manager didn't get them in those places when he should have. He initialed — signed off on — my set of older plans, and now he's denying he did. Maybe he's forgotten. Whatever is going on, since I've misplaced my set, I have no proof."

"Isn't there always proof of some kind, a trail of e-mails or texts?"

"Normally there would be, but I was working odd hours and not asking questions via text or e-mail. I had one conversation with Sanders, the project manager, right before heading out to Summer Grove."

"The busyness and stress of that time for you is just more proof to me that we were on that Thunderhawk roller coaster together." Ariana sighed.

"It was worth it, Ari." Quill shifted.

"I appreciate that's how you feel, but what's hard for me to get my head around is that your cool, calm demeanor has convinced me more than once that my turmoil didn't rattle you at all."

"Anyway" — he held one palm up as if losing his patience — "changing the subject to something more useful than feelings —"

"You don't mind us talking about feelings. But I'm starting to realize you don't like it when we talk about *your* feelings."

"If you don't stop" — Quill pointed a finger at her — "I'm going to turn this buggy around and take you back home."

Ariana burst into laughter. His Mamm had said that to them once when Quill, her brother, and Ariana were cutting up and out of control while she was taking them to town. It had caused the two boys to become rowdier, and Ariana had laughed harder, unintentionally egging them on.

"What buggy?" Ariana ran her hands across the dash.

Quill grinned, looking as if he was truly glad to be away from the job site.

"You know," Cameron piped up, "this is more entertaining than TMZ."

Quill gave a quizzical look to Ariana.

"It's a show about celebrity gossip." She pinned a loose strand of hair behind her ear. "So where does the wiring mistake leave things?"

He turned into a parking lot. "The extra work hassle is an inconvenient setback. But Schlabach Home Builders will deal with it."

He found an empty space and parked the car. "You ready?"

"I am."

Cameron opened her door. "I haven't been to one of these things since a fourth-grade field trip."

The yellow-brick building was square, but a large dome stuck up in the center of it. They entered a lobby with huge, beautiful images hanging like pictures on the walls. Ariana was drawn to the one closest to her and read the caption: "The Galaxy Earth Is In — The Milky Way."

The spiral beauty of stars and planets spread out toward the darkness like rays of light from the sun. "It's gorgeous," she whispered, but when she looked up, neither Quill nor Cameron was with her.

Quill was at a counter, purchasing tickets. Cameron was going into a bathroom.

Her heart fluttering like hummingbird wings, Ariana went to the next image. The caption read "Hubble's Deepest View of the Universe Unveils Never-Before-Seen Galaxies." The caption of the next image was "Mixed Galaxies." Then she looked at "White Dwarf Stars in the Milky Way." The caption didn't do justice to the beauty she saw. A plaque on the wall explained that cameras on the Hubble Space Telescope took all the images. One picture showed numerous galaxies inside the universe, and the Milky Way was simply one of them.

Quill came up beside her. "Blows the mind, doesn't it?"

"Ya." She tapped her chest. "And maybe the heart too. They estimate there are a hundred to two hundred billion galaxies in the universe and hundreds of billions of stars."

Cameron joined them. "Can we go in now?"

"We should. The show begins in just a few minutes." Quill pointed down the hallway.

They entered a quiet, dimly lit round room. When Ariana sat, the seat leaned back, and she found herself staring into a dome, a view of the night sky across it. Chills ran over her skin, and excitement pumped in her heart. What was she about to view?

Quill and Cameron sat on either side of her. Ariana couldn't close her eyes for fear she'd miss something, and the program hadn't even begun. With her eyes open and her lips closed, she prayed, asking God to show her more of His true self. A thought came to her, and she leaned in closer to Quill. "Don't ask me why this came to mind, but are there any security cameras near the flat files or the permit box?"

Quill's eyes lit up. "That's brilliant!" He got out his phone. "Why didn't I think of it? I'll text Dan to look into it. He knows way more department heads to contact than I do, and someone in the know will volunteer to help because Dan's a likable guy."

She giggled. "You're not?"

He hit Send. "Warm and friendly? No." He turned off his phone and slid it into his pocket.

Quill wasn't much of a people person, not like Rudy and apparently not like Dan, but inside his quiet, restrained ways, he held tightly to his ethics in dealing with everyone God put in his path.

As one of those people, she was grateful. Thoughts of Frieda returned to her, and Ariana realized her text had been too sterile, simply saying "hello" and "I'd like to communicate with you." Maybe the stiffness of the message was the reason she hadn't heard back. What if she told Frieda that she loved her and that even though she didn't know why Frieda had left, she was grateful she was brave enough to do what she needed to? Maybe she should be peppy in her texts and send some pictures. Maybe tell her some of what was going on with her.

Ariana pulled out her cell phone and held

it toward Quill. "Do you trust me?"

His blue eyes moved from the phone to her. "I do."

"Then you should give me Frieda's phone number."

He drew a breath and eased the phone from her, apparently willing to cross his confidentiality boundary for her. He pressed the touchscreen numerous times.

"And Dan's number in case I can't reach you."

He nodded and entered the information.

"And your checking and savings account numbers and their PINs."

He chuckled and returned the phone to her. "Funny."

"I thought so." She started to text Frieda right then, but the music began.

She tucked her phone back into her purse. The dim lights became even softer as planets appeared on the dome. Her heart rate went crazy. How had she been so narrow in her view of God that she'd never imagined Him as the amazing creator of such a beautiful, vast universe?

TWENTY-FOUR

A cold rain fell from dreary skies as Abram drove the final nails into the tin roof of the small, well-ventilated woodshed that would house the new generator. The generator Skylar assured them they needed. It had to have a roof over it, but it couldn't be installed in the café building due to exhaust fumes and safety hazards. He'd begun the project days ago when the weather was dry and had worked mostly after the café closed.

A horse and carriage turned from the side road onto the path between the back of the café and the small pasture where the workers' horses were kept. His pulse quickened in anticipation of seeing Cilla, and he climbed down. After the incident last Saturday, she had been out sick for three days. Despite the buzz he felt over her return, his movements dragged. Fatigue had been his only saving grace. It dulled his emotions and numbed him to a degree. He'd felt this way since he'd learned that Ariana wasn't his twin. Skylar's presence had made it worse, and something was really up with her this week. But most of all, he'd been worried about Cilla since he'd witnessed how frail she was.

When the rig came to a halt, Abram realized Cilla wasn't driving it. He went to the passenger's side and opened the door. "Where's Cilla?"

Barbie passed him a closed umbrella and stepped out. "Hey, Abram. She couldn't come today."

"Is she all right?" He opened the umbrella and held it over her.

"I think so." Barbie unbuckled a latch. "She isn't doing as well as she'd hoped, mostly because she's an optimist, and she thought she'd be on her feet within a couple of days. After Saturday's bout I didn't think she would be up to coming to the café at all this week."

"Why are you removing the rigging?"

"I'm here in her stead. She couldn't stand one more day of the café not having enough help."

"No. We're good." He passed her the umbrella and relatched the buckle she'd undone.

Barbie grabbed the buckle. "Aren't you

extremely busy and shorthanded?"

"Ya, but we'll be fine. It's our problem. Not yours."

She unbuckled it again, using one hand. "I know I'm not your favorite person, but Cilla was so upset about not being able to come that I gave her my word I'd fill in for her. She needs rest, and she's not getting enough for fretting over not being here. So I gave her the answer she needed."

Abram sighed and began removing the rigging from the horse. "Siblings."

"Ain't it the truth? Mamm had to argue with her again this morning, but her oxygen levels were just too low."

"Tell her she should always stay home when she's not feeling well."

"She likes working at the café."

"Ya, apparently she likes it enough to work without pay."

Barbie laughed, but Abram hadn't meant it as a joke. "She speaks fondly of you."

He didn't know what Barbie was getting at. Was she as surprised as Skylar that someone was interested in him? Skylar had clearly been surprised that Jackson talked to him as if he mattered. That was the kind of thing Ariana never doubted, even when he'd been more backward and withdrawn. Ariana had spent all last summer trying to help him think of ways to talk to Barbie, but now he just wanted her to be quiet.

He opened the back door to the café. "You looking forward to working seven hours for no pay?"

"I'm working to make Cilla be quiet and give me a break." Barbie's smile and raised eyebrow made it clear she was teasing. "That's far more valuable than money." She closed the umbrella.

When they walked inside, Abram saw the largest morning crowd yet. He'd been so busy working on the woodshed that he hadn't realized what was happening in here. And Barbie had arrived an hour late.

The front of Skylar's white shirt was covered with a brown stain. Foamy milk was spattered on and dripping from the countertop. Apparently her plan to add a frothy milk espresso to today's menu, using a battery-powered frothing wand, wasn't going as planned. She caught his eye and gestured, waving her hands in desperation.

"Right." He hung his hat on a peg. "Skylar, this is Barbie, Cilla's sister." He removed his coat and held out his hand to take her coat. "Barbie, you help Skylar. She won't hesitate to let you know what you need to do. I'm going to relieve Susie from running both grills." As he stepped into the kitchen, he saw Martha was juggling multiple cooking jobs too. Abram washed his hands, put on a clean apron, and grabbed a spatula.

"Before you man the grill, get some bread on the tables." Martha dumped a pan of biscuits into a huge basket. "If people have something to nibble on until their orders are ready, they'll be happier with us." Abram quickly filled four plates with biscuits, buttered toast, and jellies.

As he set them on the pick-up counter, Jackson grabbed them up. "What are you doing here, Jackson?"

He had that big, unfaltering grin in place. "Since it's raining, there's no roofing today. What happened was Skylar. I walked in, and she said that since I was your friend and you were busy trying to get the generator working, I needed to help."

"Jackson," Skylar scolded, "if you're going to lie, at least do the job you're lying about and be helpful."

"Yes, ma'am." Jackson hurried off with the four plates balanced in his arms.

"Thank you," Abram hollered.

"You're welcome," Jackson answered. He whispered something as he passed Skylar, and she smiled before glancing out the window. Over the last few days, she'd grown more interested by the hour in taking quick looks out the front window. Was she expecting someone? If so, apparently the person hadn't come yet, because each day she grew antsier.

Jackson made an about-face and told Skylar, "We'll need six warmups on table five fairly soon, please."

"Thanks." Skylar gave a thumbs-up and began brewing another pot of coffee. What would Jackson think when he learned that Skylar was Abram's twin? It wasn't something he or Skylar talked about with anyone, as if not discussing it kept it from being real. She hated it here, and he felt certain that Ariana was no happier inside Skylar's old life.

Martha set more plates of breakfast food on the pick-up counter. "You go cook and fill orders, please."

"Oh yeah." Abram went to the grill and started filling orders. While focusing on cooking eggs and breakfast meats to order, he kept thinking about Cilla. There had to be better answers, maybe beginning with a better doctor.

The breakfast rush lasted more than an hour. When no more fresh orders came in, Abram grabbed a tub for dirty dishes and a clean rag and left the kitchen.

Barbie grasped three tumblers in her

fingers while also picking up dirty plates.

"What has Cilla's doctor said about her condition?" Abram asked quietly as he held out the tub to her.

Barbie laid the cups and plates in the bin. "Same as he usually says."

"What does he usually say?" Abram set the tub on a table and gathered some dirty flatware.

"To do the breathing treatments and stay in bed when her oxygen levels are low and that the symptoms will come and go." Barbie sprayed the table with a cleaning solution.

"That's it?" Abram wiped the table with a clean rag.

"Basically." Barbie gathered more dirty dishes from another table.

Abram followed with the tub in hand. "What does 'basically' mean?"

She slid the items in with the others. "The doctor doesn't say much, and that's what I've gleaned."

The thought of an apathetic doctor treating Cilla worried Abram. "Are you sure he is a good doctor?"

"He's a doctor."

"Right, but there are good doctors and bad doctors, just like there are good and bad carpenters and farmers."

Barbie stopped cleaning and faced Abram. "He's what we can afford. Most doctors charge more if you don't have insurance, but this one doesn't. Mamm doesn't know another doctor who's willing to accept what we can pay."

The Amish community wasn't rich with doctors. It got the ones who were willing to accept what payment they could get. And the Amish didn't rely heavily on doctors, so they didn't know much about how to find a truly good one. Some of the older Amish would say that if God willed people to be well, then they would get well, doctor or no doctor. Most Amish had evolved from that line of thinking, but collectively they still had limited knowledge about doctors.

"Cilla hasn't shown any improvement with the help of the doctor?"

"She has good days and bad. She's always been this way. The doctor said that's the way it is with cystic fibrosis."

He knew the disease was rough and became progressively worse over time, but it was becoming clear that Barbie didn't question Cilla's doctor. So did their parents question him?

Could Cilla do better under the care of a different doctor? Abram didn't know enough to answer that question, but it seemed like an important one to ask.

With all the dirty dishes gathered, Abram started for the kitchen. The café door opened, and Jackson walked in, carrying a grocery bag. "I thought you were gone for the day," Abram said.

"I ran an errand for Susie."

Susie came out of the kitchen and stopped near the pass-through, motioning for them to join her.

"Thank you so much, Jackson." She took the bag from him. "We were completely out of eggs and bread. On the upside, Skylar was definitely right about serving better coffee and changing the menu to match our limited baking skills."

"Yeah." Skylar came out from behind the register. "It was a brilliant plan. I increased my work load in a job I'd rather not do."

Jackson chuckled. "I like it when people are brutally honest."

"I'm brutally honest *and* lazy," Skylar added. "It's a winning combination."

Susie shifted the brown bag in her arms. "This is a good gathering spot. We can see when the customers need refills or if anyone comes in, and we can talk without being heard. I'd like to know what's going on with Cilla."

"Barbie and I were just talking about

that." Abram took the groceries from Susie and set them on the counter. He looked at Jackson. "Do you know how to find a good doctor, a specialist?"

"Not really. I think most people rely on word of mouth or, these days, look them up on the Internet."

"Oh." That wasn't a solution for Abram.

Jackson pointed at Skylar. "I bet she could help you look up some doctors."

Skylar raised her brows. "Flattery will get you nowhere, Jax."

"Good to know, but I was actually thinking you're probably more detail oriented. According to Susie, you knew how to scour information from a supply catalog and knew exactly what this place needed to give it a boost. You searched for the details that make a difference, ones I wouldn't have noticed. Now Brennemans' Perks has the right food, the right equipment, and the right coffees that people make a racket for. If you could do that with a catalog, imagine what you could do on the Internet."

"He's right, Skylar. Would you do it?" Abram asked.

She glanced out the window before looking at Barbie. A hint of compassion flickered in Skylar's eyes. "Sure, but how? I don't have access to a computer or a cell phone."

"I have a computer," Jackson said, "and a jetpack that will give an Internet connection. But I don't have them with me."

"Sounds good." Abram nodded. "We can't have those in the house, but both would be allowed in here since it's a business."

"I can get them and be back around closing time. I doubt it would take more than an hour, maybe two, to find what you're looking for."

"Perfect plan." Abram didn't know why Jackson was always so good to him, and now he was including Cilla, Susie, and the café. But whatever the reason, Abram was incredibly grateful.

TWENTY-FIVE

Somewhere in central Ohio, Ariana gazed into a café. Beyond her reflection in the window that showed her Amish attire, she could see this place had contemporary décor and looked every bit as inviting as her own. She'd like to know how her café was doing, how Susie and Martha were doing running it, how Abram and everyone else was faring. If Rudy had talked to anyone in her family on the community phone, she would have a few answers when he arrived in about an hour.

The glass reflected familiar movement. Brandi was crossing the street, coming toward her.

Ariana turned to greet her. "You found your phone."

They had arrived in town about ninety minutes ago, and after eating at a café down the street, they'd done a little window shopping, paying particular attention to each café and diner. While in line to buy chocolate-covered apples, Brandi realized she didn't have her phone. Ariana stayed in the queue for the apples, and Brandi hurried back to the car to search for it.

"I thought maybe it'd fallen out of my purse during the drive." Brandi's eyes glimmered with pleasure. "It was under the car seat." Her breath was frosty, and she wore a hat and a knit scarf around her neck.

"Glad it was there." It would've taken them a long time to backtrack through all the shops they'd gone into.

Brandi dangled Ariana's keys in front of her. "Thanks."

Ariana put the keys in her purse. Since she'd had her license for only a couple of weeks, neither Brandi nor Nicholas wanted her driving by herself for the almost five-hour trip to this halfway point. So Ariana had asked Brandi to come with her and help navigate. She had jumped at the offer, dropping every sewing job she had for today.

It seemed wrong to admit to anyone how much she enjoyed driving. Whatever the driving situation — small towns, major highways, sunshine, or rain — she longed to get behind the wheel. Each time she felt something she'd never experienced before — a surging sense of confidence and power.

And guilt. A lot of guilt.

But the confidence was like warm sunshine melting the snow from a long winter. The cozy, wonderful feeling was the opposite of the powerlessness she'd often felt in being poor.

"Have you tried a bite yet?" Brandi asked.

"No. But I asked them to slice the apples so they will be easier to eat." Ariana opened the white pastry box.

She and Brandi would stay at a hotel tonight and go back to Pennsylvania tomorrow morning, but Rudy's driver had to leave this evening between seven and eight, which meant they wouldn't arrive home until at least midnight.

Brandi gingerly lifted a wedge of chocolate-covered apple. "I'm so thrilled to be here with you, honey."

"I feel the same way." In the past week Ariana and her mom had made a lot of progress in healing. The planetarium event had reshaped Ariana's thinking. She'd been born again in a way. Love and hope had flooded her unlike anything she'd ever experienced, and her mind felt renewed.

"Wow," Brandi mumbled around the apple slice. "That is so good."

Ariana closed the box, not the least bit hungry after her lunch.

As they strolled down the sidewalk, Ariana's mind raced. It was tempting to discount some of the experience at the planetarium as emotionalism after seeing the amazing pictures from space. But she couldn't do that, because her moment of intuition about the security cameras had proved to be spot on. Quill called to tell her the news a few days ago, and he was so relieved. The project manager hadn't put the updated plans in the permit box before Quill ordered the supplies for the new phase. The time stamp on the footage proved that, which meant all fault lay with Sanders. In addition, the cameras near the flat files at the architects' and engineers' office showed that after Quill had ordered and installed the wrong electrical system, Sanders doctored the plans and tried to cover his mistake by pinning it on Quill. Ariana wasn't familiar enough with the process to understand all of what Quill explained, but the bottom line was Schlabach Home Builders had been reimbursed for the new panels and wiring and had been paid overtime for all the rewiring. McLaren also had followed through and offered to promote them to contractors for a project that would begin next summer.

Her time at the planetarium had done just

as much for her. It had planted a thousand new and exciting seeds, and it would take months to begin to understand all that had taken root during that program. But she'd spent the week studying God's Word, history, and other cultures. It was all so fascinating she'd hardly taken time to eat.

It also was amazing, almost surreal, that Brandi and she had come this far in being comfortable with each other. Brandi took another apple slice. "When you're running the café, will you have some seasonal foods, like caramel apples in the fall and Christmas cookies in December?"

"I hadn't really thought about it, but that's a good idea. Would you help me find and test a few recipes?"

Brandi's eyes glistened. Were those tears? "I would love that, Ari."

"Me too. And Cameron can be our guinea pig."

Brandi laughed and almost choked. "She'll complain loudly and enjoy every minute of it, even if the food is horrible."

Ariana glanced at her phone, checking the time. "We better head toward the park."

"Sure."

They walked down the street, going toward the small park where Ari would meet Rudy. Her phone pinged, and she checked the text message. When she glanced at the screen, her heart leaped. She grabbed Brandi's arm, stopping her abruptly. "It's from Frieda," she squealed. "I've been texting her all week. Listen to this: 'Dearest Ari, apparently I haven't been receiving my texts. I realized this yesterday and immediately turned off my phone for the first time in forever. This morning when I turned it on again, my text box was flooded with beautiful messages from you. I've cried for joy all morning. As soon as I can stop crying long enough to think, I'll send a real message. Love you forever and always, Frieda.' "

Tears spilled down Ariana's cheeks.

"That's great, honey." Brandi studied her. "Who's Frieda?"

Ariana looped an arm through Brandi's. "She was my closest friend, the one who left home with Quill." She summarized the rest of the story while they walked. "So while I was at the planetarium, even before the program began, I saw God as energetic love, which is in line with His Word, and I got morsels of understanding about God and life."

"You haven't told me any of the specifics, only that going to the planetarium was great and amazing."

Ariana pulled her arm from Brandi's so she could use both hands to gesture. "My aha moment was that everything God did created light and order. He sent His Word to this planet to create light and order in our lives, but not for the sake of order."

Brandi took another bite of crispy apple. "You lost me."

"Yeah, I guess I'm sharing thoughts from the Old Order culture. To the Amish, order is equal to laws and rules. The question is, are we here to serve them, or are they here to serve us? In Jesus's day people had the Sabbath tied up in rules — how many steps could be taken, how one obtained food, how many threads could be tied together — and people ended up serving the day rather than God's intention, which was for the Sabbath to serve people's need for rest. So I asked myself, on some level have the conservative faithful done that with order, with our view of what's important rather than God's view of it?"

"That's pretty deep. Really good food for thought."

When she was inside the dark dome watching the movie, it was as if her feelings of intolerance for others had been physically pulled from her heart and love had flooded in, taking its place. And forgiveness for her biological parents, her Amish parents, and those who'd left the order came as easily as pulling the plug in a sink of dirty dishwater and refilling it with clean water. She felt as if she had no grudges, hurt, or anger with anyone. All that seemed to remain was love and the hope for a fresh beginning.

Brandi buttoned the top of her coat. "I've grown comfortable seeing God through my personal cynicism with the church. It's refreshing to think of Him as you just described."

"It is, isn't it?" Maybe *now* Ariana was in a place where she could share the power and beauty of faith with Brandi and Nicholas.

TWENTY-SIX

Autumn could've come and gone in a single night, and Skylar doubted that she would've noticed. Life seemed to be constant static, like an old television with a blur of black and white and a persistent buzz.

She had only one clear thought: *four pills.*

That's all she had left.

Four pills.

She lit a cigarette and leaned against the brick wall of the café. "Come on, Cody." Her hands trembled, but she wasn't sure if it was from the cold November temperature or from cutting back on the pills. Cody had come to the café just once, eleven days ago. "We're closing soon, and it's Saturday," she whispered as if he could somehow hear her.

The door to the café swung open, and Susie walked out. "Hi."

"Hey."

"You know that we really appreciate all you're doing, right? The help with figuring out what we needed to order for the café, great menu suggestions, hard work for a payday that hasn't come yet, and especially finding a doctor for Cilla."

"Potential good doctor," Skylar corrected while exhaling smoke. "That's all we know right now."

Abram had called the doctor's office, and the first available appointment was in six weeks, which stank in Skylar's opinion.

Susie folded her arms, shivering. "It's the best lead you could find, based on the reviews and Yelp. I didn't realize that they'd do a couple of weeks of testing. Abram said the follow-up visit after the testing won't happen until the first of the year. Apparently getting answers for someone with Cilla's condition is quite a process." Susie stomped her feet, obviously trying to warm herself.

Skylar inhaled. "Yeah, I did a fabulous job poking around the Internet that night."

Susie rubbed her palms over her thin sleeves. "I don't know what that means."

"Of course not." Skylar had no cause to be snippy or to talk in coded nonsense to Susie, but her mood was too foul for her to stop herself.

Two days earlier Jackson had brought his computer to the café. While the others talked and cleaned, Skylar had spent a couple of hours making a short list of potential doctors for Cilla. Once she had the list, everyone, including Jackson, discussed the information and decided which doctor to call. With that done and Jackson in no hurry to leave, Skylar had played around online. That had been a mistake. She'd gone to YouTube, as she used to do regularly, and typed in some names — hers, Cody's, her mom's. It wasn't until she searched for her dad's name that she stumbled across a clip of her mom onstage singing with Ariana while he accompanied them . . . and sang!

Skylar had no words for the hurt and anger that had rumbled through her as she watched the display of emotion between her mom and Ariana and the pride on her dad's face. Skylar thought she had talent. But Ariana's voice was remarkable, and she couldn't read music and had never had a voice lesson, at least not before leaving Summer Grove. Worse, the stupid thing had been posted Saturday evening, and when Skylar saw it six days later, the clip already had twelve thousand views and every review was glowing with positive comments.

The whole situation was nauseating, infuriating. So Skylar had exited YouTube and closed the computer, telling no one what she'd seen. She'd bottled her emotions, and now she was a jumbled mess and downing more pills than usual.

"Why'd you come out here, Susie?"

"Well, see, you're smoking out front again. Mamm and Daed and all of us are trying to be cool about this awful habit, but it can't be inviting for customers to see an employee propped against the front of the café and smoking. You showed us that we've earned a few bad reviews on Yelp, and we'd like to avoid any more."

"The reviews had nothing to do with me smoking. Ten reviews. Two bad ones based on the first week the café was open, and they said that neither the service nor the food was good."

"And you've helped set to rights the coffee, the menu, and the service. But can I ask what happened to the agreement that if you had to smoke, you'd do it behind the building?"

"Change of plans."

"Like the change that's keeping away whoever it is you keep looking for?"

She inhaled again. "Give the girl a gold star. She's not as unaware as she looks."

"Sorry, Sky, but no one is as naive as you seem to think. So this guy . . . I'm assuming it's a guy. What happens if he never shows?"

Skylar flicked her cigarette in Susie's direction, using just enough restraint not to hit her with it. "That's not going to happen."

"And if it does? I've watched you struggle a little more each day this week, and I'd really like to know what you're going to do if he doesn't show."

Skylar studied the street, wishing Cody would arrive. If the fuzzy television set inside her brain could get a clear picture for just a few minutes, she might be able to think of a decent retort. "Kill myself."

"That's not funny, but you already knew that." Susie pressed her foot against the cigarette butt, picked it up, and put it in the nearby trash can. "If you need someone to talk to —"

"I don't."

What was there to talk about? If Cody abandoned her the way her mom and dad had, she was alone, stuck inside a weird life from another century. Her bio family could barely tolerate her living with them, and her mom and dad had traded her away as soon as they found out about Ariana.

Without her parents' support there would be no acting school, but she wasn't sure she cared about that anymore. She missed her mom and even Nicholas. She ached to be their little girl again. But the oddest thing of all was that she didn't miss being onstage. Maybe it was because she'd been booted out of drama for the semester, so she wouldn't have been onstage or learning parts whether she was there or here. But she didn't even dream of singing or performing anymore. Something was happening in her. Things that used to matter didn't now.

The thing she missed most about performing was something she hadn't even been aware was a part of her. Whenever she had performed onstage, she could feel Mom and Dad in the audience pulling for her to nail every line and hit every note. During those times all of life grew quiet for them and nothing existed but her. Their focused desire toward her felt as if they'd had some sort of supernatural power, like prayer would if God were real.

Skylar overlapped the front of her coat and started walking toward the gas station. She had to call Cody again.

"Where are you going?"

"Since you seem to know so much about me, there's no need to keep my calls to Cody a secret, is there?"

Skylar kept walking. She had herself, the

cigarettes she'd bought with her tip money, and four pills.

She rolled her eyes. Life just kept getting better and better.

Maybe Cody would answer the phone this time.

TWENTY-SEVEN

Ariana and Brandi sat on a park bench. Children in coats and hats threw a football back and forth. The midday air was brisk, and the delicious aromas of late fall flooded Ariana with memories of home. The closer the time came for Rudy to arrive, the faster her heart beat. He should arrive in the next ten minutes.

Several benches away an old man and woman clasped gloved hands, a blanket over their legs, bundled against the November chill. She smiled as the elderly couple huddled together, talking. That would be Rudy and her one day, decades after all their children were grown. As comforting as that thought was, her emotions bounced between conflicting waves of excitement and melancholy. In order to get to this park today, she had done several things Rudy might disapprove of. So many compromises that she no longer saw as wrong.

Would he consider her decisions wrong? Maybe he'd be disappointed rather than pleased. However Rudy reacted, she couldn't un-learn or unexperience the many things she'd been exposed to. He might consider them worldly, and in some ways he'd be right, but they were also freeing. She could already feel herself changing, looking at life, God, and faith vastly different from before. What would that do to them?

"You're trembling. From the cold or nerves?"

"Maybe some of both."

She also worried how Rudy would take the news that she was the illegitimate child of an adulterous affair. She was at peace with it now. Could he learn to accept it? And that she'd driven to Ohio?

Brandi removed her black neck scarf with its glittery silver threading and placed it over Ariana's prayer Kapp, covering her ears.

With Ariana's hair pinned back in proper Amish style, her ears were aching with the cold. She should've worn her black winter bonnet. The warm knit felt good, and she doubted she would take it off, even if it looked a little peculiar.

In the distance a car pulled into a parking space, and she focused on it, hoping it would be Rudy. A man bundled in a coat and wearing the traditional Amish black hat for winter got out of the passenger's side and scanned the park.

"He's here." Ariana pointed.

"He's cute."

"And so good to me." Excitement pulsed through her, and she got up from the bench.

Brandi stood. "Call me when you're ready for us to meet up again."

Guilt nibbled at Ariana. She had so much she needed Rudy to adjust to that she hadn't wanted him to meet Brandi. Not yet. "What will you do with the rest of the afternoon?"

"Shop, read, eat, see a movie, call Gabe and chat like we used to do when we were dating." She grinned. "Don't worry about me."

Ariana pulled out the keys. "You should keep these and take the car for the day. We won't use it."

"Okay. I've got a car, money, and time." She winked. "Once it's check-in time, I could even go to the hotel and nap between shopping sprees." She blew a kiss and hurried off.

Ariana walked toward him, but he'd yet to spot her.

She would go back to Amish life the moment she was allowed, but she wouldn't return as the same person who'd left. A nervous chill ran down her spine. Surely Rudy would understand that.

Finally Rudy saw her, and a huge grin replaced the serious look he'd had earlier. He waved and picked up his pace. Nicholas had assured her that an illegitimate child wasn't taboo in today's times. But Ariana's home wasn't part of modern culture. She'd thought of various ways to break the news to Rudy, but she decided it would be better just to come out and say it.

Without a word he embraced her, making her stomach jump to her throat. He trembled as he held her tightly for at least a minute without speaking. He backed up only enough to see her face. "How've you been?"

"It's been rougher than I expected, but I'm adjusting."

"Are you hungry?"

"No, I've eaten. You?"

"About an hour ago." He slid his warm hand into hers and held it as they walked toward a bench. "You look great."

Ariana clutched the black shimmering scarf. "Really?"

"Absolutely." He glanced around. "Think anyone will faint, wag a finger, or call your

Daed if I kiss you?"

"I think it would be worth it."

He raised his eyebrows. "I was hoping you'd say that." He leaned in and kissed her on the lips.

How could life be so confusing and difficult one day and so perfect the next?

He put an arm behind her and pulled her close, as close as two people in winter coats could get. "You know, I could've found a driver that didn't need to be home tonight and could've gone all the way to Bellflower Creek. I wouldn't have minded."

Ariana put her head on his shoulder. "I appreciate that, but I didn't think it was a good idea."

"Why's that?"

"Nicholas might have ruined our time, cross-examining you about your faith and preaching his beliefs."

Rudy lifted her hand to his lips and kissed it. "Oh."

"It isn't you. He's that way with me too."

"He doesn't sound like such a nice guy."

Ariana soaked in seeing Rudy. His curly, rust-colored hair and dark eyes were mesmerizing. "He's different. At least from the people in our community."

He squeezed her hand. "I've been worried about you."

"That's very sweet. It's easier now, and I can't see it getting unbearable again. But I'm also counting the days until I can go back to Amish life."

"That's really good to hear. I've been trying to imagine what you do all day, but I have no idea."

"Nicholas makes lists of things I need to do and learn. And I spend time with Brandi and him. I read books and study things on the Internet. I play some video games with my stepbrothers and watch a lot of movies with my stepsister."

"Okay, Ariana, be honest. Electric heat and lights at the flip of a switch have to be great."

She chuckled, relieved that he took no offense at how she spent her days. "Ya, those are pretty hard to overrate. Oh, and thermostats. If you're cold, you press a button, and heat not only turns on, but it stays on until the room is the desired temperature."

"Don't make me jealous, Ariana. I'm living in the land of the super-conservative. Around this time next month, I'll be helping to cut and store ice so my community will have it for their iceboxes until next year's ice cutting."

"I've never seen anyone cut ice before. Is it done like Kristoff does it in *Frozen*?"

He stopped and stared at her. "Did you just ask me if I've seen a movie — a princess-type, children's movie? What are you implying?"

Ariana laughed. "Sorry."

"Sure you are. You couldn't ask if I'd seen some manly movie?"

"Like *Die Hard* and *Terminator,* right?" Ariana hadn't seen those yet, but her stepbrothers had rambled on about them during one of their mealtimes.

"Ya, like . . . What were the names of those movies again?" His grin was too cute.

She cupped his face in her hands and kissed his lips again.

"Denki," Rudy whispered. "Hey, I've talked to Susie a few times, trying to find out how you've been doing. I'd hoped to at least send a warm 'hello, thinking of you, miss you terribly' message to you. Apparently you've had no contact with anyone at home."

"None. All of us are trying to follow Nicholas's demands so no one gets sued."

"I have some good news from home. The café is doing great, according to Susie. And she said to tell you that she misses you terribly and that you should be grateful she hasn't burned it down yet in revolt."

"That's our Susie." But Ariana wanted to

shout with excitement. She'd been concerned about the café and worried about Susie. Buying the café had been her dream, and she'd made a lot of promises to Susie about the work load, ones she hadn't been able to keep. "She's not pulling out her hair?"

"She said the first week was really tough but the second was a little better. This week has been even better, so they didn't lose as much money as the first two weeks. She said Abram is practically managing it and doing a really good job."

"Abram?" Ariana couldn't picture her brother managing the café. Because of his feelings of insecurity, decision making was very tough, and he was extremely shy.

"Everyone sends their love and is eager for you to come back."

She had to cut the small talk until she told him the truths she had learned about herself. All of them. But she would work her way up to the hardest one. "I have a driver's license."

"You do? Did you drive here?"

"I did."

"By yourself?"

"Brandi came with me. Nicholas felt I needed more experience before I crossed any state lines alone. She was a lot of help when it came to merging onto highways and teaching me how to read a GPS when it's showing multiple highways at once."

He nodded.

"Are you okay with me driving?"

"It feels weird." He tapped his chest. "But I get it, Ariana. You're stuck between a rock and a hard place, trying to survive while protecting the people in your community. And trying to share Christ with your Englisch family."

"Until the last few days, I've not been a good witness at all. My plans and will betrayed me, and I pretty much cried my way through the first two weeks."

"Me too." His slight smile said he was teasing. "No real tears, but a lot of irritable howling. Just ask my family." He winked. "Maybe you haven't handled things as well as you'd hoped, but I'm proud of —"

She covered his mouth with her fingers. "Don't say that. Not yet." She lowered her hand. "I need you to listen without interrupting because I have to get through a lot of information you need to know."

It took her a while to tell him about her hair, the Englisch clothes, and Nicholas's bucket list. She explained some of the things she'd done to earn the opportunity to see him today.

Rudy's brow was heavy with concern. "I'm glad you care that much."

"It gets worse." She choked out the truth about her parents and her illegitimacy.

He stared at her briefly before exhaling and slowly leaning back. His eyes fell on the children playing nearby. "Good grief, Ariana. I can't imagine how tough this time has been for you." He put his arm around her and leaned his head against hers. "I'm so sorry, and to think you've been all alone while going through it."

Is that all he had to say about it? Maybe he needed some time to think about what she'd said.

"I . . . I haven't been totally alone. I'm allowed to see, text, and call Quill."

"Quill." Rudy's voice went flat, and he pulled back his arm. The displeasure in his eyes was obvious.

Who would've thought that was more upsetting than the other information?

He tapped the back of one hand with the palm of the other. "You have to jump through hoops to see me, but you're allowed to reach out to him anytime."

"I know. It's wrong. But to Nicholas, Quill is the ideal person for me to be around. He's former Amish with a life, career, and family outside of the Old Order."

"Quill has a family? As in a wife and children?"

"No. He has four brothers and sisters-in-law and eight nieces and nephews."

"Wait, let me guess. He's single, right?"

"I wouldn't like the situation one bit better than you if the tables were turned, but I promise you it's not like that with Quill and me."

"Maybe not today."

"Or in a year. And I'm not the only one around singles of the opposite gender. Isn't there someone your parents are pushing your way, hoping you'll stay in Indiana rather than move to Summer Grove with the girl whose actual lineage isn't Amish?"

"Ya." He nodded. "They're doing that. But there was no one for me before I met you, and there will be no one after you. So let's stick to the only real threat: Quill Schlabach."

"He's not a threat. His goal is to help me cope with the situation and to help me get back to Summer Grove. He wants you and me to marry and have children, because he knows I love you. And then we can be family to his Mamm."

Resting his forearms on his thighs, Rudy stared at the ground but said nothing.

In mid-September they had disagreed over

Quill's helping her purchase the café, and Rudy had lost all control. He'd railed with anger. But this silence was far more disconcerting. His anger she understood. Silence was harder to decipher.

"That's great, Ariana. *He* wants you to return to Summer Grove."

His sarcasm caught her off guard.

With his forearms still on his legs, he intertwined his hands and never glanced her way. "I'm working really long hours to save for our future, assuring myself that, at the end of our forced separation, we'll be together for the rest of our lives." He turned his head, looking at her. "But you're there with Quill, and I'm in Indiana. And now I'm wondering, at the end of this separation, is it going to be you and me?"

"Rudy." What was he thinking? "Ya, of course it is."

He studied her as if looking for the truth. "Promise me I'm not waiting for nothing. Promise me this ridiculous hardship your dad has put on us won't break us."

"I promise," she yelped before looping her arm through his and leaning against his shoulder. "I promise, Rudy," she whispered. "You don't need to think twice about that. And I have a few ideas about how I might get home sooner."

He kissed her forehead. "I hope they're rock-solid ideas."

"Remember when we discussed what Nicholas wanted, and we agreed that it was God's will that I obey my parents?"

"Ya."

"I'm rethinking that."

He leaned forward so he could look in her eyes. Skepticism covered his face. "You're rethinking God's will?"

He was perfectly serious. But she didn't think she was wrong. Not in this.

"No. Goodness, no. I'm rethinking our view of His will. See, last weekend I went to a planetarium, and . . ." She told him even more than she had shared with Brandi, and he seemed to understand it in the way she needed him to.

"I can feel some of those things just by listening to you talk about them." He scooted a few inches away and angled himself so he could face her. "The bottom line is you're hoping to find a balance between submitting to the scriptures about obedience to parents and following God as you feel He's leading you. That's dangerous ground, Ariana."

"Ya, I know. But isn't it also dangerous to blindly obey any individual? Nicholas has given me history books to read, things we brushed over in school. The Word says to obey those in power, and yet Hitler was once in power."

"Honoring our parents is a commandment."

"But what is meant by the word *honor*?"

His eyes grew large. "Seriously?"

"Shouldn't we at least pray about it, be sure we're not letting others use us for their purposes while telling us it's for God's purpose?" She didn't dare confess that Quill had planted that thought in her mind.

"See, this is why I want to stay under God's authority in the Amish church. No one there would try to sabotage God's ways for personal gain."

She barely nodded, unsure if he was right. The bishop had dealt severely with the Schlabachs, but none of the brothers had joined the faith. Why be so adamant about the sons not visiting their Mamm? Was that scriptural?

Ariana toyed with the fringe of the knit scarf. "But my immediate authority right now isn't the Amish church or my Amish parents. I'm under Nicholas."

"Ya, and he's threatened a lawsuit and prison time for the midwife and your parents."

"He has definitely jumbled the Word

concerning the need to obey him as a parent and the lawsuit threat together, and they have to be separated and dealt with as very different issues. He was angry and upset at the beginning, offended that his daughter had been raised Amish. Now that we've bonded some, I think he may be willing to relent. At least a little. But the question is, do you agree with me about pushing back and even disobeying him at times?"

She was asking a difficult question, and she was asking him as the future head of their household. Rudy would stand a better chance of knowing his answer if they'd been taught differently. They hadn't been taught to follow their conscience. The Word and the Ordnung *were* their conscience, but what did a person do after the Ordnung had been stripped away and the Word was being used for selfish purposes?

Rudy sighed. "Let me think about that for a bit. I want you back in Summer Grove, but I'm really uncomfortable with your idea of rethinking God's will. Your Daed agreed to you coming here. It wasn't just Nicholas."

"But there are times when God tells people to leave their families, like when God called Abraham to leave his family, despite what his father may have wanted. Jesus told a man to leave his father and follow Him."

"Ya, but every instance I can think of is God telling a man to come away. Do you know of a time when God told a woman to leave her father or husband?"

His line of thinking didn't seem right to her. "So if two boys had been born and swapped at the Amish center that night, and if I was Abram, I could challenge Nicholas, and whatever my decision was, it would be accepted as God's leading? But since I'm me, a woman, I'm stuck keeping my mouth shut? That's a little convenient for the men, don't you think?"

"When you put it that way, it just sounds wrong, doesn't it?" He drew her hand to his lips and kissed it. "Let's put all this talk away for now and enjoy our time."

"Ya, I would like that." She was ready to think about other things and have some fun.

"Maybe the answer will come to us before we part." With her hand in his, he stood. "My driver said there's a really cool café inside a place called the Popcorn Palace. Hot drinks, deli sandwiches, scones. Care to check it out?"

"I'd like that."

He tugged on her hand, and in the blink of an eye, they were toe-to-toe. He lifted her chin, gazed into her eyes, and kissed her again, making her feel beautiful and protected, just as it did each time their lips met.

And she prayed God would protect their relationship.

TWENTY-EIGHT

Abram stood behind the register and glanced at the clock. Three minutes before two on a Monday. It'd been their best day yet, and business picked up on Fridays and Saturdays. Almost closing time and no one was in line, but there were still several people at various tables, finishing their lunch. Jackson had picked up a bag of wheat berries for Susie and brought it by, and he was eating the special she'd made for him as a way to say thanks.

He counted the money again, trying to get the drawer to balance with the orders they'd filled today. Sometimes it took several tries to balance the drawer. Even so, he was pleased with how well the café was doing. They were gaining customers every day, and many were becoming regulars.

A loud crash jolted everyone.

"Sorry." Skylar knelt. Her dyed swath of black hair was growing out, leaving dirty blond roots. She kept it in a ponytail while at work, but the moment she walked out of the café, she removed the band.

Abram came out from behind the counter and saw that she'd dropped a tray of clean flatware. Jackson was getting up too.

She held up her hand. "I got it. Both of you. I'm fine." Her hand and arm were shaking, but she lifted her eyes, and they were steely cold. "Just back off."

Abram drew a breath and returned to the register. Man, he missed Ariana. Susie glanced out of the pass-through window from her cooking station. Their eyes met, and he saw her concern. This was the third time today Skylar had dropped something and then snapped at whoever was closest. Earlier a half-full coffeepot had slipped from her hands, shattering on the floor and spattering coffee.

Cilla and Martha were in the kitchen with Susie, cleaning and getting the place ready so everyone could go home shortly after closing. Cilla came out with an empty tray to help Skylar gather the flatware.

Abram caught her by the arm and shook his head. He nodded toward the register. "I can't get the drawer to balance. Would you mind trying?"

"Not at all." Cilla handed him the tray

and went behind the register.

He walked over to a table far away from Skylar. He had a few clues about what was going on with her. He and Susie had talked about it. Whoever Skylar was watching for had apparently not dropped by.

Abram began gathering the dirty dishes. Nearby a small group of customers rose and laughed as they headed for the door. "Great food as always." An older man put his hand on Abram's shoulder as he passed by.

"Glad you enjoyed it." Abram waved as the man went out the door. "Thanks for coming in."

Where were those familiar awkward feelings? The ones that made it hard to talk to people? The café seemed to have changed everything.

Brennemans' Perks.

If Ariana had known she wasn't a Brenneman before naming the café, would she have called it something else? How would she feel about the name when she returned? He looked at the coffee makers, a timer, a scale, a grinder, a toaster, a waffle maker, and a blender for frappes and smoothies. From the coffees to the menu to the electric appliances, Brennemans' Perks hardly looked like the place Ariana had set up. How would she feel about that? He pushed those thoughts aside. There was nothing he could do about Ariana right now. But there was plenty he could do to help the café be successful.

Skylar was still on her knees, gathering the scattered flatware. When her hands were full, she dropped a load on the largest table, and then she ambled over to gather the rest.

The remaining customers, three separate tables of women, glanced at her. Some whispered. Others began collecting their things.

Abram slid his tray of dirty dishes onto a table and went to Skylar, turning his back to the customers. "You need a minute? Maybe some air?"

"No. It's just stupid flatware. I got this, okay?"

"It's not just about you, Skylar. You've rattled the customers."

She peered around him, nodded, and drew a breath. "Hi, ladies. Sorry to be so noisy. Nothing personal. Well, not to you. I'd personally like to drop my ex-boyfriend like he's apparently dropped me. Two weeks ago we were good, and he said, 'See you in a few days.' Now? Nothing. Nada. Zip. He hasn't called and won't even pick up when I call. I'd like to scatter his emotions across the floor like I did the flatware."

The women reacted in a lively fashion. Some made a sad face, some clapped, some nodded. One shouted, "You go, girl." Another said, "If you want a little help, we'd be glad to break some dishes with you."

All of them were jovial and smiling by the time Skylar turned back to Abram. "Happy?" She scowled at him.

Sometimes she was like a gas burner on a stovetop, going from stone cold to blue flames with the turn of a knob.

He pushed a teetering utensil away from the edge of the table. "That helped, but you know all these have to be washed again, right?"

The hardness on her face made him think she'd like to spit on him, but she simply nodded.

Abram returned to his table and finished loading the tray. He couldn't figure her out. She had times of seeming to care about the café, Cilla, and the Brennemans. Today she was a hornet with a serious case of the shakes.

Jackson lifted his mug. "Hey, Abram."

"You've made a habit of loitering," he teased.

"I'm thinking about becoming Amish."

Abram chuckled. "Oh?"

"Yeah, I figure I come here so often I

might as well convert."

Susie walked out of the kitchen. "Here's your money." She passed an envelope to Jackson.

"Thanks," Jackson said.

"Nee, Jackson." Susie wagged her finger. "We thank you. It was very convenient to call you from the community phone."

"Anytime. And I mean that."

Skylar huffed, sounding offended. Jackson glanced at her. She looked as hard as if someone had carved her from a block of marble.

"Where's my envelope?" Abram asked.

"Ha!" Susie laughed. "Jackson picked up the wheat berries at the co-op for me, so now I can grind whole-wheat flour for fresh bread." She turned her back on them. "Continue your conversation. I have things to do."

"So . . ." — Jackson took a sip of his coffee — "how about you, Skylar?"

"Me what?" Skylar's tone was barely civil.

"Convert with me?"

"Is that supposed to be funny?" She sprayed a table.

Abram hoped to calm her. "He doesn't know, Skylar."

Her steely gaze remained on the droplets of cleaner on the table. "If you want to get rid of your truck, phone, computer, and electronic and digital devices, you can give them to me. You convert." She used the back of her wrist to push loose strands of hair away from her face. "All I want is to go back to living like a normal human again." She rubbed the middle of her forehead, making circles.

"I imagine Ariana wants to return to living human again too," Abram whispered.

"Maybe." Skylar made wide sweeps with a clean cloth, wiping off the spray.

Abram pulled out a chair and sat across from Jackson. "Thanks again for offering us a ride to the doctor's office."

Jackson nodded. "Sure. And after your initial visit and the testing, I'll be available for your appointment in January. I have the first visit marked on my calendar. With winter here and construction slowing to a crawl, I have very little work going on."

Skylar glanced up, brow raised, but she said nothing.

"I know," Jackson said. "You're thinking, 'That explains a lot.' "

"Well, I'm grateful you can take us," Abram said.

Skylar plopped the tray on the table in front of Jackson. "Nothing better to do? How is that possible? Oh, because you get to enjoy the ambiance of the Amish café, and then you get in your truck and drive to your home with its television, computer, and Internet. I had those things once. Then the parents I grew up with were thrilled to leave me in this hellhole. Anything to get me off their hands. What a stroke of luck! I turned out not to be theirs. And the poor Brennemans, my biological family, are stuck with me and are too kind to kick me out." She picked up the tray and slung the cutlery across the room. "How's that for honesty?" Skylar walked toward the front door.

Abram and Jackson started to follow her.

She turned. "Don't." She pointed at each of them. "Or I promise I'll disappear the first chance I get. Me, the cash I took from the register, and the clothes on my back."

Abram stopped cold. He didn't understand her, but he believed she was in the mood to follow through on her threat. That would break his Mamm's heart.

Twenty-Nine

The sleet was like tiny needles against Skylar's face. She crossed her arms and buried her fingers. Why couldn't she have thought to grab her coat before storming off? As much as she wanted the warmth, her pride wouldn't let her go back for it. She didn't know where she was going, so she left that up to her legs as she put one foot in front of the other.

Nausea clawed at her throat, and her head spun. She should pop her one remaining pill immediately. But if she didn't make a drug connection soon, there were tougher times ahead. Besides, the pill was a downer, and if she wanted any sleep tonight, she would need it later.

She heard a horse and buggy approaching from behind. Was it one of the Brennemans? She walked faster, but it soon came alongside her and slowed. She looked up, expecting to see Abram, despite her threat. But it was Susie, and the clear vinyl window was open.

"Where are you going?" Susie yelled over the thumping hoofs.

"Go home, please."

"Is that where you're headed?"

"I don't know. But take a hint, Susie, and go away."

Susie wasn't completely awful, but at the moment Skylar hated everything and everyone.

"Hey, at least take this." Susie slowed the horse and tossed Skylar her coat. Skylar ignored it, letting it fall on the ground. She kept walking, face forward.

"You won't get far on the money you took from the register."

"Far enough."

The road under Skylar's feet seemed to sway like a rope ladder over a deep canyon. "Consider it payment toward the hours I worked at your café."

Susie sped up the buggy. "You're really selfish, you know that!"

"That seems to be the general consensus."

"I'm not against you, Skylar."

"Yeah, right. You don't want me in that buggy any more than you want to share your bedroom with me or be my sister." Skylar refused to continue this ridiculous conversation, so she turned and started walking across an open field. That would stop Susie. The buggy couldn't follow her, and Susie couldn't yell that loud.

What to do now? Maybe she should call her mom. She wasn't against begging at this point. Even if Ariana had won her parents' hearts, they owed Skylar something — like paying for her room and board, returning her car and cell phone, and giving her some pocket money. Right?

"Skylar!" Susie breathed.

Skylar turned to see Susie running after her, carrying Skylar's coat. When Susie caught up with her, she matched Skylar's pace. "Could you stop acting like a brat and tell me what's wrong?"

"I'm done. I don't care if my biological family never speaks to me again. I don't care if I never see any of you ever again."

"I've got news for you, sis. There is no way you took enough money from the register to cover whatever plan you've come up with, especially if your boyfriend isn't around to help you."

"You don't know me. I could have a dozen friends waiting to help me."

"But you don't."

"What makes you so sure?"

"If you had someone who'd whisk you

away, you'd have left after the first night. You think everyone around here is too stupid to see the truth. We're not. We're trying to give you space, but we're not blind, Skylar."

"Well, well, Susie Q, the little Miss Old Order Amish homemaker who's too young to have a husband, has it all figured out?"

Susie tilted her head straight back, looking at the sky. "Help me!" She straightened. "You are such a pain, and the hardest part is that you enjoy it. Behind all your prickles, you're really unhappy. None of us wants it to be that way. But you don't want to do anything to change it."

"And what would I do? Convert to your religion?"

"You join the Amish church? No." Susie grabbed Skylar's arm. "What have we done to make you think we are on a mission to convert you? We'd like you to see the truth, but becoming Amish isn't what we want. You are our sister, no matter what you believe."

Nausea rolled through her, and dizziness spun her head. What were the next few days going to be like if she didn't find a supplier? Skylar pulled free and started walking again. "I've heard the same speech from our parents."

"It isn't a speech, and if you're too stubborn to see that, I don't know how else to convince you. Now come back to the buggy with me."

"No."

Susie put her hand on Skylar's shoulder. "I could barely get the horse and rig off the road. It could get hit by a car."

"Then you should go back."

"I'm not leaving without you."

"Why?"

"Because you're my sister!"

"No, I'm not."

"You're my sister whether you like it or not."

Skylar slowed her pace. Her nausea was so strong she could feel it in her throat. "I don't want to be your sister."

"Ya, well, you can't do anything about it."

"I can leave."

"And I can follow."

Skylar had to stop. She put her hands on her knees, breathing heavily. Why was the nausea so bad already? "What will it take for all of you to just leave me alone?"

"Come to the buggy for starters."

Skylar shook her head. "Why would you go to all this trouble to get me to come back?"

"Because I actually love you. So do

Mamm and Daed and Abram and Mark and Martha and everyone else. Even though you have been nothing but a problem, you're a part of the family. You can run away and never see us again, but Mamm will still pray for you and worry about you. And so will the rest of us. It's the way things work!"

Skylar's breath came in short, choppy gasps. "You didn't even know I existed until a few months ago."

"But we do now. And trust me, if I could pray away how I feel about you, I would. And just so we're clear, despite your potential to be likable, you're really not. Aside from that, for reasons only God can fathom, I love you."

Skylar held out her hand for her coat, and Susie passed it to her. Skylar slid into it, glad for the warmth. She pulled a pack of cigarettes from her pocket and put one in her mouth. "That was sweet." She lit the cigarette. "It was, but like I said, I'm done." She inhaled a lungful of smoke. "I'm just done."

"With?" Susie scooped something off the ground.

"All of this. I don't want any of it."

"Stop being such a coward."

Skylar blew smoke at Susie's sweet, prayer-Kapp-adorned head. "Excuse me?"

"You heard me."

"You don't know what it's like —"

"I know that you have an entire house full of people who love you. They love you enough to put up with your selfish nonsense."

"Do you know how cheap the word *love* is? Everyone says it. No one does it."

"You push people away and then blame them for not being close to you." Susie held up the baggie that had a lone pill. "Drop something?"

Skylar dug into her coat pocket. That's what Susie had scooped from the ground. Apparently it had fallen out when she took the cigarettes from her pocket. "I need that. It's the only one I have left."

"And the guy you've been looking for is supposed to bring you more."

"Yeah. But he's not coming, so I'm on my own, which means I need to find a decent-sized town, one with a pool hall or a dive bar."

"You would be walking all night. And even if you got there, how would you find what you're looking for?"

Skylar shrugged. "Someone is always selling."

"Then what?"

"I don't know."

"You have about fifty dollars. Will that cover even one night at a hotel?"

"I can figure it out."

Susie scoffed. "Yeah, because you've always done so well on your own."

Skylar inhaled again. "You have a strange way of convincing someone to come home with you."

"Tough love, because I'm done sugarcoating it for you." Susie removed the pill from the bag. "You can have it back when you admit it."

"Admit what?"

"That I'm your sister. That the Brennemans you so enjoy looking down on are your family."

"I only have that one pill left."

"Then you better say it, or I'll throw it as far as I can. And if you can find it in the wet weeds, it'll be a melted, yucky mess."

Skylar looked at the pill. It seemed to her that Susie was very comfortable discussing drugs, as if she'd known about Skylar's stash. "Did you know about the pills?"

"No, but I'm not surprised. Now say it."

"What difference does it make?"

"What difference does it make?" Susie mocked. "You fight for something that cares nothing about you." Susie held up the pill. "But you discount who I am as your sister.

Do you have any idea how much that hurts? Don't let something that cares nothing about you control your life. It will make you as apathetic as it is. Fight, Skylar. Decide that you, your family, and your future are worth more than these stupid pills!"

"Wow." Skylar tossed her cigarette on the ground and smashed it with the toe of her boot. "That's been building for a while."

"Ya, it's from putting up with you. You should try it sometime."

"I did. It turned me to drugs."

"Not funny."

"It was a little funny."

"Tell me I'm your sister."

"Why?"

"Because there's magic in it. Power in admitting you're connected to me, connected to the whole family. It's you choosing to care that we're sisters. Say it, because I'm hoping that will break through your apathy. Because" — Susie thudded her chest with her palm — "I need to hear it."

What had Susie done to her? Skylar's eyes filled with tears. And she was positive she heard the ice around her heart begin to crack. "You're my sister," she whispered.

Susie clutched her, holding her tight. "Denki." Susie backed away, breathing hard. "Now" — she held up the pill and slid it into her coat pocket — "let's go home."

Nausea hit so hard that Skylar gagged. She put her hands on her knees and threw up.

Susie passed her a tissue. "Hugging me wasn't that bad."

Skylar wiped her mouth. "The proof states otherwise."

Susie chuckled and wrapped her arm around Skylar's shoulders. "Kumm, you stubborn thing. Let's get you home." Susie directed her toward the buggy. She helped Skylar into the passenger seat and then hurried to the other side.

"I really don't think I can do it."

"Do what?"

Skylar sniffed. "Get clean."

"Of course you can."

Skylar looked at Susie as she drove. Despite her sister's firm words, her demeanor was soft and nurturing.

"How do you know?" Skylar asked.

"Because you're a Brenneman."

The statement thawed a little more of Skylar's heart. She rode in silence, allowing the strange sensation coursing through her to do its thing, whatever it was. Relief? Love? Hope?

When the Brenneman house came into

view, Skylar remembered the others were at the café. "What about Abram and Martha?"

"Jackson will bring them home." Susie pulled the buggy in front of the house. "Sky, don't change your mind about getting clean. The only other option is really stupid. I mean, seriously, what's the plan? To do whatever kind of drugs you do for the rest of your life?"

"You're actually pretty smart. You know that?"

"I do. It's you I've had a hard time convincing." Susie grinned and set the brake and came around to Skylar's side.

Her legs were like wet noodles. "I don't understand. I've never reacted this much this early on. I've been cutting back, and I still have some in my system."

"I don't know. Maybe you're more addicted now." Susie supported her as they walked inside and into the living room.

Lovina came down the stairs, and as soon as she spotted them, she ran to Skylar's side. "What happened?"

Skylar eased onto the couch. "I'm all right."

"Are you sick?"

"In a sense."

"Should I call a doctor?"

"No, they've got nothing for someone like me."

Susie sat next to her on the couch.

Skylar gazed up at Lovina. "I've been taking pills while I've been here."

Lovina nodded. "I know. I found a bottle of pills the day we herded the cows. And you took some of Salome's pain pills."

It was embarrassing to realize that everyone around her was aware of her shortcomings. The one day she had done something right by helping a nephew to safety, she'd marred it by dropping the bottle of pills, which resulted in Lovina finding it. Then she stole from the boy's mother.

The desire to be her best self pulled her, much like the desire for drugs. "I'm ready to get clean."

Susie took the pill from her coat pocket and set it on the beat-up coffee table.

Skylar's body screamed for more than the one remaining pill, and the miserable desire to grab it and shove it into her mouth was a clue to just how much she needed to get clean.

Lovina knelt and put her hand on Skylar's head. "How do you know you don't need a doctor?"

"Because I'm a Brenneman."

Lovina grabbed Skylar and pulled her to

her chest in a hug. "I love you," she whispered.

Maybe she did.

Despite the embrace Skylar stared over Lovina's shoulder at the pill on the table. Could she really get clean and stay clean?

Susie's words played in her head. "Of course you can. Because you're a Brenneman."

Nausea rolled. Her skin ached. And her head pounded. But was that odd feeling in her chest the stirring of hope?

THIRTY

Classical piano music filled the car as Ariana glanced up from her book to look out the side window. Just beyond the highway safety rail was a marsh that stretched to the horizon. A white egret flew from somewhere and landed in the muddy muck, its long, knobby legs keeping its body well above the murky water.

Seeing nature and historical buildings and highways that went on forever, and cafés and hotels and libraries and bookstores and museums of all kinds, and dozens of other things over the last ten days had fascinated her. Nothing looked as simplistic and as matter-of-fact in real life or in an exhibit as it did in a book, online, or in a documentary.

The smell of decomposing plants and thick, stagnant mud filled the car. She crinkled her nose. "Yuck."

Nicholas looked concerned as he turned down the volume. "What's going on, Ari?"

His kind tone was a thousand miles from where it'd been during her first week with him. He'd somehow tapped into his fatherly side, and currently he was at the ready, wanting to help her navigate anything that attacked her "gentle senses," as he called them.

She freed one hand from the book and pinched her nose. "I thought the description of marshland at the Georgia Aquarium was thorough. Once again pictures and words do not match the real thing."

Nicholas's shoulders relaxed, and he laughed long and hearty. "True."

She understood his relief that the only thing wrong was a smell. Not too many miles back she'd reacted strongly to a billboard image of half-nude women inviting men to take the next exit and visit a gentleman's club. And different women in various provocative positions had been plastered on billboard after billboard during this leg of the journey. She had heard of such advertising, but the in-your-face obscenity of it all had mortified her, making her heart race, and she couldn't keep the tears at bay.

Nicholas had tried to help her accept the reality without taking it to heart. How did a person do that? How could someone not

405

take that to heart? Before she'd come to terms with the billboards, they passed a nude bar, boldly advertising women as if they were today's special at a grocery store. The buildings were just off the road, up close and personal, and that had sliced even deeper than the billboards, dismantling all she had thought she understood of life and worldliness and meanness.

In order to get a grip, she'd buried her head in her book, distancing herself from reality. The Englisch world was a mixture of fascinating beauty and deviant horror.

"Where are we?"

Nicholas turned the radio down. "A few minutes outside of Savannah."

Ariana stretched. "What time is your friend expecting us?"

Nicholas had an old friend from college who had visited him at Christmastime the last few years, and Nicholas had promised to come here to see the Victorian home he'd been restoring. Nicholas said this meandering trip, crisscrossing parts of the East Coast by plane and car, was a perfect time to do that.

"He'll meet us for dinner, and then we'll stay with him tonight. We have about four hours to explore Savannah before then."

"Okay."

Another billboard loomed ahead, and she returned to her book. She'd found a strange new interest — psychology. She felt like a sponge, and the study of behavior and the mind was like water. Psychology seemed to be all about understanding and embracing the human experience, regardless of race, socioeconomic status, or religion. Just the term *socioeconomic status* fascinated her. But this particular self-help book was about the dilemma of obedience. It was a dilemma all right, but she wasn't sure she'd find answers in the author's opinion in black ink on glaring white pages. That would be too easy, and life wasn't easy.

"Quiz?" Nicholas asked.

She looked from her book to him, hoping not to see another naked backside on a billboard. "Sure. Go."

"Music?" He turned up the radio.

" 'I,' by Yiruma. Real name: Lee Ru-ma. He's a thirty-eight-year-old composer and pianist from South Korea. His style is somewhere between New Age and contemporary classic. Did you change playlists? Because last I heard, Ashkenazy was playing Chopin."

"I did, and you covered the history of both Ashkenazy and Chopin yesterday. Excellent." He pointed out the window. "Type of bridge?"

"Suspension. It's where the load-bearing portion is hung below the suspension cables. The first ones were built in the early nineteenth century."

"Body of water?"

"Savannah River. A major waterway in the Southeast and most of the border between South Carolina and Georgia."

"Man alive, girl, you learn fast."

"Not really, since you warn me at least a few hours or even a couple of days before you do a pop quiz. We scour museums, and you ask about things I'll never forget. And there's always Wikipedia for a quick resource on towns, bridges, and waterways."

"Do you mind the pop quizzes?"

"It's a game to me. At least so far."

He smiled. "Good. I know I've said this before, but you're very easy to travel with."

"Except for the occasional panic over billboards and dive bars."

"There is no end to learning of harsh new realities, no end to hurting anew when we learn of difficult things. It's not a bad thing to be disappointed and hurt, Ari. It still happens to me at times when I hear something on the news. I think it means we long for a kinder, more loving world."

"I guess that's a pretty good way of looking at it." She gazed out the window, watching sunlight sparkle off the water as barges and boats navigated the river. He, too, was surprisingly easy to travel with, but it would feel weird to say that.

"Favorite place in Atlanta?"

She had to mull over that one. It was only seven hundred miles from Nicholas's home to Savannah. But they'd zigzagged from here to there, hitting a few places he thought she should see. Thus far they'd gone to Washington DC, Chattanooga, Asheville, Charlotte, and Atlanta.

They'd flown to Atlanta, where they navigated the largest airport she'd been in yet. Apparently Atlanta was on his list because the High Museum of Art had exhibits of dresses, from breathtaking gowns worn by royalty in the 1860s to modern designers. Nicholas had wanted to broaden her view of clothing through the centuries. The experience had been an eyeopener, but it wasn't her favorite. They also visited the zoo, ate late in a restaurant that overlooked the city and all its lights, and went to an a cappella performance at the Fox Theatre. If there was one thing the Amish were familiar with, it was a cappella singing. But the Amish didn't sing like those performers.

Then Nicholas and she flew to Charlotte

to attend a Renaissance festival and the Southern Christmas Show, because some of Nicholas's former students were performing at both.

"In Atlanta? Fernbank, I think." The focus there was on international holiday celebrations, and by *holiday* they meant Christmas. And the exhibits showed how Christmas was celebrated around the world. Since she'd had two informative experiences about Christmas — one in Atlanta and one in Charlotte — and it wouldn't be Thanksgiving for another week, she assumed that Nicholas was pushing her to embrace the idea of a fancy Christmas. She stretched, ready to get out of the car. Something about hours in a car or plane made her feel simultaneously stove-up, tired, and energetic.

Her phone pinged, and she glanced at a text from Frieda. It had been two weeks since Frieda first messaged her. Frieda had suggested they not talk yet, concerned she might say too much and cause Ariana to change her mind about their reuniting as friends and afraid she'd cause a rift between Ariana and Quill. Ariana didn't understand Frieda's anxiety, but she didn't have to. All she had to do was respect it and give her grace. They didn't talk, but they kept the phone hopping with texts. They shared photos of their surroundings and messaged about good memories from their younger years.

"Brandi?" Nicholas asked.

"Frieda this time."

He nodded. "Maybe texting her will help her learn to trust you the way she trusts Quill."

"I don't think it works that way." One thing about traveling with a parent for an extended period was that she'd been unable to wall him out. He probably knew way too much. "I used to think the word *trustworthy* meant being an obedient, hardworking person who keeps his tongue in check at all times, regardless of how he feels."

Nicholas exited Highway 17 and banked right, following a sharp loop. "That sounds very trustworthy to me. So what's the problem?"

"It's one kind of trustworthiness. But that's all about self-control. I'm decent at that, but can I carry her difficult secrets without judging her, without faltering in my love and understanding? I doubt it, and I think that's why she's afraid to talk to me."

Nicholas came to a stop at a traffic light and glanced from the road to her several times. "First, self-control is huge. So ap-

411　·

preciate that and cut yourself some slack. Second, if anyone shares tough things with you at any point, you shouldn't have to respond exactly as that person wants." When the light changed, he turned left. "How flawless is the person who is demanding your response be flawless?"

While mulling that over, she looked out the window. For as far as the eye could see, there was a straight line of squares of sidewalk with green spaces in each one, as if each were a miniature Central Park with statues and water fountains. Huge oaks were draped with Spanish moss, and across the street from the green squares were beautiful old homes.

She rolled down her window. "No wonder General Sherman couldn't make himself burn down this place."

"I agree. It's something else."

"Park." She pointed. "Just park, and let's get out."

He chuckled and did as she said.

She jaywalked to the closest green square and put her hand on the nearest tree. "Look at this." Standing here, the trees looked like miles and miles of a flowing canopy.

"You won't believe the food here."

She focused on the end of the long street. Had Nicholas said something? "The people who live here have this breathtaking view every day, and look," — she pointed down a street — "they can take a joy walk to town or cafés." She pressed the camera icon on her phone and started taking pictures. In all her best dreams, she'd never seen anything like this. "Can we?"

"Sure. Let's go."

They walked, admiring the statues and reading inscriptions as they went. They went in and out of shops, some that seemed as old as the town and others that looked new. They came to River Street and walked down unbelievably steep, narrow stairs until they were on a cobblestone road. Some of the cobblestone was flanked by wharf buildings, and it separated the old buildings from the river. The area smelled of delicious food and history, but when the wind turned, the air hinted of saltiness, marsh, and the acrid aroma of a paper mill. As they walked, she snapped pictures and sent texts.

"Who are you sending pictures to?"

"Brandi, Cameron, and Frieda."

"Not Quill?"

"I'll send him one, but I can't be fair to Rudy and keep spending time with Quill or texting him like I do the others. I just wish Rudy had a phone. So many Amish have cell phones these days. But my district and his really frown on it."

"Religion shouldn't be used as the thread that sews everyone together like a quilt, all firmly stitched in place for life. Look around you, Ari. If God exists, He believes in diversity, and He made people to think, to invent, to make hard decisions. Now Quill, he's shown real backbone, and —"

"Hey!" She took a picture of an old brick church. This area had gorgeous trees, some live oaks and other kinds, but no moss hung from them. "Could you take it easy and not ruin a perfectly good day by preaching?" She would never get used to his rants about individualism and the importance of free-thinking.

"Sorry." He held up his hands. "I didn't realize I was being offensive."

They picked up their pace. "How about I start preaching the gospel every time you start preaching disorder to the Old Order?"

"That's fine. For every hour you listen to me, I'll listen to you."

"Except you totally discount the foundation of my beliefs, and yours aren't so easily dismissed."

"Why do you think that is? Could it be my reasoning and proof outweigh yours? Even if we both accepted that God created the universe and that the Bible is His Word,

414

no one knows exactly how He meant all the verses to be taken — literally or figuratively. Did certain stories take place, or are they metaphorical? The King James Version, New Testament, says, and I quote, 'All scripture is given by inspiration of God.' I read that last night, and all I'm saying is maybe 'inspiration' isn't the same as God literally giving every line of the Word to be taken literally."

"Wait." She paused, holding up her hand. "The Bible actually says, 'All scripture is given by inspiration of God'?" That phrase "by inspiration" meant something very different to her today than it did before the trip.

"It does. Second Timothy 3:16."

She started walking again.

"Ari, we've spent nearly two weeks seeing what inspiration does for people. You inspire me to be a better person. Inspiration causes composers to write music and artists to create beautiful paintings and writers to —"

"Ya, I get the idea." Confusion clouded her thinking. Had he planned this trip to plant that one seed?

"How can anyone tell for sure the way God meant for mankind to process certain verses? In Genesis it says, 'God blessed them and said, "Be fruitful and multiply, and fill the earth, and subdue it; and rule over every living thing that moves." ' Let's say that's exactly what God inspired to be written and there have been no alterations of meaning throughout centuries of translations. How does any preacher or priest or bishop know whether God was saying, 'Go, enjoy yourselves, procreate to your heart's content'? They don't. But your preachers teach that as if it's a command of God. And that's just one example."

He'd held his tongue for several days, and now his passion for her to find moderation in her faith poured from him. Thankfully, he'd stopped trying to totally strip her faith from her, but he still pressed her to rethink what the Amish believed. This was actually harder to discount than an overt attack on faith. Was there any truth in what he, a nonbeliever, said? It wasn't possible, was it? But he made sense, and she wished he'd never picked up the Bible to study it.

The more frustrated she felt, the faster she walked. "No matter how much I try to do what you want, it's never enough. You're always pushing me."

Nicholas matched her pace. "Don't be upset."

"You get to tell me your opinion whether I want to hear it or not, but you absolutely cannot dictate how I feel about it. Even the Amish don't do that." When her Daed gave a ruling that upset her, he left her alone to feel what she needed to and to work through it.

"You're right." He held up his hands. "I'm sorry. You're completely right. I just have so much I want you to think about."

"Could we walk in silence for a few minutes, please? Or maybe you could just stop walking with me." Was she really talking to him like this?

"As gorgeous as Savannah is, it has some really rough areas. I can't let you walk alone."

Silence, precious silence, reigned for a few blocks. Despite Nicholas's best efforts to tone down his opinions, she couldn't imagine having to listen to his freethinking views until next October. She longed for peace, the kind that would come with returning to Summer Grove and building a faith-filled life among her people.

Nicholas paused to read a street sign. "Let's cross here and go up the block. There's a place not too far from here called Back in the Day Bakery. Everything in it is the best you've ever had."

"Fine." She hated the sulky tone in her voice. It seemed that mood swings were becoming a part of her, intertwining with her personality like weeds entangling with crops. Maybe the unpleasant shift in her nature was a by-product of her love-hate relationship with this new world.

There weren't so many live oaks down this way, and none of the trees had moss. The houses and businesses surrounding them no longer looked majestic. The more modern buildings were run-down, and the feel of the Old South had disappeared. This spot could be any poor neighborhood anywhere in the country. One structure stood out, and she knew it was a dive bar.

"Wait." Pulling his phone from his pocket, Nicholas stopped walking. "I think I'm turned around."

While he messed with his phone, Ariana saw three scantily dressed women on the street corner. A man in his forties approached the youngest one of the group and motioned for her to turn around. Ariana's stomach churned. He pulled money from his wallet.

"Nicholas." Without taking her eyes off what was happening, she tapped the back of her hand against his arm. "We should do something."

"About?" He looked up.

"He's trying to buy her. We need to stop him."

"No, we stay out of it."

"Stay out of it? Where is your moral line?" Ariana started to walk toward them.

Nicholas grabbed her arm. "For hookers to be so open about what's going on, the police have to be looking the other way. It's her decision and her right, Ariana."

"Maybe she doesn't know there are better ways. We could talk to —" Ariana tried to jerk her arm free.

Nicholas tightened his grip. "If you approach that situation, you can't cause anything but trouble. It's dangerous."

"Hey," she yelled, flailing her free hand.

"Ariana, stop." Nicholas tugged at her, and she stumbled along beside him. "Be quiet and walk away."

"She doesn't have to do this!" Ariana focused on the woman.

Nicholas dragged her farther away.

She lost sight of the girl as Nicholas led her around the corner. Ariana finally pulled free, but when she tried to walk back to the bar, he stepped in front of her. "Leave it alone, Ariana." He held out his arms, blocking her.

"Fine." She stopped and gestured toward the bar. "But why is it that all you want to do is pull me away?"

"It's not your business. To her, you're the enemy — you and your middle-class modesty. If you approach her, a fight will break out, and she'll be fighting you, not the guy."

"Why?"

"Because you have no understanding of her life or respect for her rights."

"Her rights? How can you of all people talk about her rights? She's someone's daughter, like I'm yours. And I'd bet she's younger than I am!"

Nicholas wiped his brow with the back of his thumb. "Let's get out of here, and then we'll talk, okay?" He glanced at his GPS and motioned up the block.

Ariana shook from deep inside, and thoughts of the girl and so many others like her rocked her to the core. "I want to go home."

"Okay, we'll leave first thing tomorrow. We can turn in the rental and fly back tomorrow."

"No." She stopped, folding her arms tight as she tried to control her trembling. "I want to go *home.*" Tears fell.

"Come on, Ariana. We've talked about this. We have a plan in place."

"You'd let that girl sell herself because it's her right, but I can't go home to a safe place because it's too religious for your comfort zone? Where are *my* rights?"

Nicholas glanced down the block. "Can we keep walking for now and talk about this in a bit?" He clutched her arm and tugged, getting her feet moving again.

When Old Savannah looked like itself again, he slowed, and they headed to a bench in one of the green squares. She melted onto the wooden seat.

"Look, Ari." Nicholas's hands were trembling. "You have the rest of your life to live Amish, to be the wife of this Rudy person, and to please your family in Summer Grove."

"Stop diminishing my reasons for wanting to go home. Saying I only want to please my family is hypocritical. Who were you trying to please just then? I'll tell you who — the man who had the money."

"I was defusing the situation while you were being rash. It wasn't about trying to please anyone."

"Maybe, but that doesn't change that you continue to please yourself by being willing to blackmail my family if I don't stay here for a year."

"Blackmail?" He stared at her for long moments. "Okay, maybe that is what I did. But —"

"My life isn't out here. It's in Summer Grove, being Amish, marrying Rudy, living under the wisdom, guidance, and restraint of the Ordnung, where the black and white of what's on the pages of the Word matters. We take it literally, and we make it matter in literal ways, just as you do with music theory."

"That's a good, solid argument — something you wouldn't have been able to articulate without this time away from your people. But about three hundred years ago, music theory was used in literal ways. Before then and since, it's been used to understand how music works, and musicians and composers break every rule in order to free their creativity. That's all I want for you, to get free of the literal and be creative in building your life."

Once again he'd silenced her with his knowledge, turned her own words against her to make his point.

"Ari, honey, I know the Plain life feels safe, especially after what just happened, and in some ways it is safe. But it's also thwarting all you could be. You're so smart. You wouldn't look at the Plain life with such favor if they hadn't had a lifetime of teaching you their ways."

"If you'd had your way twenty years ago

when you learned Brandi was pregnant, would I even exist?"

"Point taken. Can we look at that situation a little deeper? Your mom was younger than you are now, but she was her own person when it came to making the decision to have you. She didn't kowtow to me because I was a man, or to the church, who would've been much kinder to her if she'd secretly gotten rid of you. Brandi knew every option, knew her choice would ostracize me, her own mother, and even her friends. Maybe it's different today, but twenty years ago no one agreed with teen pregnancy, not even her college friends. But she took all the information and chose what mattered most to her. Despite the sacrifice and how things turned out — with her not raising her own daughter — she was right, Ari. She was a young, mixed-up kid, and she was right."

"I have no idea how that connects to what we're talking about."

"Because all I really want is for you to truly know your options concerning life and religion and to make an informed decision that isn't molded by fear or by what anyone else wants, including your Amish family or boyfriend. For now, you are here, alive and well, and I —"

"God put me there. Look at the list of extraordinary events that caused me to be raised Amish. The Ordnung may sound manipulative and controlling to you, but I see it as God's wisdom, and the Brennemans *are* my family."

"The agreement —"

"Dad!" She stood, her words sounding like Cameron or Susie but not herself.

The word *Dad* seemed to steal his breath, and he ducked his head, shaking it. She had finally shot an arrow that penetrated his armor, striking his heart.

She fisted her hands. "Toss out all notions of suing anyone. Stop using God's Word against me. Let me go home."

He looked like a man who feared he was losing. If Nicholas came to God, it wouldn't be because she'd stayed. He was too set in what he believed, even when he was wrong.

She couldn't keep listening to him rationalize away what she believed while witnessing evils she had no power to stop. It was just too much.

THIRTY-ONE

The early morning sky was dark, and stars twinkled brightly as Skylar looked out the side window from the backseat of the carriage. It was almost Thanksgiving, and a foot of snow covered the landscape. The white layer on the road muted the thudding of the horse's hoofs. Abram drove her, Susie, and Martha toward the café. Cilla would arrive in a couple of hours since she wasn't needed until the customers started coming in. Abram thought Brennemans' Perks wouldn't be as busy today with snow on the ground and more expected by mid-morning.

Detoxing had meant four long days and nights at the Brenneman home with headaches, nausea, leg cramps, sleeplessness, crankiness, melancholy, and depression. Then, for good measure, Skylar had spent an extra week on the farm, learning to milk cows and tend the horses. The horse venture was her favorite. It was a kind of equine therapy for a former addict. Detoxing was behind her, and a lifetime of craving relief was ahead of her.

"Skylar." Martha nudged her. "You okay?"

Of all the maternal figures in Skylar's life now, her youngest sister seemed to out-mother the others. "Yeah. I'm good. You?" *Good* was an exaggeration, but Skylar had learned numerous lessons the past two weeks as the Brennemans pulled together to help her detox and find new strength to draw from. One was that love thought of others first. Martha was genuinely concerned. Step one in responding to others who cared: assuring the person she was fine. That was the easy part. Skylar lied all the time about how she was doing.

The hard part was step two: doing whatever it took to make sure she *was* fine. The *whatever it took* could be talking to someone, talking to herself, going for a walk, getting a hot bath, tending the horses, or milking the cows. She had swung from exhausted to edgy during her two weeks on the farm, and when she was edgy, she had to stay busy.

"If you start feeling jittery today, I'll make you some of my tea."

Martha's tea, a concoction of loose leaves she mixed herself before brewing, seemed quite helpful. Or maybe it was just the girl who brought it to Skylar with hope radiating in her eyes. Who knew? The only thing Skylar knew for sure was that she had too many people invested in her success to let them down.

Skylar focused on Martha, her angelic face illuminated by silvery moonlight on freshly fallen snow, and Skylar's heart wrenched. This fifteen-year-old girl was her little sister, the youngest of five girls. Since they shared a bedroom and a bathroom, along with Susie, both innocent girls had seen too much recently — Skylar puking her guts out, moaning in pain, and ranting with anger.

She put her arm around her little sister. How had this quiet wisp of a girl and Susie's humor-laced sarcasm softened parts of Skylar's stony heart? "I'm strong enough for today." She had voiced her concern at having to see people today, customers she'd been rude to or whose coffee mugs she'd overfilled or some other embarrassing thing in the weeks she'd worked at the café.

Susie turned from the front seat, and Abram looked at Skylar from the rearview mirror. All of them meant so much more to her this week than when she'd stormed out of the café two weeks ago. How had it happened? If five weeks of living with the Old Ways had made this much difference, what would a year do?

But could she hold on to her newfound strength? Love and gratefulness were like their own high even as her body ached. Her physical aches and low tolerance to pain might take months to fully go away. Odd how that worked — the body became overly sensitive to pain after using drugs to dull the pain. "I'm fine, guys. If I feel lousy, I'll let you know, and you can help me." Skylar squeezed Martha's shoulders. "Okay?"

She knew a lot more now than she did two weeks ago. She knew she needed to be in Summer Grove with the Brennemans for a while yet. They were good people, and she needed whatever weird magic they possessed. And they needed her help in the café. Other than those things, she had no idea what she wanted to do, and she'd talked to Lovina and Isaac about that. She felt new and different and weird.

Abram pulled around to the back of the café and stopped the rig. When she got out, she stayed with him, and he showed her again how to unhitch the horse from the carriage and rigging. She didn't care about a buggy and how to make it work, but after spending a good bit of time this past week in the barn with the horses, she cared about them. There was something curative about meeting the needs of such beautiful, intelligent creatures.

Using the halter she led the horse to the hay wagon and tethered it. Abram put the horse blanket over it. He'd put up a makeshift shelter of tarps and rods so the horses — their horse and Cilla's or Barbie's horse — could stay dry when there was precipitation. She hoped the thin protection for the horse was enough to keep it comfortable, but that was another lesson she had finally come to accept recently — periodically all inhabitants of Earth groaned under some type of lack, and people who were worth their salt learned to cope without taking it out on others or using drugs.

While Abram filled the trough with fresh water, she patted the horse and let it nuzzle against her. Where had her newfound understanding come from? Maybe desperation. She was seeking answers, and she had found some. Maybe the insight came from watching each member of the family serve her so humbly, reading to her when she was too antsy to read to herself and praying over her. The Brenneman family believed in prayer. Skylar didn't. But there was no denying that faith worked for them, and she was glad. They deserved the kind of peace that came with believing, and if faith in God and the Bible gave it to them, she was grateful. Of all she'd learned recently that surprised her, a greater respect for faith was at the top of the list. She didn't have to believe in faith to accept that it could be real. She didn't know everything. Her internal workings that hated religion had finally quieted. It wasn't likely that the grumblings against faith would ever completely hush, but she could reason with them, and that was enough.

"You ready?" Abram opened the café's door.

"Not really." She stroked the horse a few more times.

Despite all the progress, a large part of her was as irritable today as she'd been when she stormed out of the café two weeks ago. Apparently feeling good and peaceful would never come naturally for her. But she refused to do anything that would hurt Lovina, Isaac, or any of her siblings. And part of her ached to see her mom, to have the chance to say she was sorry for being bratty, for lying, and for all the rest. At the same time, an equal part resented the way her mom and dad had dumped her for Ariana. Now that she understood the concept of thinking of others first, she hoped she could manage some of her overwrought emotions and venomous thoughts.

"Don't go anywhere," Skylar whispered in the horse's ear. "I may need the soothing effect of patting you." She went inside, and something akin to nostalgia washed over her.

Susie glanced up and tossed an apron her way. "If you want to try your hand as an assistant baker, put that on. And if we're not too busy today, maybe you could work on organizing the loft."

"Sure." Baking didn't sound so great, but she liked the idea of cleaning the loft. It would get her away from the customers, and it would be a nice thing to do for Susie since she hoped to live there once her parents gave their permission.

She slid the white apron over her pullover sweater and jeans. The minutes slipped into hours, and soon snow began falling again, greatly diminishing the lunch crowd.

Skylar went to a table and began removing dirty dishes. Despite the lack of customers, her back ached, and her energy was less than zero.

Abram ran a broom across the floor. "You doing okay?"

"Everything hurts, but yeah." She sprayed

the table and began wiping it.

His eyes showed pride. He pointed at the snow. "It's good sledding weather. Should we close early?"

Martha came out of the kitchen, making a rare appearance in the front of the café. She had a mug in her hand. "A hot cup of tea and an egg salad sandwich."

"Thank you." Skylar took a sip. "Perfect."

"Sit. Enjoy. You've earned it." Martha picked up the tray of dirty dishes and went to the kitchen.

Skylar went to a table in the corner near the front window since so few customers were here today and she wanted to look outside. She stretched her back while sipping the tea. Snowflakes continued to fall. Would it be difficult to get home? She picked up her sandwich and turned back to Abram. "Have you eaten?"

"Ya. I ate while you were working on the loft. How's it looking?"

"Worse, much worse. Right now it looks as if a bomb has gone off. I think the loft mirrors my life. To bring order, I create utter chaos. Now I need to sort, toss, and give away."

"If it's a mirror of your life, I suggest you gulp down that food and clean up that loft."

She laughed.

The café door opened, and Jackson walked in carrying a crate. Skylar wasn't ready for this encounter and hoped he wanted to avoid her too. What had Abram told him?

"Hey, guys." Jackson's voice carried through the almost-empty café.

"Hi." Abram set his broom aside and took the box. "Thanks for getting the supplies for Susie. It's made running this café so much easier."

"Then it works for all of us."

Susie peered out the pass-through. "Today's special?"

"Please."

"You got it, Jackson. Just take a seat."

Abram took the box to the kitchen, and Jackson went to his usual table without noticing Skylar.

Cilla brought him a cup of coffee. "So how goes the sled building?"

"It'll be a speed demon, and I'm hoping to do a trial run today. Care to give it a whirl?"

Cilla laughed. "Me? On something like that?" She walked off, cackling at the idea.

Skylar's nerves were tap-dancing. Was she going to approach him or wait for him to do all the work? Before she could make herself budge, he glanced behind him, looking out the window at the snow, and spotted her. "Skylar." He spoke her name with such frostiness that ice could've formed around them.

It was suddenly colder inside than out.

He was Abram's friend and an asset to the café, and he'd been a lot of help to Susie.

She picked up her plate and mug and walked to his table. "May I?"

He rubbed his temple. "Actually . . ."

"Oh, come on. You're fine letting me sit with you." She sat. Then she fought with herself to apologize. "I'm sorry for coming unglued at you."

"Thanks."

She waited. He said nothing, and he kept his eyes on the register, the kitchen, anywhere except on her. "Is there something else I need to say, Jackson?"

"No, that covers plenty. We're good. Let's just let it go, okay?"

"I'd like that." She took a sip of her tea. "So you build sleds?"

"Not from scratch, no."

. It was apparent he was uncomfortable, and she thought about letting him off the hook by wishing him well and taking her plate to the kitchen. But she couldn't. Why was it so important that they work through this? Was it because she now realized that relationships mattered or because he was

Abram's friend or because he was a guy and she was currently without one? She needed to sort through her motivations, but she'd have to do that later.

"How then?"

His dark eyes stayed focused on the table. "I can't do this. I'm sorry." He rose. "Excuse me."

When he started to walk toward the counter, she jumped up and moved in front of him. "Wait. What's going on?"

He glanced at the customers. "This isn't the time or place."

"It is the time. Your friend is my brother, and my behavior toward you was unacceptable. We *need* to talk. Give me five minutes, either outside or in the loft, and then erect all the walls you want."

His jaw clenched. "We do this once." He raised a finger. "Only once. I won't be dragged into a second round. Agreed?"

"I guess."

"The response is either yes or no."

Where had his open, always-friendly attitude gone?

"Okay, yes. I got it." She glanced outside at the wind swirling the falling snow. Her ability to deal with physical discomfort was at an all-time low, so rather than going outside, she walked up the wooden steps to the loft.

The steps behind her creaked, and she knew he was following.

Once at the top she gestured to the lone chair.

"I'm fine right here."

"What is the deal, Jackson? Was I so rude a couple of weeks ago that you want nothing else to do with me?"

"Yeah, that's it. Can I go now?"

She couldn't believe this was the same man who'd been friendly and witty from the first day they met. "Fine. Go. Don't know why you agreed to come up here if that was all you had to say."

"Because you wouldn't let this go, and I don't want to upset the others."

She gestured toward the stairs.

He went down a few steps and then turned and came back up. His build was daunting, and she backed up as he came toe-to-toe with her.

"You . . ." He whispered, his finger pointed, and she knew his anger had the best of him. "The day we met I thought I saw pills pass from your dealer's hand to yours, but I thought *no way,* that it had to be my imagination due to my own baggage, because you were surrounded with rock-solid Amish people. I foolishly convinced myself that you were a better person than you were simply because of the company you kept." He touched his temple. "I let another druggie make me doubt myself."

"He was my boyfriend. Not my drug dealer."

"Yeah, right. I had too many questions after your outburst, so I pushed Abram for answers. Now you and I both know the score, Skylar, so don't even try to tell me otherwise. You can't imagine how much I detest that kind of stuff. I don't have it in me to let any of it slide. You have people around you that do. I just hope they don't live to regret it." He stared into her eyes, seemingly determined to totally shut her out.

"I expected you to get that this has been a really hard time for me, learning my biological family is Amish and having to leave my old life for this one. At the least I thought you'd cut me some slack since Abram is my twin."

"That's the thing about the kind of people who use. Without exception they think there's some reason their bum rap in life deserves extra grace and understanding. It's the way users think before they start using, and it allows them to believe their woeis-me and I'm-not-like-other-users bull crap. And they feel justified. They're able to live with themselves, and the rest of us can learn to cope or get out of the way. I opt for door number two, please."

"You only knew Abram from a job site, but when he quit that work, you went out of your way to be friends with him. You help with the café, and you plan to take Cilla to the doctor — all generous. But you can't deal with an outburst from me?"

"It's not about you lashing out!"

"The drugs? Good stinking grief, Jackson. It's not like I used any hard substances. I downed mostly C4s, some C2s. That's all, but they are addicting."

"Great rationalizing, Skylar. I feel so much better about this conversation now. The hardest drugs you used were just C2s. Cocaine, opium, and morphine are also C2s."

Was that true? Had she been lying to herself all this time, thinking that, because so many people used C2s as routine medicine, they weren't controlled substances like cocaine?

He turned, looking around as he put his palm to his forehead. "I can *not* believe I'm having the exact same conversation I've had too many times before. I don't want those memories resurfacing. Just steer clear of me, okay?"

"Memories?"

"Your life is on fire, Skylar, and not in a good way. I've spent half my life in a burn unit, and I won't . . . I can't do it again. Let's just leave it at that." He headed for the stairs.

She moved in front of him. "But I'm clean."

"That's good." The look on his face didn't match his words.

"You don't believe me? Ask —"

"No need." He went for the stairs again.

She stepped in front of him again, stopping him at the top of the stairs.

"I'm sorry, Skylar, that you don't get why I'm being this way, but I know there is no winning with addicts. Today's win is tomorrow's defeat."

She couldn't believe her ears. He'd just given a rousing declaration that she would fail. "You know what? Just go." As she gestured and moved to the side, her foot slipped off the top step. With her movements seemingly in slow motion, she fell backward. Jackson's hand loomed large as he grabbed for her. He clutched her shirt, and it ripped, but he slowed her momentum as she banged the back of her head against the wall. She ricocheted off the wall and flew headfirst down the steps. How could she witness every tiny movement but be like a rag doll, powerless to stop herself? Force jerked the back of her jeans, and a moment later Jackson's arm came around her waist, stopping her in midflight. They stumbled down a few steps before coming to a halt.

Jackson clutched the railing with one hand, steadying himself before he put her feet on the steps in front of him.

She grabbed the banister, panting.

"You okay?" he asked.

She rubbed the back of her head. "Yeah. Thanks." She sank onto the fourth step, shaking but grateful Jackson had caught her before she hit the floor. "Just go."

It sounded as if a team of horses were thundering through the café, and when the noise stopped, a group of Amish-clad family members was staring at them. "Is everything okay? We heard thuds," Susie said.

"Yeah." Skylar blinked, trying to clear her vision. "I lost my balance, and Jackson caught me."

Jackson sank onto the step next to her. "She needs some ice, please."

"I'll make an ice pack." Martha disappeared.

Skylar's heart raced. She could've been

seriously injured or even died. Feeling as if she were riding an ocean wave, she folded her arms on her knees and lowered her forehead to rest on them. But she saw Jackson motioning for the others to go away.

Neither of them said a word.

Martha brought her an ice pack. "You sure you're okay?"

"Yeah, Martha. I'm much too hardheaded for something like a bump on the noggin to matter."

Martha hesitated until Susie called to her.

Skylar put the ice pack against the back of her head. "I have no idea why we're arguing like this. We barely know each other."

Jackson propped his elbows on his knees and rubbed his temples. "Because I have raw, unfiltered anger against users. I try to keep it buried deep, and I gravitate toward people who don't dig it up — people like Abram and Susie."

She probably should mind her own business, but she had to ask, "Who was the addict?"

He hesitated a long time. "My mom," he whispered. He stared straight ahead, but it seemed as if he was looking decades into the past. "You and she are alike in that she used C2s — and the people who cared about her — to get her fix."

His words cut deep, but she couldn't deny they were true. "I never meant to use people."

"It goes with the territory. Users use everything. Even their own kids."

"How old were you when you learned her secret?"

"The first time I knew something was weird I was seven, sitting in a doctor's exam room, listening to my mom expound on how hyper I was and how I couldn't ever sleep."

"Oh . . . to get you diagnosed with ADHD."

"I believed I was out of control, and I started behaving like it. She gave me a free pass to do lousy in school and act out. I was thirteen before my dad began to put all the pieces together — her taking me to see different doctors, her getting the pills filled. He asked me one day how often I took them, and I said 'regularly,' just like she'd always said."

"So you took some of them?"

"Yeah, whenever she told me it was time. See, the best way to make a non-ADHD kid look hyper is to give him Ritalin before taking him to see the people who'll prescribe the stuff." He shook his head slowly as if he still had a hard time believing all she'd done. "My health records indicate that for most of my life I've taken Adderall XR and Ritalin for hyperactivity and Ativan or Xanax to be able to sleep. The thing is, she started out as a good mom. But she got so busy with sports and music lessons for my sister and me that she couldn't keep up. So she needed a boost to be the kind of mom she wanted to be. And it ended up ruining everything."

"That makes sense. I don't actually know how Cody got hold of the prescriptions he gave me."

"Happens a lot more than any of us want to admit." He shifted. "I still can't do this, Skylar. I can't hope you're staying clean, or act as if I believe it, or any of it."

"Yeah, I can see that. Could you keep your relationship with Abram and Susie, helping out as you've been doing? I'll slip out of the room when you're around, and we'll just be polite strangers."

"I feel like a shallow jerk."

"You sound like a man with PTSD, and I'm a trigger for it. We've both earned our way into that spot, and we have to deal with it. I'm here for a while yet, maybe three or four months. We can make a truce and keep our distance in the meantime."

"My fear is in those few minutes of seeing

you, I'll realize you're using again, and I won't care who's standing near us. I'll start yelling, and it'll get really loud and ugly between us superfast."

Her ability to rationalize away her drug habit had evaporated during the last two weeks. "Sounds fair to me."

Thirty-Two

The aroma of coffee and sugar filled the air as Ariana pulled a pan of cinnamon buns out of the oven. It was early morning, but Brandi stood at the island preparing the Thanksgiving turkey for roasting. The three of them had been baking off and on since yesterday morning. And the mixture of aromas was intoxicating.

Brandi clicked her tongue "Man, I forgot to buy wine."

Cameron reached around Ariana, a glint in her eyes as she stuck her finger in the icing. "You know it's a bad Thanksgiving when your family runs out of liquor before noon." She licked the sugary stuff from her finger.

Ariana laughed. "Yeah, Brandi, what's that about?"

Brandi put her hands on her hips. "You girls. Stop that. I need it for the stuffing . . . and . . . other recipes."

Cameron angled her thumb toward her mouth. "Glug. Glug. Glug." Then she gestured toward Brandi.

Ariana couldn't help but laugh. When it came to sarcasm and teasing, nothing was off-limits to Cameron, including their Sunday morning churchgoing. One Sunday in church they heard a faint noise rise and then lessen as the preacher talked. Cameron leaned in and whispered, "Do you know why it's important to be quiet in church?" She paused. "Because people are sleeping."

Now that Brandi and Gabe were going to church with them, Ariana tried to put an adult between Cameron and herself. But from the moment the service was over, Cameron kept Ariana in stitches with her observations.

When the doorbell rang, Gabe set down his newspaper and headed for the door. A moment later he and Nicholas walked into the kitchen.

Ariana and Nicholas had returned to Bellflower Creek five days ago. He'd dropped her off here, and they were both polite, but there was an uncomfortable awkwardness between them. Since they'd spent so much time together on the trip, she was scheduled to stay with Brandi until after the Thanksgiving holiday, as if she were a minor and the parents had a custodial agreement.

"Happy Thanksgiving." He sounded somber as he nodded to Brandi and Cameron. "It smells delicious in here."

Brandi washed her hands. "Thanks." She grabbed a dishtowel. "So what's up?"

"The thing we've been texting about."

Brandi angled her head, looking curious and a bit scared. "You want to talk about this today . . . on Thanksgiving?"

"I've wrestled with it since the day we dragged Ariana here last month. You've voiced the same opinion she has — to let her go home. So I'm here to give what I guess is good news."

"She gets to choose when to leave?" Brandi asked.

Ariana's heart raced with excitement. But Brandi was in no rush for her to go. Ariana knew that as well as she knew her Mamm wanted her home again. But good moms often pulled for what their children wanted over what the moms wanted, especially when the child was twenty.

Nicholas nodded, shoving his hands into his pants pockets. "Ari, I ask that you stay until after the first of the year, preferably mid-January, so that your leaving isn't hanging so heavy throughout the Christmas holidays. And I ask that you not tell your family just yet. Let's let Skylar go through the holidays before we shake up her world again, okay?"

"Mid-January sounds great." Ariana tempered her response, but her heart soared as she went to him and clutched him around the neck. "Thank you."

He held her, his palms flat against her back, like a dad who didn't want to let go. "I'm going to miss you." He drew a ragged breath.

Ariana stepped back, part of her wanting to do a little jig, but no one in the room looked happy about the announcement, especially not Cameron.

Brandi stepped forward and hugged her, more of a lukewarm congrats than a hearty one. "Good for you, sweetie."

"Thank you." She released Brandi and winked at Cameron. "We're still sisters, and it's your turn to enter my world."

Cameron rubbed each eye with an index finger, as if dust had gotten in them. "Yeah, we're sisters, and we'll stay so close that I'll be there to pick you up if you fall."

"After you finish laughing at me, right?" Ariana grabbed a bowl of icing and held it out.

"It must be time for you to go. You already

know all my jokes."

No one but Ariana looked excited or relieved. "Don't worry, guys. The bishop will ask that I have some settling-in time, but after that you can visit me. And when I prove where my heart is, I'll be allowed to visit you too." Or at least she thought so.

If Nicholas had realized how hard Brandi and Cameron would take this news, would he have waited? Did they expect her to temper her decision to get home as soon as possible?

"Brandi." Nicholas checked his phone. "We'll need to go see Skylar and have a sit-down talk between January 2 and 12. Can you look at your calendar and let me know?"

"I can do that now." Brandi got out her phone.

"It's none of my business," Ariana said, "but does it seem strange to anyone else that no one has contacted Skylar?"

"She could've called us, and she hasn't," Nicholas said. "It's best to let Skylar make those decisions. But I'm sure she'll be willing to talk by January and will be ready to come home."

While Brandi, Gabe, and Nicholas chatted, Ariana returned to the stove to ice the cinnamon buns. Cameron got a plate from the cabinet and held it out.

Ariana put a bun on her plate. "I think I should tell Quill this news in person."

No one — not her Amish or her Englisch family — would understand this victory or celebrate it correctly in their hearts the way Quill would. Added to that, once she was home, Rudy would want — demand — space between Quill and her just as she would if he had a female friend who'd been as close as Quill had become.

An idea came to her. "What did Quill say was his last day in Mingo before the family goes to Kentucky for Christmas?"

"Thursday, December 17. I remember because the next day is the last day of school before the holiday."

"Perfect."

While the Schlabachs were at the job site that day, she would go to the trailer, let herself in with the key Dan had told her about, and make Quill his favorite meal. But she'd make enough for all his brothers. It would be her way of thanking him and celebrating her victory of going home and saying a proper good-bye, although she'd probably catch glimpses of him here and there. She might even stumble into him at Berta's house one evening while he was visiting, and she'd stay and talk with him. That pattern was sure to repeat here and there over the decades until they grew old.

In two shakes of a lamb's tail after the first of the year, she was going home! Rudy would be thrilled when he found out and so very relieved that, rather than being gone a year, she'd be home after less than three months.

Cameron sat on the counter beside Ariana and dangled her legs. "You sure about this?"

"Am I sure?"

"Yeah, about going home so soon. You looked excited for a few minutes, but right now your eyes don't reflect any thrilled-ness."

Ariana chuckled. "I think you may be projecting your lack of enthusiasm onto me."

"Yeah, maybe so."

But Ariana did sense an odd reservation in her heart. It had to be because her Englisch parents were hurt. Had she cheated them out of nine months with her they could never get back? Was three months enough in God's eyes?

With the café closed for the day, Abram flicked soapy water at Cilla. She squealed and grabbed a kitchen sprayer and held it up to threaten him.

"I dare —" Cold water splashed his face.

Cilla burst into laughter, dropped the nozzle, and scurried toward the door.

Abram went after her and slid between her and the doorway. "Going somewhere?"

"I was hoping to, ya. But you'd have to move out of my way."

He wiped a hand down his wet face. "Back to the sink. We have dishes to wash."

She dropped her head, looking defeated, and started walking that way.

"Children, is there a problem?" Skylar called from the loft, where she and Susie were doing inventory.

"Cilla." Abram called back. "She's the problem."

"Cilla," Skylar scolded, "don't let him get away with any nonsense."

Cilla laughed.

"Thanks, sis." Abram couldn't see Skylar from here, but he was sure she was chuckling.

"Anytime," Skylar offered.

No one was in the café but the four of them. He returned to the kitchen sink. Today, like several days late last week, were good days for Cilla. She had energy, and laughter came easily and often. He longed for good days to be the norm in her life.

Her doctor's appointment was two days away, right after work, and he'd yet to tell her. He wasn't sure how she would take it, and because of that, he'd decided to tell her at the last minute. *Now* was pretty much last minute. He removed a stack of clean plates from the rack. "Can we talk?"

"Sure." Cilla continued washing the plate in her hand.

"Privately."

Her smile vanished as he closed the covering to the pass-through. Then he closed the swinging kitchen door.

She grabbed a hand towel. "Is everything all right?"

"Ya, of course. I just need to talk to you." He tried to find the words he'd been rehearsing, but they had scattered. Maybe if he opened his mouth and started talking, the right words would gather. "It's nice having you on the days you feel good, and then you and Barbie on other days. You two work well together."

"Ya, I know what needs to be done, and she's capable of doing it. She says that together we make the perfect woman."

"I'm glad she has you."

Cilla chuckled. "You said that wrong. I'm the weak one, so you're glad I have her."

"What good is being able to do physical things if you don't know what to do?"

She chuckled. "I like the way you think,

even when it's wrong. So what's this about?"

He cleared his throat and started explaining about the doctor's appointment she had on Wednesday afternoon. Tests would be run afterward, and then she was scheduled for a follow-up visit after the first of the year.

Cilla's face reminded him of cut stone as she questioned and balked, assuring him that she appreciated the gesture but that she was fine and he needed to spend his money in better ways.

"It's done, Cilla. I've already committed to paying the doctor."

That wasn't completely true. Was it necessary to lie to her? He'd agreed to pay cash after the visit, and he would owe a fee if they canceled, but he wouldn't owe for the full visit if she didn't go.

She stared at him, and he wondered what her next reaction would be. Would she storm off? yell? A moment later she tackled him with a hug. Too shocked to move, Abram let his arms hang limply by his side.

"You are the sweetest person I've ever met, Abram. Denki." She sniffled. Was she crying?

Abram wanted to return the hug, but he stood there like a goof, smiling.

The door opened, and Cilla backed away, wiping her cheeks.

Skylar stepped into the kitchen. "Oh." She looked at Cilla. "Sorry, I didn't think . . ." She pointed a thumb at the seating area of the café. "I'll just go back that way," she said as she disappeared.

Cilla beamed at Abram while wiping tears. "*Gross dank,* Abram."

Abram couldn't speak, so he nodded.

THIRTY-THREE

Quill slipped out of the model home McLaren was using for the workers' Christmas party. When the door closed behind him, he felt so relieved. He'd taken care of his responsibilities. He'd talked with McLaren and the other bigwigs. Then Dan had interrupted the conversation and told the men there was something pressing Quill needed to tend to at the temp house. His brother had run interference so Quill could get his nonsocializing personality out the door.

Quill pulled his keys from his pocket while crossing the parking area. The ground was slick, as if a layer of ice had formed under the fresh snowfall. He got the snow brush from his car and removed about eight inches of the white stuff from the windshield. He turned on the radio and drove toward the trailer. The tires lost traction for a few seconds here and there, but unlike five years ago he was now reasonably skilled at driving in this kind of weather.

His thoughts returned to Ariana. There was no way of avoiding that, especially when his day grew quiet. They'd texted some since their trip to the planetarium seven weeks ago, but he'd not heard from her in two weeks. He wouldn't break the silence. She was Rudy's. For her sake, he didn't want it any other way.

When he reached the trailer, he saw a clunker car in the driveway. A light was on in the trailer, and through the narrow beige blinds, he saw movement inside. Who was here? Their temporary housing didn't have much worth stealing, except his dog. Quill hadn't taken her with him today since it was so cold and he would have needed to leave her in the car while he was at the party. If he'd known Dan would help him slip out so early, he would've kept her with him.

He quietly got out of his car and walked up the few steps to the trailer door. The lock hadn't been jimmied. Was that food he smelled? He turned the door handle and saw Lexi near the kitchen, wagging her tail. Quill relaxed. "Hello?"

Ariana stepped out of the kitchen, her eyes meeting his, and he knew she was thriving. "Hi." Her blond hair was loosely pinned, with most of it hanging down, and she had on a thick tunic sweater over a flouncy red-and-purple floral dress that hit midknee and red cowgirl boots.

He had to smile. "What are you doing here?"

She walked to him. He expected her to stop, but she put her arms around his shoulders. "I came to say thank you."

He held her tight, closing his eyes and breathing in the moment. How many times had he prayed they would rebuild a comfortable friendship? She held him in a sweet, strong embrace — the best hug he'd ever had.

After a moment she released him.

"You couldn't just call or text?" he teased.

"I texted Dan."

"So he wasn't teasing about something going on here at the trailer."

"Well, he wasn't supposed to send you home early. I just needed to be sure you guys didn't stop to eat somewhere on the way here. Speaking of Dan, I also asked him to get the family to send pictures to my phone or Brandi's e-mail address so I can make a photo album for your Mamm. You'll make sure your brothers and sisters-in-law do that, right?"

"I will."

"Are you hungry now? I could fix us a small meal and bake theirs later."

"I love that plan. Whose car?"

She motioned for him to follow as she returned to the kitchen. The countertops were covered with various foods — unbaked piecrusts, cubed chicken on a chopping block, green beans in a bowl, and pretzel dough rising in pans.

"Nicholas originally bought it as a starter car for his youngest stepson, who isn't sixteen yet. He intended to get the body-work done and new tires, but since I've never driven an automobile in this kind of snow, he suggested I use it." She picked up a wooden spoon to stir a large saucepan filled with white roux. "And, boy, do I have stories to tell about my first snow-driving day. I slid into the ditch twice on my way here." She laughed, her cheeks growing pink.

"Are you hurt?"

"Not a bit. They were gentle but very scary slides both times."

"Scary, and yet you didn't turn around and go home."

"I was tempted, but I couldn't think of one man I know who would have, so I didn't. I looked up a towing service on my trusty phone and called the same tow truck to get me out both times." She pulled a plastic card from her dress pocket, either a debit or credit card. "These things are really nice."

"They are."

She lifted a piecrust off the counter and put it in a small pan. "I've never had one before, but it seems especially nice that someone else pays it off. An upside to Nicholas is he's excited to pay bills when I spend money handling things on my own or buying books, clothes, or whatever." She poured the roux into the piecrust. "Who knew spending money could be so much fun for the spender and the payer?"

Was she really in his kitchen, relaxed and happy and chatty?

He washed his hands and dried them before going to the cutting block where she had carrots, onions, mushrooms, and a knife waiting. "What's going on with Nicholas and the revised bucket list?"

Her smile warmed his insides. "I won. He's not going to sue anyone, and I get to go home next month."

"Really?" His tone sounded hollow. He wasn't ready for this.

"Uh, a little more enthusiasm, please."

He dropped the knife on the counter and did a jig.

"All right!" She clapped, beaming. "You could dance in the snow and make it even better."

"I'd need more good news to be willing to do that."

"Rudy and I are officially engaged . . . well, as official as it gets for the Amish before instruction class and such. But you know what I mean."

He knew. It meant by this time next year she would be married and possibly expecting her first child. "Congratulations, Ariana."

"Denki."

It also meant that when the church leaders learned she was engaged and living in Summer Grove again, her every move would be examined until she was wed. Did she realize that? Should he warn her? He decided he shouldn't. Maybe the church leaders wouldn't do that to her, and friends didn't give cause for concern in the distant future when there was a celebration going on.

"Going home next month."

She grinned. "I know. Can you believe it?" She dusted her hands together. "Enough about me. Tell me all the details of the supposed mistake you made and what Sanders really did."

Their conversation continued, covering a

thousand miles and only a few inches simultaneously. She told him of her travel adventures, and they laughed as they compared stories of adjusting to Englisch life. The weight of years of guilt and months of anxiety fell from him, and he felt as if he were floating at times.

Frieda had said he could tell Ariana anything he chose to, and he couldn't hold back, not anymore. So while he filled glasses with ice and water and put flatware and napkins on the table, he told her all about his life during the years right after he left, leaving out as much personal information about Frieda as he could.

They sat at the table and talked until the timer rang.

"You amaze me." She filled their plates with his favorite foods — piping hot turkey pie, baked sweet potatoes, roasted green beans, and homemade pretzels.

When she sat again, she held out her hand for his, and he knew it was for the mealtime prayer. The moment their fingers touched, she bowed her head, but he couldn't find his voice.

She squeezed his hand. "Are we doing the old-fashioned Amish silent prayer?"

He nodded, and by the time the silent

prayer was over, he'd regained his composure.

She put a napkin in her lap. "Frieda still doesn't want to talk."

"She will in time. She loves getting your texts. And you were her sunshine when you were teenagers."

"Was I?"

"Yes. And you wouldn't doubt that if you had read the letter we wrote to you to make that time easier. But I'm glad you destroyed it rather than turn it over to the bishop as he insisted. If he'd read it, it would've caused a lot of problems for Mamm." Tranquillity shone in her eyes, and he knew she was past judging what he or Frieda should've done . . . or would do in the future. "What do you remember about Frieda living with Mamm and me?"

"The church leaders came to visit often, and afterward Frieda was always quiet, brooding. It seemed her feelings were hurt, but she always denied that."

"My Daed knew what was going on long before I did. She wanted it kept from me too, but after he died, she needed my help."

"Please don't tell me she was assaulted and the church wanted to keep it quiet. I've heard of such things."

"No, nothing sexual took place."

Ariana released a deep breath. "Denki, Gott." She pursed her lips, compassion radiating from her. "I could never stand alone like you did. Not ever. You should be pleased with yourself. If I'd known the truth about why you left, I would've gone a little easier on you" — she held her thumb and index finger an inch apart — "when you returned five years later."

"Only a little easier?"

"Hey, I feel very deeply, and those emotions have to go somewhere." She poked his shoulder. "Apparently you are a trusted target."

"Somehow I'm both honored and terrified."

"Terrified? You?" She laughed. "So are you at all impressed with what you accomplished by leaving with Frieda at twenty years old?"

"No. I handled too much wrong, caused so much pain."

"You were young, without anyone except a sick young woman who needed you. Now that things are right between us, look at every other mistake, and tell it to kiss off. You couldn't have accomplished what you needed to if you had tiptoed around everyone's feelings."

"Kiss off? I think I just heard Nicholas Jenkins loud and clear."

"He's not so bad for someone who thinks he knows everything."

Quill chuckled. "Like father, like daughter."

"You know, you should be nicer to me. I have the number to the phone you leave on twenty-four seven. I could call you with an SOS at two in the morning every day for a year." A phone buzzed. "Speaking of calls, is that you or me?"

Quill pulled his cell from his jeans pocket. "Not me."

She went to the kitchen counter and got her phone from her purse. She burst into laughter. "It's from the towing business. You know, the people who got me out of the ditch twice today." She walked toward him, holding out the phone so he could read the text.

Are you in for the evening? My wife would like me to come home for supper.

Quill burst into laughter, and Ariana joined him.

All those years of her being hurt and angry with him no longer mattered. Her learning she wasn't a Brenneman and being pulled by the roots from her Amish home — that no longer broke her. She had a joy unlike anything he'd seen since before he and Frieda left.

If helping her get to this place was the only thing he ever did right in his life, it was enough.

THIRTY-FOUR

Christmas music played throughout the fluorescent-lit store. Ariana followed the prompts on the computer screen. Again. "What is wrong with this thing?" she mumbled, glancing up to see if Cameron was finished shopping and heading her way.

Cameron was nowhere to be seen, so Ariana returned her focus to the touchscreen. It was Christmas Eve, and there was a party at Brandi's house tonight. Cameron and Ariana were on a tight schedule, and now this. Worst-case scenario she'd skip getting pictures made until after Christmas, but she should have time to work on the album during the party. The Schlabachs had done as she'd asked and had e-mailed photos to Brandi. Ariana would put them into a photo album for Berta, a gift she'd stealthily give to her when she was back in Summer Grove. With Cameron's help Ariana had loaded the images onto a flash drive, which she'd inserted into this machine ten minutes ago.

From the corner of her eye, she saw someone come up behind her. "Problem?" Cameron asked.

Relief washed over her. "Thank goodness it's you."

"With that kind of greeting, who needs a dog?" Cameron pushed her brimming shopping cart to the side. "I got the snow globe we talked about and the photo albums. So what's the prob, Bob?"

"You said this thing was user-friendly, and then you abandoned me."

Cameron reached in and pressed the Start Over button. "I apologize. I should've known a woman who actually said the words 'What's a USB port?' less than a month ago wasn't ready to fly solo." She pressed a few buttons and slid the credit card through its spot. A popup with the word "Success" on it appeared on the screen.

The first picture slithered from the machine into a tray at Ariana's waist.

Cameron picked it up while another one printed. "See, the computer is very user-friendly."

"Or maybe it was giving me a sign that I shouldn't try to give a photo album to an

Amish woman."

"Maybe. There are signs everywhere. Like the one somebody put on an acre of dirt near my friend's house. It says, 'Keep off the grass.' Or the sign on the side of a convenience store that reads 'Eat Here, Get Gas.' "

Ariana burst into laughter and quickly covered her mouth. "You're so bad."

"But I'm good at getting Timmy out of the well."

"What?"

"Never mind. Lassie didn't want to rescue Timmy anyway."

While the pictures continued to print, Ariana checked her phone for the time. "Brandi and Gabe will be out front in fifteen minutes."

"I'll go check out." Cameron grabbed the shopping cart by the handle. "A Christmas party of people from Dad's work and some of Brandi's stage-production teams. Can I just poke myself in the eye instead?"

"That bad?"

"Not if you hide out in your room like I do." Cameron shoved the cart. "Meet you out front."

"Okay."

The week had been busy, brimming with the new experiences of cutting down and trimming a Christmas tree and decorating Brandi's and Nicholas's homes. If she never saw another twinkling light or Christmas tree ornament, she wouldn't miss it. But this time was special. She and her two Englisch families had spent a month observing every Christmas tradition Ariana had missed in her lifetime — going to Christmas parades, riding through magical places decorated with Christmas lights, and binge watching Christmas movies. *It's a Wonderful Life* was not on her list of favorites, although she wasn't sure why. She'd watched *A Christmas Carol* with Patrick Stewart twice and wanted to see it at least one more time, but again she wasn't sure why. She'd attended special church services with Brandi and family and, on a different Sunday, with Nicholas and family. And the main pastime had truly been shop till you drop, which often happened for the Amish too, just not her family. The Brennemans made most of their gifts by hand, including baked goods, or they bought something used and fixed it up. She was so ready to see her family, and she would in three weeks. That seemed even closer than it sounded, because the Christmas holiday had begun, and the week between Christmas and New Year's always felt more like a day than a week.

When all the pictures were printed, she grabbed them and hurried out front where Brandi was waiting. Cameron came out a few minutes later, and they were off to the next place on their list.

The day moved briskly as they wrapped gifts and prepared for the Christmas party, making hors d'oeuvres, dips, and platters of finger foods. Ariana made a few specialties, and when the doorbell rang, she retreated to her room. This was an annual thing for Gabe and Brandi, but very few people knew who Ariana was, and she'd asked to keep it that way.

Christmas Eve noise soon filled Brandi's house, and Ariana set aside the snow globe she'd dismantled. It was a birthday gift for Quill that she would mail to him months from now. She tiptoed from her bedroom to Cameron's, hoping Brandi didn't hear her and ask her to come downstairs. She tapped and waited.

"Come in."

Ariana opened the door.

Cameron was on her bed, watching television. It appeared she had a game of some type on the screen. Cameron hit Pause, stopping the movement on the screen. "What's up?"

"I don't want to spend the evening alone,

and I don't want to go downstairs."

Cameron lifted her controller. "You want to play?"

"Tetris?"

"Not this time, oh novice one. It's a game called Halo."

"That sounds pleasant. Is it Christmassy with angels and halos?"

"Listen, Giselle." Cameron tossed the control onto the bed and batted her wide eyes. "Halo's got nothing to do with angels unless the people shot go to heaven."

Ariana grabbed a pillow and hit her with it. Cameron rolled off the bed, and Ariana plunked onto the bed and grabbed the control. "Can this thing make you shut up?"

"Oh yeah." Cameron sat next to her. "I can zone out and be quiet for hours. But not tonight." She took the control and pressed a button.

The screen animated an explosion, and a character flew limply through the air. "I'm in a team death match right now."

"Turn that thing off. I'm not watching you shoot anyone on Christmas Eve."

"Fine." She sounded angry, but she wasn't. In some ways Cameron was the Englisch version of Susie. Cameron pressed the center button, going to some kind of menu, and then a different game came on the screen. "We can play Minecraft."

"Deal. I've played that with Trent and Zachary."

"Are Nicholas's stepsons any good?"

"They're better than me."

Cameron laughed. "Which tells me absolutely nothing." After a few moments Ariana and Cameron had small pixelated characters on the screen, and they began building stuff, getting materials by punching trees.

Tonight was reminiscent of so many other nights she'd spent with Cameron. After her homework was done, they often watched a movie. Sometimes all four of them — Brandi, Gabe, Cameron, and Ariana — would watch together. Usually they stuck to Disney films, and she loved the PBS miniseries *Anne of Green Gables* with Megan Follows. A memory of a movie Quill had suggested came to her. "Do you own *The Village*?"

"No, but I've seen it, and I'm sure we can download it. Seriously, you want to watch *The Village*?"

"Quill said that it's a good metaphor for how the Amish live and that if I watched it, a lot of things about myself would make more sense."

"As much as I'll laugh hilariously watching you tense and jump and gasp throughout that movie, I gotta say I'm confused. You're going home soon. Why would you want to watch it now?" She grabbed the remote control and pressed a few buttons.

"To understand what Quill meant about it."

"It's not the type of thing people watch this time of year. There's a certain feeling to holidays and traditions. Fall is notorious for horror flicks because of Halloween. Christmas has a warm and fuzzy feel to it, so people usually stick to warm and fuzzy movies, like . . ." She puckered her lips and narrowed her eyes. "Oh, I know, *The Chronicles of Narnia*. We haven't watched that one yet. We can watch *The Village* on New Year's Eve or something. People like to scream and shoot off fireworks then, so the mood of the movie will sort of match the mood of the neighborhood."

"Okay. *The Chronicles of Narnia* it is."

There was a tap on the bedroom door. "Girls?"

"Yeah, come on in," Cameron said.

Brandi had on a sparkly burgundy shirt and lots of pretty jewelry. "Gabe's coworkers have all left."

"So soon?" Cameron looked at the clock on her nightstand. "How is it already nine o'clock?"

474

"I'm fun and entertaining. That's how," Ariana said. "But isn't nine a little early to end a party?"

"Not on Christmas Eve," Brandi said. "We've had this same party for years, and most people need to leave between eight and nine. That's why we begin at five." She shifted, jiggling the doorknob. "But, Ari, the friends I told you about are still here. The ones who know about you and Skylar. I was hoping you'd be willing to meet them."

Cameron made a face that said Ariana should go.

"Can we watch *The Chronicles of Narnia* later?" Ariana asked.

"Sure." She dropped the control onto the bed.

Brandi winked at Cameron. "I have Chex Mix and sausage cheese balls."

Cameron jumped off the bed. "I'm there."

Ariana's nerves were on edge as she went down with Brandi. Should she change clothes? She still had on the jeans and sweater she'd slid into after they returned from shopping. Jeans were so much warmer than a dress.

A small group of men and women had a plate of food or a drink in hand, and half of them were wearing jeans. Those who looked up smiled at Ariana. Cameron navigated to her dad, and Gabe held out an empty plate. She took it and went to the spread on the table.

Brandi introduced Ariana to several people, and soon a casual circle surrounded her.

"Your mom said you've been traveling with your dad. How'd that go?"

"Good. I liked it. A lot." She doubted if she and Nicholas would go on another trip between now and when she went home, but maybe.

"What was your favorite part?"

There was a lot she liked about it. Listening to books and music and then talking about those things, researching the history of the towns ahead of time, and reading historical markers. Staying in different hotels, eating at nice restaurants. But she had a definite favorite. "Going to museums with exhibits on history and culture. When we began, I thought I would most enjoy going to various cafés. And that is fun. But piecing together the tapestry of who we are and how we've changed over the centuries is the best."

"Ariana owns a café in Summer Grove." Brandi put her arm around her.

"Had you traveled before?"

Ariana shrugged. "Some." She'd gone to

her cousins' homes in Pennsylvania and Ohio, mostly in search of a spouse. "Not very much."

"What was your favorite city?" a man asked.

Ariana had an instant answer. "Actually my favorite was also my least favorite: Savannah, Georgia."

"Best and worst? Why's that?" the man asked.

Ariana shared all that she liked and then told of watching the man pay a hooker and how disturbing it was to witness.

The man nodded. "I've only been to Savannah once. It felt a bit like New Orleans to me. Have you been to New Orleans?"

"No." And chances were, she never would go there or much of anywhere else once she returned home. She and Rudy might splurge and go to Niagara Falls. A lot of Amish couples did that.

Gabe came to Ariana, smiling at the small group talking with her. "Excuse us for a moment." He put his hands on her shoulders and led her to the table. "Fill your plate, and you're welcome to stay or disappear. I understand there is a movie on the docket for tonight."

"It's okay, right?"

"Sure. Cameron loves watching stuff with

you. Skylar would've loved it even more. She's the real movie buff of the family."

"How is she?"

"Your mom talked to, uh, your Amish mom for a minute a few days ago. She said Skylar was doing really well. Much like you, she's adjusted. Brandi and Nicholas are planning a visit in two weeks, the week before you return home."

It seemed strange to think of Skylar and her swapping places again, as if this had all been a social experiment of some kind. Ariana glanced into the other room, seeing the Christmas tree adorned with shiny bulbs, tinsel, and multicolored lights.

Cameron threw something at her, grabbing her attention. A pretzel fell from Ariana's chest to the floor.

Cameron nodded upstairs. "The movie awaits."

When Ariana left home, she'd had no idea she might actually miss this kind of life by the time she returned. She nodded at Cameron, but Ariana couldn't make the muscles in her face form a smile.

She had grown to like this crazy, mixed-up family where only she and Brandi carried the same DNA, but Gabe and Cameron had worked their way into her heart. She liked Nicholas's family too. His wife was quiet and his stepsons were loud, but they were family.

Ariana would never have another holiday like this — Christmas music, festive lights, and sparkly decorations everywhere. But all would become very quiet later tonight as they went to a candlelight service and honored the birth of Christ.

Was she sad at the thought of leaving? Did some part of her want to stay?

THIRTY-FIVE

Abram rolled the boring magazine into the shape of a cylinder and tapped it on his leg. The doctor's office smelled of illness and air freshener. Jackson had dropped off Cilla, Emma, and Abram about ninety minutes ago and said he'd be back around five. Would Cilla be done in thirty minutes? They had been in the room with the doctor for nearly an hour.

This was the day they'd been waiting for. After the initial visit and weeks of tests, the doctor was sitting down with Cilla and her mom to give them her diagnosis as well as a prognosis. Abram's nerves were taut. Could Cilla be helped? Could the severity and frequency of her bouts of illness be lessened? He tossed the magazine onto a table and looked out the window. There hadn't been a fresh snow in a couple of weeks, so what was there was dirty and half-melted, and today was unusually warm for the first week in January.

A door opened from the doctor's pod into the waiting room, and finally Cilla walked out with Emma behind her. Cilla's beautiful smile said she was pleased, but her eyes held a hint of sadness. A dagger of fear shot through him. But Emma was beaming. Had the doctor given mixed news?

Abram rose. "You ready?"

Cilla nodded. He wanted to know far more than that, but there were too many people around them. He held out their coats and put on his own. Without a word they walked through two sets of sliding glass doors and continued down the sidewalk until they were well away from the building entrance.

"How did it go?" Abram asked.

The three of them formed a small group, and Cilla smiled. "It went very well. There's no way to thank you, Abram."

If it had gone so well, why did she seem rattled?

Emma grabbed Abram and hugged him. "The doctor gave Cilla a prognosis of living into her fifties, which is twice as long as any other doctor has given her."

Abram scooped up Cilla and hugged her. "That's fantastic!"

"It is." Cilla held on to him. "It truly is."

Abram released her, ready to hear some specifics, but Cilla only smiled. Was that hesitancy in her eyes?

"It was the best doctor's appointment ever." Emma put her arm around her daughter's shoulders. "She pinpointed some of the reasons Cilla has struggled over the years, and she's made changes in Cilla's protocols that should make her bouts milder and less frequent. Apparently our other doctor was using older medications and protocols, but she should've been seeing a specialist all along. That's so apparent now." Emma grabbed him again. "Denki," she whispered.

Over Emma's shoulder he studied Cilla. She was smiling and nodding yes with every thank-you her mother spoke, but something was wrong.

Emma held him for a few moments, and he allowed it. They had received excellent news, worthy of a long hug from a very concerned Mamm who'd thought for years she would lose her daughter in her mid-twenties. When Emma released him, he scanned the sidewalks. Benches were here and there, mostly for the sick or elderly to sit on while their caregivers drove up to the building to get them. Abram pointed to one that was just a few feet from where they stood.

"Emma, Jackson will be here in twenty minutes or so. Could Cilla and I have this time to talk — alone?"

Emma clutched his shoulder. "You may have whatever you want." She grinned, showing her overwhelming joy. Before she walked off, she kissed Cilla on the cheek. "Focus on the gift you have been given."

There was only one reason for Emma to say something like that. What didn't she want Cilla to think about? Abram gestured toward the bench, and they took a seat.

"What's the bad part your Mamm doesn't want you to think about, Cilla?"

She fidgeted with her fingers. "I'm so very grateful. Let's talk about that." Her eyes filled with tears, and soon she was wiping them from her cheeks. "I'm sorry. It's all very emotional."

"The bad part?"

She shook her head. "It's nothing, really."

Abram watched cars pull into and out of parking spaces as he pondered what he'd learned thus far. "I've heard that when a young person learns they only have a few years to live, it's life altering in every way. Sitting here now, I realize the same is probably true if that young person believed she only had a few years and suddenly was told she had twenty-five more. It changes all your expectations, and maybe that is an adjustment."

She nodded.

He put his arm around her. It felt so right. He wasn't bumfuzzled, awkward, or confused with her in his life. Being himself came easy, and before her, nothing came easy.

"What is it, Cilla?"

She wiped away tears. "I'm a horrible person not to be totally thrilled with today's news. Please forgive me, and let's talk about something else."

"You're forgiven. Now talk to me, just two friends saying what's on their minds."

She looked unsure. "You're more than a friend to me, and I know I shouldn't admit that. But I have to in order to say I don't want to put you in a position where you do or say anything out of pity or for any other wrong reason."

He thought about her words. He supposed he should've known she liked him before now. Well, maybe he did know. "I won't let anything you say corner me. So just say it already. We'll both feel better."

She drew a deep breath. "It seems as if all my life I've known I would do well to live to be twenty or a little older at the latest. At an early age I adjusted to the notion that I wouldn't fall in love or marry or have children. When you think you're going to die young, it's easier to accept those things. But now . . ."

"But a longer life means you'll have the time to do those things, right?"

"Not really. The doctor says a good regimen will lengthen my life expectancy by decades, but I'll undo all that improvement if I marry."

"Marrying is bad for your health?"

"No, but having babies is." She covered her face. "I shouldn't be talking to you about marriage."

Abram clasped her wrists and gently lowered her hands. "Can we slow down just a tad? Your timetable for life was just extended, but you're mourning what you'll never have during that extra time? I guess you'll have to learn to live like the rest of us — with a long road of unknowns ahead of you."

"You're right. I know you are. It's just I . . . I'd hoped we would have a chance, a real chance, where I wasn't sick. And if we fell madly in love, we could marry and have babies."

Abram laughed. "You are as honest and

open as the winter is long. You know that, Pricilla Yoder?"

"Pricilla! No one has called me that since before I went to school."

"I had planned to ask you out when the time was right. If we fall madly in love, we'll figure it out then. Look at all that's happened because of a simple Internet search. New medicines and new protocols are always being developed. And maybe by the time you're thirty-five, some newer medicines and treatments will increase your life to sixty or seventy or more. Right?"

"That's true. Why didn't I think of that?"

"If we like dating and decide to marry, the only part of your hopes that we have to avoid is you having babies."

"That's forbidden. The church would never agree to —"

"Cilla." Abram put his forehead against hers. "You have to slow down all the what-ifs. Let's enjoy today for what it is and not put expectations on tomorrow or our relationship or the church leaders. *If* we decide we're right for each other, we'll know. And God will give us wisdom for the next step, just as He did to get us to this point with your amazing news."

THIRTY-SIX

From inside the café Skylar sprayed the vinegar solution on the window and wiped the glass with an old cloth diaper. Eerie silence filled the vacant place, and she feared this kind of emptiness would soon fill every part of her life. She'd spent almost three months growing accustomed to the bustle of the work load and the camaraderie with her stranger siblings. Both this place and her weird Amish family filled a gaping hole inside her. Somehow.

But it was time to go. They'd helped her, and she needed to give them their lives back. How hard would it be to live in her isolated world again?

Staying with the Brennemans had meant she was only alone in the bathroom, and time in that tiny space was limited. If she took longer than fifteen minutes, a sister would knock and enter anyway, or her brothers would pound until she yielded the room. Tempers flared at times, usually hers, but even if the human contact was an annoyance or an argument, she'd grown comfortable with the endless interaction.

But the Brennemans and their contradictory ways of loving-kindness and neverending moral codes couldn't help her get through the next hour. Her parents, the people who'd raised her, were on their way. She had to face them on her own, and she had avoided it for as long as possible.

Something thudded against the back door, and the lock jiggled. The door popped open, startling her. Jackson came in with a large box in both hands. January winds swept in too, and he had on a heavy coat, hat, and boots. The ground had two feet of snow.

He spotted her. "Hey." He sounded a bit leery and maybe confused. "A shipment came in, and I . . . I thought the place was empty."

"Not a problem. Just leave it."

"Okay. But there's more than this one."

She nodded, and he took the box to the loft. She continued with the windows. Staying busy was cathartic. In this bizarre world, being useful was admired and appreciated, much like getting good grades or having an outstanding performance was in her normal world. She'd come to enjoy all sorts of work

— from whatever was needed at the café to feeding livestock, milking cows, and occasional gardening. But the horses were still her favorite. She'd had no idea people did anything to a vegetable garden in October, but apparently some produce, like kale, red cabbage, beets, and Brussels sprouts, was harvested. Looking back, she realized that the first time she pulled items from the garden and they used them to make a meal, the connection between the earth and the kitchen table had an addictive feel to it, much like spending time with the horses. When the last of the produce had been gathered for the fall, she thought that work was done, but evidently November was the season to spread organic matter, turn the soil with a hoe, wait a few weeks, and repeat with a different organic matter. Seemed a bit crazy, but she liked working the garden. Well, at least looking back on it, she liked it. At the time she'd been annoyed by it because, for her, drugs murdered all pleasure other than using. She still hadn't heard from Cody, and she was grateful he'd abandoned her.

Jackson bounded down the steps. He was very agile for his size and build. "I'll grab the last two boxes and be gone."

He barely glanced at her. She nodded

anyway. The strain between them was still tangible, but it had seemed different lately. His body language and the way he watched her when he didn't think she noticed made her think that he no longer wanted to avoid her even though he continued to do so. Not that it mattered. She reminded him of his mother. Besides, it'd been ten weeks since she'd last seen Cody, and she'd survived just fine without a guy in her life. Actually, she liked it — liked that she was managing her emotions rather than the other way around, liked that she was beginning to feel somewhat whole without a guy stroking her ego and promising her she ruled her world. No one ruled their own world. Some thought they did, but she knew better.

She poured cream into a container and set it on the counter along with the sugar.

Piecing together her thoughts, understanding the essence of who she was came easier these days. Living Amish was murder on a social life and all things technological, but it was good for the soul — the intense quiet, the nonstop physical work, the ocean of love. She'd been clean since November 10. Nine weeks without worldly noise, peer pressure, or parental discord had equaled time without any drugs, legal or otherwise. It was funny that the things she'd hated most about the Amish lifestyle were the things that gave her the strength to stay clean. For better or worse, the Amish were one ironclad connected group. She often felt as if she were a puppy in a large litter. It was difficult to breathe as her littermates piled on top of her, but it was also a warm, safe feeling. Rather than fighting to be free, she had relaxed under the mound, able to breathe better there than anywhere else in this crazy world. But she would never, ever become Amish. They believed in a God who didn't exist, but that belief yielded a lot of love and contentment.

As Jackson walked back toward the stairs, she saw something fall from the bottom of the box, and she gasped for fear it was breaking open.

"What?" Jackson stopped, looking at the floor around him.

She walked over to him. "Oh, nothing. Sorry." She picked up several packing peanuts. "I thought the box was breaking." She held them out. "It was just these."

"You okay?" Jackson remained in place. If he really wanted much of an answer, he would set the box on a table for a few minutes.

"I'm swinging from preoccupied to jittery."

"I sorta picked up on that. Why?"

"My parents, the non-Amish ones, are coming here today."

"That explains your overreaction to a falling packing peanut."

She and Jackson sounded like really bad actors reading for parts — monotone and awkward.

Quiet stress wasn't her only issue. Anger and hurt churned inside her much like they used to do every day, and now the emotions made more sense to her. It came naturally to her to feel that her best efforts in the arts and school were never good enough, that she was a disappointment to her parents. But she didn't want to blame them.

Jackson seemed to be waiting for her to assure him he could go. Maybe teasing would help. "I'm not intense. Just really, really alert."

"Yeah, real stress is when you suddenly sit up in bed screaming, only to realize you hadn't fallen asleep yet, right?" His eyes held understanding as he stepped around her. "Life," he said sarcastically as he headed for the stairs.

Despite their agreement to avoid each other, they inadvertently dropped their guard on occasion, and what flowed between them was usually honest, painfully so at times. But there was also quick banter and unexpected humor before they retreated to their respective corners. But not today. She was too out of sorts, and he'd been caught off guard by her being here. The interesting thing about Jackson and Skylar is they didn't need a lot of words to understand each other. That was sort of nice, and it kept her from falling into her natural state of neediness. She didn't want to be that person anymore.

"Sarcasm. Just one of the many services we offer at Brennemans' Perks," she responded, raising her voice as he went up the steps.

"Exactly," he said over his shoulder. "I'll be gone in less than a minute."

"You're fine. It feels weird being here alone anyway."

"I bet." He disappeared into the loft.

If the Brennemans were even slightly more average Americans, just churchgoing Americans, like Methodists or something, she would consider staying closer to them, maybe ask to rent the loft or find a nearby place to rent. If God was love and nothing more — not part of a bunch of archaic writings — maybe He or She did exist in a universe far, far away. At least that would explain the very real sense of love her Amish parents and siblings had inside them and gave to her. It was tangible, and she supposed it had to come from somewhere.

Headlights reflected in the window as a car pulled into a parking space in front of the café. The lights went off, and she saw her dad behind the wheel and her mom in the passenger's seat. She rubbed her forehead, wishing she believed in prayer.

Jackson came down the steps. "You can do it."

"Sure. I can do *something,* say *something.* The question is, can I make myself say the right things in the right way?"

She wanted to be kind and let them off the hook. There was no need for them to be her parents in any shape or form. After a lifetime of feeling insecure, she knew that her insecurities were to a large extent just her nature. Based on conversations she'd had with Abram, he dealt with the same kind of self-doubt she did. So that wasn't her mom's or dad's fault. It was just life, she guessed. But when Mom and Dad learned she wasn't theirs, they took back the gifts they'd given her. Removed her from college and withdrew all promises of paying for her education. If that wasn't enough, they took her car, her phone, and her allowance.

Then they dumped her here as fast as they could.

No, that wasn't actually true. They had Quill pick her up and chauffeur her as needed while they drove here to get Ariana. And those were just the highlights of her proof that they'd been more than ready to dump her and take Ariana. Her mom used to love her dearly, and their relationship had flourished. But it had been taxed the last couple of years. And when the news came that Skylar wasn't actually theirs, it was a death blow.

Dad and Mom got out of the car, and fragments of memories assaulted her — some as warm as sunshine in spring and some as harsh as winter winds. They stepped onto the curb and headed for the door of the café.

Jackson moved in front of her, blocking her view of them. "If you're worried about protecting them, don't be. Thinking that way could make you cave in to what they want. Every word should have only one goal — protecting yourself — so that when they leave, you've done nothing that will undo your progress. Be kind if you can, but do it for the right reasons — your peace and contentment." He held up his index finger. "One goal, Skylar: self-preservation. You've come too far to let anyone unravel you."

Jackson sounded like a trainer talking to a prizefighter in a boxing ring. And she realized he was pulling for her.

A tap on the glass startled her. Her mom and dad were just outside the door, waiting on her, but she couldn't get her feet to move.

Jackson gestured with his thumb. "You need me to open it?"

She drew a breath, trying to shake the feeling of being immobile. "I thought you just said I could do this."

"Sometimes we need a nudge."

She pushed his shoulder. "That's me nudging you to get out."

He stared into her eyes. "Call me if you want."

"Thanks." She didn't know much, but she knew she didn't need a man to rescue her. Not anymore. Somehow in this land stripped of all normalcy, she'd reinvented herself to a small degree.

As Jackson went out the back door, Skylar opened the front one. Mom rushed forward and hugged her. Skylar wanted both to engulf her and to step away. A moment later she returned the hug. Missing her mom had been a constant.

"I love you so much," Mom whispered.

Skylar wanted to return the words, but love for either of them seemed buried under her anger and pain. When she backed away, Mom was smiling. Skylar couldn't return the smile. That would be like an affirmation that everything between them was okay. And it wasn't.

"We've missed you so very much." She cupped Skylar's cheek in her hand.

"Did you?" Then why hadn't she heard from them?

"Yes." Mom fisted her hands tight, making them tremble. "Love you with all my might."

Skylar remembered them making that gesture and saying those words all the time when she was little. Often several times a day.

Dad looked uncomfortable, but he moved forward and hugged her. Skylar's arms hung limp at her side. When he released her, she gestured to a table. As they took a seat, she went behind the counter and poured two mugs of coffee.

"This is a really charming café, isn't it?" Mom smiled while looking around.

Skylar set the steaming mugs on the table. "It is." She grabbed the cream and sugar off the counter and sat down with them.

"How are you, Sky?" Dad asked.

"Good. Better."

"Then everything is okay?" he asked.

Everything? He was kidding, right? She hated the angry sarcasm that churned inside her. It had seemed to melt away in the last couple of months, but here it was again, making her feel like an ungrateful brat. "No, everything isn't okay. But some things are."

"Sweetie." Mom's voice burrowed deep. "You said you're better, which is great. Do you mind if I ask in what ways?"

"I'm clean. Completely."

Dad clapped, making a thunderous sound. "That's great, honey."

When had she become *honey* to him? He hadn't wanted her mom to have her, and he hadn't given a dime of child support until she was four or five years old. The story she'd heard was that his new wife had influenced him to get involved in Skylar's life. A perfect stranger to Skylar had wielded more power over her dad than she ever had. She longed to mutter, "I'm not your honey."

Mom reached for her hand. "We wanted to see you before you come back. You know, to make some plans for the future."

Skylar eased her hand free and slid both into her lap. "So it's true. Despite everything, you didn't manage to get Ariana to stay even three months."

"She wanted to go home, and we thought maybe you were thinking the same thing." Her smile quivered.

"Skylar," — Dad softened his voice almost to a whisper — "now that you're clean —"

"I'm your daughter again?"

He flinched as if she'd hit him.

"You've always been our daughter," Mom said, her eyes filling with tears.

"Really?" Skylar pulled out her phone and went to the YouTube clip of them singing with Ariana. She turned it toward them. "Look at your faces. Listen to the passion in your voices as you sing to her. She's your daughter."

Dad lowered his eyes. "She's one of our daughters. You are our daughter also, Sky Blue. And for those times I've not treated you as though you were or as you deserved, I'm so very sorry. I'm hoping you'll forgive me and give me another chance. If I were you and I saw that clip, my feelings would be hurt too. And I'm not sure what to say to help you see how important you are to us."

Skylar couldn't believe her ears. He was apologizing for being a jerk most of her life? Had his coziness with Ariana melted his frozen heart?

He pushed his coffee to the side. "But

your mom doesn't deserve for you to question *her* love and loyalty. She could not have loved you more, sticking to you like glue, enjoying being your mom, working so hard to support your dreams. It sounds as if you're angry at us for sending you here. You're clean now. So I would say this has been a success."

"Stop!" Skylar was shaking as she covered her ears. "Are you pleased with yourself about this success? Your child, who isn't even yours, is clean. So now you want to return to pretending you care?"

Mom reached across the table, trying to touch Skylar's arm. "Skylar, please —"

"You dropped me like a hot potato, Mom. Did you want to do that, or did you let him bully you into one more thing you disagreed with?"

"I . . . I thought you were doing well here. Has it been that bad?" he asked.

"No, actually it hasn't. But this isn't about the Brennemans or how I'm doing. This is about you two shoving me out the door, taking everything away from me, and not checking on me once these past three months!" Why was she yelling at them? What happened to not blaming them?

"Sky, honey." Mom's eyes held disbelief. "You came here instead of rehab, and we took everything, just as we would have if you had chosen rehab. But there are phones, and we were giving you space to call or not call as you saw fit."

"But I see how it must've looked," Dad added. "In my mind you pushed us away, Sky. You were angry, told us to give you space, and didn't even want us to drive you here, insisting Quill do that."

Was that accurate? That's not at all how she remembered it. Then again, she had been high a lot back then.

"We've made mistakes, a lot of mistakes. Me most of all," he said. "None of them was a declaration that we didn't care about you. We're here now. Let's talk and figure out what *you* need so we can move forward."

She shook her head. "No. You wanted a new daughter, and you got her."

Mom wiped away tears. "You can't really believe that's what happened."

Skylar pointed a finger at her dad. "I think that's what he wanted, and I think you were hopeful about having a clean slate with someone who wasn't me."

Maybe Skylar was wrong, but his green eyes seemed to hold a truth he would never say — that he and Ariana had bonded in ways he and Skylar never would. Never could.

"I deserve your resentment," he said. Then he lowered his voice. "I was a jerk to your mom for years, and I ignored you. I regret that. When I look at how I acted, my heart literally hurts. When Lynn and I married, she poked and prodded me until I began to understand how wrong I was."

"See, I don't get that. Why would Lynn be the one to make you understand that I had some value to you?"

"I . . . I don't know. I was self-absorbed, and until her children entered my life, I'd never been around children enough to realize how vulnerable they are. Even then I bumbled in being a parent to you. Often causing a lot of pain. I tried to control your mom and you rather than nurture you. That's been made abundantly clear to me, and if I could go back, I'd do it differently. I promise I would. But your mom gladly gave up every opportunity for herself in order to make your life as good as she could. Criticize me if you want to, but you're not being fair to her."

Skylar hadn't prepared herself for him accepting any blame or respecting Mom, who was crying. Is this what Skylar wanted — to hurt them the way they'd hurt her? Remorse flooded her.

"Mom, I'm sorry."

She rushed to Skylar and pulled her to her feet. "I love you, Sky Blue. I've missed you so much." She held her tight. "Not a day has gone by without Gabe saying how the house feels so empty without you."

That felt good to hear, but Skylar was sure Cameron never said anything like that.

Skylar hugged her back. "I love you too, Mom." At least she thought she did. She wasn't good at understanding what it meant to truly love someone. Still, it was the right thing to say. "But I don't think I'm coming back anytime soon."

Mom grabbed her shoulders and backed up, staring into her eyes. "What?" She looked at Dad as if to say, "Fix this!"

Had he been more of a support to her mom over the years than Skylar knew?

He stood. "I've changed, Sky Blue. I'd like a chance —"

"I can't." Skylar should hug him, but all she managed was a brief smile. "I appreciate it, though."

"Is this your way of rebelling against me?" he asked. "Ariana is returning to this nightmare of a religion, and you're choosing to stay?"

Was it? "I don't think so."

"I can't imagine any other reason you wouldn't want to come home."

"I'm not fully sure why either, except this has been a fresh start for me, and I'm not ready to leave."

"So you're staying with the Brennemans?"

"No." She would, except that Ariana, the queen of everyone's heart, was returning in two weeks. Emotions were light and merry.

Dad choked up. "Where will you go?"

"I don't know." That was the great question. She had no interest in returning to college and no interest in pursuing a career onstage. "I only know what I'm not going to do. I'm not coming back right now."

THIRTY-SEVEN

Ariana pushed the last straight pin into place, weaving its sharp tip between the fabric of her cape dress and black apron. Finally it was time to return to Summer Grove, nine months ahead of Nicholas's original time line.

"Yep." Cameron was sprawled across Ariana's bed, her head propped up on her hand. She lowered her eyes, flipping through the photo album they'd made together. "When you arrived, you looked just like you do now." She reached out and nudged Ariana's open and almost-full suitcase. "You emerged as if you'd traveled through time to get here."

Cameron could be depended on to be honest at all times.

"Yeah, I get that time traveler thing a lot. But God is timeless, and evidently so are the Amish." Ariana moved to the full-length mirror, checking to see if everything was in place. Her reflection was jarring. Emotionally she felt modern, slightly traveled, and decently informed on numerous topics, but she looked puritanical and severely religious. She inched forward, staring into her eyes, and she suddenly felt at odds with herself.

Who was that young woman peering back at her?

Maybe a better question was, why did she feel so different now that she had on her Amish clothes? It had taken three months of extraordinary effort and patience to win the right to go home. And she felt weird.

"Cameron." Ariana moved closer to the mirror, trying to catch a glimpse of the girl she used to see. "Is it normal, you know, for the Englisch to be unsure exactly who they are?" She didn't think it was for the Amish, or at least it hadn't been normal for her. Decisions and viewpoints were limited to two choices: the right one as set forth by the Amish church and the wrong one as set forth by any views outside of the Amish church. That's how she'd regarded everything until recently. Now each subject splintered into a thousand viewpoints, many with reasonable validity.

Cameron sat upright. "Are you second-guessing whether you want to go back?"

"No. Of course not." Ariana held her gaze

in the mirror, asking herself that same question. Pleased at the measure of reassurance she felt, she lowered her eyes. Still, even without looking at herself, she felt displaced somehow. The odd feeling began a few days ago, or maybe it began the day she arrived. "I long to go home, but I'm second-guessing every thought I've ever had about life in general."

Cameron pulled her feet onto the bed and crisscrossed her legs. "I'm lost."

"Yeah, I guess so." Ariana opened a drawer and pulled out a stack of neatly folded black stockings, none of which she'd worn in months. "Whatever thought comes to me these days, I immediately counter it with oppositional data."

"Like?" Cameron studied her, listening carefully.

Ariana tucked the stockings into the suitcase. "When I woke up today, I was looking forward to attending an Amish Sunday meeting, and, *bam,* I was struck with memories of what I've read concerning home churches and the negative effects of obsessive dedication. Then I thought how wonderful it'll be to come under Daed's authority again and, later, Rudy's, when we marry. And, *bam,* I was hit with a dozen facts about giving up my autonomy, a word

I didn't even know existed until I came here."

"The horse blinders you grew up with have been ripped off. You've been forced to see the world around you, and you've learned that everything has multiple sides. Welcome to the new millennium. That sort of stuff happens to me all the time."

Ariana plunked on the bed beside her. "Yeah, I guess I now have a gazillion new ways of viewing myself, religion, people, and even God. It's not much fun, is it?"

"My grandpa always says getting old is no fun, but it's better than the other option. Having so many new ways of looking at things may not be much fun, but it's better than the other option — knowing only what you've been told. I would rather wade through a ton of 'oppositional data' and use it to decide for myself what I believe."

"And if a person just wants those thoughts to leave her alone?"

"I guess she'll do her best to tune out anything outside her chosen area of focus. That part will get easier once you're back inside your insulated life, right?"

"I don't know. Nicholas calls it a filter of analytical thinking. Some of the books refer to it as freethinking. Whatever it's called, I'm not sure I'll ever make it stop."

"But it'll grow fainter. You'll just need a little time."

"Yeah, I guess." Ariana picked up the photo album and flipped through the pages. The images of Berta's sons and their families made her heart raw. They were good men, and Berta had much to be pleased about, but the consequences and devastation from the sons leaving the Amish made it seem more like an act of war than adult children merely moving away.

"You okay?"

She turned the pages, seeing the Schlabachs celebrate birthdays and holidays as if they'd never been raised Amish. "Something keeps nagging at me, and I can't figure out what it is." She tapped her finger on a picture of Quill. He was in a porch swing, clearly unaware his picture was being taken, and he looked peaceful. "I bet he would know what's eating at me."

"Call him."

She shook her head. "No. Like a lot of things, I need to figure this out on my own. I'm just not sure I know myself well enough to figure it out anytime soon."

"See, that kind of talk worries me. Maybe you're going back before you should."

"Ha." Ariana nudged her shoulder into Cameron's. "Not soon enough is the problem. The answer is to go home and begin anew the only life I've ever wanted."

"Maybe. My dad has a cardinal rule: even if something is legal, I have to be old enough to know myself before I'm free to make a decision that has sticking power — like getting a tattoo or quitting school. Neither of those things has the kind of sticking power that joining the Amish faith and getting married does."

Cameron's words tightened around Ariana's neck. She drew a deep breath, trying to settle her frazzled nerves. Why was she just as nervous as she was thrilled about returning home?

Ariana stood and put the album in her suitcase. "It's a transition, and they are always hard." She felt really anxious in leaving behind, at least for a while, this world and the people she'd come to love. In some ways she was leaving them forever.

Cameron shrugged, looking sad. "Just about the time Princess Jasmine understands her new world, she leaves it." She wrapped her arms around her bent legs. "I'll miss watching movies with you."

"Ditto," Ariana said. "Come visit me as soon as I get permission, okay?"

"How long will that take?"

"I doubt even the bishop knows the answer to that. I'll go through a proving time, and the length will be determined by how well I do or how well they think I'm doing. Probably six months or more."

"That's not very long. Can I bring a generator with me? I'm not sure I'd do well without electricity or movies for an entire evening."

Ariana exaggerated a sigh while closing her suitcase. "Kids these days."

Someone tapped on the open bedroom door, and when Ariana turned around, her Englisch parents were standing there, looking vulnerable and resigned. Skylar had refused to return home to them, and now Ariana was leaving.

She lifted the suitcase off the bed and set it on the floor. "There's a bright side. I talked to Susie last night." Ariana pulled her cell phone from the hidden pocket of her apron and held it up. "Skylar is still living at the house and working at the café. Maybe that will give us a chance to get to know each other. And with a bit of time, I can find ways to assure her that you love her and want her to come home."

It was easy for Ariana to see where Brandi and Nicholas had made mistakes that left Skylar feeling abandoned and unwanted. But they loved Skylar just as much as if she were their own child. Ariana believed that as strongly as she believed in Rudy's love.

Nicholas and Brandi began a sentence at the same time and then stopped. "You first," he said.

Brandi looked from the suitcase to Ariana. "I was going to ask the obvious — if you had packed everything."

Ariana's parents were as changed as she was. They easily yielded the floor to each other, and they were supportive rather than combative. They hardly reminded her of the people who had been at each other's throats when she arrived.

"This isn't the end, guys." Ariana looked each in the eyes, trying to assure them of her words.

They nodded.

"Once I've gone through the proving time and joined the faith, I'll have more freedom to invite you to visit. When I'm married, you can come to my place, and I can come to yours." At least she hoped it worked that smoothly.

As far as the church and community were concerned, Nicholas and Brandi had a long list of strikes against them — threatening to sue the Amish, having sway over her as her biological parents, and living in sin with their new spouses. The church leaders wouldn't consider her relationship with Brandi and Nicholas to be the same as most interaction between Amish and Englisch friends. It would be more complicated, with more objections to her having contact with them. But it could be done.

And may God help her navigate these murky waters if the church leaders learned that Nicholas was an atheist. Did God want her to cut him off because he wasn't a believer? She didn't think so. What better way for Nicholas to see that faith has value than to witness it in a believer's life? But for a while, maybe for always, the church would see to it that Ariana and her Englisch parents didn't have complete freedom to visit each other. Still, with Rudy's support, the church leaders' permission, and careful steps, Ariana was sure they could make periodic visits.

Brandi fidgeted with a dangling earring. "I'll hear from you about the wedding next fall, if not before, right?"

"Yes, of course."

Ariana was sure Rudy wouldn't mind her extending wedding invitations to her Englisch family. Not a lot of Englisch were invited to Amish weddings, but a few were. For some reason, attending Ariana's wedding was very important to Brandi. Ariana doubted Nicholas would come, not because he didn't love her, but because he did. Since he felt she would be stripping herself of all her reasonable rights, he would be hard pressed to attend her wedding. She had yet to understand why she enjoyed his company when he was so far off base about things. Maybe God had placed that fondness for him in her heart.

She put her hands on Brandi's shoulders. "You aren't losing me. I'm moving away, and you will come when I get married and have babies and at other times too. But Amish life is what God intended for me."

Nicholas picked up her suitcase. "You always have a place with either of us. Know that. And don't let what the church teaches keep you there out of fear." He shifted, looking more perturbed than sad. "Remember all that we talked about. How to analyze and think independently."

"I won't forget." How could she? But Ariana was weary of being talked to about life and God in ways that drained and challenged her. She longed to get back to Summer Grove.

She had said her good-byes to her stepsiblings at a family gathering last night, an event that included both households — Brandi's and Nicholas's. She turned and waved at Cameron. They had said all they knew to say, and Cameron wasn't a hugger. Cameron returned the gesture, and Ariana walked down the hall of Brandi's house. Gabe was at the bottom of the stairs, watching his wife more than Ariana. This had to be difficult for a man who loved his wife so much and only wanted to make her life better.

Once they were beside Nicholas's car, Ariana hugged Brandi and Gabe, and then she got into the car and waved as he drove them away. During the drive Nicholas talked about different aspects of the long trip they'd made together and some of the things he'd learned from her. She prayed for him — silently, of course. He talked about his regrets with Skylar and how vicious his regret would be if Skylar never gave him a chance to make up for his years of apathy and hardheadedness. Finally they entered Summer Grove.

An idea suddenly hit her. Ariana had planned on seeing Berta tomorrow, but maybe today would be better. She reached into her coat pocket and felt her phone. "Could we stop somewhere first?"

"Sure, where?"

"Turn left at the next stop sign. I'd like to go by Quill's mom's home."

"Berta," he said. "The one Cameron helped you make a gift for."

"Yeah. The Schlabachs gave me a lot of pictures to share with her, and Cameron helped me put them into albums." She pulled out her phone. It was an amazing piece of technology, and the word *phone* didn't seem at all accurate. It was like a handheld computer that could do remarkable things.

"Take the next right." She pointed out the huge farmhouse that sat mere feet off the road. Being so close to the main road was largely why it was so difficult for the Schlabach brothers to sneak in to visit her.

Nicholas pulled onto the driveway. "Doesn't it bother you that she can't have open visits from her family?"

"It's a way of life every member has agreed to."

He turned off his car. "Quill didn't, and yet he's banned from seeing his mom."

"It's complicated. No one wants it to be that way."

"I beg to differ. Someone wants it that way, or it wouldn't be that way. And my guess is it's those in power and those who back them. They've banded together to use those situations to gain more power. How many leave when they know the catastrophic damage they will cause if they do so?"

"You make valid points, and I don't have all the answers, but may I respectfully request that you zip it?"

"Sorry."

"Any organization — from school systems to medical facilities to family units — is marred by flaws, but as the saying goes, 'Don't toss out the baby with the bathwater.'"

"The difference is we keep trying to improve those systems. No one, and I mean no one, is standing as the gatekeeper, saying, 'This is how we agreed to do it a hundred years ago, and we intend to keep it that way. If you stand against us, we'll shun you. And if you leave, we'll ban you for life.' There's dialogue and debate, and each gender has an equal say."

"Okay." Ariana raised her hands in surrender. "It was a bad analogy. I should've known to do solid research before tossing out a thought."

They got out and went to the trunk. She unzipped her suitcase, and a moment later she had the gift in hand. "Give me ten minutes, okay?"

"This is likely to be the last parent-type thing I get to do for you for a long time. So take all the time you want."

Thankfully, Nicholas hadn't asked why she needed to do this now.

She hurried up the stairs, and feelings of nostalgia and being home were so strong it was as if she'd stepped through a portal into a new land. She knocked and opened the door. "Hallo? Berta?"

"Ari? Is that you?" Berta rushed out of the living room. "Ariana!" She put her arms around her and squeezed, rocking back and forth. "Oh, my girl is home!"

The word *home* struck deep. This big old house with this lonely woman felt like home. Memories of time spent here during her childhood washed over her. The delicious aromas, laughter, and long talks. Sunlight dancing across the floor as the wind lifted the sheers, and silvery moonlight making the room glow while she and Frieda talked the night away.

Ariana held Berta tight. "You and this wonderful old house make me feel like I'm home."

Berta released her. "You're welcome here anytime and all the time."

Ariana chuckled. "Dan said nearly those same words to me."

"You saw him?"

"There are no more secrets, Berta."

"And yet you're here."

"Without anger or judgment."

Berta's eyes filled with tears, and she hugged Ariana again. "Denki, my sweet girl." She released her and then gave her the once-over. "You look the best ever. I heard you were arriving today, but, child, what are you doing here?"

"I just *had* to see you." They were connected in ways Ariana didn't understand, but she could feel it as she stood there. She passed her the gift. "From your sons, daughters-in-law, grandchildren, and me. My stepsister had to help me too. I'd never seen a photo album before. Be careful no one sees it."

Berta nodded, holding it tightly to her chest. "Denki."

"Your boys, all of them, are such fine men. And they've chosen good wives and have beautiful, loving families. You have much to be grateful for." Ariana pulled her phone from her coat pocket. "If the bishop knows I'm returning today and if he's talked to my Daed, I may be required to give up my phone before I even enter my house. But first . . ." She pressed the necessary icons to call Quill.

"Hey, stranger." Quill's voice was strong and peaceful. "I haven't heard from you in a while."

That was true, and it would only get worse from here. She'd called him on Christmas Day, and they hadn't spoken or texted since. Quill wouldn't take the initiative to contact her. The ball was always in her court. She assumed he did it that way to avoid causing issues between her and Rudy.

"Hi. I'm in Summer Grove, and I have someone here I think you should talk to."

Berta looked puzzled, as if the little box in Ariana's hand couldn't be a phone. "Say hello to your youngest son." Ariana put the phone in her hand and eased it to Berta's face.

Berta's hand trembled. "Quill?"

"Mamm! Hi! How's the best mom in the world doing today?"

Berta grinned, looking thrilled, and yet there was pain etched on her face. Tears brimmed in Ariana's eyes.

By the time Mamm and son were finished talking, Ariana had been at Berta's for almost thirty minutes. She hugged Berta one last time. "I'll be back tomorrow." She hurried out the door. Nicholas was in the car, doing something on his phone. Maybe he was doing some research, gearing up for a last-ditch effort to convince her not to join the Amish faith.

As she got in the car, he slid the phone

into his pocket. "You're beaming, and it took longer than expected. Clearly all went really well. Is there anywhere else you'd like to stop?"

"No, but thank you. It's time to go home. By the way the crow flies or this girl walks, my house is just over that ridge. But with luggage in tow, I better ride there."

Nicholas pulled onto the main road, and she gave him directions.

"Ari, shouldn't there be empirical evidence for such bold faith in God?"

"So you've returned to that line of defense, huh? No more tiptoeing around, saying, 'Let's just say that God does exist, then what about . . .' " She folded her arms. "I give you points for being tenacious." She directed him to take the next right. "I've considered all you've had to say about God's Word and disproving God's existence, and in exchange for that, you've gone to church numerous times. If we had an eternity together and you kept quoting every external source available to mankind, I would still have my faith. I know He exists because of what's in my heart that He placed there. You love Skylar, but is there empirical evidence for that?"

"Unfortunately, no."

"Then how does anyone know it's true?"

He drew a slow breath and nodded, conceding her point. "I know it because of what my heart holds for her."

"Exactly. And I know in my heart that God exists. I also know it because of His Word and because my heart, mind, and soul are better for His presence in them. That's enough proof, and it's more proof than I deserve."

Nicholas tightened his grip on the steering wheel. "I'm out of words."

She chuckled. "And it only took three months." She pulled the cell from her pocket. "My guess is that you better keep this or it'll be confiscated."

"Some Amish have cell phones."

"I know, but I'm not likely to be one of them, not while I go through the proving time after being in the Englisch world for three months."

"Do you agree with such a sacrifice?"

She would have agreed before leaving. It would've been easy to categorize it under submission to God's authority. Since seeing the universe through the Hubble's eye, she no longer viewed God as a one-dimensional being who demanded obedience concerning modern-day conveniences, but she wouldn't say that to her dad.

He clasped his hand around hers, squeezing the phone into her palm. "Get permission to keep it at the café as a business phone, or hide it somewhere, maybe at Berta's. Could you do that much? I'm asking that of you as your father. Doesn't that count? I need to know you can reach me whenever you need to."

"There's a community phone nearby."

"It's not the same. The church can monitor the phone shanty. But if you have your own cell, we can talk whenever you want."

She couldn't believe the word coming from her mouth. "Okay." She put it back in her pocket.

"Can you keep it charged?"

"Yeah." Most Amish barns had a solar panel or two with wires that could be connected to a battery and a converter, which could be used like an electric outlet. Her family didn't have one, maybe because phones were frowned on or maybe because they were poor. Probably the old cooperage building at Berta's would be the best and most secretive place to recharge her cell.

Her home came into sight, but rather than excitement or relief, she felt apprehension, like astronauts reentering Earth's atmosphere. "The next driveway to your right."

Nicholas squeezed the steering wheel, looking as uptight as she felt. "Would you at least send a text every week to let me know you're okay?"

"I'll try. It might be closer to every two weeks." A lot would depend on whether her visits to Berta's were restricted.

"Every two weeks, then." The lines in his face deepened, and when he glanced at her, she saw raw concern in his eyes.

"I'll be fine. This is what I want."

"I know. But I've never dealt with these kinds of emotions. I wasn't there for Skylar, not to release her hand on the first day of kindergarten or to witness her heartaches and triumphs. I have no practice in letting go."

She pointed at the driveway to her house, and he turned on his blinker.

Was his anxiety crossing over into her emotions? Was that why she, too, felt it was hard to breathe? "I'm safe here. You know, a lot of parents would be at peace about this kind of decision."

He started to say something else, but instead he drew a deep breath and put the car in Park. "Home sweet home." He pulled the trunk release lever and paused, waiting for her to say something.

When she opened her door, he opened his. They got out and met at the trunk.

He pulled out her one piece of luggage

and set it on the ground. "If you need anything . . ."

She hugged him. "All I have to do is call." When she released him, she saw a bevy of siblings, nieces, nephews, and her Mamm and Daed gathered on the porch, just beyond the front door, giving Nicholas and her time to say good-bye.

Susie's eyes caught hers, and she screamed, "Ariana!" Susie ran for her.

In a flash Ariana was engulfed in hugs from everyone.

Abram held her the longest. "I have no idea what all this fuss is about."

She backed away. His eyes held confidence, and his stature was that of a self-assured man. Had he changed that much?

He winked. "Glad you're back, sis."

"Denki." She barely got the word out before the rest of her siblings and nieces and nephews were pawing at her.

When the scuffle was over, she saw Nicholas looking at the house. Ariana followed his line of sight. A beautiful young woman who favored Salome was standing at a second-story bedroom window, looking at her. *Skylar.* Then her eyes moved to Nicholas, and he waved. Skylar returned the wave and faded from the window.

An eerie sensation pricked Ariana's skin,

as if she saw for the first time part of her new reality. She couldn't move back into her home. This was where Skylar was supposed to have been raised, and Ariana would do Skylar a disservice to waltz back into the house and make her feel like an unwanted guest.

No one budged, as if there was nothing to say beyond this greeting. And those few slow-motion seconds revealed an elephant-sized awkwardness between her and her family. Their stares seemed to ask if they still knew her, and the silent answer that rose from within terrified her — she no longer knew herself. Or maybe she had never known herself but had only known what she'd been taught.

As she stood in the midst of her Amish family, she realized just how far removed she was from the girl she used to be, from the simple faith of believing the black and white of the Old Ways.

"Why is everyone so quiet?" Abram made a face while shaking his head. "Kumm. We have a surprise for you." He grabbed her wrist and tugged her toward the house. A man stepped onto the porch.

Rudy!

His smile melted her heart, and they hurried toward each other. His strong arms gently wrapped around her. This was the homecoming she'd been dreaming of since before she left Summer Grove.

THIRTY-EIGHT

The noise from the celebration over Ariana's return echoed off the kitchen walls and off Skylar's nerves. She should have left a week ago. Why was she still here? She tuned out the questions Ariana asked about the café. And while Susie and Abram fielded the queries, Skylar focused on why she hadn't left.

Had she stayed out of fear? She'd never been on her own before. Did she want more time with *her* family? And they were hers, not Ariana's. And there was something inexplicably powerful in spending time with those who carried the same DNA.

"Wow. You guys are even more amazing than I thought. And that's saying a lot," Ariana said.

The excitement in Ariana's voice pulled Skylar from her thoughts.

"You don't mind about the generator and

the lineup of electrical appliances?" Martha asked.

"Not a bit. I bought a café and left you here to run it, and run it you have." Ariana pushed food around on her plate more than eating it. "I'm so impressed the café is doing that well."

"We were stuck in the mud, spinning our wheels, and then Skylar had some ideas, and we got traction," Susie said.

"Skylar," — Ariana pinned her with a warm stare — "thank you."

"Who knew that Mom's love of cafés would one day come in handy?"

"She'll love hearing that."

Lovina left the table and returned with a cake that said *Welcome Home* in buttercream frosting. She cut the cake and placed slices on plates, which were then passed down the table. The conversation about the café grew quiet, and Skylar realized that no one had asked Ariana anything other than how she was.

"Skylar," — Ariana broke the chain of passing the cake to the next person and handed the plate to Skylar instead — "I'm really glad you're here."

Skylar took the plate. No wonder everyone spoke so highly of Ariana. Not many people in her situation could say those words and sound totally sincere. "Thanks." Skylar set the plate in front of her. "It's been an interesting three months. I'm completely surprised you figured out a way to get back home so much quicker than Dad planned."

And now Skylar knew why she hadn't left. She had been absolutely positive Nicholas would make Ariana stay the full year. But with Ariana here now, all the awkwardness Skylar had worked through since her arrival months ago was back again. But she couldn't leave tonight. She wouldn't do anything that would take away from the family's joy over Ariana being home again. But soon, maybe tomorrow or the next day, she would pack her bags and say good-bye.

Skylar took a bite of cake. "So what was your favorite part of living English?"

Everyone sitting at the table froze. Tension appeared from nowhere. Much like adding hot water to instant coffee, things went from clear to murky. Was Ariana supposed to forget her experiences as she prepared to join the faith?

Ariana angled her head, looking thoughtful, as if she was fully aware of things Skylar could only guess at. "Earning a visit to see Rudy."

The room erupted in words of agreement and applause. Ariana smiled at Rudy before returning her focus to Skylar. "What has been your favorite part of being here?"

"I'm not sure." But she was. It wouldn't be right to say, "Your family, all of them. They are my littermates, and I can breathe when they're around. Your mom's wisdom stole my heart. Susie's tough love is irresistible. Martha's maternal nature overwhelms me. And Abram has actually started to feel like my twin." The girl who'd arrived here three months ago would've said those things just to annoy Ariana, but Skylar wasn't that same girl. "I like working at your café."

"*Our* café. It's called Brennemans' Perks for a reason." Ariana smiled and took a bite of cake.

"Well, that's nice of you to say. But I should've been gone by now," Skylar said.

"That's not true." Mamm plunked another piece of cake onto a plate. "I know you're not used to tight quarters, Skylar. But that room can easily fit more. It once held all five girls. It can certainly hold four again. We just need to get the bunk bed out of the attic. We should've done it already, but the frame needs a new mattress that we won't be ready to buy until Isaac's next paycheck."

"Actually," Ariana said, "rather than you adding a bed . . . I'd like to stay at Berta's."

Lovina immediately stopped. Was she even breathing? She finally blinked. "Ari, this is your home."

"Absolutely, and all I've dreamed about since leaving. But Summer Grove is also home." Ariana wiped her mouth with the napkin. "And I'm talking about living just across the back field, give or take an angle or two. This house is small and brimming, and hers is large and practically empty. I can be here for supper every night if you want me to."

Isaac cleared his throat. "It's best if you stay here until you marry."

Ariana blinked, staring at her dad. She lowered her fork until it rested on the plate. "Berta's been faithful to the Old Ways her whole life, and there is no reason for anyone — not you or the church leaders — to feel I need to avoid her."

No one answered, but Skylar had the feeling there was a reason they wanted her to avoid Berta. Usually when Skylar felt an undercurrent in a situation, she would wait until Martha was asleep and then ask Susie to explain it. But she couldn't do that if Ariana was going to be in the room.

Ariana looked from one person to the next, concern in her eyes. "My time with

Berta never bothered you before. Why now?"

"While you were away, it became apparent to the church leaders that she's had contact with her sons over the years." Lovina took a sip of her water.

Ariana's eyes reminded Skylar of her mother's eyes . . . or rather Brandi's eyes. Right now those eyes reflected disbelief and maybe a challenge, as if Ariana wanted to say, "So?"

Ariana rubbed her forehead. "Her faithfulness to God is being judged because she allowed a few visits from her sons?"

"You have your answer about staying with her, Daughter," Isaac said.

Skylar had heard the phrase "you have your answer" a few times while staying here. It meant the conversation was over.

"Ya, Daed," Ariana said. "I got that part, but I'm waiting for a reason."

Isaac studied her, as if deciding whether he owed her more than his final say in the matter. "You've been *draus in da Welt,* and your movements, all of them, will be restricted for a while."

What was draus in da Welt?

"I planned on that," Ariana said. "I didn't return home to be willful, but I'd like to understand. Berta is more like me than you might want to think. We both have ties to the outside world — people we're related to and care about who live Englisch. Will I be suspect all my days too?"

"No, of course not. She's disobeyed the bishop."

Ariana's eyes narrowed, seemingly not with disdain or contempt, but with thoughtful consideration. "What if the bishop's opinion is clouded and he's not sharing God's will as much as his own?"

Isaac's palm smacked the table, making the utensils rattle. "God gave the bishop final say over all of us."

"Did He?" Ariana asked. "Because it seems to me that three names went into the lot, and with or without God, one of those three men was going to be chosen."

"Ariana!" Lovina gasped, her eyes wide.

Ariana closed her eyes tight and covered her mouth. "I'm sorry," she mumbled through her fingers. She looked up. "Daed, Mamm, forgive me. I had no right —"

"You've been away. Things were different there." Isaac rose, moved behind Ariana, and rested his hands on her shoulders. "But it sounds as if you need a refresher on what we believe and why."

Ariana looked uncomfortable with that idea, and Skylar could only imagine how much Nicholas had tried to sway her to discount her faith. "Maybe so."

Maybe? That struck Skylar as the wrong word to use. Did anyone else at the table feel that the word *maybe* coming from Ariana right then was very telling of how she really felt? She didn't blame her. No one had come at Skylar with such strictness.

Isaac kissed the top of Ariana's head, pressing his lips against the rim of her prayer Kapp. "I'm so very grateful you're home." He cupped her chin, causing her to look up at him. "We'll use some of our time each day talking about the tenets of our faith, okay?"

Ariana gave a weak smile. "I'm just tired, Daed."

"Still, we will do as I said." Isaac squeezed her face lovingly, winked, and returned to his seat.

It struck Skylar as odd that Ariana hadn't assured Isaac or the family that she needed to hear the tenets of her faith once again. Instead, she seemed reluctant.

Rudy set his napkin beside his plate. "That was delicious. Thank you." He took Ariana's hand into his. "If you don't mind, could we be excused? I think a long walk would do us both some good."

"Ya, go." Isaac motioned toward the door.

Rudy and Ariana grabbed their coats off the pegs and went outside.

The room grew quiet, but the glances between her siblings gave clues as to how deep the undercurrent of discomfort was running. No one had been prepared for Ariana's desire to stay with Berta, and no one had expected Ariana to question the bishop's authority.

Clearly Ariana's time outside the Amish had left its mark. Skylar hadn't seen this side of Isaac before, the attitude "you'll take the Amish way or the highway." It was enough to cause a question to nag at Skylar. Was Isaac as controlling as Nicholas when challenged? When she was ready to leave, would it be a struggle to free herself from her biological family?

THIRTY-NINE

Struggling to breathe, Ariana stepped onto the porch. Rudy followed her, but as he was closing the door behind them, Mamm called to him.

Rudy glanced at Ariana. "I'll be right back."

She nodded, moved to a step, and sat. Why had she blurted out her negative thoughts about the bishop's authority? What had come over her?

Her cell phone vibrated, and she pulled it from the hidden pocket of her apron. It was a text from Quill with two simple words:

Thank you.

She glanced behind her and then quickly responded:

My pleasure.

Giving Berta the photo album and using a

cell phone so mother and son could talk had been inexplicably gratifying. She was just beginning to realize how much her belief system had changed since she had left here, and she couldn't really wrap her head around it right now. It began when she realized she didn't know God like she'd thought she did. She had once believed she'd known who He was and what He wanted, but that had been shattered when He removed her from her insular world and His will no longer seemed perfectly clear. Her view of Him changed again at the planetarium with Quill. But the most uncomfortable change was realizing how many times God's Word had been translated from one language to another. And once it was in English, it'd been translated from Old English to Middle English to modern English. So believing in a completely literal translation only made sense if the preachers studied the original transcripts to determine the intent, and no Amish preachers had any training in such matters. And the Bible the Amish studied most of the time was the German Bible. Was it the one that had first been translated to English in the Middle Ages or the Gothic translation? She wasn't sure what the difference was, but it seemed there needed to be more grace and less legalism about exactly how to live.

Rudy walked outside. "Are we sitting?"

She slid the phone into her pocket. "Apparently. Do you mind?" She felt as if her legs had been cut out from under her. Her energy was zapped, and her whole body felt as heavy as the conversation she'd just had with her Mamm and Daed.

"Not a bit." He sat beside her.

She hadn't meant to challenge her Daed. The words seemed completely justified at the moment, but after she'd spoken them and had seen the look on her parents' faces, she knew there was no defense for speaking her thoughts. And what was wrong with her that all these thoughts about the Word were pummeling her now rather than while she was living Englisch?

"You're home." Rudy gestured at the homestead — the house, the land, and the barns.

"I am." But the whole time she was pushing Nicholas to let her return, she'd expected her homecoming to be filled to overflowing with peace. Why was the opposite happening? Her head roared with voices that weren't coming from the Old Ways. Was she now a heretic?

"What did Mamm want?"

"Nothing important." Rudy entwined his

arm with hers. "So what's going on?"

"Not much." Should she tell him about the number of thoughts bombarding her, conflicting ones from the Amish, Nicholas, Brandi, Quill, scientists, and even those taught from the pulpits of non-Amish churches? The list of opinions vying for the top spot in her heart seemed to include every possible group. Worse, she had no idea which one or ones she agreed with when it came to obeying the bishop. With every new voice that rose from within, she wavered, uncertain which was right.

"Not much?" Rudy leaned in and kissed her cheek. "That doesn't sound accurate, does it?"

"I guess not." How could a person spend three months struggling to get back here and then feel this overwhelmed with churning, adversarial thoughts?

He raised her hand to his lips and kissed it. "I'm not here simply to welcome you home. I made sure I was here when you arrived because I knew returning would be an adjustment."

His words worked their way through her, and she took a deep breath. But then she realized that even he knew her better than she knew herself. She had thought she would be thrilled, ready to begin her life of happily-ever-after.

"Ariana, talk to me."

If she started talking, he would naturally give his opinion. It's what people did in a heart-to-heart conversation. But she couldn't stand knowing one more opinion right now. She was filled to the brim with what others thought, and everyone except her seemed to know themselves and their opinions quite well.

She curled her hand over his, holding it tight. "I can't. I've been so busy trying to get home, to get back to you and our future that I haven't processed all this new information."

He frowned. "You can't talk because . . . why?"

"I need some time to think, to decompress and integrate all I've learned with who I am."

"That's a lot of big words, and I'm not sure they explained much of anything."

What could she say directly? Everyone had been waiting for her to return. Her siblings didn't just keep the café afloat. They'd made it a success. Rudy had uprooted his life twice, and he was here to support her.

"Sorry about that. I guess what I'm saying is I've spent my life being told who I am and what I need to believe. Am I still that person?"

"Who else would you be?"

"Good question."

Rudy moved away from her a bit, angling his body, presumably to have a better view of her face. "This is a scary conversation, Ariana, and nothing like what I thought we'd be talking about tonight."

"I'm sorry. You're right." Is this what her life would become — one long series of apologies as she tried to repress any thought that slightly challenged the Amish faith? She took Rudy's face into her hands and kissed him. "Ignore me on all points but this one: I love you."

"That's what I needed to hear." He hugged her, and they settled back onto the steps, staring across the pastures and at the horizon. The sun was setting, causing the sky to glow with orange and lavender clouds. If she hadn't known what time of day it was, she might have thought it was dawn. Life could look like a lot of things it wasn't. A person had to know a few grounding pieces of information, a few absolutes that could be relied upon. She knew who had created this world and who died for it, but did she believe in the Old Ways?

As she sat and held Rudy's hand while they stared out at God's green earth, she knew what she needed just as sure as she knew her Creator. She needed time away from everyone, every person she'd ever known, so she could sort through the noise and find peace between God and her and discover who she really was. But doing that would take courage. Did she have it in her to tell her loved ones she needed time away from all of them as well as her Englisch family?

She studied Rudy. It would be the hardest to tell him. Did she possess that kind of strength?

Moreover, if she did, would he wait for her?

GLOSSARY

ach — oh

Bischt allrecht, Liewer? — Are you all right, dear?

Bobbeli — baby

Dabber schpring — Run quick

Daed — father or dad; pronounced "dat"

denki — thank you

draus in da Welt — out in the world

Englisch — non-Plain person, a term used by the Amish and Plain Mennonites

Gott — God

Grossdaadi — grandfather

gross dank — many thanks

Grossmammi — grandmother

gut — good

hallo — hello

Ich bin gut. — I am good.

Iss sell du? — Is it you?

Kapp — prayer cap or covering

kumm — come

Mamm — mom or mother

Mammi — grandmother
mei Lieb — my love
nee — no
Ordnung — order; set of rules
rumschpringe — running around
ya — yes

MAIN CHARACTERS

Ariana Brenneman — A dedicated but inexperienced twenty-year-old who was raised Amish. The truth surrounding her birth and the threat of a lawsuit against the midwife who delivered her have recently ripped Ariana from her beloved Amish roots.

Abram Brenneman — A loyal and supportive brother to Ariana who, until recently, thought she was his twin.

Isaac and Lovina Brenneman — A poor Amish couple that are dairy farmers. They have ten children, some grown and some minors. They raised Ariana, believing she was theirs.

Salome Brenneman Glick — The eldest Brenneman daughter, who is indecisive but loyal. She's married to Emanuel, and they have five children, including Henry, James, Esther, and Katie Ann. They live in the same home as Isaac and Lovina.

Susie Brenneman — The eighteen-year-old daughter, who is sassy and determined.

Martha Brenneman — The fifteen-year-old daughter, who is sweet and maternal in nature.

Abner, Ivan, Mark, and John Brenneman — Along with Abram, the sons of Isaac and Lovina.

Brandi Nash — The Englisch mom who twenty years ago gave birth to Ariana in a birthing center a few minutes before Lovina Brenneman gave birth to twins, a girl and then a boy. She is now a sincere, trendy, and fit mom who has raised Skylar as well as a stepdaughter, Cameron.

Skylar Nash — The talented but hurting addict who was raised by Brandi Nash in a non-Amish home. She is the biological child of Lovina and Isaac, and the Brenneman children are her biological siblings.

Gabe Crespo — Brandi's husband and Cameron's father.

Cameron Crespo — Gabe's fifteen-year-old daughter, who befriends Ariana.

Nicholas Jenkins — Ariana's biological father, who helped raise Skylar Nash.

Lynn Jenkins — Nicholas's wife.

Quill Schlabach — A twenty-five-year-old man who grew up in Summer Grove with Ariana and was a close friend. But he has left the Amish.

Berta Schlabach — Mother to Quill and his four brothers — **Dan, Erastus, Leon,** and **Elam** — who have also left the Amish. She is also a matronly friend of Ariana's.

Cilla Yoder — A young Amish woman who has cystic fibrosis. She helps out at Brennemans' Perks and cares for Abram. Her Mamm is Emma, and her sister is **Barbie.**

ABOUT THE AUTHOR

Cindy Woodsmall is a *New York Times* and CBA bestselling author of numerous works of fiction and one of nonfiction. Her connection with the Amish community has been featured widely in national media. She lives in the Foothills of the North Georgia Mountains with her family.